Belinda Alexandra has been published to wide acclaim in Australia, New Zealand, the United Kingdom, France, Germany, Holland, Poland, Norway and Russia. She is the daughter of a Russian mother and an Australian father and has been an intrepid traveller since her youth. Her love of other cultures is matched by her passion for her home country, Australia, where she is a volunteer rescuer and carer for the New South Wales Wildlife Information Rescue and Education Service (WIRES).

Also by Belinda Alexandra

White Gardenia
Wild Lavender

Silver Wattle

BELINDA ALEXANDRA

HarperCollins*Publishers*

HarperCollins*Publishers*

First published in Australia in 2007
by HarperCollins*Publishers* Australia Pty Limited
ABN 36 009 913 517
www.harpercollins.com.au

HarperCollins*Publishers*
25 Ryde Road, Pymble, Sydney, NSW 2073, Australia
31 View Road, Glenfield, Auckland 10, New Zealand
77–85 Fulham Palace Road, London, W6 8JB, United Kingdom
Hazelton Lanes, 55 Avenue Road, Suite 2900, Toronto, Ontario M5R 3L2
and 1995 Markham Road, Scarborough, Ontario M1B 5M8, Canada
10 East 53rd Street, New York NY 10022, USA

National Library of Australia Cataloguing-in-Publication data:

Alexandra, Belinda.
    Silver wattle.
    ISBN 978 0 7322 8134 2.
    1. to come. I. Title.
A823.4

Cover design: Darren Holt, HarperCollins Design Studio
Cover images: Woman and couple courtesy of Getty Images
Arcade theatre courtesy of www.argoodman.com
Typeset in Sabon 11/17 by Kirby Jones
Printed and bound in Australia by Griffin Press.

70gsm Bulky Book Ivory used by HarperCollins*Publishers* is a natural, recyclable product
made from wood grown in sustainable forests. The manufacturing processes conform to
the environmental regulations in the country of origin, Finland.

6 5 4 3 2 1   07 08 09 10

For Mauro

ONE

——

We Czechs have a saying: 'Do not let evil take you by surprise.' I wish I had paid more attention to that warning. But then we also have a proverb: 'After the battle, everyone is a general.' It is easy to see what one may have done differently in hindsight.

When I remember Prague, I think of chestnut blossoms bursting out on the trees of Petřín Hill. I see shutters thrown open to blue skies and smell lilac wafting in on the breeze. I hear my sister, Klára, playing Chopin on the Petrof grand in our house at the foot of the Castle. My mother is there too, busy at her easel — blocking in the sky, roughing in a foreground, dabbing in the finer details of her latest painting. The book of verse falls from my lap while I listen to the music drift on the air as delicately as the lilac scent. Klára's fingers glide over the keyboard. From the time she first sat at the piano, my younger sister confounded music teachers by playing complex pieces with a subtleness that belied her age. She has a certain touch, a way of caressing the music that is best described as 'silky'.

My mother and I could listen to Klára play for hours on those mornings we spent together when my stepfather was away on business. And, being an indefatigable practiser, Klára readily obliged us. Even now, all these years later, when I think of her playing a sense of peace washes over me.

Later in the day, my mother, Klára and I would eat potato soup and fruit dumplings while Mother read the newspaper to us. We were interested in developments in our newly born state, Czechoslovakia. It had come into existence with the collapse of the Austro–Hungarian Empire at the end of the Great War, which had finished the previous year. But if Aunt Josephine arrived for a visit with her poodle, Frip, the newspaper was put aside and the spirited spinster and her black-furred companion given our full attention.

'Ah, look at you two girls,' Aunt Josephine would say, addressing Klára and myself. 'You grow more lovely each time I see you!'

Klára and I would exchange a smile. Aunt Josephine visited us three or four times a week and always said the same thing with an exclamation of surprise. 'But what do you expect?' she asked when we reminded her of this fact. 'With such a glorious mother.'

Although Mother had been friends with my father's sister for years, she was embarrassed by the compliment. Mother's round face was not classically beautiful but her bowed smile and pink cheeks gave her a certain charm. She dressed superbly in shades of violet and, although she was close to forty, there was not a strand of grey in her blonde hair or a wrinkle on her creamy skin.

Some afternoons, Aunt Josephine arrived earlier than usual and in a state of excitement because she had received a letter from Uncle Ota. Mother would invite her into the drawing room with us, where we sat down on the gilded chairs like royal ladies on our thrones. Frip would plonk himself at Aunt Josephine's feet.

On one of these visits, Mother and the cook had made apple strudel that morning and Mother's maid, Marie, was called to serve the pastry along with a pot of tea. When the strudel was presented to Aunt Josephine, she lifted her palm to her cheek in horror. 'With my waist?' she cried, patting her belly, but accepted the plate Mother passed to her anyway. The smells of cinnamon and sultanas filled the air. The strudel was too tempting for anyone to resist.

Silence reigned while we ate the strudel, although Aunt Josephine kept glancing at her purse, impatient to share the contents of the latest letter. Frip, who was on a strict diet, lifted his nose in the air, but when he saw that none of the dessert was coming his way he rested his head on his front paws and fell asleep.

'Hmm,' said Klára, closing her eyes and relishing the strudel.

'You must include this recipe in the box-supper fundraiser,' Aunt Josephine told Mother.

At the start of each season, the women in our district baked their fanciest desserts and wrapped them in boxes covered with silk and decorated with ribbons, hearts and flowers. The boxes were auctioned off to the highest bidders and the money given to the church to help the poor.

Mother smiled and turned to me and Klára. 'I fell in love with your father that way. He always offered the most money for my Sunday bábovka.'

It was a story that she had related to us a hundred times but we never tired of hearing it. I looked around the room. The house was every inch my mother with its velvet curtains, tapestry cushions and floral scrollwork, but the drawing room had touches of my father: the bronze stallion on the mantelpiece with its front hoof raised and its head thrown back; the acanthus leaf tea chest; the Turkish rug with its beasts of the forest motif.

'A man who has daughters has a family, and he who has sons has strangers,' Father used to say whenever someone expressed their sympathy that he had no male heirs. It was an unusual sentiment for a man who had been a captain in the army, but it was true that Father had loved Klára and myself as dearly as he would have loved male children. For a moment, I saw us all together again at the country house in Doksy on Máchovo jezero. My father did not like to hunt and would take us riding through the woods in the early morning instead so that we could observe the deer and the otters. I smelt the damp of the mossy earth mixed with the summer air as clearly as if I were there.

'And where has your mind wandered to, Adélka?' Aunt Josephine asked. I woke from my daydream to see that everyone had finished their dessert and was looking at me. Klára hid her smile behind her napkin. At nine years of age, Klára's features had already formed into the ones that would be with her all her life. The pointy chin and soft waves of golden-brown hair growing upwards from her forehead created the shape of a heart. It was a shape true to her character, because Klára was all heart, even under her sometimes cool exterior.

'Adélka is a great one for dreaming,' said Mother, smiling at me. 'She has a writer's imagination.'

Aunt Josephine clapped her hands. 'Ah, to be sixteen again.' I was expecting reminiscences about her youth, but instead she reached into her purse and pulled out the letter. 'Your uncle has written to us again,' she said, her eyes sparkling. 'It is a most interesting letter.'

Klára and I leaned forward. Uncle Ota was Aunt Josephine's and my father's brother and an adventurer who had avoided going into his father's sugar business by proposing he 'travel for education' before settling down.

Mother once explained it to me. 'Your Uncle Ota started soberly enough with sojourns to Italy and France. But soon these trips extended to treks in Egypt and Palestine, from where he sent back pictures of himself in Arab dress and vivid descriptions of the temples of Karnak and Luxor. When his father called him home, Ota claimed that a fortune-teller had told him that if he ever stopped travelling he would die.'

Klára and I had grown up unaware of Uncle Ota's whereabouts, until he began corresponding with us through Aunt Josephine after Father was killed in the war. Yet his letters were so enthralling, it was as if we had known him all our lives. His salutation was always 'To my dear ladies' and, although it was not clear if he intended the letters to be read by Mother as well as Aunt Josephine and ourselves, there seemed no harm in their being shared with everybody.

My stepfather called Uncle Ota a *povaleč*, a useless loafer, but we paid him no attention. Klára and I were captivated by our uncle's descriptions of his journeys up the Nile and the Ganges and his visits to civilisations that had never heard of words like 'national revival' and 'independent state'.

> To my dear ladies,
>   I am sorry for my tardiness in writing but
> I have been three weeks on the deck of a ship
> bound for Bombay, then a further week
> tied up with self-important customs
> officials ...

'India again?' said Klára, tracing her finger along the map Aunt Josephine brought with her. 'Perhaps he intends to travel overland to China this time?'

Aunt Josephine read Uncle Ota's letter with great expression and Klára and I hung on every word about the devout of India who bathed in the holy rivers and the medicine men who healed simply by opening their palms.

> *The things I have seen here, one could not imagine …*
> *a five-legged cow wandering through the markets, a*
> *holy man making a pilgrimage on stilts, a ritual dance*
> *in which the worshippers throw coconuts into the air*
> *to crack them on their heads …*

Mother's reaction to the wonders Uncle Ota described was more reserved on these occasions. She nodded at every turn in the adventure, but all the while her face was blanched of colour as if she had received a shock. I could not imagine what it was about Uncle Ota's letters that made Mother change so. The family photograph albums were full of pictures of my father and his older brother arm in arm, from their childhood until just after the time my father and mother married. Mother had adored Father who had in turn worshipped his brother. My father, according to Aunt Josephine, had been inconsolable when his own father disinherited Uncle Ota.

'Do Uncle Ota's letters bother you?' I asked Mother when we were alone in the drawing room after Klára and Aunt Josephine had taken Frip for a walk in the park.

Her face did not change but her eyes flashed with surprise. 'No,' she said, shaking her head. Her voice trailed off when she added, 'Ota sounds very happy.'

* * *

When I remember Prague, I try not to think of my stepfather, Miloš. If I do, my stomach turns to knots and his voice booms in my head.

'Marta, I want that useless maid sent away this afternoon!'

I see him in my memory, pale blond like an ice prince, stamping about the house and admonishing my mother because Marie had over-starched his collar and he could not button it.

'I don't know how your mother could have married him after Antonín,' paní Milotová, the Russian music teacher who gave Klára piano lessons, confided to me one day after my mother and stepfather had returned from their honeymoon. 'He doesn't want Klára to play anything challenging, only decorative pieces. He broke a string on the piano just because I was teaching her Fauré's Le Voyageur.'

The question of why my mother would marry a man like my stepfather was on everyone's lips. 'He's seven years younger than you and has no position,' Aunt Josephine had warned Mother the day their engagement was announced. 'He is after your money.'

'My daughters need a father,' Mother replied. 'And he is cultured.'

Mother's stubbornness on the issue was legendary; perhaps it was a kind of madness that came from the terrible grief she had suffered when the telegram arrived announcing Father's death in the first year of the war. It was to Aunt Josephine's credit that she remained Mother's friend after her second marriage, although our aunt would never visit us when my stepfather was in town. Mother and Miloš married in 1917. All I remember of the day is being annoyed that Miloš's mother said that because Miloš was fair like me, everyone would think I was his natural daughter. My father had been as dark as an Arab.

Each time my stepfather, a partner in a firm of interior decorators and plasterers, returned from one of his business trips, our easy meals of soup and dumplings gave way to a table covered with a white cloth, candlesticks and platters of roasted duck with sauerkraut, marinated beef and saddles of oozing venison, which Klára refused to eat.

'If you don't eat meat, Klára,' my stepfather would say, pointing his finger at her, 'not only will you fade away but you will cease to be Czech.'

Why Mother had thought that Klára and I needed the kind of culture that Miloš was capable of teaching us escaped me. While he played the violin and danced more elegantly than any other man in Prague, one got the impression that he had never shaken the stigma of belonging to a trade. It was clear from my mother's pained expressions and silences one year into her new marriage that this truth had dawned on her. But there was nothing to be done now. Divorce was social suicide and she had spent a fortune on buying Miloš his partnership in the firm.

Klára was usually unmoved by our stepfather's admonitions against her vegetarianism until his fierce blue eyes shifted to Mister Rudolf swimming in his tank on the sideboard. Miloš had threatened to dump Klára's pet carp into the Vltava, where he would die of cold, and just his glance at the fish was sufficient to make Klára scoop a slice of beef onto her plate and nibble at it. Her face was always impassive, but I knew that her stomach was retching. Miloš did not understand what it was about Mister Rudolf that stopped Klára from eating meat or fish, but he sensed the connection and found it a useful threat.

Czechs eat fish for Lent and our farmers have been breeding fat, thick-boned carp for centuries. Carp and potato salad are the traditional Christmas dishes, and it was with the intention of buying a juicy fish for Christmas that Mother, Klára and I set out, canvas bag in hand, one frosty December evening.

It was the first time Klára had accompanied Mother and me to the Christmas markets. She reached out one hand to Mother and one to me, and skipped along between us through the streets. When we reached the market, her eyes widened and she let go of us, running towards the brightly decorated huts. 'Look, Maminka. Look, Adélka!' she cried, pointing to the rows of wooden toys and straw and paper ornaments. The Christmas lights danced in her eyes like tiny flames.

After a sip of the hot spiced wine Mother bought from a vendor, Klára grabbed my hand and pulled me towards the nativity scene, where both of us patted the heads of the clay donkeys and sheep. Mother reminded us that we had to hurry because she had other things to prepare at home. The fishmongers were at the far end of the square. The cobblestones became slicker the closer we got to the stalls, and the air was especially chilly around the wooden vats where dozens of silvery carp swished together. Klára brought her face close to one, watching the fishes' mouths gaping for air. The enchantment on her face disappeared.

'Adélka, they are drowning,' she said.

'How do you want it?' a fishmonger asked an old woman, dipping a net into the vat and scooping up a fish. 'You'd be best to let it swim in the bathtub until Christmas Eve. It will be fresher that way.'

The woman pulled her shawl tighter around her head. 'I don't have a bathtub. Kill it for me, please.'

Mother always brought our Christmas carp home to swim in the bath as the fishmonger had suggested. I had never seen one killed. Somehow I had missed the connection between the live fish that came home with us and the fried one that appeared on a platter on Christmas Eve.

The fishmonger dropped the writhing fish onto a pair of scales and from there to a wooden block. It stared up at the man with a bulging eye, as if begging for mercy. The fishmonger held the fish and lifted the mallet. Klára clenched my hand so tightly that her fingernails pierced both of our gloves. I tried to stretch my free hand over her eyes but was too late. The fishmonger slammed the mallet down. The 'bang' sent a jar through me. He sliced off the fish's head and wrapped it with the body in a cloth which he handed to the woman.

After the woman left, my mother lifted her bag to the fishmonger. 'Ours will be going in the bathtub for a few ...' She stopped short when she saw that the fishmonger was looking beyond her, not listening. She turned and saw Klára backing away, gazing from myself to Mother with tear-filled eyes. Her mouth moved as if she wanted to say something, but no sound came out. She reminded me of the fish we had just seen killed, writhing and wriggling away from me each time I tried to grab her hand.

'Klárinka, what's wrong?' my mother asked, rushing towards her but looking at me for an explanation.

'The fish,' I stuttered. 'She saw him kill the fish.'

Mister Rudolf, the carp we brought home from the markets, swam in our bathtub for the next three nights. Mother had promised to keep him as a pet, secretly hoping Klára would turn her attention to something else. But Klára watched over the fish vigilantly, regarding anybody who went to the bathroom to wash their hands or sponge their face as a potential murderer. When we wanted to take a bath, we had to do it quickly, because Mister Rudolf needed to be moved to a bucket, and he would often flip himself out and onto the floor. Finally, in exasperation, my mother bought a tank for Mister Rudolf and served another, less fortunate fish from the markets for Christmas dinner. But Klára was not fooled that the cooked fish had suffered less than the one she had seen killed at the markets. Mother and I realised then that Klára was seeing us differently, and that we would have to win back her trust. After that, my mother indulged Klára's whim to never touch meat or fish and instead fed her nuts, dates, figs, grapes, raisins and mushrooms as substitutes. As for Mister Rudolf, carp were supposed to die a while after being removed from their pond, but he thrived in his tank.

While our stepfather took exception to Klára's eating habits, he used our mealtimes to improve my education. The impromptu lessons made me so nervous I could not swallow my food.

'Adéla, what is that allows a ship to stay afloat?' Miloš asked me one day. He always used my formal name, never the diminutive, Adélka, as the rest of my family did.

I stared at the plate of beef soup and liver dumplings that were our meal that day, unable to think of the answer. He had explained it to me the previous summer when we were walking alongside the Vltava River. I knew it had something to do with the boat pushing water out of the way and some ancient Greek who had discovered the principle of displacement. But beyond that I could not explain it exactly, and a precise answer was the only kind my stepfather would accept.

Sweat gathered under the arches of my feet.

Miloš closed his eyes and repeated his question so slowly that my face burned with shame. It was unfair of him to say that science was for men and then teach it to us in dribs and drabs. Klára still attended a school for young ladies three days a week, but Mother was mainly responsible for our education. She encouraged us to pursue our natural strengths. That was music for Klára and literature for me. I had read everything from the Czech poets to Chekov's plays, and Uncle Ota's letters were an education in themselves. If my stepfather had asked me about the geography I had learned from Uncle Ota's travels, I could have answered him. But he was not interested in other countries and their cultures.

'So you don't know? Then I suggest you look it up and give me an answer tomorrow,' he sighed, before turning to Klára. 'And you, young lady, what is the difference between a butterfly and a moth?'

Klára thought for a moment before answering. 'Moths fly by night and rest during the day. Butterflies love sunshine. A butterfly rests with its wings closed but a moth sleeps with them spread open.'

Klára was in her element. She had an eye for the wonders of nature: the fall of light on a landscape, the rustle of wind through the trees. She loved to watch living creatures and could spend an afternoon studying an army of ants or an evening listening out for nightingales. But Miloš was interested in facts, not poetry.

'Anything else?' he asked.

'Moths are not as colourful as butterflies and have a fatter shape.'

Miloš gave a satisfied laugh and returned his attention to his food. I glanced at Mother. Her face was expressionless, but I saw the glint of tears in her eyes.

Mother's hand on my shoulder stirred me from sleep later that night. 'Adélka,' she whispered. I struggled to open my eyes and focus on her standing next to the bed in her dressing gown and holding a lamp near her face.

'What is it?' I asked, glancing at Klára who was sleeping beside me. 'Is anybody sick?'

Mother put her finger to her lips and shook her head. She moved towards the door and then turned, indicating that I should follow her. The house was silent except for the creaks of the floorboards under our feet and the occasional groan of its ancient walls. It had been in our family for nearly a century and had been left to Mother by her parents. My father had owned a family home too, where Aunt Josephine now lived, but had resided in Mother's house for, while it was not the grandest in Prague, it was one of the most beautiful. The exterior walls were pale blue with white portals and dormers decorated with carved birds and flowers. The house resembled a jasperware vase, and its rear courtyard was a secret garden of ivy-covered fountains and benches. Once you had lived in the 'blue house on the corner of the square', you were spoiled to live anywhere else.

I followed Mother down the hall and wondered if we would meet any of the family ghosts on our journey. There was Great-grandfather Francis who coughed before dashing from one room to another and then disappearing; and Great-aunt Vera who appeared whenever a change was made to the house. She either slammed doors in disapproval or left petals on the doorstep to demonstrate her pleasure. The ghost of Aunt Emilie, who I saw every few years, was the most intriguing. Her face was young and tranquil and there was no inkling in it that her life had ended tragically. One Christmas, I came across Emilie when I thought I had heard Klára singing carols in the music room. I opened the door to find a woman by the piano. She vanished in an instant but I recognised her as Emilie from the picture in the locket Mother wore around her neck, which also contained a snippet of Father's hair. Mother, who was not able to see the ghosts, was happy when I told her that I had discovered her younger sister in the house. She was comforted that Emilie seemed to have found the peace that had eluded her in life.

We climbed the stairs that led to the attic. Mother opened the door and put the lamp on a table.

'Here, sit,' Mother told me, indicating a chair covered with a sheet. She switched on the attic light.

The attic was crowded with furniture of generations past that could no longer fit in the main rooms: a beechwood armoire with brass-banded doors; cherrywood bedheads; a refectory table with lyre-shaped legs. A corner of the room was cordoned off like a chamber in a museum. That place was devoted to my father's favourite pieces for which Miloš had found no use in his rooms. They were arranged exactly as my father had positioned them in his study. I cast my eye over the walnut desk and matching bookcases, the gilt bronze inkstand, and the tall-case clock with the hands stopped at twenty minutes past eleven, the time we had received the telegram informing us of Father's death.

Mother slipped a key from her pocket and opened a mahogany chest with a bear carved on it. I caught a glimpse of Father's sword, Bible and officer's helmet. Mother lifted a black case from the chest and placed it on the desk.

'I was going to give this to you when you came into your inheritance, but I can't see any reason to wait.'

She opened the case and produced a box Brownie camera and passed it to me. I recognised it was the camera Father had bought before he left for Sarajevo. It was a simple design with a rotary shutter and a meniscus lens. My father had never been anything more than an amateur photographer. Yet, I felt his spirit as soon as I touched it. I was taken back to those rides in the countryside around Doksy. I remembered the way Father regarded me with his gentle eyes when he helped me to mount my horse. I was sure that no other human being would ever love me as much.

'Thank you,' I said, looking up at Mother. One glance at the hopeful expression on her face and I understood the meaning of the gift. She was trying to compensate me for having married a tyrant in place of the angel who had been my father.

'Your mother is one of those women who can't not be married,' Aunt Josephine told me the following day when I arrived at her house to show her the camera and to take pictures of her and Frip. 'She was lucky with my brother, but her second marriage ... what a mistake!'

It was not the first time Aunt Josephine had lectured me on the subject of marriage. The women in my family did not always make good choices.

'Men can be so charming before marriage and so terrible afterwards,' Aunt Josephine continued, positioning herself on the sofa with Frip sitting beside her. 'My own father had an atrocious temper and used to order my poor mother around so much that I am certain it was he who sent her to an early grave.'

If Mother had known that Aunt Josephine lectured me against marriage her hair would have turned white. For Mother, marriage was a woman's highest achievement. Not so with Aunt Josephine. Since the time I was old enough to visit her on my own, my aunt had plied me with articles from newspapers and magazines about women who had established themselves in occupations that had been previously forbidden to them: women physicians, astronomers, chemists, journalists and mountain climbers.

'No, give me the free life,' said Aunt Josephine, holding her straight nose in the air and lifting her chin as I depressed the shutter on the camera. 'It might be simple but it's mine.'

I walked the cobblestoned streets home and thought about Aunt Josephine. She lived more humbly than we did. Her house had been left to her by my father, but in order to keep it in good repair she lived on one floor and rented out the others. She had one maid, a stern but loyal German woman called Hilda. Aunt Josephine was always in good temper but the economies in her 'simple' life were obvious: daisies instead of roses in the vases; sponge cake instead of bábovka; cotton instead of silk handkerchiefs. Could I be happy without the financial security a man gave? Then I thought about Mother, and the drain Miloš was on her fortune as well as her happiness, and wondered if Aunt Josephine might be right.

Before returning to the house I walked around Petřín Hill. Mother could not have given me a better gift than the camera. I had always seen the world in images but had been frustrated by my lack of ability to draw or paint. Suddenly I had a means of expression. I took pictures of trees, of couples sitting on benches, of elegant dogs with their equally elegant mistresses. One Afghan hound stopped on the path in front of me and held his chin in the air.

'I think he is posing,' I told his mistress. 'Do you mind if I take a photograph?'

'There is no opportunity Prince would miss for some attention,' she laughed.

I loved dogs. As a child, I asked my parents every Christmas why we could not have one of our own.

My mother's mouth would set in a firm line. 'You know why,' she always replied, turning away from me while my father attempted to distract my wilful demands with promises of birds and goldfish. It was only when I was older that I was made to understand why my mother refused to own a dog. It was a front to save her family's reputation, for Aunt Emilie was supposed to have died of madness brought on by a case of rabies after she was bitten by a stray dog.

Because Mother knew many wealthy people and Miloš's clients were rich, we often attended parties in grand homes. One of these was the villa of paní Provazníková, on one of the most exclusive avenues in the fashionable suburb of Bubeneč. When Klára and I followed Mother and Miloš up the marble staircase, past rows of manservants and maids dressed in black, we knew we were in no ordinary house. French doors opened into a reception hall complete with Greek columns. For her first party of the season, paní Provazníková, the heiress to a coal fortune, had converted the hall into an indoor garden. Trellises of vines hung from the ceiling; a weeping willow drooped over an artificial pond with live ducks bobbing on it; and a path bordered by pots of golden azaleas led the way to paní Provazníková. The hostess sat on a floral throne surrounded by admirers perched on stools while a string quartet played Haydn in the background.

'There he is,' she said, turning to welcome Miloš. 'There is the genius who made all this happen.'

In her pink gown and dainty slippers and with ostrich feathers in her hair, paní Provazníková was a fairy princess. Her dark hair was streaked with silver but her face was young and, despite the frivolity of her outfit, her eyes had an intelligent gleam.

'The house is a masterpiece,' agreed one of paní Provazníková's companions. A woman sitting next to him squinted at us and produced such a tight-lipped smile that I cringed. 'Marta, it is nice to see you,' she said to Mother. 'It has been a long time. And you brought your children.'

Mother introduced the woman as paní Doubková, a friend of hers from finishing school.

'Such lovely girls,' said paní Doubková, her eyes narrowing on us like a hawk. 'One blonde, one dark.'

Klára flinched and I wondered if paní Doubková's high-pitched voice was grating on her sensitive ears. In the house next to ours lived an old man who liked to whistle whenever he watered the flowers in his window box. But there was no tune to his serenade, which sounded about as musical as a squeaking wheel, and Klára would cup her ears and wince in pain whenever she heard him. Then I realised that she was staring at the glass eyes of the fox stole paní Doubková wore around her neck. The animal's feet hung limply at the woman's stodgy throat, its once wild claws manicured into tiny points.

If paní Doubková noticed my sister's disgust, she did not show it. She patted Klára on the head and introduced her husband, who was named Václav Doubek. When he stood up to greet us, he stooped so badly he must have measured half his true size.

'Why don't the children get something to eat?' suggested an old lady sitting near paní Doubková. She had the kindly eyes and apple cheeks of a storybook grandmother. That was the only kind of grandmother I knew, because my maternal one had died before I was born and my only recollection of my paternal grandmother was the whiskers on her chin, which prickled me whenever she kissed me.

I returned the woman's smile, not minding that she had referred to me as a child although I was nearly seventeen. I took Klára's hand and led her to a table spread with cheeses, breads, apple pastries, chocolates and marzipan sweets shaped into crowns. We returned with our plates to sit beside Mother. Miloš was gone. I surveyed the room and found him talking to an elegant woman in a brocade dress. She glanced in our direction before turning away. Her gaze fell on us for only a second but it sent a shiver down my spine.

'She's pretty, isn't she?' whispered paní Doubková. 'She is paní Beňová, widow of the army officer, the late Major Beňo. Her family used to be one of the wealthiest in Prague, but her father gambled their fortune away. I've heard she is on the lookout for a better situation.'

'She is a talented pianist,' added pan Doubek.

'Klára plays the piano beautifully,' my mother said. 'She is exceptional for her age.' There was a sense of strain in her voice. It mirrored the anxiety creeping up on me that I could not explain.

'Is that so?' asked the old lady, who was called paní Koutská. 'I do so love music and children and these days have neither in my home. Perhaps, paní Provazníková, you could introduce me to paní Beňová and I can ask her and Klára to play at a soirée for me one day?'

I turned to look again at Miloš and paní Beňová. The young woman was beautiful, with raven-black hair, a long neck and a tiny pout for a mouth. She was like a swan. But it was my stepfather who most caught my attention. Gone was the stern look on his face. He lowered his eyes and whispered something that made paní Beňová laugh. Then he laughed too, his eyes sparkling with gaiety. That must have been Mother's first impression of Miloš, I thought. For I was convinced that she would not have chosen such a humourless man to be our stepfather had she known what he was really like.

The invitation to attend paní Koutská's soirée came a few weeks later. Klára was finishing up her lesson with paní Milotová. They had been working on Beethoven's last keyboard work, the Six

Bagatelles, Opus 126. It was a mature work for Klára to be studying but she played it with deep feeling. I listened from the dining room where I was helping Marie lay out the table for lunch. Paní Milotová was a friend of my mother's and she stayed to eat with us each Wednesday after Klára's lesson. When we were seated at the table, Mother handed her paní Koutská's invitation.

'Do you think it is too soon for Klára to perform for an audience?' she asked. 'Will it take away her enjoyment of playing?'

Paní Milotová, who Mother called Lída but who we addressed formally because she was a teacher, studied the invitation. 'Klárinka is a natural performer,' she said. 'She will shine even brighter with an audience.'

Mother turned away. Paní Milotová frowned then a look of understanding crossed her face and she blushed. 'You could certainly use that as an excuse if you didn't wish to attend. But I would go, if I were you. I would hold my head up and be proud of my daughter. You are the one who nurtured her talent.'

I looked from Mother to paní Milotová. Some understanding had passed between them but I was not sure what it meant. My stomach turned. I had the premonition that something was about to happen but I had no idea what.

Aunt Josephine appeared on our doorstep with Frip soon after paní Milotová had left.

'I have a letter from Ota,' she said, holding up a thick envelope. It was not opened, and when Aunt Josephine saw that I had noticed she explained, 'The moment I touched it, I knew it was something important. So I came straight here.'

Mother showed Aunt Jospephine into the drawing room and gave Frip a bowl of water. The maid brought tea as usual. The day was warm and the curtains were closed to keep out the heat. The drawing room was stuffy and I was sure I felt the presence of a spirit somewhere near me but had no idea to whom it belonged.

While Aunt Josephine was always excited to receive a letter from Uncle Ota, she seemed more so than ever today. Her face was flushed and she had not taken as much care as usual with her toilette. She smoothed down a lock of hair that had sprung loose from her chignon and pushed her hat straight before she commenced reading the letter.

> To my dear ladies,
> So many extraordinary things have happened since I last wrote to you. Not the least is that I have married. Now, my dear ladies, I know that this is not something you were expecting to hear from me and that you are wondering to what kind of woman I have decided to devote my life. Well, let me tell you that her name is Ranjana, which means 'delightful' and sums her up perfectly ...

'Ranjana? An Indian?' said Mother, patting her neck with a handkerchief.

Klára and I leaned forward, eager to hear more. I had a picture of a marvellous princess bedecked in gold bangles and an ochre-coloured sari. We were used to Uncle Ota's eccentricities and viewed his marriage as another of his adventures. We begged Aunt Josephine to continue to read the letter to us. And after a few moments of disbelieving head shaking, she obliged.

> As you will recall from my last letter, I was heading towards Delhi from Bombay. I stopped in a village not far from Jaipur to visit a British officer and his family

*who I had met on a previous trip to the region. While
I was there, the officer was informed that a young
woman in a nearby village was intending to commit
sati. You may have heard of this custom? A widow
immolates herself on her husband's funeral pyre.
Hindus believe that a woman who dies this way is
virtuous and will go directly to heaven and redeem all
her forefathers' sins in the process. The practice was
outlawed by the British government last century and is
condemned by enlightened Indian leaders.*

*The officer asked if I would like to accompany him
and some soldiers from his regiment. When we arrived
in the village we learned that the woman and her
kindred had already left with the husband's body and
were heading towards the cremation ground. We
followed them there and viewed the party from the
cover of some nearby hills. I have seen many temples
dedicated to sati 'goddesses' and have always sought
not to interfere in anyone else's beliefs. The life of a
widow in India is a hard one. On the death of her
husband, she loses all status in the household and her
head is shaved. Her touch, her voice and her
appearance are considered abhorrent. But what we
witnessed on the field below us was an abomination.*

*The widow was no more than twenty-one. She had
been tied to a horse and was being led along by a man
in a red robe. Instead of her holding the symbols of a
sati — a mirror and a lemon — in each hand, they had
been strung around her neck. Her head was lolling as
if she had been drugged. Walking in front of her were
a group of women singing and chanting. The officer*

*told the soldiers with him to be ready for trouble
because the girl was surrounded on all sides by youths
carrying swords. They had got whiff of intervention
and were ready to prevent it.*

*We watched the party until they reached the spot
where they intended to set the pyre alight. My stomach
turned when the woman was dragged from the horse
and thrown upon the platform alongside her husband's
corpse. In her weakened state she put up the fiercest
struggle she could but her pathetic cries for help were
unheeded by the women who simply chanted louder.
The officer told me to stay some distance behind his
men, then he commanded the soldiers down the hill
between some rocks. I watched in horror as the youths
covered the woman with sticks then doused her with
oil. But before they could light the pyre, the officer and
his men were upon them. A fight ensued in which
several of the youths were shot and one soldier had his
arm wounded. While the men were having it out, I
noticed one of the youths sneak away and light a torch.
I ran down the hill and intercepted him before he
reached the pyre. I had to deliver several blows to his
stomach before I could force him to the ground and
put the fire out. I pulled the sticks off the girl;
curiously none of the women tried to stop me. When I
reached the widow, I found her fitting and frothing at
the mouth. I lifted my canteen to her lips, convinced
that she had been poisoned and was done for anyway.
But after a few moments the convulsions ceased and
she looked up at me with the richest coffee-coloured
eyes I have ever seen.*

The rest I leave to your imagination, only to tell you that after that fateful meeting of eyes we travelled to Calcutta and from there to Ceylon, where we were married yesterday amongst bougainvillea, hibiscus and gardenias in what must have been the original Garden of Eden.

My dear ladies, I am sure that this letter has you astonished but I hope that you will share with me in my own happy bewilderment. I am a man who does not change his habits easily, therefore, while my decision may have been quick, do not think it was unconsidered. Ranjana is an unusual young woman. She was betrothed at ten years of age to her husband, who was then sixty. Although the marriage was arranged, he was a wealthy businessman who did not want an ignorant wife. Ranjana often accompanied him on his trips to Jaipur, where he traded with the British Raj, and she was educated by governesses in English, French and German. She assures me that her husband would never have agreed to her committing sati and that the whole idea was dreamed up by her in-laws because her husband had made provision for her in his will, a practice unheard of in India. She is quite a linguist and her Czech is coming along nicely — much better than my attempts at Marwari and Hindi, which leave her in fits of laughter. Anyway, with Ranjana a widow and me a Czech, we cannot stay in this region for long and must find a new place soon. We are thinking of going to the fifth continent, Australia ...

'Well, I say,' said Aunt Josephine. 'He is full of surprises!'

I was startled to hear a sob. Klára, Aunt Josephine and I turned and saw that Mother had risen from her chair and was standing by the fireplace.

'Good gracious, what is it?' said Aunt Josephine, rushing to Mother's side.

Klára and I both stood, not sure of what to do. I thought of calling Marie to bring Mother a glass of water but I stopped myself. This was a sight she should not see.

'I'm fine,' said Mother, wiping at her wet cheeks. But she was anything but fine. She was trembling and there was a desolate look in her eyes. Aunt Josephine led her back to the sofa and sat down with her. Klára poured Mother another cup of tea. Mother had made a scene and she would have to give us an explanation for it.

'I'm so sorry,' she said, dabbing at her tears with her handkerchief. 'You see, I knew Ota when he was young and he said that he would never marry. His news came as shock because it took me back to the days when I first met your father. That was twenty years ago. It's a jolt when things change suddenly and you realise that you are no longer young. That so much has already passed and you can never go back and live those days again.'

Aunt Josephine patted Mother's hand sympathetically but her mouth twitched and she did not seem convinced by Mother's explanation. I thought back to Miloš unashamedly flirting with paní Beňová at paní Provazníková's party, and the mysterious conversation between Mother and paní Milotová earlier in the day. Could these be the true reasons for Mother's reaction?

I was even more puzzled that night when I passed Mother's room and heard her weeping. Not gentle tears of sentimentality but choking sobs of unbridled grief. I was tempted to knock on her door and try to comfort her, but something told me not to disturb her, to let her anguish run its course.

When I climbed into bed beside the already sleeping Klára, I found it difficult to drift into dreams. It seemed to me that Mother was grieving as bitterly over Uncle Ota's marriage as she had over Father's death.

Two

Mother accepted the invitation to paní Koutská's musical evening, and Klára and paní Milotová worked on some pieces by Mozart, Beethoven and Chopin. They chose six sonatas and preludes, rather than longer pieces, so that Klára could adapt what to play based on the mood of the gathering.

When the evening came around, I was amazed at how at ease Klára was about the prospect of playing for her first audience. She hummed her repertoire while she went about bathing and dressing as if she did not have a care in the world. Paní Milotová had been right in describing Klára as a natural performer. Mother had bestowed upon Klára and me beautiful porcelain dolls when we were growing up, but our favourites were the ones we made ourselves by painting faces on wooden spoons. We gave our divas coiffures made from wool and costumed them in pieces of lace and tulle. We created mini puppet shows together to showcase the dolls — Klára composed the songs while I penned the dialogue and storyline. But when the time came to perform for Mother and her friends, my tongue always managed to lodge itself in my throat and Klára would be left to carry the extravaganza on her own. My only consolation was that afterwards Mother would praise the story. 'You may not be a performer but you created some wonderful scenarios,' she was always quick to comfort me.

The evening of the soirée, Miloš, who had been in Brno for business, arrived home just after seven. He stood at the bottom of the stairs, glaring at his watch and yelling at us to hurry. My heart sank. Miloš was always impatient with us, but that night was especially so. I hurried down the stairs, tripping on the rug in my haste to avoid his wrath. But Klára remained unruffled. She glided down the staircase with the grace of a princess.

'You had better not act so proudly at the party, young lady,' Miloš muttered, 'or it will be your last.'

Mother emerged from the drawing room looking splendid in a lilac dress with silver beads over the bodice and hem. The scent of lily of the valley, her favourite perfume, wafted around her. She glanced at Miloš and I wondered if she had heard him, but she said nothing and turned to Klára and myself. Her face broke into a smile. 'You will be the most beautiful girls in the room.'

Mother always lavished praise on us, but from the way Miloš skulked to the car, I wondered if the comment had been made with a more pointed purpose on this occasion.

Paní Koutská's apartment was everything a grandmother's home should be, down to the Tiffany lamps, tulip-patterned wallpaper and upholstered chairs. The piano was in the drawing room, and when we arrived there were already guests drinking tea and eating honey cake. Paní Beňová, in a claret gown with an overdress of iridescent sequins, was talking to a man with white hair and peaked eyebrows. I recognised him as Leoš Janáček, the composer of

Jenufa. I had heard he was in Prague that month to attend a concert. Paní Koutská had barely a chance to greet us before paní Beňová left the esteemed guest's side and minced over to us.

'I am charmed to meet you,' she said to Mother. 'Miloš did a wonderful job of my house and I have been dying to meet the woman who inspires him.'

Mother grimaced at the compliment. The young widow was even more striking up close, with fine skin and sapphire eyes. But there was something insincere about her, like people who say they like opera when they do not. And the way she had rushed in without waiting for an introduction was vulgar. I was surprised that Miloš welcomed her so warmly, being quick to correct 'bad' manners in myself and Klára, and was even more surprised when he kissed paní Beňová on the hand.

Pan Doubek, who was sitting with his wife near the fireplace, called out to Miloš and engaged him in conversation about the design he wanted for a new hotel. While my stepfather's attention was taken, paní Beňová leaned towards Klára.

'I cannot wait to hear you play,' she said, placing her hand on Klára's shoulder. 'Would you like to be first or second?'

Klára lifted her chin. 'I would like to play second, thank you.'

Paní Beňová's eyes narrowed. She glanced at me. Although the way she held her torso and head straight made her appear controlled, annoyance flashed in her eyes. It was rude of Klára to have taken the second place as that was usually reserved for the better pianist, which paní Beňová assumed herself to be. I glanced at Mother but she simply pursed her lips and rubbed her bracelet. Normally she would have scolded Klára for impertinence, but it appeared she did not intend to say anything and I decided that I would not either. Paní Koutská's only comment was that she was going to serve another round of tea.

Paní Beňová glanced around for our stepfather. It would be out of place to make a scene so I guessed she intended to tell him discreetly to switch the order. But Miloš was involved in his conversation with pan Doubek. I could see that paní Beňová was weighing up in her mind whether she should discuss the issue with paní Koutská, but before she could say anything the old lady began a long story about her love of music. 'It all started for me when I was a girl and my family attended a performance of Bach's Brandenburg Concertos. They were sublime, everything so beautifully balanced and in proportion. Every note so right ...'

Well, if she wanted to play second, paní Beňová should not have asked Klára what she wanted to do, I told myself. She should have left it to paní Koutská, who would have placed the most senior pianist last anyway.

Paní Koutská called for the gathering to take their places in the chairs around the piano. The black gloss of the instrument and the glow from the lamps gave paní Beňová's skin a luminescent sheen when she sat down at the keyboard. Paní Koutská announced that her lovely guest was going to play two pieces, starting with Beethoven's *Appassionata*. The piece was well known as technically challenging and paní Beňová wasted no time in manoeuvring from the quietly menacing opening into the tempestuous chordal passages. The sound was explosive in the small room and I felt the hairs on the back of my neck stand on end. Although the speed with which paní Beňová approached the piece was questionable, she did not smear the arpeggios. There was no doubt that she was good.

Professor Janáček nodded to Miloš, whose face glowed with such pride one could easily have thought that paní Beňová was his daughter, not Klára. Mother's expression told a different story. She was on the verge of tears, having found the first moment when people were not looking at her to let her emotions show. I thought about paní Beňová's comment that she wanted to meet the woman who inspired Miloš. My stepfather would not have said that. He never bestowed praise on anyone else that he could accept for himself. The unsettling feelings about paní Beňová I had first experienced at paní Provazníková's party returned to me. I squeezed Mother's hand and stared at the set of Miloš's shoulders and the way his lips were pursed in boyish pleasure. I was barely a woman and not well versed in the ways of the world, but I began to guess why Miloš had become colder towards Mother and even more impatient with us. But if paní Beňová were seeking a better position, she would not find it with Miloš. He had no fortune of his own.

For her final selection, paní Beňová played *Vallée d'Obermann* from Liszt's *Years of Pilgrimage*. It was an emotionally charged piece with blazing block chords and double octaves that she played at impressive speed, although she sometimes blurred the drama of the piece. But no one could argue that she lacked technique or could not bring off sweeping gestures with ease. When paní Beňová lifted her hands from keys, there was a hush, then applause, Miloš clapping loudest of all. I remembered his lectures on tempering your applause to the size of the room, and his hypocrisy made me despise him more. Paní Beňová stood up, her chest heaving. I glanced at Klára, expecting her to be intimidated, but she wore the same calm expression that she had since the beginning of the evening.

After more cake and tea were served and everyone was seated again, paní Koutská introduced Klára and announced that she would play Mozart's Fantasia in D minor, Chopin's Prelude in D flat, and Beethoven's *Moonlight Sonata*. I heard Miloš and paní Beňová snigger. Not only was Klára's repertoire shorter, but compared to what paní Beňová had attempted the pieces were standard fare.

Klára sat at the keyboard. The gathering giggled when she stood up again to readjust the stool so that her feet were comfortably on the floor. My face burned. It was bad enough that my mother was being humiliated but I could not stand people laughing at my sister. Unlike paní Beňová, who had constantly smiled and tossed her head, Klára simply set her hands over the keys, paused, then began playing. The condescending smiles vanished and wonder came to the faces of the listeners. Klára's fingers fluttered over the keys. Her nimble touch gave the introduction of the Fantasia a shimmering quality. The music was not complicated, but Klára played so elegantly and with such poetry that it was hard to believe we were listening to a young girl. The piece was carefully shaped and Klára's handwork so neat it was mesmerising. She made every note count. Those qualities were the result of her dedicated practice, but the way she found something fresh in the passages was uniquely her own.

The audience did not murmur or fidget when she began Chopin's Prelude in D flat. The piece was referred to as *The Raindrop* because of the repeated A flat or G sharp notes, and was thought to have been composed when Chopin, who was in Majorca for the good weather, was kept in his house for days because of rain. It was one of the first recital tunes children learned to play, and could be heard any time of the day flowing out the open windows of Malá Strana, but somehow Klára managed to breathe new life into it. She played the light and dark sections with such emotion it unsettled me. Paní Milotová said that the piano, more than any other instrument, gave away the personality of the player. I saw aspects to Klára I had never witnessed before. The girl at the keyboard was still frightened there might be monsters under her bed, but in music she was a force of nature, causing the audience to tremble with emotion.

It was the same with her *Moonlight Sonata*. The piece was lyrical, vivid, tragic and haunting all at the same time. I glanced at paní Beňová. Her smug expression had faded. Klára was not using effect as an end but was making the music live. When she finished, the audience was unable to react until paní Koutská stood up and led the applause. She requested one more piece from Klára and I understood why. Klára had taken us to a place where it was too beautiful to stay. We could not exist there; she had to bring us back to the world with its brutality and trivialness. Did Klára understand this? I didn't know, but she politely obliged with a lively mazurka.

The tension between Mother and Miloš escalated the moment Klára stepped away from the piano and Professor Janáček rushed towards us and not paní Beňová.

'What a magnificent child! What a talent! Surely you will send her to the Conservatorium!' he exclaimed.

Mother's face lit up. But her joy at the compliment was quickly quashed by Miloš. He puffed out his chest. 'There is no future for a female pianist beyond the drawing room,' he said.

Professor Janáček stepped back. 'On the contrary,' he said. 'There is always a future when the talent is so exceptional.'

Miloš glanced over to paní Beňová, who, although talking to paní Doubková in a gay manner, looked peeved. She had proved herself accomplished but Klára had outshone her. Miloš realised that and turned back to Professor Janáček. 'Pianists propagate like rabbits, my honoured professor,' he said. 'Those who cannot make careers as soloists become teachers and so produce more pianists. The cycle begins again.'

Mother, who would never contradict a man or make a scene in public, held her tongue until we were in the car. There, she could not contain herself any longer.

'Does paní Beňová restrict her talents to the drawing room?' she asked, rage constricting her vocal cords. It was painful to see her this way because she was not an angry person by nature.

'Be quiet,' Miloš said.

'I am only saying what everyone else is thinking. Do you call yourself discreet? You'll bring shame on all of us, fawning over a woman with a reputation.'

'A reputation as what?' asked Miloš.

Mother shook her head. 'A marriage mercenary. Everyone can see it. No decent man will have her.'

Miloš did not respond. We drove home in silence. As soon as we were inside the front door he ordered Klára and me to bed. While Klára slept, exhausted from the excitement and attention as only a nine-year-old could be, I listened to the muffled voices of Mother and Miloš arguing in the parlour. When the clock by my bed struck two, I could bear it no longer. I crept down the stairs. When I approached the parlour doors the words became clearer.

'Never forget that I made you what you are!' Mother told Miloš. 'And that this house and my fortune will go to Adéla and Klára.'

Miloš's answer was faint but I heard him leave the room by the other door. A few minutes later, a car started up in the street and sped away.

My mother had done nothing wrong. She had merely reminded Miloš that her daughters came first. But her words had been spoken in a rage, and if she'd had the chance to think things through, she may not have voiced those sentiments so definitely.

* * *

The strain between Miloš and Mother was conspicuous throughout the following week. We ate dismal meals together, Miloš sitting with a furrowed brow, Mother barely saying anything. When they did speak to each other, it was usually with an undertone of criticism.

'Where are *you* going?' Mother asked Miloš one afternoon as he hovered near the front door, pulling on his coat and checking his appearance in the hall mirror.

'Where did *you* put my riding gloves?' Miloš asked in return. He had indirectly answered the question and at the same time implied that Mother's orderliness caused him great inconvenience.

Klára, who had not seen the storm coming and was too young to understand paní Beňová's role in it, thought that the antagonism between Mother and Miloš was because of her performance at the soirée. She played peacemaker, embracing Mother at every opportunity to comfort her while trying at the same time to placate Miloš. One day, Miloš decided to criticise one of the younger maids by pointing out every fingermark on the walls, and Klára followed behind him with a sponge, ready to remove the stains he found.

'It's not your fault,' I told her.

I wanted to protect my sister from the hurts of the world. It was a mission Mother bestowed on me when she revealed the truth about her younger sister.

'Emilie was gentle and kind — and a talented musician,' Mother said, showing me the necklace she had kept as a memento: a gold chain from which a filigree medallion with a centre of blue crystal dangled. 'But she was susceptible to slights. I was her older sister but I did not watch her closely enough. When she was nineteen, an infatuation with a scoundrel sent her spiralling downwards. Emilie started hearing voices. My father called the best doctors and she was confined to bed. But she thought her fingers were talking to her and cut them off. She was committed to an asylum but she died that winter of pneumonia.'

I shivered. So the story about the rabid dog had been to hide Emilie's insanity. The truth about my aunt's death pained me.

'After I am gone, you must protect Klára and keep her safe,' Mother instructed me. 'When I look at her delicate face I see Emilie all over again. Do not lose sight of Klára the way I lost sight of my sister.'

But how does a sister — even a loving, devoted one — protect her charge from the facts of life? One morning I found Mister Rudolf floating upside down in his tank. As nothing in his diet or conditions had changed, I assumed his death was due to natural causes. I had no idea how to break the news to Klára. I considered buying another fish, but Klára was almost impossible to fool and it would be difficult to find a carp even half the size of Mister Rudolf so far from Christmas. I resigned myself to introducing her to a sad reality of life.

'He didn't suffer,' I assured Klára when she stood before the tank. 'And you gave him a longer, happier life than he otherwise would have had.'

Klára lifted her chin stoically but tears pooled in her eyes and slid down her cheeks.

I pressed her close to me. 'It's acceptable to cry,' I said. '"Goodbye" is the saddest word in the dictionary.'

Klára and I wrapped Mister Rudolf's body, which had taken on an opaque sheen, in muslin. We then walked along the winding streets and past the baroque houses of Malá Strana to the woods of Petřín Hill. I dug a hole in a spot where the light filtered through the avenue of maple trees, while Klára collected stones and blossoms to place on the grave. 'Face him towards the path,' she said, when it came time to lay Mister Rudolf in the ground. 'So he can see the people walk by. He liked to watch us when we passed by him on the way to the parlour.'

I took a photograph of Klára standing by the grave, and afterwards we strolled around the park and on to Hradčany. It was a warm day with a gentle breeze and the least I could do was to give Klára pleasant memories of Mister Rudolf's burial. When Mother's friend Anuše died in childbirth several years earlier, I was plagued for weeks by nightmares of the funeral. The sickly smell of incense and coffin wood and the stern face of the priest had confused me with their morbidity. My image of Anuše while she was alive was of her bright smile and the sound of her raucous laughter.

Klára and I walked the cobblestoned streets of the Castle district, stopping occasionally for me to photograph the medieval house signs. We tried to guess what they represented. Before houses were numbered, tradesmen and merchants used these emblems instead of an address. There were shoes for cobblers, crowns for nobles, violins for music makers and keys for locksmiths. We had enjoyed walking here ever since I was old enough to take Klára on my own, and we always seemed to discover new signs in the endless nooks and alleys.

Klára was patient with my picture taking. I waited until the clouds in the background were right, or the sunlight was in a good position, before taking my shot. But when her pace slowed, I understood she was tired. I bought some cherries and we ate them on our way home. At the base of the Castle we stopped to look over the panoramic view of Prague. It seemed reposeful with the Vltava flowing under the Charles Bridge and the dome of St Nicholas and the Gothic tower of the town hall rising up through the red roofs. Prague was my home and the vista from the Castle was as much a part of me as my hands and feet. I took Klára's fingers, sticky with cherry juice, and clutched them in my own. I re-avowed silently that I would guard her well-being with my life.

My birthday that year marked the end of summer and the beginning of autumn. The day before had been sunny and warm, but on the morning of 21 August, I looked out my window to see that fog had settled over the city. I washed my face and hands in the basin and hurried downstairs to have breakfast with Mother and Klára. In the dining room, the maids were laying out bread rolls and assorted jams. There was also a vanilla cake with pink icing. I was surprised to see Miloš sitting at the table reading the paper. Things had settled down between him and Mother to a cold courtesy. But I did not know if it was because Miloš had given up on paní Beňová or whether Mother had chosen to turn a blind eye to his indiscretions in order to keep the peace.

'*Všechno nejlepší k narozeninám*!' Klára wished me happy birthday and pulled out the seat next to her.

'Klára and Josephine helped me choose your present this year,' said Mother, passing me something soft wrapped in tissue paper with a purple bow. I opened the gift to find a shell-pink silk scarf, almost as large as a shawl, with a fringed hem and peach blossoms embroidered in each corner.

'It's lovely,' I said, pressing the fabric to my cheek.

'You are a young lady now,' said Mother, with a proud smile. 'You should only wear beautiful things.'

Aunt Josephine avoided our house when Miloš was in town, so she invited the three of us to her home for afternoon tea that day instead.

'Has Uncle Ota not written to you at all these past months, Aunt Josephine?' Klára asked when we sat down in the parlour.

While our drawing room was all French windows and Delftware porcelain, Aunt Josephine's parlour was more comfortable. The wall panels were a rich mahogany, and crimson drapes with gold tassels framed the ceiling-to-floor windows.

Aunt Josephine glanced at my mother. 'I have in fact just received a letter,' she said. 'But we have all been so busy that I didn't have the chance to tell you about it.'

Klára's eyes flew open with delight but I knew that Aunt Josephine, usually so scrupulously honest, was not telling the truth. The first thing she did whenever she received a letter from Uncle Ota was rush to us to read it.

'Please, go ahead,' said Mother, folding her hands in her lap. 'Ota's letters give the girls such pleasure.'

Aunt Josephine shifted in her seat. Perhaps she was nervous that Mother would start crying again. But she was put at ease when Mother remarked that she enjoyed Uncle Ota's letters because 'his adventures far surpass any excitement we know in Prague, despite the concerts and galleries'.

'Very well,' she said, rising from her chair and leaving the room. She returned with a crumpled envelope and sat down. Frip rested his chin on her shoe. Aunt Josephine unfolded the letter and commenced to read.

> *To my dear ladies,*
> *After a voyage of seasickness and storms, Ranjana and I are now in Australia. It is the most mystifying country I have ever seen. Its beauty is both lush and dry. Its people the same. We are presently in Perth, on the west coast, and were greeted in the city not by people but by dozens of black and white birds called 'magpies' sitting on the docks and fences. Ranjana has*

fallen in love with the plant and bird life and has taken up 'botanising'. It is wonderful to watch her pressing the specimens of flowers and seeds into her album. Even with her sari and dark skin, she is more attentive than any European lady I have seen.

We will sail on to Sydney in a few days' time where I will try to find work as the passage here swallowed most of my funds. Ranjana and I have decided that if Sydney is to our liking, we will stay. Intellectuals are not valued in this harsh land, so I may need to work with my hands. I once said that I would never stop travelling but I have decided that if I choose to live in a foreign country, one so different from my native homeland, it does not count. There is a raw sense of adventure and possibility about this country that makes me think it is the place for us to live. Not that it was easy to be accepted past the boarding officers. That, my dear nieces, was a feat greater than passing examinations at the University of Prague. Not so much for me, as the colour of my skin is more acceptable than Ranjana's! Australians would like to keep anyone from Asia — and most non-English-speaking Europeans — out of their country, and would succeed too if not for British objections to the insult it would be to their subjects in India. Because Australian officials cannot legally discriminate against anyone who is not suffering an infectious disease, is not a criminal or a menace to society in some way, they have come up with a dictation test. Being given a test in English, the national language, I can understand. But the test may be administered in any

*prescribed language. A Maltese applicant was given a
test in Dutch; a Spaniard a test in German; and a
German fluent in several languages was eventually
failed when he was tested in Gaelic! The poor man
was sentenced to six months' jail for being an illegal
immigrant. You can see what Ranjana was up against.
Luckily, she passed the test in English and French and
was finally let through when they could not find
anyone to test her in Russian!*

*We will send you more news and an address when
we get to Sydney. Meanwhile, Ranjana has asked me
to enclose a book about the birds of Australia. We
believe little Klára is particularly interested in these
things.*

Yours lovingly,
Ota and Ranjana

Mother's reaction to Uncle Ota's letter was the opposite of how
she had responded to the previous one. 'Ranjana sounds
delightful,' she said, 'and very suited to Ota.'

She poured out the tea while Aunt Josephine cut the koláč.

'I hope we may meet them one day,' I said.

Mother sat down again. 'You would like Ota very much. I
remember his keen mind and his quick wit. But it doesn't sound
as if he intends to return to Prague any time soon.'

Aunt Josephine placed a slice of koláč in front of Klára, who
adored the dough-bread sweet. But she was absorbed in the book
on birds Ranjana had sent for her and even the scent of the
cheese, stewed prune and apricot filling did not stir her. Soon she
was telling us that the brightly coloured rainbow lorikeets had
brush-like appendages on their tongues for eating nectar, that

willy wagtails sang when the moon was bright, and that galahs mated for life.

'We were never ones for travel, were we, Marta?' asked Aunt Josephine, studying Mother's face. 'Oh, we had our seasons in Florence and Paris but that was enough for us. We learned the languages so we could pronounce the foods we served at dinner parties, but we never found anywhere that made us as happy as home.'

Mother blushed but held her own under Aunt Josephine's gaze. 'That's right,' she answered. 'That's why I waited for Antonín to finish his training before I married him. I was lonely without him, but I would have been useless away from my mother and home.'

Aunt Josephine searched Mother's face once more before sitting back. 'I want to change these drapes,' she said, clutching the velvet curtains. 'They are too heavy. Maybe you could suggest something, Marta? You have good taste.'

I sensed that Aunt Josephine had been trying to find out something but became afraid of going too far. Mother and Aunt Josephine were as different as apples and oranges but they had been friends for twenty years. They would have died for each other if it ever came to that.

I was as confused about Mother's behaviour as Aunt Josephine. I wondered if Mother had been in love with Uncle Ota once. But anyone who had seen my mother and father together could not have doubted their bond: Mother's face had lit up whenever Father entered the room, and nothing could distract her attention when he was speaking. As for my father, witnesses said it was Mother's name on his lips when he died.

I picked up Uncle Ota's letter and read it for myself, trying to discover the man behind the swirling handwriting. In the pictures

I had seen of him, Uncle Ota was the opposite of my father: tall with a shock of hair and keen, light-coloured eyes. But no matter how many times I read the letter or stared at the lines, I could not solve the puzzle.

Not long after, another letter arrived from Uncle Ota.

> *To my dear ladies,*
> *Ranjana and I are in Sydney now. And what a city! We loved it the moment we set eyes on it. The magnificent buildings of golden sandstone took our breath away. We know their names now: St Mary's Cathedral; the Lands Office Tower; the Town Hall; and the Queen Victoria Building. True, one sees Europe in their Classical and Renaissance styles, but there is also something different — something 'other' — about the place. Perhaps it is the natural setting: the opal-blue harbour with its coves and beaches, the ochre villas set amongst the silvery-green bushland. And the trees! Our first purchase in the city was a botany book and my lovely wife has already recorded descriptions and the botanic names of the fascinating species. These are some of the gum trees that thrill us with their gigantic trunks and branches that reach out like the arms of a Hindu goddess, embracing all manner of bird life:*
> *Sydney red gum, Angophora costata*
> *Red bloodwood, Eucalyptus gummifera*
> *Scribbly gums, E. racemosa and E. haemastoma*
> *Sydney peppermint, E. piperita*
> *The birds make a deafening chatter in them in the mornings and evenings: white parrots with massive*

beaks and claws, and smaller ones that are coloured like tropical fruit. Your mother would certainly have inspiration enough for a thousand of her paintings if she were to see all this beauty. We have rented a house on part of the harbour known as Watsons Bay. It is a ramshackle dwelling that is falling to bits around us, but it is the best we can do for now. Although Ranjana swapped her sari for western dress and speaks more refined English than most of the resident population, our joy is tainted by the prejudice against her. When we approached landlords about places they had advertised, they were nearly all friendly to me, but changed tune as soon as they saw Ranjana. There was one man, who was leasing what amounted to a tin shack in a yard full of coils of wire and blocks of discarded wood, who almost came to blows with me simply because I made him an offer. This behaviour is inconsistent with Australians in general, who are mostly egalitarian and carefree. Perhaps it is the location — so far from the British Isles, from where nearly all of them come — that makes them so afraid of Orientals. The only people who welcomed us were the artists of Kings Cross, but I did not fancy making Ranjana live in a rat-invested hovel. So after some frantic searching we found this place. We are renting it from an elderly blind woman and her daughter. The end of it all is that for the first time in years I have a permanent address, which will make it easier for you to write to me. I look forward to hearing the news about you and your lovely mother, although I notice my sister does not mention your stepfather much.

How is he these days? Still up to his ears in
chandeliers and chinoiserie motif fabrics?
   Our love always,
   Ota and Ranjana

From his wording, it was finally clear that Uncle Ota had meant his letters for Klára and me. He had never mentioned Mother and Miloš directly before. I wondered what Mother would say about the matter. For the past few months she had been lethargic and withdrawn. Even her paintings had been lacklustre in recent times, variations on the view from our window. But this recent letter seemed to have a positive effect on her. The following morning she was up at dawn, sketching the birds from the book Ranjana had sent. Later in the day, Mother donned a dress of violet *crêpe de Chine* and asked paní Milotová to keep us company while she ran some errands. She returned in the afternoon with truffle chocolates and a set of watercolours. The next morning she was at the dining table, surrounded by paper, paints and water jars, working on a picture of a superb fairy-wren.

Klára sat beside her reading out the habits of the bird, in quite good English considering that Mother had only recently started giving her lessons. 'Male superb fairy-wrens have blue and black plumage above and on the throat. The birds give a series of high-pitched trills, which the male extends into a full song. They are often found in urban parks and gardens in eastern Australia.'

My mother acted like someone who had carried a burden that had suddenly been lifted. It was as if she had been given a second chance at life.

*   *   *

A few nights after Klára's tenth birthday in September, Mother suffered acute stomach pains. The family physician, Doctor Soucek, was called.

'Now what ails your dear mother that you should disturb an old man's rest?' was the first thing Doctor Soucek said in his raspy voice when he arrived on our doorstep.

His manners were surly but his hands were gentle. He had no son to take his place and the pauses in his speech and the twist in his spine put him well beyond retirement but he was the only doctor Mother trusted, having brought not only Klára and myself into the world but her as well.

'He may act like a stablehand but he cures like the hand of God,' she said.

After examining Mother, Doctor Soucek spoke with Miloš and me in the drawing room.

'I cannot find a physical cause for the pains,' he said, casting his eye over Miloš. 'It would seem to me that they are due to anxiety and a lack of exercise.'

'Whenever they can't find a physical cause they put it down to nerves,' Miloš said to me after Doctor Soucek had left.

If Mother was feeling anxious, I had no doubt who was the cause of it. But Miloš surprised me. The weather had turned bitterly cold and Mother could not walk outside. So every morning and afternoon, he would link arms with her to stroll around the house.

'I feel like a tourist in my own domain,' Mother laughed.

Miloš laughed too. I would never like him, let alone love him as much as I had loved my father. But I was glad things had improved between them.

By Christmas, Mother was feeling better and Miloš remained attentive. He also taught Klára to play chess and me how to dance the Viennese waltz without becoming dizzy.

'Don't trust him,' Aunt Josephine warned me when I went to visit her on New Year's Day. 'He's just worked out which side of the bread is buttered and has decided to be more pleasant. Paní Beňová couldn't keep him in the same style as your mother does and he knows it. You and Klára will inherit your mother's house and fortune. We may not yet have the vote in this new republic, but we are still the mistresses of our property — married or not.'

I turned away. I never liked to talk about inheritances or wills. I could not imagine life without Mother. I wanted her to live forever.

Aunt Josephine, in her efforts to introduce me to the world of independent women, arranged for us to take typing lessons in the spring together. It was a strange exercise as neither of us needed to work, but Aunt Josephine was fascinated by women who were ambitious to improve their place in the world through means other than marriage. So once a week, under the pretence of sewing together, Aunt Josephine and I travelled over the Charles Bridge to the medieval streets of Staré Město where we joined the typing class at the back of a leather-goods store. While Klára produced beautiful music under the guidance of paní Milotová, Aunt Josephine and I sat in a cramped room with the ambitious daughters of shopkeepers and postmistresses and learned to touch type. I was amused by my aunt who, having lived the privileged existence of an upper-class lady, was so enamoured of women who worked for their living.

I enjoyed the lessons and the chatter of the girls before class, even though our instructress, paní Sudková, was a tyrant. At first, her cold stare made me so nervous that when she looked over my shoulder, my fingers slipped and I ended up with a jam of keys all trying to print at the same time. 'You must train your fingers to press and lift independently,' she said, raising her thick eyebrows and slapping my wrist with a ruler. 'And strike the keys harder.' Nonetheless, once I sped up to twenty words a minute, I found myself looking forward to the classes. There was something about the rhythmic clack of keys striking the platens and the 'ding' of the bells when the students reached the end of a line that was hypnotic. It was not long before I progressed from drills to typing letters.

Summer that year was more pleasant than the previous one had been. There was no sign of paní Beňová, although Aunt Josephine was adamant that Miloš was only being more discreet. Mother, however, was much happier. Her stomach pains disappeared and she and Miloš attended summer balls and parties together. Aunt Josephine and I graduated from secretarial school and Klára excelled in her lessons with paní Milotová. But by the end of summer, Mother's pains returned more severely than before. She was bedridden for days at a time. Then the unthinkable happened. I was on my way home from Aunt Josephine's when I turned the corner to the square and saw Klára sitting on the front steps of our house. She was leaning with her head against the stone balustrade.

'Klára!' I cried, running up to her. 'Mother will have a fit if she sees you sitting out here like an urchin!'

Klára lifted her face and the terror in her eyes sent me reeling backwards.

'Mother,' she said, pointing to the second-floor window. The curtains were drawn. A sickening feeling rose in my stomach.

'What's happened?' I asked. My chest constricted so tightly I could barely get the words out.

Klára trembled. 'Mother collapsed soon after you left. Miloš said Doctor Soucek was hopeless and called another doctor to see her. Doctor Hoffmann examined Mother and said her appendix is on the verge of bursting. He didn't want to risk taking her to the hospital. He is operating on her now. There is a nurse with him, and Paní Milotová is helping too.'

The ground shifted beneath my feet. The pinks, yellows and greens of the houses of the square melted together. When I had left, Mother was sitting in the morning room, writing letters. I was running late so I blew her a kiss before heading towards the door. She called me back and when I peered into the room, she smiled and said, 'I love you.'

I grasped Klára's hand. 'Come inside,' I said.

The eerie quiet of the house was a contrast to the hammering of my heart. Paní Milotová rushed out of the kitchen carrying a saucepan of boiled water. She wore a white kitchen apron that was smeared with blood. I nearly fainted.

'Pray for your mother,' she said, before running up the stairs.

I guided Klára to the parlour and sank to my knees. Klára threw herself down beside me. My head was swimming too much to pray but Klára closed her eyes and pleaded with God for Mother's life, offering up everything dear to her if he would save her. She even promised to give up music if that was the sacrifice God wanted.

Half an hour later, Miloš trudged down the stairs. His shoulders were slumped and his eyes were bloodshot. Without his arrogant air he was almost unrecognisable.

'Your mother is gravely ill,' he told us, just as the priest arrived. 'The doctor will try to save her.' He led the priest upstairs but did not ask us to follow.

Klára and I clung to the sliver of hope that Mother would survive the operation as fervently as we clung to each other while we awaited further news. There was a knock at the door and Marie hurried to answer it. I cried out when I saw Aunt Josephine standing in the hall.

'Marie sent for me,' she said, throwing her arms around us. 'Has anyone made you supper?'

'I can't eat,' wept Klára.

'I'm not hungry, Aunt Josephine,' I said.

Aunt Josephine embraced us again. Her face was ashen and the lines around her mouth seemed to have deepened since I saw her only a few hours ago. She was distressed. But instead of obeying an impulse to rush upstairs and find out what was happening, she did exactly what Mother would have asked her to do: she took care of us.

After making us drink some tea and eat two shortbread biscuits each 'for strength', Aunt Josephine returned us to the parlour. 'Let's pray,' she said. My mind calmed in her presence. Aunt Josephine's prayer was a more peaceful appeal than the desperate petitions Klára and I had made. She shunned the church as hypocritical and followed her own path. 'I'm spiritual but I'm not religious,' she always said. Now, she thanked God for the beautiful person my mother was and prayed he would watch over her and her daughters. It occurred to me that she spoke to God as one does a friend, although her voice broke on the 'Amen'.

A short while later the doctor came down the stairs. He was nothing like doddery old Doctor Soucek who usually attended Mother. He was younger with black hair and long sideburns. Aunt Josephine was surprised not to see Doctor Soucek and I quickly explained why Miloš had chosen someone new.

'The girls had better come up now,' Doctor Hoffmann said.

The smells of iodine and blood pervaded the air of Mother's bedroom. The priest had finished administering the last rites and the expression of pity on his face made me buckle at the knees. A nurse stood in the corner washing and wiping instruments.

Paní Milotová hovered beside her, weeping. When she saw us she reached out her arms. 'They opened her up but it was too late,' she whimpered. 'They could do nothing but sew her up again.'

In the dim light, I saw Mother lying on her bed with a sheet pulled up to her neck. She was so pale she looked like a marble statue on a church crypt.

'Mother?' I sobbed, moving towards her.

I was not sure if she heard me, but then she murmured, 'Adélka, come here.'

I pressed my cheek to hers. It was cold. 'Chest,' she whispered to me. 'Look in the chest.'

Mother turned to Aunt Josephine and tried to say something to her, but lost her strength. She was fading before our eyes.

The doctor sat down on the bed next to Mother and listened to her chest. 'Her heartbeat is faint,' he said. 'She is close to death.'

Mother's eyes closed as if she had fallen asleep. Suddenly they opened. 'Emilie,' she said. 'Look, Emilie is here. She is as beautiful as ever.'

Mother gasped for air, but as quickly as the spasm started, it finished. Her eyes glazed over and the breath rushed out of her in what seemed like a long sigh.

My legs shook and I pressed my palms against my forehead, trying to stop myself from fainting. 'What's happened?' Klára cried. Aunt Josephine sank into a chair and buried her head in her hands. I returned my attention to Mother's face, desperately searching for a sign of life. Doctor Hoffmann pressed his fingers to Mother's throat, feeling for a pulse. He found nothing and closed her eyes.

Then the surreal became the real and the walls pressed in on me. The doctor gave Miloš some instructions, and the priest began a prayer, but their voices sounded distant and hollow. The nurse stepped forward, made the sign of the cross, and folded Mother's arms across her chest. I felt the veil of separation slip between us and Mother. The person on whose bosom I had drawn my first breath had breathed her last. I turned to Klára, who was trembling from head to foot. I wanted to throw my arms around her, to comfort her and have her comfort me. But I was frozen to the spot.

THREE

Mother was laid out in a dress of shimmering indigo. The windows were draped in black curtains and the Delftware porcelain replaced with candles in silver holders. The exterior of our house was still blue with white trimmings, but inside it was as gloomy as night. Miloš, Aunt Josephine, paní Milotová, Klára and I, all dressed in mourning attire, took turns sitting with Mother who lay in her rosewood coffin for three days before the funeral. I stared at her impassive face, not able to believe that her eyes would not open at any moment and that she would come to life again.

Despite my grief, I held to my promise to watch over Klára, who had reacted to Mother's death with stunned silence. She had barely said a word since the terrible event. On the second night after Mother's death, when Aunt Josephine and paní Milotová watched over her coffin, Klára and I lay in bed together, listening to a storm brewing. Drops of water slid down the windowpanes. I ran my fingers through Klára's river of hair.

'Mother is with Father now,' she whispered.

I wrapped my arm around her. Her skin smelt sweet, like vanilla cream, and I thought of the cake Mother had intended to make for the following day, which was Klára's birthday. Lightning flashed and I saw Klára's tear-filled eyes. I was thankful that she was handling Mother's death so courageously.

'When our mourning period is over we will celebrate your birthday,' I promised her.

Early in the morning I was awoken by screams and the sound of glass breaking. Marie rushed into the room. 'Slečna Ruzicková!' she cried, addressing me formally. 'Your sister!'

I leaped out of bed so quickly that the room turned white and I had to grip onto the wall. I ran after Marie down the stairs to the kitchen. My breath caught in my throat. Klára was standing barefoot on the black and white tiles surrounded by broken glass. Her nightdress and hands were stained red. I imagined Mother discovering Emilie in the sewing room after she had cut off her fingers, but then I realised that the stains had clumps of seeds in them. They were not blood but raspberry jam. Across the benches and floor were strewn the smashed jars of jam Klára had made with Mother the previous month.

Klára snatched another jar from the shelf and raised her arm, intending to throw it to the floor.

'Don't,' I pleaded. I had not had time to put on slippers and I stepped gingerly towards her through the broken glass.

She stared at me, her mouth twisted into a muted cry of rage. Tears filled her eyes and she began to sob. 'Why?' she cried. 'Why?'

Her voice had such a beseeching tone that it snapped my heart. I reached her without cutting myself and threw my arms around her. Her thin frame trembled in my grasp.

'I don't know,' I said, burying my face in her neck. 'I don't know.'

* * *

Even more disturbing than Klara's violent outpouring of grief was the arrival of Doctor Soucek the day after Mother's funeral. Marie had no idea what to make of his request to see Mother, so she asked him to wait in the drawing room and called me.

'I came as soon as I heard,' he said, rising from his chair, still wheezing from having run up the stairs to our front door. 'I was away visiting my daughter.'

'We buried Mother yesterday,' I told him, bewildered by his presence. I asked Marie to call Aunt Josephine, who was still staying with us. I could not understand why Doctor Soucek had come. He had misdiagnosed Mother's appendicitis as anxiety pains. If he had recognised the true cause of her discomfort, she would have gone to hospital in plenty of time and she would be sitting in the room with us now.

Doctor Soucek's face fell and he lowered himself into the chair again. 'No chance of an autopsy then,' he said.

His words hit me with such force that I was on the verge of being sick. Of course there would be no autopsy on Mother. We knew why she died.

Doctor Soucek rushed towards Aunt Josephine when she entered the room. 'Paní Valentová was a robust woman,' he said, using Mother's maiden name. 'She should have outlived all of us. What sort of infection was she supposed to have died of?'

Aunt Josephine glanced at me. I had managed to compose myself enough that morning to start some sewing, and now Doctor Soucek had arrived and was saying terrible things. The tears I had tried to hold back flowed down my cheeks. Aunt Josephine drew herself up as if preparing for battle.

'She died of appendicitis, Doctor Soucek. When the doctor operated he saw that the infection had spread to her other organs. There was nothing he could do.'

Aunt Josephine said the words matter-of-factly but the undertone of blame was there. Doctor Soucek studied her with his rheumy eyes.

'You had better get her exhumed,' he said quietly.

I reeled back in horror at the suggestion. Mother? Exhumed after we had just buried her in holy ground?

'Let the dead have their peace,' I said, my voice rising in agitation.

'Doctor Soucek,' said Aunt Josephine. 'You are not making any sense and you are upsetting my niece who has already had a terrible shock.'

Miloš passed the drawing room and saw Doctor Soucek with us. He frowned. 'What brings you here?'

Doctor Soucek's lips pinched together as if he had nothing to say to Miloš.

'If you do not have anything to offer us, Doctor Soucek, I think you had better leave,' Miloš said, his lip curling the same way Frip's did when he saw a menacing dog.

Doctor Soucek glanced from me to Aunt Josephine. There was a tremble in his hands and I felt sorry for him. He had been good to our family over the years. I was not angry at him for misdiagnosing Mother, only sad. She had thought so highly of him. She had been a breech birth and, as a younger man, he had saved her and her mother. But this time round, he had been negligent.

Doctor Soucek turned to me as though he wanted to say something else, but another hostile glance from Miloš made him think better of it. He picked up his coat and hat. 'I will be going,' he said.

I accompanied him to the hall and helped him with his coat. 'Goodbye, Doctor Soucek,' I said, opening the door. He looked over his shoulder to check we were alone then grabbed my arm. 'You dressed her for the funeral, didn't you?' he asked. 'You saw the scars?'

The pity I felt for him turned to revulsion again. I remembered the stitched scar that had twisted across Mother's belly like a braided roll. I tried to push Doctor Soucek away but he gripped me more firmly. I thought he must have gone mad.

'Did you see the scar under it? The fine white one?'

'I'll call my stepfather,' I warned him, looking back into the house.

Doctor Soucek loosened his grip and I stumbled. He rushed down the front stairs and raised his arm to hail a cab. One arrived and he was about to step into it when he turned around. 'Appendicitis!' he snorted. 'Find out what really happened, will you? I removed your mother's appendix myself when she was eighteen years old.'

It took minutes before Aunt Josephine could bring herself to speak after I reported what Doctor Soucek had said. The news knocked the wind out of her as it had from me. She leaned on the table where Mother's coffin had rested and shook her head.

'We must be careful not to jump to conclusions,' she said. 'Doctor Soucek is old and even your mother said he was sometimes forgetful. Perhaps he is confused. Perhaps it was Emilie's appendix that he removed. I don't recall your mother ever mentioning it and that would have been not long before I met her.'

I sat back, overtaken by another wave of nausea. I wondered, with all that had happened in the last few days, if I would ever feel the vitality of my age again. But what if Doctor Soucek was right? What did that mean? Doctor Hoffmann's face floated up before me. He had been professional in his manner and did not appear to be someone who would misdiagnose an illness and then try to cover it up.

I told Aunt Josephine what I was thinking.

'No, I don't understand what it means either,' she said. 'We must speak to paní Milotová. After all, she was there.'

We were surprised to find paní Milotová wearing her mourning dress when we arrived at her apartment. Only immediate members of the family were expected to dress in black after the deceased's funeral.

'Marta was my dear friend,' she explained. 'I can't forget her.'

We sat down at paní Milotová's dining table and watched while she served tea from a samovar. She had left Russia before the Revolution and I had always been fascinated by her collection of lacquered boxes, Fabergé eggs and bear figurines.

When the tea was served, Aunt Josephine related Doctor Soucek's words to paní Milotová, whose face turned as green as the jade handles on the teaspoons. The pitch of her voice, an octave higher than normal, conveyed her shock.

'I arrived at the house at eleven o'clock to give Klára her lesson,' she said. 'Marta had collapsed and Marie was leaving to fetch Doctor Soucek. Miloš stopped her and scribbled down the address of Doctor Hoffmann. When the doctor arrived I was impressed at how he took control of the crisis.'

Paní Milotová paused, as if she were seeing the scene unfold in front of her. Then she continued. 'He examined Marta and told us that emergency surgery was needed. Marie was despatched to fetch Doctor Hoffmann's nurse. "I have medical training," I told him. "I was a volunteer nurse during the war."

He stared at me as if considering the proposition. "Then you know how to sterilise instruments?" he asked. I told him that I did and that I would help in any way I could. Marta was anaesthetised. I don't believe she felt a thing.'

Paní Milotová hesitated. A troubled look furrowed her brow. 'At the time everything seemed professional ... but I was struck by how little the doctor said to the nurse. I was with doctors during the war to clean wounds and they were always giving me instructions. But Doctor Hoffmann asked nothing of his nurse.'

The three of us fell quiet, wondering about this observation. Perhaps Doctor Hoffmann and his nurse, having performed many operations together, did not need to speak.

'Where was Miloš?' Aunt Josephine asked.

Paní Milotová considered the question, then said, 'He was pacing outside the door most of the time, but every so often he looked into the room. It was only when Doctor Hoffmann had sewed Marta back up and she was starting to come to that he told us there was no hope.'

It was terrible to hear all these things about Mother's death, but I was compelled to find out the truth. After paní Milotová had told us all she could, Aunt Josephine and I decided we would visit Doctor Soucek and ask to see his medical records. Before we went to see the doctor, however, Aunt Josephine suggested we seek the advice of our family lawyer, Doctor Holub. Mother's final testament was not due to be read until the following week, so he was surprised when he saw us waiting in his office.

'God be with you at this time,' he said, leaving aside formality and embracing us. Doctor Holub had been Father's best friend and had a soft spot for our family. 'What can I do for you?'

Aunt Josephine related the story about Mother's appendix. Doctor Holub listened carefully, rubbing his bald patch with one hand and taking notes with the other. When Aunt Josephine finished speaking, he folded his hands under his chin, deep in thought.

'It's possible the doctor misdiagnosed,' he said. 'Then tried to cover his mistake. I will make some enquiries into his character and medical record. I will also see Doctor Soucek myself.'

Doctor Holub re-read his notes and his face turned dark. He looked at me. 'Your mother and stepfather ... they were happy?' he ventured.

Everyone knew that Mother and Miloš were far from happy so I was taken aback by the chill the question sent through me. A thought that had not occurred to me until that moment gripped me like a vice. My breath caught in my throat when I tried to speak. I turned hopelessly to Aunt Josephine, who gave a better considered answer than I could.

'The marriage was not a success. Marta hoped for a companion to relieve her loneliness and to be a father figure to her daughters, but pan Dolezal did not fulfil those longings. He is simply too vain and too selfish. But if you are suggesting he plotted with Doctor Hoffmann to kill Marta ... especially in such a heinous way ... I could not accuse him of that. Miloš is an overgrown child, not a murderer.'

Aunt Josephine's logic calmed my mind and I began to breathe more easily. She was right: Miloš was a conceited fool but not a villain.

'Paní Dolezalová's will is to be formally read out next week,' Doctor Holub said to Aunt Josephine. 'In the event of her death, she appointed you as the guardian of her children until the youngest of her daughters, Klára, comes of age. At that time the fortunes of the Ruzicka and Valenta families will transfer to the young ladies. Pan Dolezal is to receive an allowance until this time, with the expectation that his business will eventually make him self-sufficient.'

'I wonder if he knows that?' asked Aunt Josephine. 'I think he was expecting to be "kept" in the event of Marta's death.'

Doctor Holub's eyes did not move from Aunt Josephine's face. He was trying to tell her something he did not want to say in front of me. But I could guess what it was. If my mother's will had not been altered since the time of her marriage to Miloš, then my stepfather would be the beneficiary should Klára and I both die before she reached twenty-one.

I found it difficult to sleep that night. My dreams were haunted by images of Mother dying, her grave covered in lilies, and Miloš. I felt no love for my stepfather but his grief at Mother's death seemed sincere. Now Doctor Holub had put terrible ideas in my head and, despite Aunt Josephine's assurances, I could not forget them.

Aunt Josephine looked as tired as I did the following day. Neither of us spoke over breakfast, which left the conversation up to Klára and Miloš and they did not have much to say. Aunt Josephine had stayed with us since Mother's death, and I wondered, as she was to be our guardian, whether we would continue to live in our house or move to hers. Later in the morning, when I was in the courtyard garden, the question was answered. I heard Aunt Josephine talking with Miloš through the library window.

'I understand that you are grieved by Marta's death,' Aunt Josephine said, 'but the funeral was a few days ago and it is unseemly for you to continue to live under the same roof as your stepdaughters.'

Aunt Josephine was being tactful and treading carefully. Miloš answered immediately.

'Yes, I have prepared for that. I have taken an apartment. But I hope that I will have your permission to call on the girls? I have grown fond of them.'

Miloš had never been fond of us. But perhaps he regretted his behaviour towards Mother and wanted to make up for it. I did not hear Aunt Josephine's reply. But what could she have said? As unseemly as it would appear if Miloš continued to live under the same roof as us, it would be just as unseemly if all relations were suddenly cut off.

'I will move my things tomorrow,' Miloš promised.

That night, I tossed and turned and had nightmares again. Although paní Milotová had assured me that Mother had been given sufficient morphine, I dreamt that she had been cut across the belly and was screaming. I woke with a start.

What if Miloš *had* hired Doctor Hoffmann to kill Mother? It was far less suspicious to die of a medical condition in the presence of a doctor than to be poisoned or stabbed. If Mother had been murdered in those conventional ways, the suspicion would have immediately fallen on Miloš. I thought about whether the police could do anything, and decided they probably could not with only accusations and no evidence. Doctor Soucek's demand for an autopsy would also be fruitless. The violation of Mother's body would not prove anything: she would not have an appendix either way. Doctor Soucek would claim that he removed it years ago, and Doctor Hoffmann would say he'd had the diseased organ incinerated. My head swam with the appalling possibilities, but in the end I kept coming back to one thing. Miloš was arrogant, self-seeking and unpleasant, but was he capable of such an evil plan to get rid of Mother?

I thought about Mother's last day and how she had seemed well when I wished her goodbye in the morning. A few hours later she died in her bed.

'Look in the chest.'

Goose bumps prickled my arms. Those had been Mother's last words to me. I had thought she was delirious and talking about a pain in her chest. Now I remembered the night she gave me Father's camera from his chest in the attic.

I climbed out of bed and opened the door. The hall was dark and quiet. I did not need a lamp to guide me because the bathroom was at the other end and I knew the route there by heart. But I would need light to negotiate the attic stairs. I searched about for a candle, found one in the dresser drawer and lit the wick.

There were no ghosts in the hall and I crept towards the attic stairs. I passed Miloš's bedroom and heard him sigh. A glimmer of light flickered beneath the door. He must be reading in bed, I thought. I held my breath and prayed that no creaking floorboards would betray me.

The room felt closed when I entered it. My candle gave only a small circle of light but I dared not turn on the switch as the new electric globe was twice as bright as those downstairs and Miloš might notice it if he left his room to go to the bathroom.

The chest was still there but where was the key? I searched the drawers of Father's desk and under the rug but had no luck finding it. I heard the door to Miloš's room open then shut. I froze to the spot, listening for further sounds. But then I heard his feet on the floorboards and realised he had not left his room. I felt under the chest and found only cobwebs, then around the inkstand. My fingers touched the thin metal barrel of a key and I grasped it with triumph. I tried it in the lock. It fitted.

I lifted the lid gently so it would not make any noise. The smell of wool rose up from the chest and then a sweet smell too. I recognised it as rosemary. Father used to drink an infusion of it every morning. He believed it improved his memory. He also laid a sprig of it on Mother's pillow on their anniversary each year, as a symbol of his fidelity. Mother had tucked sachets of the herb around the sides of the chest. I held up the candle so I could see better, careful not to drop wax onto Father's uniform. I saw an envelope addressed to Aunt Josephine lying on top of Father's coat. The handwriting was Mother's. I picked up the envelope and found another one for Uncle Ota beneath it.

The sound of footsteps on the attic stairs jolted me. I tucked the letter in my hand into my nightdress, closed the chest and blew out the candle. I had just slid behind the armoire when the door opened and Miloš crept in, holding a lamp.

I wondered if he had been disturbed by sounds in the attic and if he would smell the lingering scent of wax from the candle. Fortunately, the room held such a mixture of odours — dust, wood, musty cloth — they must have masked the wax for Miloš seemed unaware of my presence. I had closed the chest but had left the key in the lock, and the letter for Uncle Ota was still lying on top of Father's uniform. For a moment, I had an urge to reveal myself and make up some excuse for being in the attic, but something in the set of Miloš's face stopped me. I was not sure if it was a trick of the light but the contours of his cheeks and chin looked sharper than usual.

He did not turn on the electric light, but placed the lamp on Father's desk and began searching through the drawers. I realised that he had not come because he had heard a noise but rather to look for something when he thought we were all asleep.

When Miloš did not find what he was searching for in the

desk, he turned to the shelf and leafed through the books. After the bookshelf yielded nothing of interest, he looked at the chest. My heart skipped a beat when he opened the lid, then picked up the lamp so that he might see more clearly into it. He discovered the letter and ripped open the envelope.

Miloš showed no emotion while reading the letter. I was surprised that he could read correspondence from his late wife to the brother of her first husband so impassively. I understood little of men and women then, but knew enough to realise that men could be jealous. Miloš studied the letter like someone committing facts to memory for an examination. Every so often he would look up, his lips moving as if he were taking particular note of a place or name. When he had finished reading, I hoped he would discard the letter, but he rolled it into a tube and lit it with the wick of his lamp. The paper flared brightly and I thought he was intent on burning the house down. But before the flame reached his fingers, he extinguished it. He dropped the remains to the floor and stomped on them before taking up his lamp again and leaving.

I remained in my hiding place for half an hour after I heard the door to Miloš's room close and quiet descended on the house. As dawn broke in the sky, shedding silvery light through the dormer window, I crept out and picked up the blackened remains of the letter. There was one piece that had been unharmed by the flame. I gently unfolded it, afraid it would crumble in my hand, and read the words my mother had written:

> Whispered of love the mosses frail,
> The flowering tree as sweetly lied,
> The rose's fragrant sigh replied
> To love songs of the nightingale.

I recognised the lines — they were from the famous love poem 'May'. It was about a young man with an unfaithful lover. He kills his rival and later learns that it was his own father.

I wondered why my mother would have included the poem in a letter to Uncle Ota. I leaned forward and the letter Mother had addressed to Aunt Josephine jabbed me in the chest. Perhaps the answers would lie there.

Aunt Josephine sat in the courtyard garden and read the letter from Mother. I chased Frip around the fountain. I did it to keep warm, but also to stop myself from interrupting Aunt Josephine before she had finished. I thought she would call when she had read the letter and was surprised when I turned around and saw her with the letter on her lap, staring out in front of her. One look at the grim expression on her face and I understood it had revealed something terrible.

'Aunt Josephine?' I sat down beside her. Frip sensed the gravity of the moment and sat still.

Aunt Josephine did not move. Whatever she had read in Mother's letter had come as a blow.

'What is it?' I said, gripping her arm and feeling the tremor there. 'Read it to me.'

She shook her head. 'I can't. You must read it for yourself,' and she handed me the letter.

I was so afraid, I had to inhale a few times before I could focus on the words.

> *Dear Josephine,*
>   *I am writing to you because I know that you do not like to visit us when Miloš is at home — and, as you know, he is at home more often than not these*

days! At first I thought this change was due to a recovery of his devotion to me, or perhaps because he had given up the 'thorn in my side'. For that immoral woman has ceased to appear at social functions, so I am free from her stares, and no longer reserves seats at the theatre so near to us that I can feel her breathing down my neck. Lída tells me that she has been seen folding bandages at the veterans' hospital — an occupation much more suited to a widow of her position than pursuing other women's husbands.

But it appears my husband's attention is not so endearing. He watches me with an interest that suffocates me. I cannot leave the house or make contact with a friend without a dozen of his questions. I do not flatter myself that this watchfulness is a sign of jealousy. No, he is studying me, but for what reason I do not know. I have these spasms of anxiety in my stomach that the doctor cannot cure, although I know the cause: the daily state of being in fear.

What is worse is that this watchfulness now extends to my daughters. He teaches Klárinka to play chess and Adélka to dance, but not from fatherly tenderness, as I had once hoped. I am sure he has some other purpose in mind. I have seen Emilie in my dreams. She stands on the other side of a river and calls out to me, warning me of something, but I cannot hear what she is saying.

My dear friend, I almost smile as I imagine you shaking your practical head, wondering if I am reaching the troublesome stage of motherhood when the children are growing up and one sees danger in every corner as a result of their increasing independence. But when I tell you what has provoked my anxieties, I am sure you will understand.

Yesterday morning I awoke as dawn was breaking, having suffered another dream about Emilie. The room was stifling and I went to open the window. I looked down to the street and thought I must be hallucinating. There was that woman sitting in her car with her driver. At first I thought she might be preying on Miloš, but then I realised she was staring at the house. She was not regarding it as might a jealous mistress who has been shut out of her lover's domestic life, but rather as a woman admiring property that will soon be her own.

Josephine, you know that if anything should happen to me you will be the guardian of my daughters. An income, which I hope will be considered generous by you, has been set aside for this purpose. But I fear for my children's safety should they stay in Prague. Ota is a good man, and so far away that I feel they will be out of danger with him and his wife. If you fear for their safety too, I beg you to send them to him.

There is a matter between Ota and myself that has never been settled and which I have never discussed with you. But in his latest letter he enquired after me so kindly that I cannot but hope he has forgiven me. In any case, he seems to have a keen interest in the welfare of his brother's daughters. I have written to him expressing my hopes. I will explain all when I see you next.

I will ask Adélka to take these letters to you as, for obvious reasons, I do not wish my husband to have knowledge of this correspondence. Please come and see me as soon as possible, and please let Doctor Holub know that I would like to see him too. There are clauses in my will that I must amend immediately.
All my love,
Marta

I covered my mouth with my hand and leaned over. I retched but could bring nothing up. Aunt Josephine gripped my arm.

'Marta knew he was going to kill her,' she said. 'She only did not expect it to happen that day.'

I pressed my head into my hands, struggling to breathe. 'He must have given her something to make her collapse. Then they overdosed her with morphine.'

What we had found too terrifying to believe was real. The appearance of paní Beňová in events explained everything.

FOUR

Aunt Josephine and I showed Doctor Holub the letter. But his news threw us into confusion again.

'Doctor Hoffmann has a perfect medical record,' he informed us. 'He was decorated for his services during the war, and his nurse has been with him for ten years. He has a beautiful wife and lives in a house in Vinohrady with glass ceilings and Italian barocco-style furniture. He is not a candidate for being bribed into murdering for money.'

Aunt Josephine shook her head. 'Then what about Doctor Soucek's claim that he had already removed Marta's appendix?'

Doctor Holub shrugged. 'He is still insistent on that fact and says that if paní Dolezalová had died of a ruptured appendix, as Doctor Hoffmann suggests, then the time from the onset of her symptoms to her death would have been a few days, not months. But when I asked him to show me the records, the operation was not entered. He said it may not have been included because at the time his wife was pregnant with their second child and was not feeling well enough to keep account of all his operations.'

'How can he be certain then?' I asked. 'He is getting old. Surely he does not expect us to trust his memory?'

Outside the window behind Doctor Holub, the leaves of the cherry trees had turned gold. The light flickered through them as the leaves were stirred by the breeze. Appendectomies were not common in Mother's day, so Doctor Soucek may well be right that he remembered the operation even if there were no records. It occurred to me that if he had not come to our house with his story about Mother's appendix, then we would be mourning her loss with peace and not suspicion.

'Doctor Soucek says he remembers it well because he operated on paní Dolezalová the same night the German emperor died.'

I leaned back and sighed. Doctor Soucek sounded senile. I had been sure of a conspiracy between Miloš and paní Beňová, but that belief suddenly seemed not only unfounded but ridiculous. Had Mother truly thought that Miloš was going to kill her? Or did she only fear that he and paní Beňová would find a way to get us out of the house? Pain gripped my stomach and I winced. I was suffering the same anxiety spasms that had afflicted Mother.

'I fear this is too much for you,' said Doctor Holub.

I shook my head. 'I want to know the truth.'

'What do we do now?' Aunt Josephine asked. 'My nieces' lives may be in danger.'

Doctor Holub scratched his head. 'There is nothing to be done for now,' he said. 'There is no evidence that paní Dolezalová was murdered, despite her frightened letter. Only a confession would change things and that is not likely to happen. You must watch pan Dolezal carefully. He may give something away.'

* * *

The day that Mother's will was read, I studied Miloš's reaction. I noticed that Doctor Holub glanced at him when he read the part about Miloš being given an allowance. My stepfather did not bat an eyelid.

'Your mother was a most generous woman,' Miloš told me afterwards, when we shared tea and cakes in Doctor Holub's office. 'I shall always be grateful to her. Our marriage was short but she brought me much joy.'

I winced. I resented being unable to speak my mind, but I had to tread carefully with Miloš. Aunt Josephine was our guardian until both Klára and I came of age, but the allowance to be paid to her for our care had to be signed off by Miloš as well as Doctor Holub at the bank each month. I understood why Mother had originally organised things that way: she did not think a woman should be troubled by money matters and had wanted to put Miloš in a fatherly position. But her good intentions had left us in a difficult situation. We were dependent on Miloš for our financial welfare until we came into our fortune.

Later, Miloš asked Aunt Josephine about Klára's musical education and whether she would send us to finishing school abroad. Anyone listening to him would have thought him a devoted stepfather. I tried to read his mind but could see nothing beyond his handsome face. But is that not what they say about cold-blooded killers? You can never tell them from ordinary human beings. On the surface, at least. If Miloš murdered us, how would he do it, I wondered. Would he use Doctor Hoffmann again? Or would he simply strangle us in our sleep?

Some time later, Hilda, Aunt Josephine's maid who had come to stay with us too, informed us that there was a letter from

Australia. Uncle Ota had sent us a pressed flower stem inside a sheet of tissue paper. Klára held it up and we admired the plant's silvery-green leaves and its balls of golden flowers. A fragrance similar to lilacs lingered in the paper. The envelope also contained a coloured drawing of the plant — silver wattle — by Ranjana. The accompanying letter from Uncle Ota asked that the flower be placed on Mother's grave. *Although I had not seen Marta for nearly twenty years, I remember the vibrant young woman who was so devoted to her family*, Uncle Ota wrote. Then, on a separate page, he had written:

> *In shadowy woods the burnished lake*
> *Darkly complained a secret pain,*
> *By circling shores embraced again;*
> *And heaven's clear sun leaned down to take*
> *A road astray in azure deeps,*
> *Like burning tears the lover weeps.*

A shiver ran down my spine. They were lines from the poem 'May' that followed those I had read in the remains of Mother's letter to Uncle Ota.

'It is ironic that he should quote Karel Hynek Mácha,' Aunt Josephine told me when Klára was out of earshot.

'Why?' I asked.

'Because the poet is thought to have died of appendicitis, but mystery still surrounds his death.'

The months passed, but our pain did not. Klára worked on her pieces with paní Milotová with an even greater intensity than before. Because she was sensitive, we kept Doctor Soucek's claim from her. As a result, her grief followed a more even path than

Aunt Josephine or I managed. I fell apart one afternoon when I found a hairbrush with Mother's blonde strands still intertwined in the bristles. Aunt Josephine did the same when she was rummaging through the sewing box and discovered a pin cushion she had made for Mother when they were young. The only clue to Klára's inner anguish came when she practised on her own. If she could not learn a piece by her third attempt, her playing descended into a tumble of chords, as though she was shrieking out her pain through her instrument. Yet, on the surface, she remained as calm as always.

Miloš visited us on Christmas Eve. Aunt Josephine seated him in a chair opposite the sofa where she sat with Klára and myself. She would not leave him alone with us. Aunt Josephine and I were in two minds about my stepfather. If we never saw him again, we would not be sorry; on the other hand, we needed to watch him and see if we could find any clues as to whether he had played a role in Mother's death. For his part, Miloš may have been keeping up an appearance of caring about us to maintain propriety and divert any suspicion. More chillingly, he could have been trying to stay close enough so he could kill us.

Miloš had brought presents: a wide-brimmed tea hat for Aunt Josephine, which I knew she would think too showy; a crystal lamb for Klára, which was ironic considering Miloš had no love for animals; and a gold necklace with a diamond pendant for me. I held up the chain and the diamond sparkled in the lamplight.

'I bought it for your mother ... for our anniversary,' said Miloš. 'You are so much like her. I hope that its beauty flatters your own.'

My gaze drifted to the extra setting at the table. It was a Czech tradition to make a place for the recently departed, who we believed to be with us in spirit. I turned back to Miloš but could not tell if the glimmer in his eye was a tear or a glint from the fire's light.

We ate dinner in silence. The cook was away, so Hilda had prepared cabbage soup with potato salad and vánočka. Normally the soup was delicious, but with the tension in the air it tasted bitter. Aunt Josephine did not lift her eyes from her bowl and Miloš clenched his spoon so tightly that each time he moved it to his lips the action looked mechanical.

At last it was time for Miloš to leave. Despite our efforts to be hospitable, he had sensed that he was unwelcome. I watched him walk down the snow-covered street and remembered a proverb my father was fond of reciting: 'Keep your friends close, but your enemies even closer.'

Not long into the new year, we received a letter from Uncle Ota and Ranjana.

> To my dear ladies,
> I cannot tell you the joy the arrival of our boy has brought us. Ranjana was at her job at a stocking factory when this little one decided to arrive a few weeks early. Despite this, his lungs are strong and his fingers have a grip like a monkey's. He has my nose and chin, but I am happy to announce that he has his mother's eyes. He is the most delicious colour — like a caramel toffee. Because he was born in Australia, we have decided to give him a distinguished English-sounding name: Thomas James. I have also changed my surname to 'Rose' as 'Ruzicka' is proving too difficult for anyone here to pronounce ...

Perhaps Uncle Ota had not told us that he and Ranjana were expecting a child because of the news of Mother's death, but after receiving the letter Aunt Josephine set us to work knitting booties and jackets for our new cousin.

'It's warm in Australia,' Klára tried to explain.

'It doesn't matter,' said Aunt Josephine. 'They don't have much money and we must do what we can to help them.'

On the days Klára went to school, I walked her there. In the afternoons she used to walk back with a group of friends, but since Mother's death I met her at the school door and accompanied her home myself.

If she did not have a music lesson after school, Klára and I visited patisseries and sweet shops on our way home. It was on one of these visits that I noticed the man.

Klára and I were in paní Ježková's patisserie eyeing the vanilla rolls, poppyseed koláče and cream puffs displayed on silver trays. We settled on linzer biscuits with marmalade centres and vanilla rolls dusted with icing sugar. Paní Ježková was no more than four foot tall and had to stand on tiptoes to see over the counter to take our order. She had the inquisitive eyes and well-rounded body of the animal from which her name derived; when she moved around the display, picking up the rolls and biscuits, I could imagine a hedgehog snuffling around a rosebush. Paní Ježková made the best nut cake in Prague and, as we were expecting paní Milotová to visit later in the afternoon, we bought one.

Paní Ježková turned her back to place the cake in a box. I heard the tinkle of the bell as the door opened and another customer entered, bringing a breath of chilly street air with them. The newcomer hesitated before approaching the counter to stand beside us. I turned to see a man about Miloš's age. He was tall, thin and dark in the face. His clothes were not the finest quality but they fitted him well. His hair was combed and his face was shaven but there was something about him that seemed out of place in paní Ježková's glistening mahogany and brass shop. I could not imagine someone with such a dour expression sinking his teeth into strawberry creams or sucking on vanilla buttons.

Paní Ježková handed me the cake box and our sweets wrapped in paper and wished us good day before greeting the man, who was staring at us with his pale eyes. I grabbed Klára's hand and hurried her out the door, but as soon as we were on the pavement I could not resist the temptation to look over my shoulder. Through the window I saw that paní Ježková was trying to attract the man's attention but he had his back to her and was watching us. On another occasion, I might have thought he was simply curious. But the man's half-smile sent a shiver down my spine.

'Come on,' I said to Klára, who was already munching on a biscuit. 'We have to hurry home.'

After that encounter, Aunt Josephine or Hilda accompanied us everywhere. But one day, when Hilda had come down with a cold and Aunt Josephine was suffering a severe migraine, our aunt reluctantly agreed to let Klára and me go to a piano recital in the Old Town on our own. The pianist was a famous one from Hungary and Klára did not want to miss the performance.

'You walk across the bridge in view of the crowds and directly to the hall without dawdling or getting side-tracked,' she told me. 'Under no circumstances must you or Klára be alone.'

Spring was awakening and the day was breezy. Klára and I held on to our hats as we passed the fishermen and pottery pedlars on our way across the Charles Bridge.

'Let's put our hands on Saint John,' said Klára.

Before I had a chance to stop her, she rushed towards the bronze statue and became caught up in a group of school-children and their teacher.

'Legend has it that Saint John of Nepomuk was trussed up in armour and thrown off the bridge at the order of King Wenceslas after he refused to reveal the Queen's confessions,' the teacher announced to her students. 'It is said that if you rub the statue, then one day you will return to Prague.'

'But we live in Prague,' I muttered to myself. 'And we are already late.'

I walked towards Klára, but before I reached her a man stepped behind her. He turned to the side and I recognised his face: the man from the patisserie. My heart leapt to my throat.

I bounded towards Klára and yanked her by the hand.

'Why?' she protested, tugging against me.

The man turned towards us. I dragged Klára away and broke into a run, still holding her hand. I was grateful she did not resist me this time for she had seen the man too and had sensed something was wrong.

We dodged the cars and the people walking their dogs and the nannies pushing prams on the bridge. We were only a short distance from the tower to the Old Town but Klára began to wheeze. She stumbled and I stopped to catch her. We were two young girls who had run with all our might. I was sure we had lost the man amongst the traffic, but to my horror he was almost upon us. Aunt Josephine had told us to stay with the crowds but no one seemed to think anything of two girls being chased by a man. I saw a youth sketching pictures, but we would not have time to reach him and explain our situation before our pursuer caught up with us.

There was a fruit and vegetable market near the tower and I told Klára that we must run there. She took my hand again and we weaved between the tables and boxes of cabbages and horseradish. On the other side of the market I saw an inn. The cellar doors were open and a man was loading beer kegs onto a cart. He was not looking so I pushed Klára into the cellar and followed after her. We squeezed ourselves behind some full kegs, the coldness of the metal like ice burning our chests and cheeks. After a few moments I saw the legs and boots of the man who had followed us. They stopped outside the cellar door. My breath caught in my throat. I felt like a rabbit with a fox sniffing outside its burrow. The man bent down and peered inside. From the way he was squinting I realised that it was too dark in the cellar for him to see us.

'Looking for something, sir?' I heard the cartman ask our pursuer.

'Yes, I think my dog ran inside your cellar. Do you have a light?'

The sound of the man's voice chilled me. I had been expecting a rough dialect of the street. But he spoke Czech like an aristocrat. He could have been someone Mother would have invited to afternoon tea.

'I didn't see a dog run in there,' replied the cartman. 'And I've been standing out here the whole time.'

'Oh?'

I hoped our pursuer would accept the cartman's word and move away, but he stayed put.

'I did see two young girls running past though,' said the cartman. 'Are they looking for the dog as well?'

'Why yes,' said the man. 'They are my nieces. You saw them?'

My breath caught in my throat. I pulled Klára closer.

'Yes,' answered the cartman. 'They nearly knocked me over. They ran down that way, back towards the river.'

'Thank you,' said our pursuer.

I waited a few seconds after the man's legs disappeared from sight, then told Klára to hurry out with me lest the cartman close the cellar doors on us. But before we could move the cartman poked his head into the cellar and called, 'Now, you rascals. I don't know what you stole from that gentleman but I don't care. Run home now.'

Klára and I climbed out of our hiding place and made our way through the kegs to the door.

'Go on! Go!' said the cartman. 'And don't do it again!'

He did not need to tell us a second time. I grabbed Klára's hand and we ran with all our strength towards the bridge and the safety of home.

When we reached our house, having missed the recital, I realised that Klára would need an explanation. I had never lied to my younger sister and I did not intend to start. But how could I explain to her our suspicions about Miloš? She was eleven years old and had struggled valiantly with her grief over Mother. What would it do to her mind if I told her we suspected Mother had been murdered and that our lives were now in danger too?

'It's not "lying" to protect a child's innocence,' Aunt Josephine told me while Klára was washing her hands and face. 'You must simply tell her that you are two wealthy young women in a town filled with thieves, and that you recognised the man from a picture in the newspaper of an infamous thief known for robbing children.'

The fact that Klára believed my explanation with as much trust as she had taken my hand when we fled across the bridge earlier that day did not settle my mind. I lay next to her that night trying not to imagine what 'the assassin' intended to do with us once he caught us. I remembered his well-spoken voice and shivered. Then I thought about Doctor Hoffmann, who I was now convinced had killed Mother. Miloš had the knack of finding gentlemen to do his dirty work. Did he know something about these men that other people did not?

The weather at the beginning of spring was unpredictable and even though the day had been breezy it had also been warm. Then, after dark, the temperature reverted to winter and snow fell. At first it was light and dusted the roofs and statues with a fine powder. But then gusts of wind started to rattle our doors and windows and the snow fell more heavily.

The lights flickered then went out. Aunt Josephine lit a lamp and we read together in the parlour for a few hours before the room grew cold and Aunt Josephine suggested that we go to bed.

Frip scratched at the door and stared at Aunt Josephine who rubbed her eyes and yawned.

'I'll take him outside,' I told her.

The courtyard garden was covered in snow and I tugged my shawl around my shoulders. Frip scampered to the flowerbed and crouched. He did not like the cold either so finished his business quickly. I was about to open the door so we could go back inside when he growled and circled my feet. I looked up and saw in the moonlight the silhouette of a man at the courtyard gates. I could tell from his stance that he was staring at me. My fingers trembled so badly that I could barely turn the door knob. Finally I managed to grasp it and, once Frip was inside after me, I slammed the door shut.

A few seconds later there was a knock at the front door. I stifled a scream and ran to the bottom of the stairs. 'Aunt Josephine!' I cried, with all the voice I could muster for I was breathless with fear. From the sound of the floorboards creaking above me, Aunt Josephine was preparing for bed and had not heard me.

The knock sounded again. Frip barked. The creaking of the floorboards stopped. Aunt Josephine must have heard it this time. I picked up the lamp Aunt Josephine had left for me and ran up the stairs as fast as I could.

'Aunt Josephine!' I cried from the landing. 'The man ... the man I told you about is at our door!'

The knocking continued, becoming more insistent with each rap.

Aunt Josephine appeared at the top of the stairs in her nightdress, a lamp in her hand. 'One moment,' she said, sounding as breathless as I did. I heard her open the door to the bedroom I shared with Klára and tell her to lock the door. 'Don't let anyone in but me or Adéla,' she said.

Aunt Josephine ran down the stairs. 'Get Frip's lead,' she told me.

I grabbed the lead from the hallstand and placed it around Frip's neck. Hilda, who had been woken by the commotion, was already at the door. We had no time to warn her before she opened it, revealing the dark face of the intruder. He barged inside, shaking the snow off his coat.

Frip lunged forward, barking furiously. I was not sure whether to keep holding on to his lead or to let him go for fear he would choke. Hilda shut the door but lingered near it.

The man took off his hat and brushed the snow from it. He peered at us through the gloom. It was not the man from the patisserie but another man: much older, with stringy grey hair. 'I've come to warn you!' he said to Aunt Josephine. 'Someone is after your nieces.'

He spoke with the lilt of a Polish accent.

'Who are you?' demanded Aunt Josephine.

'I am Henio Tyszka,' the man answered. 'But you will

understand better if I tell you I am the stable manager for Doctor Hoffmann, and the husband of his nurse.'

Aunt Josephine and I responded to the man's statement with stunned silence. Eventually Aunt Josephine gathered her will to invite the man into the drawing room and asked Hilda to make tea.

Pan Tyszka stared at the bronze horse on the mantelpiece before sitting down on the sofa. Frip sniffed his boots, then, sensing the danger had passed, sat by me.

Hilda brought the tea and placed it on the table. After she had left, Aunt Josephine turned to pan Tyszka. 'Well, you had better explain.'

Pan Tyszka, who had refused to give his hat to Hilda and now sat with it clenched in his hands, wasted no time getting to the heart of the story. 'Doctor Hoffmann has debts. Gambling debts. He lives elegantly, and his wife, who is expecting their first child, and his father-in-law have no idea of the depth of his trouble — that his home and riches are on the verge of being carted away by ruthless debt collectors. The desire to preserve his public image is a powerful motivation for an otherwise decent man to become a murderer. A man might do anything to save his own family, especially if the victim is painted to him as an adulteress and a cruel mother.'

I reached for Aunt Josephine's hand. She grasped mine. Pan Tyszka had described a world different from the one we inhabited. A place where life was cheap.

Pan Tyszka studied our faces. 'It looks to me that you have already guessed what I am going to tell you. The girls' stepfather furnished Doctor Hoffmann's house, that's how they met. The doctor needed money quickly if he did not want to find his wife at the bottom of the river.'

The worst I had imagined was now confirmed. I felt ill when pan Tyszka verified Mother's death had been from an overdose of morphine. He told us that his wife had been so horrified at the deed performed by her employer — which she was unaware of until overhearing a conversation between Doctor Hoffmann and Miloš — that she ran straight to her priest. But her confession and prayers could not bring her peace. Then she overheard another conversation in which Doctor Hoffman was seeking an assassin on Miloš's behalf.

The idea of an assassin had seemed a fantasy when I thought about it; now it was nightmarishly real. I longed to be a child again, when my world had been Mother and Father, puppet shows and an adorable baby sister. My throat was raw and I found it difficult to swallow. 'Why?' I asked, unable to stop the tears falling down my cheeks. I was about to tell Aunt Josephine that money did not matter, that I would give my inheritance away to keep us safe. But what pan Tyszka said next changed my mind.

'You do not have much time. It is your stepfather's mistress who is urging him on. She wants this house and hounds him daily about it.'

I imagined paní Beňová sleeping in Mother's bed, pawing over her jewels, sitting in her chair. Paní Beňová would not touch any of those things as long as I had breath in my body.

'Will you go with us to the police?' Aunt Josephine asked pan Tyszka.

If Aunt Josephine had stuck pan Tyszka with a needle, she could not have made him rise faster. 'No, that is not what I have come for. That is not what I will do.'

'But surely ... your wife is religious,' stammered Aunt Josephine. 'Do you not think God needs to punish the men who killed a mother and now plot to destroy her daughters?'

Pan Tyszka backed towards the door and shook his head. 'I have got the safety of a wife and four children to look out for.

What you do to protect those girls is your business. I came to warn you and I have taken a risk to do that. If you tell the police I said anything, I will deny it all.'

No amount of tears and offers of money could persuade pan Tyszka to change his mind. It was two o'clock in the morning and the snow was still falling when he bade us farewell. 'I came and warned you,' he said. 'My conscience is clear. The rest is up to you.'

I remembered Klára was still in her room and ran upstairs. She opened the door then retreated to the bed again, sitting with her knees to her chest and the blankets pulled around her.

Aunt Josephine followed after me, her face grim. 'It's all confirmed now and there's nothing to do but what I dreaded most. I must send you girls away. God in heaven knows I'd do anything to keep you with me. You are like my own daughters. But I must think about your welfare, for it is better to have you far away and in safe hands than close by and in danger.'

The lamp I had placed on the side table flickered. The flame died then ignited more brightly than before.

'There,' said Aunt Josephine. 'It's your mother. She's telling me she agrees with my decision.'

'What decision?' asked Klára, her eyes wide with fear. She had no idea what had passed.

Aunt Josephine grabbed our hands and squeezed them in her own. 'I'm sending you to Ota. To Australia.'

Klára and I hardly had time to grasp what Aunt Josephine had said before Hilda appeared at the door. Aunt Josephine nodded to her. 'We must get them out of Prague without Miloš knowing.'

FIVE

The next weeks were full of secrecy and fear. Doctor Holub was our co-conspirator. He organised our passports through the British Consulate, and correspondence from Aunt Josephine to Uncle Ota was to pass through him to avoid leaving a trail from her to Australia.

'I have booked tickets on a ship sailing to New York in the young ladies' names, as well as the passage to Australia, to throw anyone off the scent,' he explained to Aunt Josephine when she and I went to see him to make the final arrangements. 'But there's one problem. Pan Dolezal will not be inclined to sign permission for the girls' allowance if he does not know where they are.'

'What do you suggest?' asked Aunt Josephine. 'I can wire them money.'

'Enough to last them until they are twenty-one?' asked Doctor Holub.

Aunt Josephine's inheritance was tied up in her house and I was horrified at the idea that she might sell it in order to support

86

us. I was relieved when Doctor Holub added, 'Wiring money might be too much of a risk. Someone at the bank may contact Miloš and the girls will be traced.'

'But I cannot ask Ota to support them,' said Aunt Josephine.

'Is he so very poor?' asked Doctor Holub.

'He is not starving,' said Aunt Josephine. 'But he is not well off either.'

'Well,' said Doctor Holub, 'send the young ladies with as much money as they can safely take with them. They will have to live simply until they come into their fortune. The important thing is to get them out of the country.'

'I wish we could go to the police,' I told Aunt Josephine on our way home. The flower sellers were out on the streets and everywhere I looked there were buckets of roses, lilies and daffodils. But the colours and scents of the flowers could not cheer me.

'We can't, without evidence or witnesses willing to testify,' replied Aunt Josephine.

We walked by Madame Bouquet's drapery, which had been Mother's favourite shop. We admired some glazed floral chintzes and gold-embroidered silks. Every time Mother and I had passed this way, we stopped to look at the fabrics. It occurred to me that I may never see the shop again. Everywhere I went in Prague these days, I was bidding some well-loved pleasure farewell.

'Won't you come with us?' I asked Aunt Josephine. 'When we are gone you won't be safe in Prague. What if Miloš threatens you to get information ...'

I stopped. I could not bring myself to imagine what Miloš or the assassin might do to Aunt Josephine to make her talk.

'I have Hilda and Frip,' Aunt Josephine replied. 'I can't adapt to foreign countries and I am too old to change. But you and

Klára are young and speak English. Uncle Ota will look after you. I know that, and your mother knew it too.'

When Aunt Josephine used to read Uncle Ota's letters to us, I often thought that it would be marvellous to travel the world. I had not been anywhere outside of Czechoslovakia. My debut into society and my education in Paris and Florence had been halted by the war. But now that I was going away, I found the idea daunting. I thought of the wretched convicts the British had transported to Australia, and imagined their faces peering through the ships' portholes at their homeland as it disappeared in the distance. Klára and I were not convicts but we were fugitives.

I recalled paní Milotová's reaction when we had taken her into our confidence. 'Australia?' she said, her eyes wide with horror. 'It's a wild place. What about Klára and her music? She will have to come back to study in Leipzig otherwise she won't amount to anything!'

When we returned home, I found Klára sitting in the garden with Frip. My sister was not the innocent child she had been until I was forced to tell her the truth about Mother's death and why we were leaving. The change was not in her smooth skin, her soft hair or her agile hands. It was in the way she looked at things. There was hatred in her gaze, and I had never known Klára to despise anything. I sat down next to her and wanted to promise I would restore the joy she had once taken for granted. But I could not guarantee anything. I was unsure of the future myself.

'What are you thinking about?' I asked her.

She raised her eyes to meet mine. 'When I am old enough, I will make Miloš and paní Beňová pay for what they did.'

Her voice sent a chill through me. She did not sound like Klára any more.

'You've been brave,' I told her. 'And we must be careful to hide our feelings. You mustn't let Marie or anybody else know that we are leaving. We must behave as if everything is the same as it always has been.'

'It's not,' said Klára, leaning down to pat Frip's head. 'Nothing will ever be the same without Mother.'

Klára was right. Even without the murder and the price on our lives, the chasm Mother's death had left would still be there. I longed to be reborn in another, happier life. I wanted to believe that might happen in Australia. But I doubted it. Klára and I might have been able to rebuild our lives in Paris, London or somewhere in America. But the fifth continent? We may as well have been going to darkest Africa.

The morning of our departure, Aunt Josephine and I waited in the parlour for Doctor Holub. He was to take Klára and me to the train station. The story given to our servants was that we were departing to our summer house early with paní Milotová and her husband. Klára was sickly and needed fresh air and a change from Prague. We had a local maid in Doksy and Marie would follow later.

'I will keep visitors away and live here until I have received word you and Klára are in Australia,' Aunt Josephine explained to me. 'Then I will close up this house and put it in the hands of a caretaker until your return.'

Aunt Josephine planned to move back to her own house. She would be safer amongst her high-society tenants than she would be living alone.

The arrival of paní Milotová and her husband in travelling dress added to the surreal atmosphere.

'Doctor Holub has been delayed,' paní Milotová informed us. 'An urgent business matter came up but he will be here before ten o'clock.'

Aunt Josephine glanced at her watch and frowned. 'That will be cutting things fine. The schedule is tight.'

Klára appeared from the garden with some Perle d'Or roses in her hands. 'Look,' she said, holding out the golden-pink flowers. 'They are starting to bloom.'

Perle d'Or had been Mother's favourite rose because of its fruity perfume. She had grown those in our garden from seed but had never seen them come into flower.

Paní Milotová put her arm around Klára. I hated my sister looking so drawn but at least her appearance was convincing as an invalid in need of country air.

Pan Milota asked me about my camera and mentioned the photographic exhibitions that would be showing in the warmer months. He was trying to relieve the tension but his conversation made me sad. I would not be seeing exhibitions in Prague for many years.

We heard a car pull up in the street and readied ourselves to leave. We were startled when Marie entered the room with Miloš. 'Pan Dolezal is here,' she said, looking annoyed that Miloš had not waited in the hall to be announced, even if he had lived in the house previously.

'I came as soon as I heard,' said Miloš.

'Heard what?' asked Aunt Josephine, keeping her voice steady.

'About Klára's illness.' Miloš stepped towards Klára and knelt beside her chair. 'I wish I had heard it from you first, Josephine,' he said. 'She *is* my stepdaughter.'

We had not seen Miloš since Christmas. He explained his absence as a business trip but I suspected that he was lying low until his assassin had finished with us. It is a dreadful thing to face the killer of one's mother, and my hatred of him sent my heart thumping in my chest. I glanced at Klára. Her mouth was pinched into a tight ball. We were so close to foiling Miloš; I prayed she would not do anything to give us away.

Miloš put his arm around her. 'I have a better offer than boring old Doksy,' he said. 'I will take my stepdaughters to Venice.'

I glanced at the clock on the mantelpiece. It was a quarter to ten and Doctor Holub would be arriving at any minute. The train to Genoa was due to depart at twenty-three past the hour.

'They can't go anywhere with you without a chaperone,' said Aunt Josephine. 'And I am not going to Venice.'

Miloš had taken this into account. 'But you weren't going to Doksy either,' he said. 'I'm sure that pan Milota and his wife would prefer Venice?'

'The main concern is Klára and her health,' said paní Milotová. 'Venice is full of rats and cholera. She needs fresh air.'

Miloš turned his back to us. 'What do you have to say for yourself, Klárinka?' he asked in an affectionate tone that he'd never used on her before. 'Where do you want to go?'

Klára lifted her chin and looked into Miloš's eyes.

'Stepfather, you are kind. But perhaps we can go to Venice in the summer?'

'Well, that's an idea,' Miloš said, a victorious note in his voice. He was oblivious to how Klára had triumphed over him with self-control.

Marie opened the door and Doctor Holub strode into the room, bringing us back to our senses. His eyes narrowed on Miloš. Aunt Josephine explained that he had made an offer to take Klára and me to Venice. Doctor Holub's expression remained calm but I wondered if he was thinking the same thing I was: Miloš had intended to arrange some sort of 'accident' in Venice.

Doctor Holub put our suitcases and those that paní Milotová and her husband had brought as decoys in the car. Miloš lingered and I thought he was going to offer to join us for the drive to Doksy. But after Doctor Holub had turned the motor he waved and said, 'See you in the summer then.'

It was difficult to be sure how much Miloš knew about our plans. He had read Mother's letter to Uncle Ota before destroying it, and Mother had said that if we were in danger she wanted us to go to Uncle Ota. But did Miloš know that Uncle Ota was in Australia or would he believe he was in America? It was terrible to be making the long journey without being sure that we would be any safer in our new home.

Miloš's unexpected visit had left us with little time for goodbyes at the station. Klára and I had only a few minutes to farewell the people who meant so much to us and who we would not see for many years. I pulled out my camera to take a picture but the conductor whistled and called us aboard. Hilda too, as she was accompanying us to Genoa.

'Goodbye!' Klára and I called from the train window. My last glimpse of Prague was Aunt Josephine weeping on paní Milotová's shoulder and the stained-glass windows of Hlavní Nádraží station.

For nearly two months the first things I saw on opening my eyes every morning were the fan above my bed and the thermos flask that sat in a holder above the washbasin in our cabin on the ship bound for Australia. We had boarded in the morning after a night in a backstreet hotel in Genoa, where we had sat with the lights off. In my dreams I saw Miloš hiding in the crevices behind the armoire and under the desk, waiting to snatch Klára away from me. It was a relief when we finally stood at the gangway to the ship and saw the steam flying from its funnels.

'Look after your sister,' said Hilda, adjusting my scarf to fit more snugly around my throat. She took the cross from her neck, kissed it and placed it in my hand before bending down and stroking Klára's cheek. 'And God be with you both.'

Once we had climbed the gangway, Hilda did not wait to see the ship depart from the dock. That might have drawn attention to us should Miloš have a spy among the crowd bidding farewell to their relatives. I watched Hilda's stout figure disappear into the throng, my hand clutching the cross that was still warm with her body heat. When I could no longer see her, and the ship began to move, I felt like a drowning person being washed out to sea.

'*Buon viaggio! Buon viaggio!*'

The passengers were mostly Italians making their way to Australia for work or disembarking at one of the ports along the way. We would have liked to speak to them, even though their dialects were often different from the literary Florentine our mother had taught us, but fear of being traced and found out made us reserved about who we spoke to, even amongst the other first-class passengers.

Our journey passed slowly, measured in sunrises and sunsets. Aunt Josephine had asked us not to leave the ship to visit the ports, so Klára and I wrote a list of activities to keep ourselves occupied. We crammed the schedule with as many occupations as possible and listed them at breakfast as if each one were a delight to look forward to, although we did them every day.

Walk the promenade deck.

Read *The Wind in the Willows* out loud to each other to practise English.

Two games of shuffleboard.

Two games of quoits.

One game of chess.

Listen to ship's orchestra at afternoon tea.

Take a photograph of something we have not noticed before on the ship.

Klára to read and hum music for an hour.

Adéla to write a page in her journal.

To dispel our boredom and relieve our fears, Klára and I mostly relied on our imaginations.

'What are you doing?' I asked one afternoon when I woke up from a nap to find Klára sitting before her berth and lifting and dropping her fingers on the side of it.

'I'm playing Chopin's Nocturne Opus 72,' she answered. 'What are you doing? It looked like you were sleeping.'

I sat up and wriggled my feet. 'I wasn't sleeping. I was at the markets.'

She smiled. 'Which markets?'

'The ones in Colombo. See,' I held out my arm to her. 'Smell my sleeve. It's infused with the scents of saffron and turmeric.'

'Did you bring me back anything?'

'Of course I did.' I took the clasp from my hair and handed it to her. 'I brought you this silver engraved bangle.'

Most of the time Klára and I were content in our self-contained world. But at other times the isolation of our existence and our fear of our stepfather became unbearable. Once, after the ship had docked at Port Said, Klára was convinced that Miloš had boarded.

We were walking along the promenade deck when she clutched my arm. 'It's him.'

'Who?' I asked, looking at the passengers sitting in the deckchairs, reading books or sleeping.

'Miloš!'

My heart skipped a beat. I examined the faces and found no one who resembled our stepfather.

'Klára, are you all right? Have you had too much sun?'

Klára did not answer me. I tugged her sleeve and she stared at me as if she did not recognise who I was. There was a distant look in her eyes. She was like a stranger and that was even more frightening to me than being pursued by Miloš.

We sailed into Sydney Harbour on the last day of May. The sky was the same brilliant duck-egg blue as the sky in Prague, but the sunlight was brighter. It sparkled off the crests of the waves that swirled around our ship, the funnels and the decks. We leaned over the railing to catch a glimpse of the city. The intensity of the light made me squint. I searched the foreshores for the buildings Uncle Ota had described. But all I could see were stone outcrops from which sprouted trees with white trunks and silvery-green leaves. Some of the headlands had been cleared but many were lush with shrubs and trees.

I gripped the railing. This is our new home for the next ten years, I told myself.

The customs procedure at the port was not as arduous as I had feared and we were not given the dictation test. Having Uncle Ota as our guarantor and the letter of support Doctor Holub had obtained from the British Consul General had helped. Klára and I were the first passengers to emerge into the sea of faces waiting to greet the ship.

A man moved towards us. He was so tall he had to stoop under the arrivals banner. Following him was a woman with dark skin holding a baby. Until that moment, Uncle Ota had been a man with his arm around my father in photographs and in stories read out by Aunt Josephine. Ranjana and Thomas had been characters in a dream. Now Klára and I were about to meet them in the flesh.

When they reached us, Uncle Ota removed his hat and clutched it to his chest. It was frayed at the edges and there were dark spots on the crown. 'Gentleman's spots' Mother had called those marks on a man's hat, because they suggested that the wearer was prone to lifting his hat frequently, especially to passing ladies.

'You are the image of your mother,' Uncle Ota told me. 'I could see straightaway that you are Marta's daughter.'

I wanted to cry and laugh at the same time. Uncle Ota's voice was just as I had imagined it would be: warm, debonair, charming. He looked young for a man in his late forties, with a smatter of freckles across his cheeks and a mass of tousled hair framing his inquisitive face.

'Yes, I am Adéla,' I said, standing on my tiptoes to receive his kiss. 'And this is Klára.'

Uncle Ota turned to Klára and stopped in his tracks. His eyes danced over her face as if he were in some sort of dream. 'Emilie?' he muttered.

Klára climbed on top of her suitcase so she could put her arms around Uncle Ota's neck. He must have noticed the puzzled look on my face and recovered himself.

'I am pleased to meet you, lovely Klára,' he said, returning her embrace. 'My sister often writes about your exceptional talent.' Uncle Ota turned to the woman and child. 'Let me introduce you both to my wife and son.'

After the exotic images I had kept in my head about Ranjana, I was surprised that she was wearing a simple floral dress, flat shoes and spectacles. Rather than the Oriental princess I had imagined, she could have been the librarian of a ladies college if she was not so dark-skinned. But the proud tilt of her chin and the way she stood with her feet balanced on the ground and her shoulders straight did give her a regal bearing despite her plain clothes.

'*Dobrý den, moc mě těši, že Vás nebo Tebe? Poznávám,*' she said in Czech. She was pleased to meet me. I was astonished to hear perfect pronunciation from someone whose native language was so different from my own.

'*Děkuji. Jsem ráda, že jsem tady,*' I replied. 'Thank you. I am glad I am here.'

Ranjana held up Thomas, who was fat and, although not as dark as his mother, had her bright eyes. He gurgled and swiped at my cheek.

Uncle Ota suggested that we take a couple of hansom cabs to his house. 'There is no more elegant way to be transported in Sydney,' he said, leading us to a line of horses and ebony carriages. 'Watsons Bay,' Uncle Ota told the driver at the head of the line. The doors to the cab were open and Klára and I peered at the shabby leather seats and faded carpet.

The driver swung his head and saw Ranjana. He shut the cab doors, almost catching Klára's fingers. My cheeks burned with shame but I acted as if I had not noticed to avoid embarrassing my aunt. Ranjana stood with her eyes straight ahead, as if the driver's reaction had nothing to do with her.

Uncle Ota put his arm around his wife. 'What a rude fellow!' he said. 'Horses are nice but I don't think we want to give someone of that level of intelligence our money, do you, my dear?'

Before Ranjana could answer, a voice came from behind us. 'I can take you.' We turned to see a man with a red face and an upturned nose leaning out of a motor taxi. 'I can fit you all in here.'

I tried to place his accent: Russian? Polish? It was hard to tell because some of his words had taken on a nasal tone that was not part of either of those languages.

The taxi was newer than the hansom cab and in better repair. The seats were plush and the chrome trims were polished so brightly that I could see my reflection in the wheel guard.

'Ha!' said Uncle Ota. 'Never stoop to answer a slight and soon the truth will come to light.'

Ranjana's face broke into a smile and Uncle Ota stepped towards the taxi. He offered the driver a price and they haggled good-naturedly until they agreed on the fare. The driver stepped out of the car to open the doors for us and put our luggage in the boot. Ranjana and Thomas sat in the front with Uncle Ota while Klára and I climbed in the back. Uncle Ota opened the window and said loud enough for the hansom cab driver to hear, 'I have changed my mind about the most elegant way to travel, and this is it. In a hansom cab, one feels oneself too close to the horse's backside.' He let out a booming laugh. The hansom cab driver's nostrils twitched and he turned away.

The taxi driver put his foot on the accelerator. Klára clasped my hand and squeezed it. At first I thought she was frightened, but she stared out the window, fascinated by the chaos that was unfolding around us. The streets were congested with every form of transport, all travelling at different speeds. At one intersection a policeman tried to exert control over the mayhem, but his gestures were futile. The barrowmen, pushing their trays of fruit and flowers, got in the way of the cars, whose drivers beeped their horns and shook their fists to no avail. A tram rattled across our path with a horse and dray clomping after it. And everywhere were blockboys, risking their lives to dart among the traffic and shovel away horse manure.

I was intrigued by the people on the footpaths. Some were dressed in dove grey suits or pleated drop-waist dresses, but most looked like workers. There were men in checked shirts with their sleeves folded to the elbows, and women, both young and old, in aprons and white stockings. We passed a grocery store where a man in overalls was painting a window with an advertisement for Bushells tea, while opposite another man was scraping away one for Mother's Choice flour.

Before long we found ourselves passing along serpentine lanes lined by terraced houses whose front doors opened straight onto the street. There was something seedy in the reek of damp and mud and the way the pale children stared at us from gutters and doorways.

'There are slums in this city as poor as those in London,' Uncle Ota explained over the noise of the engine. 'You'd never come this way at night. Gangs roam the streets, ready to slit your throat with a razor for a bit of money.'

I gulped, my fingers instinctively reaching to protect my neck, but before I knew it we were out in the open air again. My glimpse of the dark side of Sydney was forgotten as we travelled along a road bordered by walls covered in ivy. Beyond them we could see mansions with shingled roofs and bay windows. There were forty-foot-tall maple-like trees on either side of the road, crimson in leaf, and pink-orange-barked trees with sinuous limbs that Ranjana said were called red gums. Before long the vegetation thinned and we found ourselves passing through rocky terrain. Bungalows sat on blocks of lawn with nothing to differentiate them except the position of their rusty water tanks. The only relief from the starkness was an occasional glimpse of the sea.

A few miles on, Uncle Ota directed the driver to turn into a narrow street with houses on one side and a low forest on the other.

Dozens of brightly coloured parrots squawked and somersaulted on a tree with leathery leaves and golden flower spikes. Two broke away from the group and swooped low over the taxi's bonnet.

'Rainbow lorikeets,' said Klára, pressing her face to the glass.

'We studied the book you sent us,' I explained to Uncle Ota and Ranjana.

The taxi stopped outside a weatherboard cottage bordered by a picket fence. A large black bird with a white nape and underwings sat near the letterbox. 'Magpie or currawong?' Ranjana asked Klára.

'Magpie,' Klára answered. 'Currawongs have black necks.'

The driver removed our luggage from the boot while Uncle Ota opened the passenger doors for everyone. He gestured towards the house. 'Welcome to our humble home,' he said.

Paint curled in flakes from the cottage's walls. The roof was mottled with rust patches and the stairs to the front door were cracked. But the house had a strange charm. A camellia tree with soft pink flowers decorated the tiny front yard, with a cheery border of marigolds along the fence. The two front windows were framed by green shutters which made it look as if the house had a face with eyes and the door was its nose.

After Uncle Ota had paid the driver, Ranjana opened the front door and we tramped in single file down a corridor whose sole light came from the kitchen at the end of it. The kitchen had been painted primrose yellow and had a modern stove, but when we were seated at the table I noticed the ceiling was soot-stained and that the enamel cups Ranjana placed before us were chipped. I glanced at Klára and wondered what she was thinking. The house was a few steps down from the way we had lived in Prague. But my sister seemed happy and did not take her eyes from Thomas, who Uncle Ota was bouncing on his knee.

Ranjana set down a plate of scones on the table along with vanilla slice. Klára picked up the pot of sweet-smelling jam that Ranjana had placed next to a bowl of cream. 'It's lilly-pilly,' Ranjana told her. 'To put on the scones.'

'I am a vegetarian,' replied Klára, in English and with so much dignity I wanted to laugh.

Ranjana patted her head. 'I made it from the berries of the lilly-pilly tree in our back garden. I'm a vegetarian too, so we'll get along fine.'

After we had finished our afternoon tea, Ranjana showed Klára and me to the room we were to share. It was the second-largest room in the house and faced on to the street, but it was still tiny. Two single beds had been crammed against each other but there was barely room to open the doors of the battered armoire. I could see Ranjana had tried to make the room cosy with a vase of marigolds on the side table and a magenta sari in place of curtains at the window. My legs trembled and I sat down on the bed.

'Are you all right?' Ranjana asked.

'Just sea legs,' I said, trying to shake off the fainting spell. I knew my lack of balance was not because my legs were unused to land, but because the room was confirmation that this was our life now; Prague was far away and Mother was gone forever.

When I felt better, Ranjana continued with the tour of the house. Uncle Ota, Ranjana and Thomas shared the room next to ours. The bath was in the laundry shed in the long, narrow garden at the rear of the house. Next to this, standing in a shed of its own, was the toilet. I was the first to use it. Considering it was only a seat with a pan, it did not smell as bad as I had feared and the chilly breeze under the door seemed to ventilate it. A picture of a white-tiled and brass-fitted bathroom from *Home* magazine was pasted to the back of the door. I took it to be an example of Uncle Ota's humour. Next to the toilet was a basket filled with squares of torn-up newspaper, the use of which I did not need to guess. A hairy spider had fixed itself in a web in the corner of the roof. No doubt Klára would be fascinated by it, but I sat the whole time with the fear that it would spin down a line of web and land on my head.

After Klára had made use of the 'dunny', as Uncle Ota called it, Ranjana showed us the room at the rear of the house. It was the largest room and, from the joins in the walls, it looked as though a sitting room, a third bedroom and an enclosed balcony had been combined. Here, between its Victorian-style red walls, Uncle Ota kept the treasures he had collected from his travels. There was a Turkish pipe and an African drum leaning against a stone elephant in one corner, and an ostrich egg perched on a stand in front of a gold mirror in another. On the shelves stood miniature wooden dolls with primitive faces and human hair. Glass cabinets held collections of books, African masks, maps, Chinese scrolls and shells labelled into their classification families. Two cabin trunks served as side tables. Uncle Ota opened them to show me his collection of glass-plate negatives stacked together. From the number of photographs of temples and palaces that adorned the walls I could see he was as keen about photography as I was. The most macabre object in the room, besides the medieval cauldron, was a set of jaws four feet high and five across, with serrated teeth. Uncle Ota saw me looking at it and explained that it had come from a shark that been caught off the shore from Gibsons Beach, which was down the road. I shivered at the thought of such a monster lurking under the surface of the sea. I was surprised when Uncle Ota said, 'The fishermen should have let it go. Sharks are the keepers of the ocean.'

Uncle Ota tapped the floor in the corner of the room nearest the back window. 'We shall place your piano here when it arrives, Klára,' he said. 'The acoustics will be good and the floor won't give way.'

The following day, because he did not have to work at the Australian Museum — where he was 'in charge of dusting shelves and mopping floors' — until the afternoon, Uncle Ota led us on an expedition around the harbour shoreline and showed us rock pools where we found anemones, worms, sponges, snails and fish of every colour living amongst the ribbon-like seaweed.

He also took us to the Royal Botanic Gardens, where we stretched our necks to look at the fig trees and Norfolk Island pines and wandered around the lawns, duck ponds and rose gardens with the backdrop of the harbour beyond them. Klára was captivated by the grey-headed flying foxes that gathered in the palm groves. There were so many of them that the trees looked black.

'They are intelligent animals and vegetarians like us,' Ranjana told her. 'They eat berries and blossoms and are pollinators of native plants. If you look closely you will see some of the females have a young one tucked under their wing.'

'They invite sporting clubs in after the park closes to shoot the poor creatures,' said Uncle Ota.

'Why?' I asked.

'Because they eat the exotic plants,' Ranjana answered, hoisting Thomas higher up in her arms. 'But there are other ways to deter them. They hate sudden loud noises.'

'I've never understood why my sex finds it so terribly manly to slaughter harmless creatures,' said Uncle Ota. 'If you want my opinion, women are superior in respecting life.'

'Because we are the ones who work so hard to bring it into being,' said his wife.

Klára did not take her eyes from the colony of bats. She leaned against the trunk of a giant angophora. 'Australian trees are so beautiful, why would you want to plant anything exotic?' she said. 'I wonder what would happen if the hunters were hunted.'

Uncle Ota gazed at Klára for a long time. I thought he might be intrigued by her perception of things. Her commitment to vegetarianism had forced me to examine my own attitude to animals. 'Everything on this earth is connected,' she had told me. 'If we harm other living creatures, we ultimately harm ourselves. As long as we show them no compassion, we ourselves will continue to suffer in our minds and bodies.' As it turned out, her belief protected us from the only outbreak of disease on our voyage to Australia — an eruption of food poisoning attributed to the salted beef.

Uncle Ota looked as if he were going to ask Klára to elaborate on what she meant, but Ranjana reminded him that he had to be at the museum in ten minutes.

'Yes, that's right,' said Uncle Ota, shaking his head as if Ranjana had woken him from a dream.

I looked from Klára to Uncle Ota and wondered what it was about my sister that so entranced him.

SIX

Prior to our arrival in Australia, Uncle Ota had received a letter from Aunt Josephine dated two days after our ship had departed from Genoa. It had been prompted by Hilda's report of our safe boarding. Klára's piano arrived not long after we did. According to the shipping notice it had been sent by Doctor Holub three weeks after Aunt Josephine's letter. Since the letter and the piano we had heard nothing. I waited for the postman every day, twice a day, for news from Aunt Josephine. Each time I was disappointed. By July, I had stopped waiting and started praying that she was safe.

For the first month in Sydney, Klára and I had been nervous. We jammed our bedroom window closed and jumped each time we heard someone open the front gate. But we soon learned that in Sydney there was always someone opening the front gate. Firstly, at dawn, the milkman arrived with the 'clink' of glass bottles. He returned in the afternoon with butter and cream. Then there was the iceman, who came rain or shine with a slab of ice on his back. The postman blew his whistle twice daily and the baker's visit was heralded by the scent of fresh bread and the 'clop, clop' of his draughthorse. The clothes prop man sold us gum saplings to support our washing line, and there was also the scissors and knife-sharpening man, the cobbler, the sanitary man, the newspaper boy and the travelling salesman who arrived each week with a suitcase filled with fountain pens, sponges, candles, needles and threads and mosquito coils. Once a month the bottle man announced his beer delivery at the gate with the cry 'Bottle-oh!' Like most Czech men, Uncle Ota preferred beer to wine or spirits.

'You can't be a hermit and live in Australia,' Klára said.

'No,' I agreed.

In Prague, we had become used to not going anywhere alone. So when Klára began attending school, I rode with her on the tram to Waverley every morning and was there to pick her up at three o'clock each afternoon.

'You have to stop that,' Ranjana told me one afternoon when she was showing me how to bake naan bread. 'You must stop living in fear.'

That was impossible to do. Uncle Ota had not written to Aunt Josephine because he wanted to wait until he had word from her. Each morning I awoke with questions running through my mind. How did Miloš react when he found out we were gone? Did he threaten Aunt Josephine? Was he trying to trace us? Had he been tricked by the decoy tickets to America or was he on his way to Australia right now?

'You can believe me,' Ranjana said, kneading the dough. 'I know about fear.'

I watched her divide and roll out the bread. Ranjana had beautiful hands, strong but graceful. I had seen pictures of Indian people in books and had thought they looked fragile. But not Ranjana. She was like a tree rooted in the ground. I could not imagine her being afraid of anything. But I understood that the sati pyre had left scars; if not on her body, then on her soul.

To ease my mind, I threw myself into photography. I took pictures of the native birds and Ranjana collected leaves and flowers for me to photograph for her botany books. I also did portraiture.

'You capture the essence of your subjects beautifully,' Uncle Ota told me. 'As well as things others perhaps would not notice, such as Ranjana's penetrating glance and Klára's sylph-like hands.'

He was surprised to learn that I had never developed my own photographs and relied on studios to produce my prints.

'My dear Adélka, development is half the art,' he said. 'Follow me.'

Uncle Ota led me into the back garden to the laundry shed. Next to the copper and washtub was an enlarger fashioned from tins. The windows and doors had black curtains on them to block out the light.

'The chemicals and trays are here,' Uncle Ota said, indicating a crate on the floor. 'I'll give you a lesson in the process, but the art you can learn by yourself. Use this room any time you like, except Mondays when Ranjana does the laundry.'

Ranjana returned to work at the stocking factory and left Thomas in my care. She and Uncle Ota took afternoon shifts and Uncle Ota worked some evenings as well. I had put some of the money Aunt Josephine had given me aside to pay Klára's school fees and for musical tuition once we had found a suitable teacher. I wanted to give the rest to Uncle Ota but he refused to take it.

'Hold on to your money,' he told me. 'You might need it. And we have all that we need here.'

It was a strange thing that Ranjana and Uncle Ota worked hard and had few material items and yet lived more abundantly than some of the richest families in Prague. They never went to balls or parties, yet their lives were filled with more good humour and fun than I had seen in any damasked and gold-leafed parlour.

One afternoon, Klára and I were collecting the washing from the line in the back garden when I sensed someone watching us. I turned to see a woman peering through the pencil pines that bordered our house and our neighbour's. She was so pale that if I had not known better I would have thought her a ghost. The woman was perhaps three or four years older than Ranjana, but in her brown house dress and with bags under her eyes she looked worn out.

'Hello,' I said.

The woman started. Despite her appearance, her eyes were bright and alert. 'Hello,' she replied. Her mouth trembled as if she would like to say more, but she thought better of it and turned on her heel and scurried away.

'How extraordinary,' Klára said. 'She's like a little mouse.'

'That's Esther,' Ranjana explained when she returned home. 'The daughter of the woman we rent the house from. She's terribly shy. I think it's the strain of looking after her mother. The woman has been blind for ten years.'

'Lonely souls need comfort,' Mother always said. She had won Father's admiration, and irritated Miloš, by visiting neighbours who were suffering misfortune. She could not help herself. She had been born with a generous heart. I decided that I did not just want to look like my mother, I wanted to emulate her. So the following afternoon, Klára and I decided to visit our reclusive neighbour. We packed a basket with jars of Ranjana's lilly-pilly and kumquat jams and headed next door.

The house that Esther and her mother shared was twice the size of ours, with a second storey, but was much drearier. In the front garden a fountain had crumbled into mouldy ruins overrun by ivy, and the veranda was a mass of cobwebs with tree roots poking through the boards. But the back garden, from what Klára and I had managed to glimpse through the gaps in the paling fence, was an overgrown Eden of silver gum and bloodwood trees knotted with flannel flowers, lilies and lantana. We would have loved to explore it.

I knocked on the door. A butterfly with turquoise wings rimmed in black flitted over my wrist to the knocker then off again. The creature was a thing of beauty set against the shabbiness of the house. We heard feet shuffling down the hall. The door opened a crack and Esther peered at us.

'We wanted to introduce ourselves to you,' I told her. 'I am Ota Rose's niece, Adéla, and this is my sister, Klára.'

If Esther heard me she did not acknowledge it. She stared at us without saying a word. Klára held up the basket of jams and Esther looked at it as if she did not know what it was. A mouse, Klára had called her. I half expected Esther to sniff the contents, twitch her nose, then run away.

'We will leave the basket here,' I said, pointing to a dusty table on the veranda. Esther's shyness was crippling and I did not want to impose on her too long.

But to my surprise a smile came to her face. With her small face and large eyes she was a pretty woman, but the dowdy clothes and unkempt hair hid it. 'You play the piano?' she asked me.

'Klára does,' I replied.

'It's beautiful,' Esther said. 'It gives Mother a lot of pleasure.'

We had to take care that the sea air and the dramatic temperature changes of late winter did not put the piano out of tune but from that day on we opened the window a crack whenever Klára sat down to play piano. On my nineteenth birthday, we were celebrating with a chocolate cake in the back room when Klára looked out the window and noticed that a window in Esther's house had opened a crack too. The following month, when the temperatures steadied, both windows opened to halfway. Then, in October, Esther opened her window all the way and took down the curtains. When the light was at a certain angle, we saw an elderly woman reclining in a chair with her back towards the window.

One day a note appeared in our letterbox: *Mother says that you are rushing the fugue. You should try to play it more evenly.*

Then the following day, another message arrived: *Mother says that if you want to achieve a singing sound, you must relax your arms more. Move your fingers as little as possible from the keys and follow every movement of them with a downward and upward motion of the arm.*

After that a note appeared that read: *Acquiring a good technique is as much a mental process as a physical one. Make sure you do not let your mind wander.* This was soon followed by: *Before you start your piece, sit in front of the piano and imagine how you will play it from start to finish. If this makes you feel impatient, you must keep doing this until you can sit before your piano and be relaxed. Never be in a rush to commence your piece without having settled your mind first. This is the reason you are playing the Schumann too fast.*

The tuition from Esther's mother proved right. Whenever Klára applied the advice, the quality of the piece she was practising improved.

After a while, we could not contain our curiosity.

Esther, I wrote at the bottom of one of the notes before returning it to the letterbox, *Klára and I should very much like to meet your mother. We would like to thank her for the help she has been giving Klára.*

There was no reply with the following day's note, but the morning after that, when I was leaving to go to the grocery shop, I found Esther hovering near the gate. She was wearing a wool skirt that rolled around the hemline and a brown sweater.

'Mother says you can come at three tomorrow afternoon,' she said. She trembled when she gave the invitation and seemed relieved when I said that we would be there. She turned to go and a blue butterfly, like the one we had seen near her door, appeared. It rested on her shoulder, unnoticed by her, before flying off again.

Ranjana was making chocolates and told us that we could take some for our visit to Esther and her mother. Klára and I watched Ranjana blend the chocolate, vanilla and milk and pour the mixture into heart-shaped moulds. I thought of Prague, where the house had smelt of roasting cocoa beans for days before Mother blended her chocolate. Uncle Ota arrived home and tried to taste a piece before it had set. Ranjana shooed him from the kitchen.

'Thomas is better behaved than you!' she said, and chased him down the hall with a saucepan, laughing.

Given the rundown appearance of the house, I expected the interior of our neighbours' home to be as decrepit and to find Esther's mother sitting amongst cobwebs and dust like Miss Havisham in Dickens's *Great Expectations*. So when Esther opened the door for Klára and me and invited us in, I was surprised to find that the house was orderly although gloomy. We followed Esther down a corridor, past bedrooms with the curtains drawn but with enough light seeping in to catch glimpses of neatly made four-poster beds and carved mahogany wardrobes.

We arrived at a room at the back of the house, where Esther's mother was sitting. She wore a black dress with leg-of-mutton sleeves and a high collar. When she heard our footsteps, she turned in our direction. Her eyes were cloudy. I had seen the condition in an old dog once. It was cataracts and there was nothing that could be done about them.

'Mother, your guests are here,' Esther said.

Her mother nodded. Her skin was wrinkled, with deep crevices running from the corners of her mouth to her chin. The lines gave her the comical appearance of a ventriloquist's doll, but there was nothing humorous about the woman.

'I am Mrs Bain,' she said, without asking our names in turn. 'Sit down.' It was more an order than an invitation.

Besides the armchair in which Mrs Bain sat, there were four walnut chairs set in a circle around a faded rug. Klára and I sat ourselves in two of these while Esther placed the dish of chocolates we had brought on the table before disappearing down the hall. The room gave me a queer feeling. There was a cast-iron fireplace decorated with lion's-head mouldings and the chairs we sat in had carved heads of nymphs on the crests and arms. The wallpaper was patterned in a peacock-feather design, which gave the effect of dozens of eyes staring down at us. The woman in the room was blind and yet I felt that we were being watched from every angle.

Esther returned with a tray of cups and a teapot. I turned to Mrs Bain. 'I have to thank you,' I said. 'Your help has been invaluable to Klára's progress.'

I restrained myself from asking questions but I was curious to know who Esther's mother was. There was a burled walnut piano in the corner of the room, its lid closed and covered in a white cloth. The piano appeared to be in good condition but, from the porcelain figurines that had been arranged on the lid, seemed to have not been played for some time. There were no photographs in the room or other personal mementos to give us a clue to the identity of Mrs Bain and what made her an authority on music. The only thing I was sure of was that Esther and her mother had not always resided in Watsons Bay. The elaborate furniture was out of place in the wooden home and out of keeping with the area, which was mostly fishermen's cottages and labourers' huts.

Mrs Bain returned my gratitude with a tight-lipped smile. Esther placed some chocolates on a plate on her mother's lap. Mrs Bain picked one up and smelled it, but not in the timid, mouse-like way her daughter explored things. She gave the impression of a wolf sniffing the air before commencing the hunt. She put the chocolate back on her plate without touching it. Who could refuse one of Ranjana's delicious chocolates? I felt sorry for anyone who had lost a sense so precious as sight, but Mrs Bain's behaviour made me wonder if she had been an insensitive person all her life.

'Your sister has natural aptitude,' Mrs Bain said to me. 'But genius is a jealous god and demands sacrifice.'

The conversation continued in an awkward manner. I managed to elicit from Mrs Bain that she had studied music in London and Vienna and, although she had never performed in anything more public than a soirée herself, she had taught piano and many of her students had gone overseas to forge careers. I wanted to ask her what to do about Klára's musical education and whether she thought the Conservatorium High School would be a suitable institution. I had assumed Esther's mother might be interested to know that we were from Prague, the city that had produced great composers and inspired foreign ones. But Mrs Bain talked about herself — about how her life had been ruined by the loss of her sight, how her status in society had been reduced by her husband's death and his family's scrambling for the assets. She did not say outright that Esther had blighted her life, but she left us with the impression that she had been enjoying a 'long youth' until her daughter came along.

From the awkwardness with which Esther went about serving the tea, pushing the plates around the table and nearly spilling the sugar, I sensed that we were the first visitors to the house in years and a fresh audience for what Esther must have listened to every day. While Mrs Bain might not be as rich now as when she lived with her husband in Point Piper, she was not exactly in the poorhouse. Her home could have been a lovely place to live, despite her blindness. But Mrs Bain was determined to live miserably, and to make Esther do so along with her. The visit passed slowly, and we were relieved when it came time to leave.

'Poor Esther,' Klára said when we returned home. 'What a joyless person she lives with. I am benefiting from Mrs Bain's notes but I see now that she is not sending them out of generosity. She just wants to show off.'

After listening to our story, Uncle Ota agreed. 'It's Esther who enjoys Klára's playing, I think. The poor thing is starved for beauty — and company. We need to entice her here more often.'

Klára continued to open the window when she practised and Mrs Bain continued to send notes. But we were in no hurry for a return visit to our landlady's house, although I could not help thinking about Esther. I sensed she had potential for a bigger and better life. But was it her mother alone who had made her so frightened and drab?

It was the milkman, our educator on everything we needed to know about Australia from its politics to redback spiders, who gave us the answer. 'Esther's a nice girl,' he told us. 'She fell in love with a Protestant and her mother wouldn't let them marry. He died in the war. When Esther received the news, Mrs Bain said it was just as well and Esther could forget all about the boy now. Poor love, I don't think she ever got over that. She closed down and shut out the world.'

I felt for Esther. The sight of ex-soldiers wandering the streets, many missing a limb or an eye, still wearing their service badges on their shabby suits, was heartbreaking. The war had finished only a few years ago and yet they had already become invisible. The world had moved on. But they must have been painful reminders to Esther of her lost love. Perhaps that was the reason she rarely went out.

There was still no word from Aunt Josephine.

'If something bad has happened, Doctor Holub would have told us,' Uncle Ota assured me. 'As they used to say in the war, "No news is good news."'

Uncle Ota, however, received some information from the director of the Australian Museum about his job. And it was good news indeed. He beamed when he told us: 'I've been promoted to a guide.'

I was glad for Uncle Ota, and sorry for him too. He was over-qualified for the job. He had a university diploma and had mastered several languages during his travels. He wanted to be a teacher but had been unable to obtain a university post because he was foreign. Still, the promotion meant that he would not be performing menial cleaning jobs any longer.

Uncle Ota proved to be a popular tour guide and enjoyed his work so much that Ranjana suggested we invite people to our house each Tuesday evening for a lecture-cum-soirée.

'For a small fee, we can treat guests to a recital by Klára, canapés courtesy of me, and a lecture by Ota based on his experiences travelling the world,' she said.

Other intellectuals would have come to Australia and baulked at its working-class ethic and the lack of cultural institutions. Klára and I had been disappointed by the dearth of art exhibitions, theatre plays and philosophical lectures in Sydney compared with Prague. But Ranjana and Uncle Ota saw what was required and created it for themselves.

While Klára and I set out the chairs for the inaugural meeting, I wondered who would show up. At exactly seven o'clock, I heard the gate open and footsteps come down the garden path. Within minutes our back room was filled with an eclectic mix of people: a university professor and his wife; an artist; three shopkeepers; a grazier who was in town for the week; and an SP bookie who had seen Uncle Ota's advertisement in the window of the local grocery shop asking for 'interested people to travel the world and expand their minds for one evening a week'.

That first night, Uncle Ota gave a talk on African tribal masks and their spiritual meanings. The talk was well received, and word spread so quickly about the Tuesday lectures that for future meetings we had to take advance bookings due to the lack of space.

When Uncle Ota needed a break he invited a 'guest' to speak about their area of expertise. Ranjana gave a lecture on vegetarianism along with a cooking demonstration, while Klára talked about Chopin's hand technique. Uncle Ota made me give a lecture on 'Pictorialism versus Modernism in Photography', which went well but caused me so much gut-twitching agitation that I refused to do one ever again.

We invited Esther to the meetings. At first she declined, but one evening she arrived in a neatly ironed dress with a butterfly brooch on her shoulder. Although she shied away if anyone tried to speak to her, the physical transformation was dramatic — aside from the leaves in her hair, which Klára subtly picked out when she was not looking.

The next Tuesday, while Ranjana and I were in the kitchen preparing the supper, we saw the kitchen window of Esther's house open. A few seconds later, Esther clambered out. That explained the leaves — she had to make her way through the overgrown back garden instead of taking the front path.

'She's sneaking out of the house like a naughty adolescent,' Ranjana said.

'Wonderful!' said Uncle Ota when we told him. 'A few hours away from the dragon will do her good.'

We never mentioned to Esther that we knew her secret for fear it would embarrass her and stop her from coming. But Uncle Ota was sure to hang some lamps in our garden and prop a ladder against the fence so Esther could find her way home without tearing her clothes.

Seven

Our first Christmas in Australia was our second without Mother. In some ways it was easier because a summer Christmas was different from any we had experienced before and we could not be nostalgic. The eighty-six-degree heat wilted the tree, and us along with it. Uncle Ota cooked 'billy can pudding' over a fire in the back garden and Ranjana made spicy samosas and tongue-burning curry. I cooked a dish of mushrooms and barley called *houbový kuba*, but the mushrooms were not as sweet and I realised that Uncle Ota's subversion of traditions and creation of fresh ones was based on sound reasoning: better the novelty of the new than the shadow of the old.

'I'm enjoying my Australian Christmas,' Klára told me. 'I don't have to look at the poor carp at the markets.'

I wondered what she would have said if she had seen the fly-speckled leg of ham that the butcher had delivered to Mrs Fisher down the road that morning.

It was four days into the new year when the notes from Mrs Bain on piano technique stopped. She'd had chest pains before Christmas, but we were still surprised when we saw the undertaker and his assistant leave Esther's house with a coffin. Esther was nowhere in sight, but we could imagine her watching her mother's departure from behind the curtains. There was no obituary or funeral notice in the newspaper and we were at a loss about how to approach Esther to show her our support.

'Esther may not want anyone else to be involved,' suggested Uncle Ota.

'I know Mrs Bain was not kind to her but she must feel the loss,' I said.

We became alarmed a few days later when a furniture removalist arrived at Esther's house and began carting away chairs and tables.

'I hope Esther's not in trouble,' said Uncle Ota. 'We must visit her and see if there is anything we can do to help.'

We planned to pay Esther a visit the next day but she turned up on our doorstep that afternoon. She twitched nervously when she spoke but there was a light in her eyes that was new.

'I have cleared the top floor of my house,' she said. 'I never use it. Would you like to live there instead of in this house? I'll reduce your rent if you help me clean the house and fix up the garden.'

Esther's offer stopped us in our tracks. She rubbed her chin and her eyes darted from her feet to our waists before she could settle her gaze on our faces. 'It's time for a change,' she said. 'I could do with some company.'

Esther's house was more comfortable than the one we had been renting from her. There was a sitting room upstairs with a view of the street, and I could observe people at the front gate without them seeing me. Klára and I shared a bedroom, which overlooked the garden and had a silver gum outside the window. I would have liked to climb onto one of its branches, but Ranjana forbade it.

'You want to break your neck, you can do it out of my sight,' she said.

Ranjana and Uncle Ota slept in the bedroom next to ours with an alcove for Thomas's cot. Esther remained in her bedroom downstairs, but cleared the parlour so we could put Klára's piano there along with Uncle Ota's artefacts. I thought it was generous of Esther to give us so much space, especially as she already had a piano in the sitting room at the rear of the house.

'And, of course, you must continue your Tuesday nights,' she said.

The camel-back sofas, burgundy velvet chairs and tapestries downstairs were Victorian in style and when I passed them to go to the kitchen or bathroom, I knew what Klára meant when she said, 'We are living on the set of an Oscar Wilde play.'

One night I woke up and could not go back to sleep. I went to sit in the room with a view of the street. The bush across the road was silver in the moonlight and I saw a tawny frogmouth swoop down on some prey. Then I noticed the man standing by the gate. He wore a khaki military uniform and a high-domed hat with a narrow brim and a strap under his jaw. The man had a pale, youthful face and innocent eyes. He seemed to be looking into the garden for something. I reached for the latch to open the window so I could call to him, but he vanished into thin air.

The following morning I told Klára about the ghost. We had been brought up in a superstitious culture and the existence of a spiritual world that paralleled our own was something we were at ease conversing about. After all, our house in Prague had been full of spirits.

'He might be one of the young men who did not come back from the war,' Klára suggested.

I stood at the window in the sitting room every night for the next week to see if the man would appear again. But he did not.

The Tuesday night meetings grew in size and Uncle Ota could now afford to invite a paid guest lecturer each week. The first was a palaeontologist who showed us prehistoric vertebrate fossils that had been discovered in Western Australia. He was followed by a member of the Horticultural Society who espoused the wonders of kikuyu grass, and an architect who implored us to 'stop promoting Romanticism in a modern city'. The most fascinating of all, however, was the talk by a lecturer from the University of Sydney's anthropology department about his travels in Outback Australia. It was not just the subject of his address — the Aboriginal tribes of the inland — that captured our imagination but also the medium he used to convey it. Doctor Parker turned up on our doorstep with two suitcases and a screen. Uncle Ota and I helped him set up his projector and, after his introduction, Ranjana turned down the lights. The reel began with a train journey through mountains. The picture had been shot from the front of the train and gave us the sensation that we were travelling on it. I stifled a scream when the train zigzagged around a tight bend with a precipice on one side, so real did the illusion appear. We saw open plains with kangaroos bounding across the grasslands, and isolated homesteads in stark but beautiful landscapes. Finally, Doctor Parker showed us footage of Aboriginal corroborees and tribal women preparing food on sheaths of bark. If we had seen photographs, we would have been engaged by such exotic sights, but it was the film that brought them so vividly to life. When the images shook and the tape came to an end with a 'click', it was a shock to find myself sitting in the parlour.

After the screening the audience asked questions about the Aboriginal tribes Doctor Parker had studied, and Uncle Ota and I also questioned him about the filming: what kind of camera he had used; what kind of film; how he had kept the camera steady during motion shots. He was flattered by our interest in such details and spoke with us long after the other guests had left, about varying shot depths and how to edit scenes for maximum impact.

'I've seen kinetoscope parlours and nickelodeons at fairs but nothing like the quality production we saw tonight,' Uncle Ota told me. 'They say it's only a passing fad but I believe moving pictures will be the art form of tomorrow.'

I thought back to an afternoon in Prague when I had been running errands and had passed a cinema with a poster of Pola Negri starring in *Gypsy Blood* in the glass display case outside. The actress's smoky eyes seemed to me the essence of glamour. Miloš had forbidden us to go to the cinema — he described it as 'cheap entertainment for the masses' — and even Mother had said she would prefer it if we went to the theatre or opera. That afternoon I watched the people line up at the box office and longed to follow them up the stairs and into that secretive world where stories were told in moving pictures. I had enough coins in my pocket to cover the ticket. No one would have noticed if I disappeared for a few hours. But I remembered Mother's warning never to attend entertainment on my own and could not disobey.

Uncle Ota announced that we would be going to the cinema the following Saturday. Esther volunteered to mind Thomas.

While our landlady's personality was eccentric, her dedication to my cousin's welfare was not. When Thomas started crawling,

Esther was vigilant that nothing was left on the floor that he could choke on and any sharp surfaces were either turned to the wall or padded with wads of brown paper. Thomas could not be left in safer hands.

Although we could only afford tickets in the stalls, we were going to the Saturday night session and dressed for the occasion. I wore a cocktail dress trimmed in turquoise sequins, while Klára dressed in a voile blouse with lemon piping and a matching skirt. Uncle Ota put on pinstriped trousers with his black tails and, to hide their worn appearance, added a new top hat and polished shoes. Ranjana did not own an evening dress, so I bought her one a few sizes larger than I could wear and pretended I had brought it from Prague with me. 'It's too big,' I told her. 'And I haven't had time to take it in.'

Ranjana lifted her chin and stared down her nose at me. I did my best not to flinch. She was proud and I was afraid to offend her. She and Uncle Ota would not take anything material from me. They said my contribution to the housework was enough. I had never cleaned anything in Prague — although Mother had taught us to sew, cook and be tidy — but I did the sweeping and dusting of Esther's house and most of the gardening. Ranjana had also lived a privileged life in her first marriage, and Uncle Ota had been born into a wealthy family; it was ironic that we should have all ended up washing our own underwear and scrubbing the floors. But I did not mind it. I enjoyed the meditative quality of housework.

'Thank you,' said Ranjana, trying on the dress.

The red satin sheath I had chosen was stunning against her dark skin.

'You look like a queen,' I told her.

She rolled her eyes. 'Let's just see if they let me in.'

Although in Prague we had regularly attended the opera and theatre, a ripple of excitement ran through me when we entered the foyer of the cinema. My eyes took in everything: the green carpet, the brass trimmings, the glittering chandeliers. Uncle Ota picked up our tickets and we lined up at the marble counter for our box of Fantale chocolates and malted milk. I took a breath when we stepped through the red curtains to the stalls and an usherette in white gloves led us to our seats. The entry to the stalls was flush to the screen so it was not until we reached our seats that I could make sense of the images on it. Slides for local businesses popped up in succession. While the others chatted, Klára and I read the slogans aloud: 'Lipton's Green Label Tea — only sixpence a pound'; 'Nutone nerve tonic will cure all your ills'.

When the patrons were seated, the curtain closed over the screen and the usherettes shut the doors. The house lights dimmed. A door under the proscenium opened and a man with sheet music under his arm stepped out. The audience clapped and the man sat down at the piano and flexed his fingers. The audience rose when he began the national anthem, 'God Save the King'.

After the last crescendo was reached and the pianist lifted his hands from the keys, the audience reseated themselves. The usherettes opened the doors to let in latecomers. A couple took the seats in front of us. The woman placed a presentation box of chocolates on her lap. 'All the ladies who came with a man have one,' Klára whispered. She was on the brink of adolescence and showed romantic inclinations. Her observation was correct. The women accompanied by a man had chocolate boxes with pink bows on their laps while the families and single people were content with Jaffas, Jujubes and Columbines. Uncle Ota guessed what Klára and I were whispering about. When the lolly boy came by with a tray of sweets strapped around his neck, Uncle

Ota purchased three presentation boxes. He gave one to Ranjana, one to me and one to Klára.

'Some men here only have one lady companion,' he said with a smile. 'I am lucky to be escorting the three most beautiful women in the room.'

When everyone had settled down, the pianist struck a dramatic chord and the curtain parted. Although we had come to see *The Four Horsemen of the Apocalypse* starring Rudolph Valentino, we were enthralled by the short film that preceded it. Although it was a cartoon, I was captivated by Felix the Cat bouncing around the screen chasing Skiddoo the mouse. It was miraculous to me that a picture could move. When Felix and the mouse became pals after taking to a flask of drink, the audience burst into laughter. The curtains closed again.

Green lights flashed up around the pianist and I saw that he had been joined by a violinist, a flautist and a trumpeter who had turned on their music-stand lights. A hush fell over the audience when the musicians began playing a tango and the opening credits for *The Four Horsemen of the Apocalypse* appeared on the screen. I was lost to the hypnotic play of light and shadow of the picture. I had thought a film might be something like a theatre play without dialogue, but it was different. The actors were apparitions, not people, and the way they conveyed their emotions — a lean towards an object to indicate interest, the tilt of the head to express love, the raising of an eyebrow to show surprise — was much closer to ballet than theatre. Their make-up was otherworldly too: ashen face powder, blackened eyes and cupid bow pouts painted on their lips. The anti-war theme of the film stirred me, reminding me of what had happened to Esther's love and the broken men I had seen in the streets of Prague and Sydney. I was amazed at how the story of two cousins who find themselves on opposite sides in the war could be brought to life so poignantly with moving images interspersed with titles. When Valentino danced his famous tango scene, Klára dug her fingers into my arm, and when the credits appeared and the audience applauded I had to blink a few times to come back to the real world.

After that first night we were hooked. We went to the pictures every Saturday evening and during the week when we could afford it. Sometimes, as a treat, we went to the city cinemas, where the pictures were preceded by vaudeville shows with chorus girls, comedians and singers. We saw everything on the program and I soon realised that my first taste of film had been a production of superb quality. There was plenty of melodrama showing as well and we often found ourselves in fits of laughter at over-gesticulated actions and implausible plots. Klára and I would analyse why these films were so terrible.

'The intertitles described things we could see for ourselves,' said Klára. '"Oh look, Margaret. The train is about to go off the tracks."'

'The best intertitles are the ones that voice the important lines then cut back into the same action shot,' I agreed.

Often Klára and I giggled because someone in the audience was reading the intertitles out loud, although if the picture was particularly incredulous the entire audience did so in unison to override the boredom.

There were no language barriers in silent pictures and we watched films from around the world, clutching our armrests through the creepy *The Cabinet of Doctor Caligari*, and weeping over *La Terre*. But the films that captivated us most were Australian. They were realistic and had usually been filmed outdoors. We loved Franklyn Barrett's *A Girl of the Bush*, not only for its plot but also because the picture was punctuated with footage of horse mustering and sheep shearing. *The Sentimental Bloke*'s portrayal of love among Woolloomooloo's poor pulled our heartstrings, although the intertitles, based on the poet CJ Dennis's popular verse, mystified us.

'*The world 'as got me snouted jist a treat: Crool forchin's dirty left 'as smote me soul*', Uncle Ota read out. 'What on earth does that mean?'

Even Ranjana, with her dictionary-perfect English, could not enlighten us. But the intertitles were not important. The leads, Arthur Tauchert and Lottie Lyell, told the story with their eyes.

The afternoon and evening cinema sessions ran set programs, but in the mornings films were shown on a continuous basis. We could attend the morning sessions when Uncle Ota and Ranjana had afternoon shifts. Women often brought their young children along, so we invited Esther to join us while Thomas slept on Ranjana's lap. Unless we arrived at exactly ten o'clock, however, it was impossible to time which picture was screening and so we sometimes took our seats halfway through a film and then had to wait until it ran again to pick up the story at the point where we had entered.

To reach the cinema we travelled by tram then walked three blocks. There was a pub on our route that was crowded no matter the time of day. The first time we passed it, the weather was pleasant and the male patrons spilled out the doors onto the street. At first I thought they had gathered for a political meeting, as I had seen in Prague before the war when the Czech nationalists were vying for independence. But it was not politics on these men's minds; from the shouts I heard through the open windows I realised they were sharing tips for the dog and horse races and drinking themselves blind. When the pub doors opened

I caught glimpses of men in serge suits, counters stacked with glasses turned upside down on towels, and barmaids rushing to take orders. At times, the reek of hops, urine and vomit was overpowering and we crossed the street to avoid it.

One Saturday morning a cold rain was falling. It was not enough to saturate our clothes but it was enough to chill our bones. We alighted from the tram and hurried towards the cinema. Ranjana cradled Thomas to her chest and Uncle Ota wrapped his arm around her shoulders. We passed the pub and I heard a burst of voices as the door opened and closed. Two men hurried by. They walked in front of Uncle Ota and Ranjana, who headed our group with Esther, Klára and me behind. The men had made a point of overtaking us but I assumed they must also be hurrying to the cinema. Then one of them, a lanky man with red scratches over his cheeks, turned, forcing us all to stop. The other man, shorter and with a squashed nose, fixed Ranjana with a hostile stare.

'Black bitch!' he muttered before turning to Uncle Ota. 'Can't you stand a white …'

The blood pounded in my ears. I did not understand the meaning of the words the man used, only that they were obscene. The other man grabbed Ranjana by the hair, forcing her to the ground. Klára and I screamed. Ranjana flung her arms around Thomas, shielding him under her body, anticipating the kick the man shaped up for. But before he could hurt Ranjana, Uncle Ota punched the man in the jaw. The man's head snapped back and he fell to the ground.

The commotion caught the attention of the pub patrons. Some men ran outside while others gathered at the windows. I thought the men who had come out were going to help us but I was mistaken. The fat man punched Uncle Ota in the ribs and the spectators cheered. 'Show the bloody foreigner what you've got!'

My mind flashed back to a scene I had witnessed in Prague when a Jewish student was set upon by some brutes. The men had kicked and punched the youth until his mouth bled and his face was as blue as a berry while my mother and I had shouted for the police.

There was no one but these thugs around us now. Although Uncle Ota was against violence, he'd had to defend himself in dangerous situations during his travels. Being taller than his attacker, he had the advantage and gave the fat man as good as he got. Then I heard a glass break. The hairs on my neck stood on end. A man held a broken tumbler from the window and one of the men outside took it and passed it along with the aim of getting it to the fat man. I tried to shout a warning but my voice cracked. I rushed towards the fat man. Everything turned to slow motion like a strange dream. A man in the crowd held up the tumbler and stepped towards me. He's going to cut my throat, I thought. Uncle Ota threw a punch that knocked the fat man out cold and at the same time my foot shot up and delivered a kick to the man with the tumbler's groin. He collapsed to his knees clutching his crotch. The other men looked shocked that their burly mate had been downed by a woman.

Uncle Ota seized the moment to pick up Ranjana and Thomas, grab Klára's hand and scream to Esther and me to run.

We made it to an alley before we realised that we were not being pursued. We crouched in a dark corner and caught our breath. A police siren wailed and we heard voices shouting abuse at the officers. Perhaps we should have returned to give our side of the story. But we were terrified. We hurried to the end of the alley then made our way to a tram stop a few streets away. When we were safely on board a tram, Klára dropped her head in her hands. There would be no pictures that day. When the tram passed by the pub on our trip home, the closed sign had been posted in the window. I looked at my shoe and realised I had split the sole when I'd kicked the man.

We never again attended the cinema near the pub. Instead we took the tram further along the line to another suburb. I had been in love with my new country. After the attack my relationship with Australia was uneasy. I was wary of Australians, wondering if they would lash out at me. Ranjana and Uncle Ota no longer walked side by side in public. Uncle Ota marched in front, his eyes scanning the streets for possible trouble. Ranjana, with Thomas in her arms, stayed a discreet distance behind. Anyone looking on would have assumed that they did not know each other.

'Ranjana and I knew we would face this when we got married,' Uncle Ota explained to me when I expressed my disgust at the situation. 'We endure it because we love each other.'

'If Beaumont Smith's film about a white man and a Maori girl is so popular, maybe people will accept marriages like yours,' I said hopefully.

Uncle Ota dispelled the idea. 'Beaumont Smith's leading lady isn't a Maori,' he said. 'She's as white as the Queen Mother. They have smeared blackface over her. That's why people accept it; it's not real.'

The attack had shaken my confidence in Australians but I was proud that I had defended myself. Ranjana stopped speaking to me like a child and treated me with respect. But Klára had been badly affected by the incident. She often woke up in the night screaming that she wanted to go home.

'We are safe from Miloš here,' I told her.

'We are not safe,' she wept. 'We are not safe anywhere.'

I was at a loss as to how to make her feel secure again.

Klára's nerves were not helped by the letter we received from Prague. I was sitting in the parlour, watching the street and listening to Klára play a Brahms waltz, when I saw Ranjana walk to the front gate to collect the mail from the postman. He handed her a letter in a brown envelope. She looked at the postmark and ran back inside the house.

'Ota!' she called. 'Adélka! Klárinka! A letter from Prague.'

Klára stopped playing and Uncle Ota rushed into the room with Thomas under his arm. He had been feeding Thomas and had pumpkin stains on his shirt. Ranjana handed Uncle Ota the letter and took Thomas from him. She sat down on the sofa and bounced her son on her lap. Uncle Ota opened the letter and sat down next to Ranjana to read it out to us.

> *My dear brother,*
>
> *It has been almost a year since my last correspondence to you and I know you must have been worried by the silence. Please forgive me. Doctor Holub checked with the shipping company that Adéla and Klára had arrived safely and were accepted into Australia. I had to content myself with the knowledge that my nieces were out of harm's way for I now understand what their dear mother meant when she said she was being 'watched'. Doctor Holub was with me when I informed Miloš that I had sent Adéla and Klára to America to be with their aunt and uncle, explaining that I had done so because Doctor Holub had received information that the girls were in danger. Of course, we did not reveal that we knew the source of this danger was Miloš himself but instead hinted at an anonymous kidnapper who was aware that the girls are heiresses to a fortune.*

*I had expected Miloš to be enraged but instead he
thanked us for acting so quickly in regard to the
protection of his stepdaughters. This calm response
unnerved me. Is it possible he believes that we
suspect nothing? Miloš said that he would like to
correspond with Adéla and Klára, which I assumed
was a ploy to find out where they are living. Doctor
Holub explained that for the girls' security he was
the only one who was entrusted with their address
and correspondence would put them at risk. Miloš
became hostile then and refused to sign the
allowance at the bank. Now we find ourselves in a
stalemate.*

*Since that meeting, Doctor Holub has found
that his mail is being tampered with, while I live
with a mysterious man posted daily outside my
house. Because of this, Doctor Holub and I are
reluctant to contact you and the girls lest we give
away your whereabouts. I hope that the money I
sent with the girls proves sufficient for their upkeep
a while longer.*

*Please let my nieces know that even when I do not
write I think of them with love every day. Each
morning I go to the church and light a candle for
them. Tell Adéla and Klára that Frip sends a lick.*

With all my love,
Josephine

Although the thought of Doctor Holub's mail being tampered with
and Aunt Josephine being spied upon were discomforting, at least
now we had a reason for the lack of correspondence from Prague.

If I could change one thing, however, it would be that Uncle Ota had not read out the letter in front of Klára. She became more nervous than ever, and so fearful for Aunt Josephine's safety that I awoke one night to find her pacing the bedroom floor.

'Klára, come back to bed,' I told her.

She shook her head and continued to walk. 'I'm praying,' she answered. 'I'm praying for us all.'

I had enrolled Klára at the Conservatorium High School for the following year. We had enough funds to cover the musical tuition, but if Klára or I should need anything else, I did not want to have to ask Uncle Ota for the money. I thought about the typing lessons I had taken with Aunt Josephine in Prague. I cared for Thomas in the afternoons, but I wondered if I could find a morning or night job to bring extra money into the household. Before I had a chance to start looking, another opportunity to contribute to the household arose.

The new cinema we attended was a smaller affair and shabbier, but the selection of films was interesting. We saw a flashy version of *Camille*, starring Rudolph Valentino and the Russian actress Alla Nazimova, who we all agreed resembled Klára. But most of the time it showed a selection of quality European films and local productions.

One Saturday night, when we were leaving the cinema, Klára voiced her disappointment that there had not been a live pianist to accompany the program, only a gramophone.

'I agree,' said Uncle Ota. 'The story was flat without a musician. A pianist can make or break a picture.'

'Perhaps Klára should have offered her services,' Ranjana said with a smile.

'Could she?'

We turned to see the cinema manager in the doorway of his office. We shuffled our feet, embarrassed because we had not seen him standing there.

'Seriously,' he said. 'Could she?' The manager's facial hair was trimmed to follow the line of his chin. He looked like a wizened Abraham Lincoln. 'I cannot get anyone for Saturday night. The big cinemas offer too much money.'

We chuckled at the suggestion. Mother had instilled in Klára and me a sense of dressing well and, although she wore no make-up, Klára appeared mature for her years.

'My sister is a fine pianist,' I replied. 'But she is only twelve years old.'

The manager's mouth opened as if he were on the verge of apologising when he was seized by another idea. 'What a novelty that would be!' he said. 'No one in Sydney has a pianist as young as that.'

He introduced himself as Mr Tilly and urged us to return to the auditorium so he could hear Klára play. We obliged him. Klára rarely declined an opportunity to play and the acoustics of the cinema would be a new experience for her. Mr Tilly led Klára to the piano while the rest of us took seats in the front row. He opened the fallboard and Klára warmed her hands with a scale. I marvelled at my sister. If I had been put on the spot like that, I would have fallen to pieces.

Klára commenced Chopin's Mazurka No 23 in D major from memory. Mr Tilly's jaw dropped. Something about Klára's poise and her ability to concentrate gave her the air of a serious musician, but I doubted he was expecting her to be as good as she was. When Klára finished the piece he could not contain his excitement.

'Bring this young lady back for a proper audition on Monday night,' he said. 'Some of the Hollywood films have scores she can practise, but for most of the films we show here the pianist needs to be able to improvise with whatever comes out of the projector. If she can keep up with the intertitles, she can have the Saturday night slot. I will pay her a fair wage and you can have free tickets.'

The offer was tempting, but I had doubts. 'It might ruin her chances of being taken seriously as a concert pianist,' I whispered to Uncle Ota.

'On the contrary,' he replied. 'She can put the money towards extra tuition at the Conservatorium High School.'

'Please let me take the audition, Adélka,' Klára said.

Klára was excited by the idea of playing for films and she practised all the next day to the neglect of her homework and household chores. The city cinemas had orchestras and chorus lines but Mr Tilly's suburban cinema relied on a single pianist. The Saturday night session was the most important of all and it was obvious he was going to use Klára's age as a drawcard. Klára selected pieces from her repertoire to suit different moods — suspense, romance, weariness, confusion. She wrote out captions on pieces of cardboard — 'The villain escapes', 'The heroine enters' — and asked me to swap them quickly until she could slip from one piece of music to another without hesitation.

On Monday evening Uncle Ota and I accompanied Klára to the cinema for her audition.

'My father was a picture showman,' Mr Tilly reminisced while guiding Klára to the piano. 'My mother and I travelled with him to the country towns where he'd set up his posters and limelight projector. They never wanted us to leave. It might be months before they saw another moving picture.'

Mr Tilly nodded to the projectionist. The lights dimmed and a picture we had not seen before appeared on the screen, *The Man from Kangaroo*. It was full of drama and romance as well as fight scenes and horse chases. The film turned out to be a six-reel feature. Mr Tilly already knew that Klára had the talent but he wanted to be certain that she had the stamina. Klára matched the action without a slip and even continued to play during the reel changes.

When the lights came up, Mr Tilly's face was flushed with excitement. 'I'll have posters made,' he said. *'The youngest talent in Sydney plays at Tilly's Cinema.'* He turned to Klára. 'What's your last name?'

'Rose,' she replied. That was Uncle Ota's anglicised name and, in a way, it was Father's name too. Uncle Ota seemed pleased. I decided I would make my surname Rose too.

Uncle Ota and Mr Tilly discussed the terms of Klára's employment while Klára and I ate coconut macaroons in the cinema office. When the two men had agreed on a fee, Mr Tilly offered Uncle Ota a cigar and they sat back, blowing smoke rings into the air.

'Who was the director of the film we saw?' Uncle Ota asked Mr Tilly.

'Wilfred Lucas. An American,' Mr Tilly answered. 'Caroll-Baker Productions brought him and his scriptwriter wife to Australia. They hoped that using American talent would secure an American market for the film.'

'Did it?'

Mr Tilly shrugged. 'The picture show business isn't like it was before the war. Australian pictures were cheap to make then, and Australians wanted to see their own country. We had a bigger local industry than France or America. Now we have permanent cinemas and the overheads that go with them, as well as the largest picture-going population in the world. Showmen need a constant supply of films and the only ones who can give us that are the Americans.'

'I should like to make a film about Australia one day,' I announced. I was surprised by my own words. Where had that idea come from? I enjoyed taking pictures with my camera but I did not know the first thing about making a film.

'Why not?' said Klára. 'You've always been good at telling stories, Adélka.'

Mr Tilly smiled at me. 'Make it a good picture then, young lady, and I'll screen it for you.'

After announcing my intention to make a film, I was obliged to follow through, especially as Klára had shown faith in me. It never occurred to us that being nineteen years old and a foreigner might hamper my progress. Mr Tilly gave me a list of Australian directors and I wrote to them asking where they obtained their cameras and for how much, and how they found actors. I kept their suggestions in an indexed journal. Most of them advised me to use sets sparingly to save money, and to film outdoors to take advantage of Australia's bright sunlight rather than using costly studio lights. Raymond Longford wrote that if I kept my technical team to a maximum of four, I could make an acceptable film for two thousand pounds. Beaumont Smith undercut this with suggestions on how to make a box office smash for a thousand pounds. In Prague I might have had access to that amount of money, but I could not afford to be frivolous with our funds here in Australia.

One thousand pounds, I sighed to myself. Well, that's the end of that.

Mr Tilly's posters featuring the 'young virtuoso Klára Rose' drew in the crowds, not just from the eastern suburbs but from other localities as well. The *Daily Telegraph* took a picture of Klára.

Her performances were so popular, Mr Tilly asked to extend her
performing nights, but I would not hear of it.

'She's still a young girl. She needs her rest,' I told him.

In winter that year, Klára complained of headaches and I
wondered if she needed glasses. One afternoon she came home
early from school looking pale. 'You need fresh air,' I told her.
She agreed to come to Nielsen Park with Esther and me.

When we arrived at the park, we found the gardeners busy
planting Moreton Bay figs and brush box along the pathways.
The park had been cleared of bushland and the caretakers had
realised too late that the result was stark and there were no trees
left to give shade. We spread out our picnic blanket near one of
the few remaining tuckeroo trees. Klára and I tugged off our
shoes and strolled to the water while Esther lay on her side on
the rug. A blue butterfly landed on her hip. I was intrigued why
Esther was a magnet for butterflies, and remembered that it was
unusual to see butterflies this time of year.

Esther had changed since her mother's death. She was still
quiet but she enjoyed going to the pictures with us. She gushed
over sheiks, swooned at Pacific Island romances and cheered for
the dancing girls. Perhaps having been robbed of her chance for
love, Esther was living vicariously.

'It's good to look at the horizon,' I told Klára when we reached
the shoreline. 'I had eye weakness when I was your age from too
much reading. Aunt Josephine told me that close work tightens the
muscles and I needed to relax them by looking into the distance.'

The wind off the water was chilly and there were no
swimmers, but dozens of boats bobbed in the waves. A musical
chirp trilled in the scrub above the rocks.

'Look!' I said, pointing out a blue bird flitting amongst the
branches. 'A superb fairy-wren.'

My mind drifted to Mother sitting at the table in our Prague house with her paints and water jars. The picture of homely bliss lifted my spirits. Then I was hit by a pain in the pit of my stomach that struck whenever I thought about Mother. Miloš had not only killed her, he had also destroyed my happy memories. If I remembered Mother, the joy was blighted by the thought of how she had died.

'Blood!' cried Klára, lifting up her hand.

I grabbed her wrist, thinking that she must have cut her hand on an oyster shell while my mind had been distracted. But there was no cut there. No sign of blood.

'Blood! Blood! I can see her face!' Klára screamed.

'Whose face?' I asked.

Klára took a step back and stared at me with the same vacant eyes she had shown me that day on the ship when she thought she had seen Miloš.

Esther ran up to us. 'Is something wrong?' she asked.

'Blood!' Klára cried again.

I grabbed her arms. 'Klára!' I said, shaking her. 'Klára!'

Klára began sobbing.

'Come,' said Esther, putting her arm around Klára's shoulders and nodding towards the road. 'We'd better go home.'

We would not have been able to get Klára back to the house in that condition on the tram, so Esther found a taxi. I was glad she was there to think for us. I helped Klára into the taxi and wrapped my coat around her.

'I was her older sister but I did not watch her closely enough ... Emilie started hearing voices in her head.' I remembered Mother's description of her sister's madness. 'After I am gone, you must protect Klára and keep her safe ... Do not lose sight of Klára the way I lost sight of my sister.'

Klára muttered inaudible sentences and tugged at her hair. It cannot happen so suddenly, I thought. It was as if the balance of the world had shifted and my sister and I were standing on the edge of a cliff, about to topple off.

EIGHT

Doctor Norwood's rooms in Macquarie Street were as quiet as a church. Uncle Ota and I watched the clock tick minutes away into an hour. Every so often the secretary tapped out something on the typewriter. Uncle Ota's lips moved silently as he read the framed certificates on the walls. Psychiatry was not a well-known specialty in Australia. It had come into practice during the war, to treat the soldiers who were 'shell-shocked'.

Despite the elaborate names that were now being used for it, the word 'madness' frightened me. Visions of the asylum in Prague with its high walls and barred windows loomed. I had found the rumours of rat-infested dungeons and hapless patients shackled in chains chilling then. Now that Klára had become ill, I could not stand the thought of it.

'That's not where your Aunt Emilie was sent,' said Uncle Ota when I told him my fears. 'Your grandparents put her in a private asylum in the countryside. But her mind weakened her body and she caught pneumonia.'

The tortured expression on Uncle Ota's face when he mentioned Aunt Emilie worsened my anxiety. Surely Klára is not insane, I told myself, although that was the first thing that leapt into my mind when she had her attack. Since then I wondered if she had simply suffered a nervous breakdown. After all, our mother had been murdered, we'd had to leave our home, and she had witnessed our family being attacked by a group of thugs.

I was grateful that Uncle Ota and Ranjana agreed to find Klára the best help they could. Ranjana and I wanted to care for Klára at home but the local doctor who saw us the afternoon of her episode would not hear of it. 'Should she wander outside in her present state of mind, she might be reported to the police,' he said. 'Then she will be certified to a mental asylum and you will have trouble getting her back.'

Doctor Norwood called us into his office and invited us to sit in the Chesterfield chairs. The oak-panelled walls and lace curtains gave the room a sense of coolness but my heart was racing and I broke into a sweat. Through a crack in the door to the examination room, I caught a glimpse of Klára lying down on a bench with a nurse leaning over her.

Doctor Norwood was in his early fifties with skin the colour of old ivory. His manner of speech was decisive. 'A sudden episode of psychosis,' he said. 'A delayed reaction to a shock.' He went on to tell us that if we did not get hospital treatment for Klára, her health would become worse. 'I will write you a referral to Broughton Hall. It is much better that Miss Rose goes to a voluntary clinic rather than a mental institution. I do not think the company of incurables does anything for one's equilibrium.'

The following day we took Klára to Broughton Hall in Rozelle. The weather was overcast and the grey sky matched the gloominess of my thoughts. Doctor Norwood had sedated her for the journey, which we took by taxi, not willing to risk any outbursts on the tram. She slept most of the time, her head resting on my shoulder. Each time Uncle Ota looked at her, his eyes clouded over as if he were remembering something painful.

With my impressions of the asylum in Prague, I had been afraid of what the clinic might look like. But there was nothing frightening, at least on the surface, about Broughton Hall except its proximity to Callan Park Mental Hospital, where the certified cases were sent. The grounds we passed through on our way to the admissions office were picturesque with flowerbeds and ponds. Palms and pine trees shaded the road while the rolling lawns were dotted with peacocks pecking at the grass.

A nurse in a white apron greeted us on the stairs of the converted Georgian mansion that now served as the admissions building. 'Good morning,' she said to us. She nodded to an attendant who pushed a wheelchair towards us and held it while Uncle Ota helped Klára into it. Inside the admissions office, Uncle Ota filled in the paperwork for Klára.

'I'm sorry,' said Klára, clinging to my arm. It dismayed me to see her looking so lost.

I stroked her hair. 'You have nothing to be sorry about. It is not your fault.'

Although Doctor Norwood had described Klára's behaviour as 'psychosis', she was admitted to the clinic as 'suffering from melancholia brought on by shock'. This meant she would not be restrained and would be free to wander the grounds in the company of a nurse.

'You are to visit her only once a week, on the supervising doctor's orders,' the admissions nurse told us. 'With the first visit not to take place within a fortnight of today.'

'Why?' I asked, upset that Klára was being kept from us.

The nurse's mouth twitched in a way that suggested she did not like to be questioned. 'Many patients remain ill as long as they have their family to show them sympathy. With the family removed, they often decide to cure themselves.'

With the paperwork done, the time came for Klára to be weighed and put into bed. Watching her being led away from us was like having my heart torn into pieces. Before she passed through the ward door, she turned to us. The vague look left her face and she smiled. 'I will get better as quickly as I can,' she said. 'I love you.'

For a moment Klára was herself again. It was like catching a glimpse of the sun on a cloudy day. My spirits lifted. But the moment was lost with the sound of jangling keys and the turn of a lock and my sister disappearing from view.

Uncle Ota and I returned to Broughton Hall a fortnight later, this time with Ranjana, full of hope to see Klára recovered. But when the nurse brought her out to the visiting room, her hair was flat and dull and her skin was grey. I remembered the way Klára had always glided into rooms, her poise commanding attention. But that day the best she could do was to shuffle in and collapse into a chair.

I knelt beside Klára and she kissed my cheek but it was a reflex action rather than a loving gesture. Her hands trembled like an old woman's.

On the second visit I went alone as Ranjana and Uncle Ota had to work and Esther was looking after Thomas. Klára was no better than she had been the previous week. She barely recognised me.

'Where is the doctor in charge?' I asked the ward nurse, a thin girl with sinewy limbs.

'Doctor Jones is doing the rounds this morning,' she said. 'He comes to the women's ward in the afternoons.'

'I want to see him now!' I told her. 'I want to know why my sister is not any better.'

'He is not your sister's doctor,' the nurse told me. 'She is being looked after by Doctor Page. He is in the men's convalescent ward at the moment.'

'Is he a senior doctor?' I asked.

'No,' said the ward nurse. 'He is a junior medical officer. But he is very good. In fact he is the —'

I did not wait to hear the rest of her sentence. I rushed through the hall and into the reception room. The admissions nurse called after me when I hurried by her in the direction of the men's convalescent ward but I ignored her. My blood was on fire. A junior medical officer indeed! My sister was seriously ill. She needed to be treated by someone with experience. There were no locks in the convalescent wards and I burst through the swing doors before stopping in my tracks. The curtains had been drawn around some of the beds but they did not reach all the way to the floor. Dozens of white, hairy bottoms squatting over bedpans shone back at me. The sulphurous smell mixed with scents of chlorine and pine oil knocked the charge out of my stampede.

'Can I help you?'

I averted my gaze from the male backsides and saw that the voice came from a doctor in a white coat at the far end of the ward. He was standing with a nurse by the bed of a patient.

The colour rushed to my cheeks. 'Are you Doctor Page?' I asked, trying to hide my embarrassment with a veil of superiority.

The doctor handed the nurse the patient's chart and instructed her to give him a warm bath, then walked towards me. 'Yes, I am,' he said. As he drew closer, I realised how young he looked. His jaw and his cheekbones were masculine but his hair was a rich chestnut colour and his complexion was what would have been called 'peaches and cream' in a woman.

'I am Miss Rose. Miss Rose's sister,' I said, blushing again when I realised how foolish my self-introduction sounded. 'Why are you treating my sister instead of Doctor Jones?'

Doctor Page, undeterred by my abrupt manner, smiled and his dimples showed. 'I had some experience with shell-shocked patients in the war,' he said. 'He thought I would be the best person to treat her.'

The war? With his slim neck and rosy cheeks Doctor Page looked too young to be out of school. But I realised that to have finished his medical training he would have to be at least eight years older than me.

'Why is she so lethargic?' I asked.

Doctor Page's face turned serious and he guided me to the door. 'If you will come to my office, I can explain your sister's treatment to you.'

I followed him down a corridor and into a room that was the size of a cupboard. The folders on the bookshelves were neatly arranged, and the desk held only a telephone, writing pad and a glazed Chinese figurine. But between the cupboards and the visitor's chair there was barely room to spread out my elbows. It seemed that junior doctors did not command large offices at Broughton Hall.

Doctor Page offered me a chair then squeezed behind his desk. The figurine was of a Chinaman sitting on a rock and fishing. His smile was lopsided and the glaze of his hat had run down one cheek. He looked like he was weeping.

'Tea?' Doctor Page asked me.

I nodded. A warm drink was exactly what I needed. The smell of bowel matter still lingered with me and I had a taste of metal in my mouth.

Doctor Page picked up the telephone and seemed to have trouble persuading the person on the line to bring some hot water. He succeeded, however, and a few minutes later an orderly appeared with a tray of cups and a pot of tea and he squeezed past me to put the things on the desk. Had I not been so worried about Klára, the clatter of crockery in the tiny room and the man with burly arms handing me a delicate china cup might have been comical. The orderly left and Doctor Page turned his attention to me.

'The standard treatment with any patient brought into care with hysteria is to sedate them,' he said, donning a pair of spectacles and pulling out a file. 'They lose their appetite and become lethargic. I am reducing your sister's medication but I have to do it gradually. While she is sedated she cannot explain to me what caused her to have an attack, and until I know that I cannot help her.'

Doctor Page glanced at me. His blue eyes were even bluer behind the glasses. 'I see here that you and your sister are from Prague. My father went to Bohemia on his grand tour and speaks highly of it. How is that you came to Australia?'

I realised Doctor Page was questioning me. He would need to know, wouldn't he? Someone would have to tell him about Mother's death and about our leaving Prague. I had never imagined mentioning those things to anyone outside the family. Who was Doctor Page and could I trust him?

He must have sensed my discomfort because he did not push me further on the matter. Instead he glanced back to his file. 'Once your sister regains her stamina, I will get her involved in activities and you will start to see progress then. I believe she plays the piano?'

'Klára is exceptionally talented,' I told him. 'She has mastered pieces that most girls her age could not tackle.'

Doctor Page smiled and his dimples appeared again. He made a note of what I said in the file. His hands were slim and neat. I became aware that one of my nails was broken and hid it by placing one hand on top of the other in my lap. Mother had been so particular about grooming and I was becoming careless.

'What a marvellous talent to have,' he said. 'I wish I had some sort of musical ability. But my father says I sing like a foghorn.'

Despite the anxiety I was feeling, I could not help laughing at the image. 'Surely your singing is not that bad,' I said.

'I don't think so either,' he said, with a mischievous grin.

I found myself blushing. I had stormed into the men's ward ready to attack Doctor Page, and now I was charmed by him. His calm, thoughtful manner had won me over. What did it matter that he was young? He was obviously the sort of doctor who cared about his patients.

He glanced at his watch. 'I'm sorry, but I will have to get back to my ward duty. However, do make an appointment with me with the admissions nurse. I would like to speak to you further about your sister.'

I rose from my chair and Doctor Page inched past me to open the door. 'Your sister will be having her nap now. Why don't you come back tomorrow?'

'Tomorrow?' I exclaimed. 'But the nurse said I could only come once a week.'

'Good gracious, no,' said Doctor Page, walking out into the corridor with me. 'Come every day if you wish. It will do your sister good. I only try to keep away relatives who are part of my patient's problems.'

On our way to the reception area we passed a nurse assisting a male patient back to the ward. The man's haggard face transformed when he saw Doctor Page.

'The nurse tells me that when I've put on a few more pounds you are going to let me play cricket with the other patients?'

'My word, Mr Cameron,' Doctor Page said, patting the man's back. 'And I should very much like to watch the match.'

I bade Doctor Page farewell and walked out of the grounds through the tall gates into the bustling street. I turned back to look at Broughton Hall. I had entered these gates feeling desperate for Klára. Now Doctor Page had given me a glimmer of hope.

Although my conversation with Doctor Page gave me a brighter outlook regarding Klára's recovery, the healing was slow and the months that she was in Broughton Hall were lonely for me. I had not realised until her absence that in all we experienced in fleeing Prague and coming to Australia, Klára had transformed from my charge into my best friend. But perhaps I had confided in her too much?

To find relief from my pain I went to Mr Tilly's cinema in the mornings before visiting Klára. Mr Tilly gave me free tickets and asked the usherettes to keep an eye out so that I would not be bothered by men. He did not know Klára was in Broughton Hall; he thought that she had glandular fever.

'Give my best to her,' he told me. 'We miss her playing here on Saturday nights.'

When the lights lowered and other worlds flashed on the screen, I had some reprieve from my worries. Afterwards I would eat a sandwich in the foyer café and watch the people coming and going from the cinema.

My other favourite distraction was the Vegetarian Café on George Street in the city. When I felt the need for something different after the cinema, I went there.

Australians were as carnivorous as Czechs: mutton, bacon and beef were the staples of their diet. Vegetarianism was a belief on the fringe of society. Uncle Ota commented that while it was not considered bizarre to pass a butcher and see men in aprons up to their elbows in blood and intestines, or to view the gory display of body parts in the windows, 'to announce oneself a vegetarian is to defy the belief that man was designated by God to have dominion over animals'.

Because of the subversive nature of vegetarianism, the café attracted an interesting mix of people: artists, philosophers, actors, dancers and athletes. There were many charity workers and socialists too. The charity workers argued that the meat industry debased the working class by forcing men to perform brutalising work, while the socialists believed more people could be fed better-quality food if land was used to cultivate crops instead of producing meat.

I would peer over the rim of my cup of chicory coffee and build theories about the people around me. One of these was a beautiful artist's model whose skin was like ivory satin even though she must have been close to seventy years old. 'Imelda' I named her in my imagination because of her exotic taste in clothes, and made up a story in which she was wondering if she would take another lover or travel to Italy this year. I had just seen Fritz Lang's *Der Müde Tod*, so my head was full of the glamorous locations like Venice and China. I created histories for the young women sharing recipes and the groups of men studying together. But there was one man whose past I was afraid to touch. Although he did not wear a military uniform or a badge, I could guess from his age how he had lost his leg. I often saw him there in the corner booth, his trouser leg pinned to his thigh and his face twisted into a scowl. Occasionally he was joined by a skinny man with ruddy cheeks who wore a cap and scarf even when the weather was warm. On these occasions, it was the skinny man who made conversation while his friend nodded or grunted. Most of the time, the man's companion was a cockatoo with a dropped wing that sat on his shoulder and bobbed up and down whenever he fed him a piece of apple. In those moments, the man's face softened and he would scratch the bird under its chin. They were a poignant couple. One could not fly and one could not walk.

One day I arrived at the café before the young man. I was finishing my salad when the door swung open and I looked up to see him manoeuvring himself over the step with a crutch to support his leg. I had never seen him move before and was surprised that he also carried a wooden tripod under the same arm that held the crutch. A camera bag, much larger than the one I used, was slung over one of his shoulders while the cockatoo perched on the other. The man was so burdened under his load that I wanted to help him by either holding open the door or pulling out a chair for him. From the way some of the customers glanced up when he hobbled past them, I wondered if they were thinking the same thing. But nobody moved. There was something in the man's eyes that forbade help.

When he reached the booth, he sank into the chair and grimaced as though trying to hide the exhaustion his efforts had cost him. I could not help staring when he slipped his crutch under the table and laid the tripod next to it. My fascination was with his camera case. He swung it onto the table and clicked the locks open. When he took out a Pathé moving-picture camera my heart jolted. Ever since my interest in making films had been piqued, I had been studying camera catalogues and I recognised the model. It was the same camera that Billy Bitzer used — the cameraman who had created films with DW Griffith. From that, and the way the man checked the adjustments and cleaned the lens, I deduced he was not an amateur. I was so absorbed in my observations that I did not notice the pair of eyes that were studying me with interest.

'Hello, pretty! Give me a nut!' the cockatoo squawked, bobbing its head in my direction.

I turned away but was not fast enough to avoid catching the man's eye. He held my gaze but did not smile.

'He is a beautiful bird,' I said, embarrassment raising the pitch of my voice.

The man did not answer. I was sure he thought I had been staring at him because of his leg. I glanced at my watch and did some play-acting of someone who has realised they are late to be somewhere else. Although the man returned to the task of checking his camera, I felt his eyes on me when I gathered my purse and jacket. My hands shook when I rummaged for the money to pay the waiter.

'That poor man,' another customer whispered to me when I approached the door. 'I don't think he could hear you.'

I nodded to her but I was sure she had interpreted the man's reaction incorrectly. He had heard me. At the moment our eyes met, he had flinched. And in his tortured expression I had seen a mirror of what I was feeling. We were kindred spirits: two people trying to fend off despair.

* * *

I visited Klára the following day and was delighted to find her not in bed but waiting for me in the visiting room. She was wearing a dress instead of a hospital gown. The nurses had cut her hair to make it easier to manage but Klára had softened the severity of the style by wearing it swept to the side and held in place with a silver clip.

'It's good to see you,' I said. I took her hand and admired the piece of embroidery she had been working on while waiting for me.

Klára smiled and I was pleased to see the colour in her cheeks and lips again.

'I hoped I might find you both here,' said Doctor Page, striding into the room. He held a package wrapped in brown paper under his arm. 'I found this treasure today,' he said, sitting down beside me and placing the package on the table in front of Klára. 'But I have to leave directly from here this afternoon to go to a conference and I need someone who can mind it for me until tomorrow evening.'

Doctor Page indicated to Klára that she should open the package. She untied the string and unravelled the paper to reveal a Chinese figurine. This one was a bearded man with a calligraphy brush. The hands and feet were the natural flesh colour of the mud from which the figurine had been made. The model was not especially artistic or well crafted but something about his raised eyebrows made me laugh. Or perhaps it was the tongue-in-cheek way Doctor Page spoke about it, as if he were entrusting us with an antique from the Tang Dynasty.

'What sort of figurine is this?' I asked him.

'A mud-man,' answered Doctor Page. 'The Chinese use them in their bonsai scenes.'

'Do you collect them?' asked Klára.

'Oh yes,' said Doctor Page, rolling his eyes in mock-seriousness. 'This is my two hundredth mud-man. Each one is unique.'

Klára's face lit up with amusement. 'We shall guard him with our lives,' she said.

The ward nurse passed by with her trolley of medicines and sent an admiring glance in Doctor Page's direction. I could understand her attraction. He was not a classically handsome man, but in his crisp white coat and with his smooth skin and reddish-brown hair he was dashing.

'Well, I'd better be off,' he said, rising from his chair.

We wished him the best for his conference. After he had left, Klára passed the figurine to me. 'You had better take it,' she said. 'If I put it on my bedside table, the night nurse will break it. She breaks at least one glass a night and then runs around with a brush and pan making a terrible commotion.'

The following day I returned with the figurine. I also brought my camera.

'Can I take some pictures of my sister in the grounds?' I asked the admissions nurse. It was the woman who had told us we could only visit Klára once a week, and I could tell from the way she pursed her lips she was not pleased that Doctor Page had been lenient with me.

'I hope you know that your request to come every day earned Doctor Page a talking-to from the superintendent,' she said.

So visiting only once a week was a policy of the clinic? I could have told her that I had not asked to come every day; Doctor Page had suggested that himself. But I thought it best to look contrite. The nurse slapped the signature book on the desk. I took it as a sign that she had granted me permission.

'Don't be more than ten minutes,' she warned me.

I took pictures of Klára in the rose garden. The weather was sunny and the flowers had come into full bloom.

'Let's take some pictures of Doctor Page's figurine,' Klára said, setting the mud-man among the ferns and rocks. I was pleased to see her taking an interest in life again.

'I hope the photograph cheers Doctor Page up,' she said, positioning her face behind the figurine so that through the lens the little man looked as if he were about to be devoured by a giant.

'Why does he need to be cheered up?'

A shadow fell over Klára's face. 'The nurses talk about him,' she said. 'They say he is madly in love with his fiancée but she keeps delaying the wedding date.'

'Klára, that's gossip,' I told her. 'Don't get involved in gossip.'

The admissions nurse opened a window and bellowed that we had been half an hour instead of ten minutes and visiting time was now at an end.

'I'll bring the photographs soon,' I told Klára, rushing back with her towards the clinic.

On the way home I found myself thinking about Doctor Page. So he had a fiancée? I had scolded Klára for gossiping about her doctor and yet I was curious about him too. I did not have much experience with men, apart from a boy I had admired at an afternoon tea in Prague, but I could not imagine keeping Doctor Page hanging on a string. His fiancée must be very beautiful and very sure of herself, I thought.

When I arrived for my visit some days later, Klára was beaming. 'I showed Doctor Page the pictures of his mud-man and he laughed so much I thought he would never stop,' she said. 'He asked me all about you.'

I placed the bunch of daisies I had picked for her in her lap. 'What did you tell him?' I asked.

'The truth,' she grinned. 'That you are wonderful and clever but rather shy.'

I wondered if Doctor Page had been asking questions about me as part of his analysis of Klára. 'What did he say to that?'

'He laughed even harder,' said Klára. 'I don't know why.'

I thought of the way I had burst into the men's ward a few weeks ago, demanding to know why Doctor Page, instead of a senior doctor, was treating my sister. No wonder he had thought Klára's description of me as shy was funny.

When she could, Ranjana changed her shifts so she could come to see Klára with me while Esther minded Thomas. Uncle Ota came on his days off. He was with me the next time I saw Doctor Page, which was our first encounter since he had given Klára the mud-man to look after. I was pleased to find him sitting in the garden talking to her. He stood up to greet us and made enquiries as to our well-being but he was not himself. There were circles under his eyes and the roses in his cheeks had faded. His eyes met mine then he looked away. 'You will have to excuse me,' he said. 'I'd better get started on the afternoon rounds.'

'He's a nice young man,' remarked Uncle Ota, watching Doctor Page make his way up the steps to the clinic.

Klára's smile waned. 'He's out of sorts,' she said. 'He and two orderlies took some soon-to-be-released patients out on a harbour cruise yesterday to celebrate their recovery. It was a happy outing until they were on their way back. A young woman jumped off the boat and drowned herself.'

I shuddered. If Doctor Page lost a patient, he would feel it. 'He must be devastated,' I said.

I was pleased with Klára's progress under Doctor Page's care, but I had not yet made an appointment with him as I had promised.

I did not have the courage to tell him — or anyone else — what had happened to us. But the tragic incident with his patient prompted him to seek me. We sat down together in his office.

'Miss Rose, I hope to discharge your sister soon. I believe she turns thirteen on 29 September? I'd like to send her home on her birthday.'

My heart leapt at the news. Klára coming home? I could hardly believe it.

Doctor Page sent me a serious glance. 'But before I have her discharged I want to make sure that I have treated the true nature of her trauma. I lost a patient this week who I thought was cured. I won't let that happen to your sister.'

His statement made me realise the gravity of the matter. My stomach tightened.

'The patient who died was admitted because she supposedly had a phobia of spiders,' he continued. 'It's a fairly straightforward fear to address, and I consulted with the doctors here and a specialist in England. After a few weeks the patient showed remarkable improvement. I was even able to take her through the grounds and encourage her to stand close to spiderwebs without any sign of fear. What we failed to realise was that what she really feared was not spiders but the world outside. She lived in a cocoon here, safe and quiet. She could not imagine returning to that frightening world again.'

I pressed my face into my hands. I had thought when I came to Australia that I could put my life in Prague aside. I had anticipated that Klára and I would live in another dimension until she reached twenty-one. I missed Aunt Josephine and Frip terribly but I would not allow myself to feel it. Although I could never forget Mother, I forced myself to almost disregard that she had been murdered. It was as if I expected that she would be waiting for us when Klára and I returned. But things had not happened as I had planned. Klára had become sick, and it seemed that if I did not cooperate with Doctor Page she might not recover.

I swallowed. 'Doctor Page, our mother was murdered by our stepfather. That is why Klára and I came to Australia.'

Whatever Doctor Page had been expecting, he was not prepared for anything quite so dramatic. 'I see,' he said, frowning. 'Please tell me what happened.'

It took me a few minutes to gather my strength, but once I began speaking I could not stop. I told Doctor Page about Miloš and about the assassin. I even told him about Aunt Emilie, and the thought that Klára might harm herself made me choke back a sob.

'Klára never told me any of this,' said Doctor Page. 'I thought she might be a perfectionist. Very sensitive people and artists often drive themselves to breaking point striving for excellence.'

I felt tears rise up in my eyes. 'Doctor Page, do you think she will get better?'

'I don't think your sister is insane,' he said. 'The situation that you've described would break anyone. During the war I treated strong men who came back from the battlefield shattered. From what you've told me, I'm surprised that you haven't fallen ill yourself. I only wish that your sister had confided all of this to me earlier. I could have helped her sooner.'

I had never heard a doctor speak so thoughtfully. I could not imagine Doctor Soucek or another doctor saying he had sympathy for us, even if he felt it. Doctors told you what to do and you did it. I realised that I had built a shell around me and Doctor Page was making cracks in it, gently and painstakingly.

I dabbed at my face with my handkerchief, trying to control the tears running down my cheeks. 'We couldn't,' I said. 'We were afraid. We could not confide in anybody.'

Doctor Page sat back, lost in thought for a few moments. 'Is there no way your mother's killer can be brought to justice?' he asked.

My handkerchief was so damp that it was useless. Doctor Page reached into his pocket and passed me his own. I explained to him the difficulties of the case and the lack of evidence.

'I'm glad that you've told me what you have,' he said. 'I lost my mother in a fire when I was ten years old. It's a terrible burden to carry alone. I feel very much for Klára — and for you.'

I was too moved to speak. I stared at the Irish linen handkerchief in my hand and wondered if Doctor Page's fiancée had given it to him. If she did not value Doctor Page, she was a foolish woman. He was so kind, and when you had been through all Klára and I had, kindness was what you most appreciated in people.

NINE

Although Broughton Hall was not as expensive as an exclusive clinic, Klára's treatment had drained our funds. She was excited about starting at the Conservatorium High School in the new year. How could I tell her I no longer had the money for her tuition?

'I wonder if I could find work in an office,' I said to Uncle Ota one day when he was reading the paper in the parlour. 'I know how to type.'

Uncle Ota glanced at me. 'That would bore you, Adélka. You're a daydreamer. Not that it is a bad habit — if you are creative. Besides, the Czech and English keyboards are not the same.'

'I could adapt,' I said.

He gave me a smile. 'Why don't you do some work with your camera? You take exceptional portraits.'

'That will take a long time to set up,' I told him. 'I'd need film, a better camera, developing chemicals, and I'd have to find clients. The tutors' fees are due by the end of the year, otherwise Klára will lose her place with the teachers she wants.'

Uncle Ota thought for a moment before answering. 'Studios need ladies to take passport photographs. Or colourists to do touch-ups. That will bring money in and you will meet clients that way. You can use my camera for the portraits.'

My spirits rallied with Uncle Ota's suggestion. Despite all the terrible things that had happened, I was glad to be living with him. Uncle Ota did not look anything like my father physically, but he resembled him in his generosity. He was right too; I would not be good at administration tasks because my mind was always wandering.

I excused myself to cook lunch. On my way to the kitchen Esther called to me. 'Adéla, could you come here for a moment?'

She was standing in the doorway to the downstairs sitting room, wringing her hands nervously. She was still an anxious and quiet person, but not so much of a mouse. The other evening, we had gone to see *The Golem*, which was set in Prague. On our way home I was praising the film when Esther surprised us all by blurting out that she thought the film was pretentious. Although her opinion conflicted with mine, I was glad she had spoken up. But she still wore drab clothes that made her look much older than her age. I thought of the man with the cockatoo at the Vegetarian Café. War left some scars that could not be erased.

I followed Esther into the sitting room, which was much cheerier than when Mrs Bain had occupied it. Esther had replaced the heavy furniture with comfortable armchairs and installed light-shades with beaded trims. A watercolour of the beach decorated the far wall. The burled walnut piano with its lyre detailing and French legs was the only reminder of her mother's taste.

'What do you think of the piano?' Esther asked me.

'It does stand out now that you've changed the room,' I said. 'But the most important thing is how it sounds.'

'Would you play it for me?' she asked, opening the fallboard and adjusting the stool. 'I never learned. Mother said I wouldn't be brilliant so it was no use trying.'

I had not touched the piano since I was fourteen years old. With a virtuoso in the house, there had been little point. Still, I sat down and played a few bars of Sinding's *Rustle of Spring*, which had been a favourite with Mother. I was surprised that the piano was in tune. The sound it produced was beautiful, despite my amateurish musicianship. Klára's Petrof grand had a better tone though.

Esther agreed. 'This old Steinway doesn't bring me any happy memories. I've decided to sell it. To pay for Klára's tuition.'

I was stunned. That Esther would sell the piano did not surprise me, as she had sold or given away most of her mother's furniture. But to make such a generous offer!

'What else should I do with it?' she said in reply to my babbled refusal. 'I have no family. It would give me pleasure to see a lovely girl get the chance she deserves.'

Later that day, I approached Esther where she was sitting in the garden and working on a tapestry. The garden was exquisite now that I had pulled out the weeds and planted borders of native flowers and urns of lavender, geraniums and verbena.

'Esther, I want to thank you for your kindness,' I said, sitting down next to her. 'If there is a way to pay you back, I will find it.'

She lowered her eyes. 'It's not necessary,' she said. 'You and your sister were kind to me.'

A blue butterfly with black-trimmed wings settled on her sleeve.

'If Klára hadn't told me that butterflies only live a few weeks, I would swear that one is following you,' I laughed.

Esther stared at me. 'Butterfly?'

'The one on your sleeve,' I said. 'The blue and black one. I've seen one like that around you several times.'

She held up both her sleeves. 'Where?' she asked, squinting. The butterfly was resting on her elbow in plain view. Was Esther short-sighted?

'There,' I said. 'It's on your shoulder now.'

She shook her head. Tears filled her eyes. 'I never see it,' she wept. 'I never see it.'

The butterfly took off towards the sunshine. I put my hand on her wrist. 'Esther, I'm sorry. It's only a butterfly.'

Tears stained her face. 'He told me that if anything happened, he would come back to me as a butterfly. But I never see it.'

The air shimmered with a sense of the unreal. 'Your fiancé?'

Esther nodded. 'He knew that I loved butterflies. He said he would communicate to me that way. Mother's doctor often saw the butterfly, and the funeral director who buried her noticed it resting on my shoulder when I stood by her grave.'

'I wonder why, if he is trying to communicate with you, you can't see him?' I said.

Esther looked at me. 'The milkman even saw him in human form, standing by the garden gate in his military uniform.'

I remembered the man with innocent eyes I had seen when we first moved into Esther's house. In Prague, ghosts had often appeared when we made changes to the house. Perhaps Esther's fiancé wanted to see who we were and to make sure we treated Esther well.

'Tell me about him,' I ventured. I was relieved when her tears dried and a smile came to her face. In that instant, I had a sense of what she had been like as a young girl, before the war had torn the man she loved from her.

'His name was Louis,' she said. '"Like Louis the Fourteenth of France," he would say when introducing himself. "The monarch who never washed."' Esther laughed. 'He wasn't like that of course. He was fastidiously clean.' Her smile faded and a troubled look came to her face. 'Awful to think of him dying in all that mud.'

'France?'

She nodded and we fell into silence, listening to the finches twittering in the jacaranda tree. They were not native birds, those little finches. They were from Europe. They were the birds the soldiers in the trenches must have heard in moments of ceasefire — or when they lay dying.

'When the war came, he told me he had to go,' Esther said, a faraway look in her eyes. 'The regiment looked dashing in their uniforms when they marched down the street. "Your mum may not approve of me now but she'll think differently when I come back a hero," he said to me. They say he died a hero's death ... but death is still death, isn't it? Hero or not.'

I understood Esther's wraithlike existence better now. She had lost hope. Her life had stopped the day she had received the news of Louis's death, just like Mother had stopped the hands on the tall clock the morning she had learned Father was dead. Esther told me stories about Louis: the way he used to talk to dogs as if they were his friends; the way he never shut a door completely but always left a gap open. 'Curtains too,' she said with a fond smile. 'He couldn't bring himself to close anything. The cork was never quite in the water bottle, the flour jar never screwed shut, so an unsuspecting person would pick it up and find themselves dusted in powder.' Esther was telling me things that had been bottled up inside because she'd had no one to listen to her grief.

When Ranjana called out from the house that she was leaving for work and Thomas was asleep, I slipped my arm through Esther's. To my surprise, she took mine and squeezed it. I sensed that she had unburdened herself. I hoped so, at least.

A few days later, I travelled to the city to visit photographic studios and ask for work. Some studio managers were friendly but had no work; others had work but were unfriendly the moment they heard the traces of my foreign accent. I wanted to take pictures for my living. My clothes were becoming worn and were not fashionable in Sydney. Klára was coming home in a fortnight and I hoped to buy new dresses for us to wear for the family party we had planned for her birthday. I had a vision of having my hair bobbed and donning a new pair of beaded shoes. I enjoyed the bohemian life I lived with Uncle Ota and Ranjana, but I had inherited Mother's love of beautiful things.

On my way down George Street, I passed the Vegetarian Café and stopped for an orange juice. I felt at home with the aroma of vegetable soup and the clatter of opinions echoing around the room. The café was crowded with familiar faces. I looked for the man with the cockatoo among them, but he was not there.

The waitress brought my juice and I flipped through the newspaper. My eyes fell on an advertisement: *Madame Diblis: Spiritualist*.

Everyone's grandmother was a spiritualist in Prague, but the practice had grown in popularity in Australia after the war. So many people had lost loved ones and lost them young. Arthur Conan Doyle had just completed a lecture tour. He was known as the writer of the Sherlock Holmes Mysteries, but after his son, brothers-in-law and nephew were killed in the war he became an exponent of Spiritualism.

I had seen many ghosts in my life but never made contact with them. I thought it irreverent to call souls back into the world after they had departed it. I was an observer of spirits rather than a medium. I thought about Esther and her butterfly. After she had told me about Louis, we had decided that the next time I saw the butterfly I would photograph it. The following day, when I returned home from visiting Klára, Esther was in the garden planting tulips. One look at my face stopped her short.

'It's on me, isn't it?' she had said.

I nodded. The butterfly was on her forearm.

'Hold still,' I told her. I rushed into the house to get my camera. There was no film in it. I searched my cupboard for a pack. I found one and loaded it. I thought the butterfly would have disappeared by the time I returned outside, but it was still there. I pressed the shutter. I wanted to take another picture but before I could, the butterfly flew away.

'I'll develop it now,' I told Esther.

I watched with bated breath as the image came to life: Esther's shape; her face; her arm. There was no butterfly.

Perhaps Madame Diblis could help Esther see Louis. I imagined Esther would not have the courage to go to a spiritualist on her own so decided to go with her. It would be a way of thanking her for her generosity to Klára.

Madame Diblis instructed us to come in the afternoon. I did not tell Ranjana or Uncle Ota where we were headed. They were superstitious in many ways but they were also convinced that spiritualists were charlatans who took advantage of people. I told them that Esther and I were going to an exhibition at the Art Gallery of New South Wales. I did not like being deceitful with Uncle Ota and Ranjana, but I convinced myself that it was for the greater good.

Even if my aunt and uncle had consented to my going to
Madame Diblis's house with Esther, they would not have
approved of the location. The medium lived in an unsavoury
part of Sydney. Esther and I walked close together through the
dingy streets of Darlinghurst, clutching our purses to our
chests, steeling ourselves against the stink of urine that wafted
up from the drains. I eyed the weather-stained walls of what
had once been mansions now subdivided into apartments. The
remnants of a more genteel time lingered in the wrought-iron
railings and the palm trees that shaded some of the gardens.
Every so often we passed a lion's-head fountain or a statue of
the Venus de Milo, incongruous with the newspaper-lined
windows.

Madame Diblis's apartment was on the second floor of a
terrace in Forbes Street. We climbed the stairs, blocking our
noses to the stench of damp. We jumped when we saw a man
lying on the landing, his head thrown back and his mouth open.
At first we thought he was dead, but then we heard his snoring
and saw the beer bottle clasped in his hand. We slipped around
him and continued down a corridor that reeked of onions. A
woman's voice burst out from behind one of the closed doors.
'Lay orf him, I tell yer. Lay orf him!'

We hurried down the hall towards Madame Diblis's
apartment, which was the last door on the left. I rapped on the
splintered wood. Footsteps approached and we heard the clicks
of several locks being turned. The door swung open and a trace
of sandalwood temporarily masked the unsavoury smell of the
hallway. We found ourselves facing a woman with her grey hair
tucked into a scarf. The pendant she wore around her neck
disappeared down her cleavage when she leaned forward to see
who we were. We introduced ourselves and Madame Diblis held

a finger to her lips. 'We must talk quietly,' she said. 'The spirits are restless today.'

We followed her into the parlour. The furniture was draped in velvet fabrics and lace doilies. In the centre of the room stood a marble dining table surrounded by high-backed chairs. By the window hung a mirror bracketed by curves and florets. It was the type of mirror I imagined the dark queen in *Snow White* gazing into when she asked her famous question: 'Mirror, Mirror on the wall ...'

'Please sit down,' said Madame Diblis, indicating a sofa covered in cushions. She listened to our story about the butterfly and Louis's promise. When I told her that I could see the butterfly while Esther could not, the medium turned to me and studied my face before sitting back and staring at her hands thoughtfully.

'It is five years since your fiancé died,' Madame Diblis said to Esther. 'It is easier to call back those who have recently passed to the other side, but with all the activity today we may have some luck. My feeling is, however, that because he is trying to reach you in the way he promised, he may not be able to speak. But we will try.'

I tried to ascertain if Madame Diblis was a fraud. I thought of the tricks false mediums used that Uncle Ota had told me about — using strings to move objects and ring bells — but could not see anything odd in the room or around the marble table, which was where I assumed she would work. Madame Diblis's apartment was more pleasant than the others around it, but there was nothing to suggest she was making a lot of money. The gold ring with the red garnet she wore was beautiful but not expensive. She had an exotic accent that I could not place, although that could have been affected.

Madame Diblis turned to me as if she had read my thoughts. 'It's important that you are a believer,' she said. 'If you bring doubts to the séance you will keep the spirits away. We must have unity of purpose.'

I decided that she was genuine.

Esther and I took our places at the table while Madame Diblis closed the curtains. She then lit the candelabra. From a cabinet she brought out a hand bell, a maraca, a notepad and pencil and placed them on the table, explaining that spirits used different tools to communicate. I glanced at Esther whose face was as white as a sheet. I was sure, with her religious upbringing, Esther had never imagined she would be taking part in a séance. I felt uneasy myself. If Louis appeared, I would not be afraid. But an upsetting thought had been bothering me. What if I disturbed Mother or Father? I closed my eyes and prayed for them to remain at rest. They had both died in terrible circumstances: I wanted them to be at peace.

'We will hold hands to create an unbroken circle of power,' Madame Diblis said. 'Uninvited spirits can come through the door I open to the other world. Sometimes they come because they wish to do harm. It is important then that you keep holding on to me and to each other no matter who arrives to speak.'

I shivered when Madame Diblis blew out the candles and we sat in the darkness with no light coming through the curtains. Madame Diblis began an incantation in Latin. After a while she said in English, 'Spirits, come forth if you are willing. Is there anyone who wishes to speak to Esther?'

My legs became heavy and my head drooped. I thought I was on the verge of dozing off, but then my arms became leaden and it was difficult to continue to hold on to Esther and Madame Diblis.

'Who is there?' asked Madame Diblis.

The chill in the room bit at my skin and I shuddered.

'Who is there?' Madame Diblis asked again. The hairs on the back of my neck prickled. I became aware of somebody leaning over me. I wanted to turn and see if it was a trick performed by an accomplice of Madame Diblis but I could not move. A hand touched my shoulder.

'Miss Rose,' whispered Madame Diblis. 'There is a presence near you. They wish to tell you something.'

I tried to grip harder on to Esther and Madame Diblis but I could no longer feel them.

I heard piano music. It was a piece I recognised for Klára played it often. Bach's Prelude No 22 in B flat minor. Pictures whirled around my mind of places and people I had never seen: young girls in lacy white dresses; a fluffy dog; a river. I found myself before our country house in Doksy. Its white walls and red roof stood out against the sky and the enormous beech and oak trees that surrounded it. The scent of pines tickled my nostrils. It was summer and the shutters were open to the breeze. I walked through the doorway and into the house, shivering when I left the sunshine for the shade. There was a staircase in the foyer. The stone was worn at the centre from years of occupants making their way up and down the steps. I floated up the stairs towards a room decorated with olive and cream furniture. A young woman was sitting by a piano. She wore a gold dress with a white collar and banana-shaped sleeves. Around her neck dangled a filigree medallion with a centre of blue crystal. At first I thought it was Klára because of the dark hair and the slim figure, but the woman looked up and I knew it was not my sister. It was Emilie.

'Ota,' she said, tears of joy filling her eyes. 'My darling Ota. I'll wait for you until the end of time.'

Blackness covered my vision. Pain seared through my shoulder. Hands touched my face. I felt a towel being pressed to my forehead. Esther's voice was close by my ear. 'Wake up, Adéla.' Gradually I came to and I saw Esther and Madame Diblis crouched over me. The curtains were open and the afternoon light poured into the room.

'You are too open,' Madame Diblis scolded me. 'You did not tell me that you had the gift too. You can't go channelling spirits unless you know how to guide them.'

'I see them,' I told her. 'But they usually don't speak to me.'

'You come back to me and I will teach you how to communicate with the afterworld properly,' she said. 'It is a dangerous gift if you don't know how to use it.'

Esther and Madame Diblis helped me to sit up and then lifted me to a standing position. I felt like a newborn calf with my weak legs splaying in all directions.

'That spirit came from a long time in the past,' Madame Diblis said, while Esther smoothed down my hair and handed me my purse. 'She had to draw a lot of power from you to speak. She wanted to tell someone that she still thinks of them.'

My head ached so much I thought it was going to explode. Esther tugged at her hat and I noticed the butterfly brooch on the rim.

'Louis didn't appear?' I asked.

'No,' said Madame Diblis. 'Come back next week and we will try again.'

Out in the dirty street, prostitutes and pimps stared at us. Esther's shoulders heaved. She was crying.

'Esther?'

She shook her head and dabbed her eyes with her gloves.

'Let's go to a teahouse,' I suggested. 'We could both do with a warm drink.'

We sat in the teahouse in silence, each lost in our own thoughts. I could see from her pinched mouth that Esther was disappointed she had not been able to speak with Louis. I felt terrible and did not know what to say. My mind drifted to Aunt Emilie. 'Ota,' she had said. 'My darling Ota.' There had been longing in her eyes.

Mother had said that Aunt Emilie went insane after an affair with a scoundrel. I calculated dates in my head. Uncle Ota had started his odyssey the year of Emilie's death. Was my kind, generous uncle the villain my mother had mentioned? Was that the falling-out she had talked about before her death? I could not imagine Uncle Ota being anything other than a gentleman. But I knew that I would not be able to see him in exactly the same way until I found out for sure.

TEN

As promised, Doctor Page discharged Klára from Broughton Hall on her birthday. Uncle Ota, Ranjana and I arrived in the morning to pick her up. I did not have enough money for a new dress for both of us, so I had bought Klára a periwinkle frock with a plissé frill at the neck and had smartened a dress I had by adding a sash and dyeing my shoes pink to match.

Ranjana and Uncle Ota waited in the reception room while I helped Klára into her new clothes in her ward. My fingers trembled from the excitement that she was coming home.

'Here we are,' I said, walking into the reception room with Klára.

Ranjana rose from her chair. 'You look beautiful,' she said, kissing Klára.

I studied Uncle Ota. I was convinced he had stared at Klára so intensely when we arrived in Australia because of her resemblance to Emilie. I had not gone back to Madame Diblis. All I had achieved was to upset Esther and maybe I had even disturbed Emilie. I could not see that any good would come of going again, although I was curious about Uncle Ota's side of the story. But he had gotten past the shock of the similarities between Klára and Emilie. He did not have stars in his eyes when he saw Klára in the reception room. He embraced her like a father hugging his daughter.

'Thank God, you are well again,' he said.

The admissions nurse handed Uncle Ota the discharge forms. I looked to the ward doors, hoping that Doctor Page would arrive to see us off. Unless Klára became sick again, which I would pray to God every day that she would not, this would be the last time we would be at Broughton Hall.

'That's all,' said the nurse, taking the forms from Uncle Ota. She glanced at me and her eyes gleamed. She was glad to be seeing the last of me.

'Well, you are off now,' said Doctor Page, walking into the reception area and smiling at Klára.

He shook Uncle Ota's hand and told Ranjana that Klára needed adequate rest and quiet.

'Thank you so much!' I said, handing Doctor Page a package wrapped in tissue paper. 'This is something from Klára and me.'

Doctor Page opened the paper to find a mud-woman embracing the moon. His face brightened. 'I don't have a female figure in my collection, would you believe?' he said with a smile. 'She'll cause jealousy among the mud-men, no doubt.'

'We didn't know how to thank you,' I told him. 'You have been so good to us.'

'You've been supportive,' Doctor Page said. 'Your sister's recovery has as much to do with you as it does with me.'

His eyes settled on my face in such a pleasant way that I was overcome by shyness. The thought that I would never see him again left me feeling flat despite my joy at Klára's recovery. I had looked forward to seeing Doctor Page on my visits to Broughton Hall.

Uncle Ota guided Ranjana and Klára towards the door. Doctor Page stepped forward to open it. An old man in pyjamas and a dressing gown was returning from the garden. We stood aside to let him pass.

The man puffed and panted. 'Good weather today,' he said to Doctor Page. 'It will be clear tonight. You'll see the Milky Way and the Clouds of Magellan as if they were in your own sitting room.'

Uncle Ota looked at Doctor Page, his interest sparked.

'Mr Foster is an astronomer,' Doctor Page explained. 'He told me how to build my own telescope.'

'Truly?' asked Uncle Ota.

Doctor Page laughed. 'My father and I are quite obsessed. We sweep the sky every night hoping for a comet.'

'Would you and your father like to give a talk to a social group of ours?' asked Uncle Ota. 'They'd be very interested.'

My heart leapt at the thought of Doctor Page coming to our house, but he blushed and shifted his feet.

'Perhaps you can't meet with patients after they have been discharged?' I said, trying to ease his embarrassment and hide my disappointment at the same time. Why should he feel awkward about the invitation?

Doctor Page shook his head. 'As long as we are not treating a patient there is no problem with seeing them or their family outside of the clinic.' He glanced at me. 'I would be delighted to come. My father would too.'

I was glad he seemed easier about the invitation and wondered if he would bring his fiancée. I was fascinated by the idea of the woman who held Doctor Page captive.

'Good,' said Uncle Ota, pulling a notepad from his pocket and scribbling down our address. 'How about Tuesday week?'

A fortnight later, Doctor Page and his father arrived at our home. Doctor Page Senior jutted his chin out and scanned the curiosities in the parlour as a soldier might study the landscape for signs of the enemy. The turn of his mouth was grim and his hair, shirt and jacket were fastidiously neat. I had overheard the ward nurse say that Doctor Page's father was the most famous surgeon in Sydney. I glanced at his pale, tapered hands. They were not hands one expected to belong to such a solidly built man; they were as delicate as Klára's and only slightly larger.

'I am very pleased to meet you,' said Doctor Page Senior, when his son introduced us to him. He had a well-modulated voice but there was a hint of tension in it. 'Tonight we should be able to see the Milky Way from Scorpius to Orion in its entirety,' he continued. 'Centaurus is one of the most spectacular constellations. It's too far south to be seen from the northern hemisphere.'

'The Aborigines regard the Milky Way as a river in the sky world where all the bright stars are fish and the smaller ones are water lilies,' Doctor Page said, winking at Klára.

'I like that,' said Klára. 'It makes me think Mister Rudolf might be there.'

'Well, let's get started, shall we?' said Uncle Ota, helping to pick up the boxes the Pages had brought with them and leading them to the front of the gathering.

The audience was transfixed by the talk on how the Pages had built their own telescope. While Doctor Page Senior discussed the mechanics of mirror-making, his son spoke about the history of telescopes. He had an obvious regard for Galileo, who stood up to the Holy Roman Church in defence of his scientific theories about the universe.

'The professor who lectured me in psychiatry often quoted Galileo,' Doctor Page told us. '"You cannot teach a man anything; you can only help him find it within himself."'

I saw Doctor Page Senior stiffen. He disapproved of something. Was it psychiatry or Galileo?

When the formal lecture was over, the doctors invited the audience to look through the telescope at Rigel in Orion and Alpha Centauri. When it was my turn to peer through the telescope, Doctor Page adjusted it for my height. 'Rigel is the seventh brightest star and is supposed to represent Orion's, the hunter's, left foot,' he said. 'I don't think you would have liked Orion. The legend has it that he wanted to kill all the animals in the world and, to prevent that happening, a scorpion bit him. After his death he was placed in the sky.'

'You are interested in legends then?' I asked Doctor Page, stepping aside so the next guest could look through the telescope. 'Isn't that unusual for a scientific man?'

'It's through science that we understand the workings of life,' Doctor Page answered. 'But it is through legends and stories that we understand the meaning.'

Klára placed a record on the gramophone. The shimmering notes of *The Blue Danube* floated about the room. I wanted to know Doctor Page better. I was intrigued by him. I had spoken with him in his capacity as Klára's doctor but I wanted to discover more about his mind.

Afterwards, there was supper and Esther's delicious walnut cake. Everyone grouped together into more intimate conversations.

I saw Doctor Page heading in my direction. He had two cups of tea in his hands and I assumed he was making his way towards one of the other guests. But to my surprise he stopped in front of me. 'Black with a slice of lemon and a pinch of sugar,' he said, handing me the cup and saucer.

'How did you know how I like my tea?' I asked, taking it from him.

'I'm a psychiatrist,' said Doctor Page. 'You'd be surprised how much I know about you by the shape of your face.'

'Truly?' I asked. 'You can tell how I like my tea from the shape of my face?'

Doctor Page's smile beamed brighter. 'No, I asked your aunt how you take it.'

I laughed along with Doctor Page but felt foolish, although I was sure he had not intended his joke to demean me. I could feel my face turning red so I diverted the conversation. 'I am embarrassed when I think of myself bursting in on you in the men's ward,' I confessed to him. 'I should apologise for that.'

'Please don't,' he said. 'You can't imagine how glad I am that you did. It showed you cared about your sister. A lot of patients are taken to Broughton Hall by their relatives and just left there.'

'The quote you gave from Galileo,' I asked him. 'Is that how you feel about psychiatry? That you help people find the truth within themselves?'

Doctor Page took a sip of tea. 'The human mind is so complex,' he said. 'I once had a patient who believed he was a haemophiliac although there was no physical evidence to support it. He cut himself on a piece of wire one day. It was the most superficial of wounds and yet he bled to death. Psychiatry is a fascinating subject but I'm not sure I'm doing anyone any good.'

I was shocked to hear Doctor Page speak that way. He had helped Klára, and I assumed from the way the other patients' demeanours lifted when they saw him that he had helped them too. I wanted to ask what he meant, but before I had the chance Uncle Ota appeared by our side.

'Doctor Page,' he said, 'your father is interested in some photographs my niece has taken. He would like her to explain them to him. Would you care to join us?'

A faint smile appeared on Doctor Page's lips. 'Certainly,' he said. 'Miss Rose took some interesting pictures of a friend of mine. I'm most fascinated by her work.'

I wasn't sure what Doctor Page meant and then I remembered the mud-man. I laughed sincerely this time and so did he.

We followed Uncle Ota to the corner of the room where my photographs hung and where Doctor Page Senior was waiting. I had taken a series of magpies that I was proud of, and a Gothic-looking photograph of a family of tawny frogmouths huddled on a tree branch. Amongst these beauties of nature were portraits of Uncle Ota, Ranjana, Thomas and Klára. I had wanted one of Esther too but she had refused to pose.

'So you are not a pictorialist,' said Doctor Page Senior, slipping on his glasses and studying the photographs. He was looking at the portrait of Klára where I had kept the edges soft and emphasised her face and hands, filling in the dimensions with side-lighting.

'No,' I said.

'Australian photography hasn't embraced the avant garde ideas that have dominated Europe since the war,' explained Uncle Ota. 'Painterly techniques and soft, romantic views prevail here. Adéla has brought a bit of Prague to Australia.'

Doctor Page Senior turned to me. 'Do you do commissions?' he asked. 'I want a portrait of myself and my son. I was thinking of an oil painting, but having seen your style I like the idea of a photograph much better.'

I was lost for an answer. I was hardly a professional photographer and was not sure I could live up to what Doctor Page Senior was expecting. He seemed like an exacting man.

'What a delightful idea,' said Doctor Page. 'Please say you'll do us the honour, Miss Rose.'

I realised that I had been given a way to more adequately repay Doctor Page for his kindness to Klára than the gift of the mud-woman. 'I think a portrait of father and son is a wonderful idea,' I said. 'I'm honoured that you have asked me to take it.'

Doctor Page Senior frowned. 'My son will be marrying soon and leaving me. The portrait will be a memento.'

Doctor Page winced. 'Father likes to dramatise things,' he said. 'He has some idea that after Beatrice and I are married we'll forget him. Nothing could be further from the truth.'

His father smiled and I wondered if he had been seeking that reassurance from his son. 'Beatrice keeps him on tenterhooks,' he said. 'No sooner do they set a wedding date than she's off travelling again. But she's promised to settle down soon. She told me the other day that she's ready to have babies — lots of them.'

The mention of Doctor Page's fiancée unsettled me. I had been enjoying having him to myself that evening, although I was surprised that he had not brought her with him. Her name conjured up an image of a slinky brunette with exotic eyes. She would have to be someone magnificent to hold men like the Pages under her spell.

'You will have your hands full with grandchildren then,' I said cheerfully to Doctor Page Senior. 'I don't think you will be forgotten or left alone.'

Doctor Page glanced at me. There was a distinct look of worry in his eyes, but I could not fathom what had disturbed him.

* * *

After the guests had left, I helped Uncle Ota straighten up the parlour. Ranjana, Esther and Klára had already washed the dishes and retired to bed. We were alone together for the first time since Esther and I had gone to Madame Diblis's séance.

'You have your first commission,' said Uncle Ota, plumping the cushions. His face was turned away from me, but I heard the pride in his voice.

He was as good to me as my own father had been. What had Mother written to him in that letter that Miloš had destroyed? And why had they both quoted lines from 'May'? Now we were alone together, I took a deep breath and broached the subject.

'I want to ask you about my Aunt Emilie.'

Uncle Ota froze mid-action. 'Emilie?' he repeated, turning slowly. He sat down on the sofa and hummed a piece of music. It took me a moment to place it: 'Quando m'en vo' from Puccini's *La Bohème*.

He stopped humming and smiled sadly. 'Your father and I first saw your mother and aunt at the opera. They were so beautiful,' he said.

I waited for him to say something more but he started humming again.

His mind was far away, remembering something. I watched him, trying to read his thoughts. But what happened in Prague, when my mother and her sister and my father and Uncle Ota were young, was still a mystery.

The following week, I arrived at the Pages' residence in Edgecliff with Uncle Ota's camera. He was working as an usher at Tilly's Cinema most weeknights, as well as his guide job at the museum.

Klára's illness had brought home the importance of extra money. 'You make use of my camera,' he told me. 'I'm too busy.'

The Pages' house was white with green shutters and a red shingled roof with wide eaves. The maid invited me inside and I was impressed by the restful atmosphere. The floors were polished hardwood and the rugs and walls were in soft tones of sand and stone. Doctor Page and his father were waiting for me in the sitting room.

'Good morning,' Doctor Page Senior said, rising from his chair. 'I thought we would have the picture taken here.'

The room opened onto a flagged terrace with a view across Double Bay to Manly. It was pleasant, not fancy, and the natural light was serene. I was surprised Doctor Page Senior wanted to be photographed in the sitting room rather than the formal drawing room I had passed in the hall. Perhaps he was not as severe as he first appeared.

'Father and I are fond of this room,' Doctor Page said to me. 'It's like a comfortable armchair that one sinks into and finds hard to get out of again.'

'The subject of a photograph should be in their natural environment,' I said. 'Otherwise the result will be posed and insincere.'

'My sentiments exactly,' said Doctor Page.

He was looking smart in a grey suit with his hair swept back from his face. I was wearing a taupe skirt and blouse that I had sewn myself. A thrill ran through me when I caught him glancing at me with admiration. His fiancée must have many beautiful clothes, so I was pleased that he approved of my one good business outfit.

I suggested that the photograph be taken at the bureau, where Doctor Page Senior could sit and his son stand, and where the light from the window was gentle. I did not use a meter for my work. I could not afford one. But judging the light by guesswork was an advantage: it trained me to see things the way my camera would.

The bureau was cluttered with bric-a-brac that was distinctly feminine: shepherdesses and angels; a set of Royal Doulton cat figurines.

'You can move those if you think they are distracting,' said Doctor Page Senior.

'But the ornaments add personality to the scene,' I said. 'Did they belong to the late Mrs Page?'

Doctor Page Senior's lips trembled and he nodded. I was taken aback by the unexpected show of emotion. 'It would be nice then to include them in your photograph with your son,' I told him. 'It puts her in the picture with you.'

Having lost my own mother, I was moved by the mix of happiness and pain I saw on the men's faces when I mentioned Mrs Page. My eyes met Doctor Page's and I saw that we understood each other. There was something refreshing about not having to make further explanations.

After the photographs had been taken, Doctor Page Senior invited me to join him and his son for lunch. I discreetly sorted my way through the pickled meats and sausages to find the lettuce and tomatoes. But Doctor Page noticed.

'I'll ask the cook to bring you vegetable soup,' he said.

I nodded gratefully. He had gone to some trouble to make sure Klára was served meatless dishes at Broughton Hall. Another doctor might have scoffed at the idea.

The maid entered and whispered to Doctor Page Senior. He excused himself to take a telephone call. When he left the room, I asked Doctor Page if he had told his father how we had met each other. 'I mean, does he know about Klára?'

Doctor Page shook his head. 'I told him I met your uncle at the museum. Father doesn't need to know everything. Sometimes it's better when he doesn't.'

'Thank you,' I said. 'I want to put what happened with Klára in the past. I want her to have a fresh start. Illnesses of the mind have a stigma about them.'

'I know,' said Doctor Page. 'By the way, call me Philip. We aren't on formal terms now.'

'Philip,' I repeated. 'And you must call me Adéla.'

'What a lovely name,' said Philip. 'It rolls off the tongue: a-DELL-ah.'

He pronounced my name perfectly. We turned back to our food.

Doctor Page Senior's voice boomed from the hall: 'Europe again!' Then after a pause he said more calmly, 'Well, yes, I suppose if you are not well.'

Philip clutched his knife and fork. I assumed Doctor Page Senior was talking to his fiancée's mother. It sounded as if his fiancée was planning another trip.

'I want to ask you what you meant the other night about psychiatry,' I said, trying to distract Philip from the telephone conversation. 'Why do you think you can't help people? You did so much for Klára.'

A shadow passed over his face. 'I hope to change specialties,' he said, pushing around a carrot on his plate. 'I want to work with children. Perhaps if I can help people when they are young, there may never be a need for places like Broughton Hall.'

That was a beautiful vision, I thought. 'Where will you study? The University of Sydney?' I asked.

'London, most likely,' he said.

I had a sense that Philip wanted to say something more but before he had the chance his father stormed into the room. 'Well, they are off again,' Doctor Page Senior said. 'Helen plans to leave in a few months. She wants to take the waters in Switzerland even though they have just come back from France. I don't want any dilly-dallying this time, Philip. You are going with them, and I want you and Beatrice to have wedding rings on your fingers before you leave.'

The colour rushed to Philip's cheeks. 'I can't give up Broughton Hall at the drop of a hat, Father.'

Doctor Page Senior waved his hand. 'Psychiatry! It's a hoax profession. What sort of doctor doesn't heal with his hands?'

Philip glared at his father. Doctor Page Senior did not respect what Philip did and I could see that it hurt him.

I left the Pages' house that day puzzled. I understood that Doctor Page Senior's gruffness may have had something to do with his wife's death, and that he did not approve of Philip's chosen profession. But what baffled me most was Philip's relationship with Beatrice. For a man who was supposed to be head over heels in love, he did not seem sure.

I returned to the Pages' house the following week, to show them the prints.

'The tones are rich,' said Doctor Page Senior. 'And the photographs so well composed.'

Philip approached his appraisal from a psychological point of view. 'The pictures show the photographer's positive worldview,' he said. 'Father, look how peaceful we appear together. And Adéla has even managed to bring out the tranquillity of the room.'

I remembered the tension that had erupted between Philip and his father after the portrait had been taken. But Philip was not being sarcastic. Perhaps 'peaceful' was the way he preferred to think of his relationship with his father.

'Well, now we must pay you,' Doctor Page Senior said to me.
'I can't accept any money.'

Doctor Page Senior lifted his eyebrows and I realised I had
spoken too soon. As a 'portrait photographer' I should charge
him, but Philip had been kind to Klára, beyond what Broughton
Hall required of him, and I wanted to thank him. But I could not
say that so I gave another reason for why I would not charge for
the photographs.

'I have a confession to make,' I said. 'I'm not a professional
portrait artist. You are my first commission. I have only taken
pictures of my family and birds and dogs before. But I was
flattered by your invitation and did not wish to refuse. I hope
you forgive me.'

'Forgive you!' said Doctor Page Senior. 'You must let us help
you. Such a talent as yours can't be wasted.' He turned to Philip.
'Tell Beatrice about Miss Rose. I would like a portrait of her as
well. That way I shall have something to remember you both by
when you leave for Europe.'

Philip clenched his fists. I could feel another tense mood
coming on between him and his father.

'Of course I will do that,' I said, before their tempers had a
chance to take hold. 'Just tell me when.'

The following week, Doctor Page Senior arrived in his chauffeur-
driven Bentley to take me to meet his soon-to-be daughter-in-law.

'You'll like the lovely Beatrice,' said Doctor Page Senior, once
the chauffeur had packed my equipment in the boot and started
the motor. 'She's been away in France for months and I've missed
her good humour. She has a positive effect on me.'

'Was she at finishing school?' I asked.

Doctor Page Senior laughed. 'Oh, Beatrice would have none

of that. Besides, she has a charm of her own. No, unfortunately her mother is not well and they went there to take the waters and breathe the mountain air.'

A short while later, the chauffeur pulled into the driveway of a house in Rose Bay. The garden was tropical with palms and tree ferns. The plain sandstone bricks of the house were a contrast to its richly decorated interior. My eyes did not know which detail to take in first when the butler invited us into the entrance hall: the French silk wallpaper; the hand-painted cupids on the ceiling roses; the chandelier that sent sparkles of light around the floor. The butler showed us to the drawing room and my senses were besieged by the wood panelling, Persian drapes and the gold detailing on the teak chairs.

The door opened and two ladies entered. They were so different from each other that if Doctor Page Senior had not introduced them as mother and daughter I never would have guessed that they were related. Beatrice was wiry with hair the colour of wild strawberries. Her hair was so untamed it looked as though it were on the verge of escaping the gold clasp that bound it and scampering around the room. She was not the woman I had pictured.

'Ah, you are here,' she said, throwing herself towards us. She kissed Doctor Page Senior then turned to me.

'I'm excited to meet you,' she said, stepping so close to me that she trod on my foot. She was almost as tall as Uncle Ota and next to her I felt like a child. If she wanted to stand for her photograph, I would have to climb on a box.

Beatrice introduced me to her mother. Mrs Fahey was a frail woman with mousy brown hair and a waxen face. From the way she wheezed and struggled for breath, I could see that she was seriously ill. But the affection between her and the vital Beatrice was obvious from the look of love in her eyes when her daughter helped her into a chair and covered her knees with a shawl.

'How are you, Helen?' asked Doctor Page Senior, sitting down next to Mrs Fahey.

'Oh, still here,' she answered, with weariness in her voice.

I bowed my head, trying to compose myself. Beatrice was so full of life, and yet I felt for her. She was going to watch her mother die — perhaps not for another year or two, but more slowly than I had witnessed mine pass. I wished there was something kind I could say to help her bear that blow. But there were no words for such things that could be said to friends or strangers.

'I suppose we can't keep Miss Rose waiting,' said Beatrice, bouncing towards the windows and tugging the curtains apart. With the light on her face, I saw that she was about twenty-five years old — too old for finishing school — and that her white skin was covered in freckles. Most women would have bleached the spots with lemon juice or powdered over them, but Beatrice appeared to have made no such effort.

'Well, I must be off to see some patients,' said Doctor Page Senior, rising from his chair. 'I'll leave you ladies to it. The Faheys' chauffeur will take you home, Miss Rose.'

After Doctor Page Senior had departed, Beatrice laid her hand on my arm. 'Old Doctor Page told me that you are a vegetarian. Is that true?'

'Yes, that's right,' I answered.

'So you never eat meat?' asked Beatrice, sitting down on a footstool so that her knees jutted upwards and made her look like a frog on a lily pad. 'Not chicken or fish or anything?'

If Beatrice was about to ridicule me, I had no intention of being belittled for caring about lives other than my own. 'I've seen maids behead chickens, a neighbour kill a cow with a poleaxe and a butcher drive a spike between a horse's eyes,' I told her. 'Those poor creatures struggled and thrashed about in terror. It's like murder to take their lives when we don't need to.'

Beatrice's green eyes focused on my face. She was not a pretty girl but I understood what Doctor Page Senior had meant about her not needing finishing school and why Philip was in love with her. Beatrice had something about her that was transfixing. She thumped her palms on her knees. 'Well, that's bloody fantastic!' she said. 'I wish I was that strong because I feel the same way. But nobody I know — apart from you now — is a vegetarian and Mother says it simply isn't "English".'

We both looked to Mrs Fahey. 'It's not natural,' she said. 'We were meant to eat meat.'

'Well, Mother,' said Beatrice, rising from her seat, 'I'm going to invite Miss Rose to our next special luncheon and I'm going to tell the cook to make it a vegetarian one. It may be good for you.'

There was no malice in Beatrice's voice but I knew that if I had ever spoken to my mother that way — let alone sworn — I would have been sent out of the room. Mrs Fahey merely laughed at her daughter. 'Have some vegetable dishes if you wish, my dear,' she said. 'Philip and Robert will go along with you. But Freddy and Alfred will be horrified. You'd better have some lamb chops for them or they won't come again.' Then she turned to me and gave a shrug as if to say, You see what life has handed me? What does one do with such a wilful daughter?

Beatrice plonked herself in a rosewood armchair and wagged her finger. 'There are too many boys around this family. I need girls to fight them with.'

Beatrice was a magnetic character. That men might find her charming did not surprise me. She was vibrant, loud and forceful. I glanced around the room and realised that the overblown wallpaper and frilly cushions were at odds with her breezy personality.

'I wonder if you might prefer your photograph taken in the garden?' I asked her. 'The light is good. I'd like to place you in a natural setting.'

Beatrice jumped out of her chair. 'Bloody marvellous idea!' she said. 'No wonder Philip thinks so much of you!'

I was surprised and flattered at the same time. Philip had talked about me to Beatrice?

Few ladies smiled in portrait photographs and those that did rarely showed their teeth. Beatrice grinned in every pose whether I told her to or not. 'So what if it gives me wrinkles and makes my teeth look big,' she laughed. 'If I look too serious people won't recognise me.'

Afterwards, we returned to the house where Mrs Fahey was waiting at a table laid out with scones and tea.

'So you will come to our luncheon when we get around to organising it?' Beatrice asked, motioning for me to sit down. 'I'll make sure there are nice dishes for you.'

She was so captivating and so earnest in her invitation that I could not see any way I could refuse. No wonder she can keep Philip on a string, I thought. You just cannot say no to her.

ELEVEN

One evening Uncle Ota came home with exciting news for us. He asked Ranjana, Klára, Esther and me to sit on the sofa before making his announcement. 'Mr Tilly is retiring and has offered me the role of manager of his cinema!'

After a moment of stunned silence we broke into cries of elation. Being promoted from head usher to manager was a significant leap in responsibility. Mr Tilly had obviously recognised that Uncle Ota had the flair necessary to manage a cinema. I could not have been more pleased for my uncle. The Tuesday night soirées had allowed him to experiment with his entrepreneurial skills. Now, at the helm of a suburban cinema, he could put his showmanship to full use.

'Well,' said Ranjana, standing up to make a pot of tea, 'that's two family members in entertainment and one to go.'

She grinned at me.

* * *

Doctor Page Senior and Mrs Fahey were so pleased with the portrait I took of Beatrice that they were determined to find more clients for me.

'There are society ladies who require portraits of themselves and their daughters, some of whom need "help" in the looks department,' Doctor Page Senior told me. 'Helen and I are going to send you to some wealthy clients and I want you to charge them and charge them well,' he said, cocking his eyebrow. 'You have exceptional talent and most of them have more money than they have sense. If they don't spend their money on a good portrait they will only spend it on a frivolous dress. Think of it that way.'

Doctor Page Senior kept his word and before long I was photographing debutantes, society weddings and children. Word about my individual touch spread and I often undertook several sittings in one day. One society matron said I was the only photographer who could bring out the darkness of her eyes, while another claimed I had diminished her prominent chin by using the light correctly. I usually photographed my clients in their homes, and by the time Klára attended her first class at the Conservatorium High School I was being welcomed into some of the grandest manors in Sydney.

'You must make Edith look beautiful,' Beatrice told me, when she accompanied me to Bellevue Hill where I was to photograph her friend. 'I haven't got many female friends,' she said, hurrying up the gravel drive, bordered by crepe myrtles, towards the Greek revival mansion. 'Actually, the only female friends I have are Edith and you.'

I followed Beatrice past the columns to the entrance of the house. She turned the ringer. I wondered how she had decided I was her friend. I had only met her once. But it seemed to me that whatever Beatrice willed came to pass. So I accepted it as a compliment. It was no trifle for a woman who worked for her living to be befriended by a socialite.

A maid answered the door and ushered us to a drawing room with a Turkish rug and two marble fireplaces. Beatrice and I sat down on a *toile de campagne* sofa.

'Edith will be my bridesmaid and I'm determined to do something for her,' Beatrice whispered. 'She desperately wants a husband but we can't get Harold Cazneaux to agree to take her portrait for *Home* magazine. And her mother wants some pictures of the house when you're finished. If you get them into the *Sydney Morning Herald*, she will pay you extra.'

Photography had been a means of expression but now I was making significant money out of it. As Doctor Page Senior had told me, society ladies were prepared to pay generously for a flattering portrait.

The door opened and a woman Beatrice's age stepped into the room. Her skin was alabaster and her pale eyes were framed by colourless lashes. Her washed-out appearance did not bode well for a photograph to catch a husband.

'This is Edith,' said Beatrice, standing up to embrace her friend.

Edith grinned, revealing enormous teeth and an inch of gum. My mind raced to think how I could photograph her. Perhaps if I had her turn slightly away from the camera I could emphasise her long neck and straight profile. 'Shall we begin?' I asked.

After the photography session, Edith insisted we stay for tea. 'Will we have it here, in the drawing room?' she asked.

'No, let's sit on the balcony where it's lovely and cool,' said Beatrice.

Edith led us to the balcony, which overlooked the lawn, and told the maid to bring us tea. A breeze sprang up and sent the smell of gardenias wafting around us.

'So, you'll be marrying soon,' said Edith to Beatrice. 'Have you set a date yet?'

'God, don't you start,' said Beatrice, lifting her hair and dropping it so that its roll fanned out and became untidy. 'I've got everyone else on my back.'

Edith laughed. 'Oh well, reluctance keeps a man keen.' She turned to me and flashed her horsy smile. 'It's always been Beatrice and Philip, as long as I can remember,' she said. 'They were born on the same day, three years apart. Our families used to holiday every year in the southern tablelands and Philip and Beatrice had two ponies who they called Lancelot and Guinevere. Romantic, isn't it?'

Beatrice smiled. 'Philip and I spent our days by the river. He pretended to be the captain of a cargo ship and I pretended to be a pirate.'

I listened with interest as Beatrice and Edith talked about Philip. They knew things about him that I did not — the names of his childhood pets; that he had attended The King's School; that he hated sour cream.

'He wants to join an air club,' Beatrice told Edith. 'And buy his own plane.'

'How daring!' her friend replied, pouring us another cup of tea and passing around the date slice.

While Beatrice and Edith spoke, it dawned on me that they discussed Philip's sporting achievements and weekend hobbies but never mentioned his work. It was surprising, because to Philip being a doctor was everything.

Beatrice continued to intrigue me. The society friends to whom Mrs Fahey recommended me were often mothers of young men, and seemed to be living in hope that Beatrice might tire of Philip.

'Such a beautiful girl,' one matron told me, after I had photographed her sitting on a sofa with her papillon puppy. 'Wasted on Doctor Philip Page.'

Beatrice was strolling around the garden while I took the photographs, and I hoped the woman might expand on what she meant before she returned.

'That young man does not need to work for a living,' the woman continued. 'If he had any sense he would be with her all the time.'

It was an interesting observation, I thought, because it seemed to me that the difficulties in their relationship were caused by Beatrice's reluctance to spend time with Philip.

It did not take Uncle Ota long to make a success of Tilly's Cinema. He selected programs the regular cinema-goers liked; placed advertisements in the local paper; and printed handbills to give out at the end of a session that announced the following week's program. He introduced a lolly-bag promotion for a sweet shop for the children's matinée. Each Saturday afternoon, throngs of children gathered outside the cinema. Ranjana and I handed them lolly bags before they burst into the cinema like a herd of wild boars. The promotion was a success, although the sweets were often hurled at the screen or rolled along the wooden floors, to the chagrin of our cleaners.

Ranjana suggested Uncle Ota promote a weekly afternoon session for mothers with young children. She and I managed a crèche while the women watched romance pictures. For some mothers it was a chance to catch up on sleep they never got at home, and afterwards they were treated to a soothing cup of tea and music courtesy of Klára and a violinist friend before we handed their children back to them.

While the changes Uncle Ota brought to the cinema were popular with the patrons, not everyone was enamoured of him. The book-keeper, who had been with Mr Tilly for fifteen years, protested against the extra workload Uncle Ota created and left to work with a law firm. Luckily, Esther proved to be an excellent replacement and took over the book-keeping with few problems. A more drastic confrontation occurred the night the projectionist walked out. Ranjana took an interest in every aspect of the cinema. She had left her job at the factory to help Uncle Ota and she wandered around behind the scenes looking for things to do. She enjoyed watching the loading of the films onto the projector and often entered the projection room when a film was screening to watch the projectionist at work.

'I want you to train my wife to be your assistant,' Uncle Ota told our projectionist. 'If you get sick, we won't be able to have a session.'

Uncle Ota was preoccupied with running the cinema and did not notice the projectionist's pinched mouth. The following night during the screening of *Sunshine Sally*, Ranjana, unaware that her fascination with sprockets and spools grated on the projectionist's nerves, was taken by surprise when he stormed out of the room, leaving the film to wind off the projector. The picture on the screen dimmed just as Sally was about to find out who her real parents were, then flickered before spinning off. The audience booed. Klára, drilled by Mr Tilly for such a crisis, struck up a sing-along number on the piano.

'What's wrong with you?' Uncle Ota hissed at the projectionist out in the wings. 'If my wife's presence was annoying you so much, why didn't you speak up earlier?'

'What's wrong with *you*,' the projectionist spat back, 'that you can't see the colour of your wife?'

Uncle Ota's eyes narrowed. If he had punched the projectionist in the face for the insult, I could not have blamed him. But just as Uncle Ota clenched his fists for a fight, the audience burst into cheers. The picture was back on the screen, and coming out brighter and steadier than usual and at a much better speed. Ranjana waved to us from the projectionist's window.

The projectionist realised he was beaten. He snatched his jacket and ran for the door. 'Never stoop to answer a slight and soon the truth will come to light,' Uncle Ota shouted after him.

Ranjana became our projectionist, and while a female in the role could have been a novelty, we never let the audience see her in case someone objected to 'an Indian' screening the film. Ranjana wore an opera mask when she worked in case anybody glimpsed her through the projection room window. This led to tales of the 'masked projectionist of Tilly's Cinema' and speculation that our projectionist might be a criminal camouflaging razor scars or a Russian prince in hiding. The rumours were good for business and we never had an empty session. Ranjana thought the escapade amusing, especially when Union Theatres and Hoyts, having heard of the excellent projection at Tilly's Cinema, sent her letters offering positions. 'I should accept one for the fun of it,' she joked. 'Imagine their faces when I roll up demanding my two shillings per film!'

Even though I'd had to buy a Kodak folding camera and upgrade my darkroom facilities, I was coming out ahead with my portrait work. Esther had given me enough money for Klára's first year of tuition but, unless Aunt Josephine was able to send us more money soon, I would have to earn enough to cover her tuition for the rest of the time she attended the school. I wished I could write to Aunt Josephine to tell her what I was doing — earning my own living. She would be proud.

My career kept me busy and I had not been to the Vegetarian Café in weeks. I decided to take Klára there one day after school. But when we arrived, the café was crowded. The only seats left were in the booth where the young man with the cockatoo was sitting with his skinny companion.

'We'll have to come back later,' I said to Klára.

We were about to leave when a voice called out, 'You are welcome to sit here. We weren't planning on staying much longer.'

I turned to see that the skinny man was pointing towards the spare bench opposite him. Something about his bright smile made me accept his offer, although I was embarrassed about my last encounter with his friend.

'I am Peter,' the skinny man introduced himself. He was wearing his usual cap and scarf although it was hot outside. His gigantic eyes and grin made me think of Felix the Cat. 'This is my friend Hugh and that is Giallo sitting on his shoulder. Giallo found himself on the wrong side of a rottweiler and Hugh found himself in the wrong trench.'

I was surprised at Peter's flippancy. Hugh grimaced but did not seem offended. Now I was close up I saw he was a good-looking man with Irish skin and light blue eyes. He nodded to us, although he did not smile.

I let Klára into the booth and took the place next to her. 'I am Adéla and this is my sister, Klára,' I told the men. Klára flashed me a surprised look because we had all introduced ourselves to each other by our Christian names, but the atmosphere at the Vegetarian Café was very informal.

'You don't sound like kangaroos,' said Peter with a laugh. 'Where are you from?'

'Prague,' I answered.

Klára scratched the cockatoo's head. He closed his eyes and leaned towards her. 'Giallo does not sound very Australian,' she said, taking up Peter's playful tone.

'I drove ambulances in Italy during the war,' Peter said. 'The day I returned to Sydney I found poor Giallo lying in a ditch. He barely had his flight feathers and I didn't expect him to live, but I took him home and kept him warm. The next day he was lively and calling to be fed. I took him to meet Hugh, who was still in the army hospital. It was love at first sight for both of them.'

I glanced at Hugh who said nothing but did not seem as sullen as my first impression. Perhaps he was self-conscious around people, as many men who had lost limbs seemed to be. Besides, Peter was so talkative it was hard to get in a word. Peter turned out to be knowledgeable about Europe and about classical composers. He was interested in Uncle Ota's job at the cinema and nearly jumped out of his seat with excitement when we told him the story of how our uncle had saved his wife from sati. We found out that he had been an art student the day war broke out and he had become a vegetarian after the armistice was declared.

'War makes life cheap. I wanted to make it sacred again. I couldn't stand bloodshed any more … and especially not of innocent animals,' he told us.

We were talking about castles in Czechoslovakia when Hugh suddenly interrupted by asking me, 'What's your surname?'

'Rose,' I replied.

He lifted his eyebrows. 'Adéla Rose? The photographer?'

It was strange to be referred to that way. I had photographed many elite people in a short amount of time, but I found it difficult to call myself 'a photographer' let alone 'Adéla Rose, the photographer'. I considered myself an amateur who had found herself in the right place at the right time.

'I've seen your work in the *Sydney Morning Herald*,' Hugh said.

The newspaper had published the pictures I had taken of Edith's house. It was a significant professional leap for me, but Hugh would have had to have studied every picture in the paper to have noticed my credit. Although he did not say whether he liked the photographs or not, I was flattered he had remembered them.

'Hugh is a photographer too,' said Peter. 'He's shooting my picture.'

My heart skipped a beat. 'Your picture?'

Peter nodded. 'Production begins soon. I have my actors and budget sorted out. I just don't have a script girl yet.'

'What does a script girl do?' I asked.

'She's the second pair of eyes to the director,' Peter said. 'She sits beside him and times the scenes with a stopwatch. She records the takes and types them up for the editor, and she also makes notes on what the actors are wearing in each scene in case anything has to be shot again later.' He flashed a rueful smile. 'My girlfriend did it for me on my other pictures, but she's found another bloke.'

'Your other pictures?' I cried. 'How many have you made?'

Peter puffed out his chest. 'I've made two so far and I have a much bigger budget for this one.'

Klára pinched me but I did not need any prompting. 'I could be your script girl,' I told him. 'I can type and I'm very interested in the pictures.'

Peter was taken aback for a second but then his face broke into a grin. 'Truly? What luck then! And I suppose you'd be willing to take the stills photographs as well?'

'Of course,' I said.

'Settled!' said Peter.

Klára squeezed my leg, Peter grinned and Giallo did a bobbing dance. Only Hugh's grim expression gave any clue that something might be amiss.

I received an invitation to a luncheon at Beatrice's home along with an apology that it had taken her longer to arrange than she had expected and a promise that she would send her chauffeur to pick me up. The day of the luncheon, I arrived at her residence and the butler showed me to the drawing room where Beatrice and Philip were waiting with the other guests. It was a surprise to see Beatrice and Philip together as I had only known them apart. I was astonished by their mismatched heights: Beatrice stood much taller than Philip. She leapt towards me and seized my arm. 'Our guest of honour is here,' she cried.

I noticed the engagement ring on her finger: an emerald set in white gold with brilliant-cut diamonds. It was the kind of ring I would have chosen. I was not one to covet other people's things; Mother had said it was vulgar. So I was repulsed by the feelings of jealousy that rose in my heart.

The other guests stepped forward to greet me. Philip said hello before introducing an elderly couple who turned out to be Beatrice's aunt and uncle, Mr and Mrs Roland.

'Oh, no formalities, please,' said Mrs Roland, who had the same red hair as her niece. 'Call me Florence.'

'Adéla,' I said in return.

Florence blinked and I was startled to see that she had false eyelashes glued to her lids. Society ladies never adorned themselves with artifice: that was for actresses and harlots. I wondered if Beatrice had inherited not only her aunt's red hair but her eccentric manner as well. I thought of Aunt Josephine and her work ethic. Perhaps aunts have more influence on us than we realise.

'I am Alfred,' said Beatrice's uncle, a smile twitching beneath his walrus moustache. 'But don't waste time with old fogies like us. Meet the young men.'

I smiled at the two male guests. The younger, who was about twenty, wore his golden hair parted down the middle and a silk suit. His dress style was urbane but his glowing face was as innocent as a country boy's.

'I'm Robert Swan,' he said. 'And this is my friend, Frederick Rockcliffe.'

'It's a pleasure to meet you, Miss Rose,' Frederick said, in the growling tone of an American accent.

It was something of a jolt to be referred to politely. I had become used to Beatrice and her family's habit of calling everyone by their Christian name. Frederick was around thirty with dark hair and shadows under his eyes. Along with his round face and tiny nose, he reminded me of a panda bear. I should have guessed from his shirt with the polka dots on it that he was a foreigner. It was too flamboyant for a luncheon.

When we arrived at the dining room, the food was already on the table and, apart from the occasional appearance of a maid to clear dishes and refill our glasses, we served ourselves. I was glad that Beatrice was aware I was a vegetarian. My stomach turned at the sight of the platters of oily roasted quails, sautéed pigeons and jugged hare.

'What's in those?' asked Robert, pointing to a plate of stuffed tomatoes.

'Cucumber and cream cheese,' Beatrice answered him. 'And over here we have mint salad and egg noodle pie. Adéla is a vegetarian and I am one today too.'

'Good-oh,' said Robert. 'I'll tuck into that then. There's

something very clean about vegetarian food. I dare say it's better for one's digestion.'

'It isn't English,' said Mrs Fahey. She was looking better than she had previously although she still wheezed.

Beatrice leaned towards me. 'Mother is third-generation Australian but she worships everything English.' Then, turning towards her mother, she said, 'It's a good thing our ancestors were upstanding British convicts, isn't it? I was thinking of stealing a horse later today myself.'

Mrs Fahey sent her daughter a horrified look. 'Will you stop saying things like that, Beatrice!' she said. 'You know they were free settlers. Horse stealers indeed!'

Philip and the Rolands burst into laughter and were joined by Robert. Frederick and I exchanged a glance, not sure of the family humour. Philip brought order back to the discussion by asking me how Klára was finding the Conservatorium High School.

I gave him a rundown of what she was learning in her eurythmics and musical theory classes. 'Most of the lessons are taught by the head of the school, Alfred Steel,' I told him. 'With the exception of French, which is taken by Madame Henri.'

While I spoke, I was aware of how close Philip and Beatrice sat to each other. They looked comfortable together and nodded their heads in unison to show their interest in what I was saying. The jealous pang that had bothered me earlier pinched me again.

'They had a devil of a time getting the Conservatorium of Music started,' Robert said. 'They not only had to form a school out of amateurs but they had to educate the public about classical music to create an audience. There were many who said the money was better spent on hospitals and public works than "highbrow" music.'

'Robert is often invited to guest lecture at the Conservatorium of Music,' Beatrice explained. 'He plays the pipe organ.'

'Truly?' I asked Robert. The Conservatorium of Music was the tertiary institution above the high school Klára attended.

'My interest is world instruments,' he said. 'I've just purchased an orchestrion, which contains a wind section, kettle drums, cymbals and triangles to simulate the sound of an orchestra.'

'I'd love to see that, Robert,' said Beatrice, clasping her hands under her chin. Mrs Fahey coughed and Beatrice hastily removed her elbows from the table.

'Well, perhaps I should arrange afternoon tea once I've got it set up. It will take a while to arrive here from Germany,' Robert said. He turned to me. 'You could bring your sister. I would be delighted to meet her.'

Klára loved all things musical and, with Robert's interest in unusual instruments, I was sure that she would be enthusiastic to meet him. I gladly accepted.

The dessert was pêche Melba, a mix of peaches, raspberry sauce and ice-cream.

'This dessert was created for the Australian opera singer, Nellie Melba,' Philip explained to me and Frederick. 'As the ice-cream is only one element it takes the edge off the coldness and spares one's vocal cords.'

Florence turned to me. 'You took Beatrice's and Edith's portraits, didn't you?'

Before I could answer, Beatrice clapped her hands. 'She did a wonderful job of Edith! She turned her into a beauty. It's given Edith a different picture of herself. She has bought herself racy new clothes and has become quite the centre of attention.'

'Well,' said Florence, touching my arm, 'if you made Edith a beauty, you must be good. Do you only take portraits?'

'At the moment,' I told her. 'But I will soon be working on a picture as a script girl. I would like to make a film of my own some day.'

Philip looked at me. At first he seemed surprised, then his face brightened. 'Really?' he asked. 'That's fascinating!'

'Ah, well,' said Robert, nodding towards Frederick, 'there's your man. Tell Adéla what you do, Freddy.'

Frederick finished chewing the piece of peach he had in his mouth and turned to me. 'I'm here with Galaxy Pictures. I work in film distribution.'

'You're here to destroy our local industry, according to the papers,' Beatrice said.

It was difficult to get used to how Beatrice spoke at the table. I had been brought up to not contradict a guest lest it embarrass them. I had never seen an argument break out at luncheon. Tension, Mother always said, would give everyone indigestion.

'Some might see it that way,' Frederick answered. 'But I don't.'

'Well,' said Alfred, 'take the case of one of our most famous directors, Franklyn Barrett. He had to shut down his production company because he couldn't get his films distributed in his own country.'

Frederick sighed and looked at me. 'What we do is sell packages of films in advance to Australian theatre chains and independents. This country has the highest cinema attendance in the world. Going to the pictures every week is even factored into the basic wage. Cinema managers need a constant supply of films. Only the United States produces enough of them to guarantee that supply.'

'That's all well and good,' said Alfred, 'but you distributors make the cinema managers purchase films twelve months in advance and there are rumours that you fix it so Australian films can't get on the bill at all. American distributors have been accused of cutting off supplies of films to managers who dare to put Australian pictures on the program. Sounds to me like you Yankees are trying to shut down the industry here. The Americans talk about free trade and competition, but they prefer to be a monopoly themselves.'

'That's hogwash,' Frederick hissed. 'If the films are good enough, the cinema managers will show them.' He flashed his eyes at me. 'What sort of picture do you intend to make?'

Frederick had put me on the spot. Apart from the fantasy of directing a film, I had given little thought as to the kind of picture I wanted to make. 'I like the films of Hans Richter and Fritz Lang,' I told him.

'Ah,' said Frederick, laying his palms on the table and rolling his eyes. 'Artistic films that don't make any money.'

'What sort of pictures make money?' Philip asked. 'Doesn't art factor at all?'

It was chivalrous of Philip to come to my defence. Beatrice, Alfred and Frederick were shooting attacks and counter-attacks around the table as if that were a normal way to make conversation. I felt unnerved — not to mention foolish.

Frederick took a breath and spoke more calmly. 'I'm sure Miss Rose will make an excellent film. I'm only saying that Australian audiences want romances and comedies.'

Dessert out of the way, our group moved to the garden for some tea and fruit served in the summerhouse. The conversation changed from the pictures to cricket and real estate at Palm Beach. Philip sat next to me.

'If Australians don't make films about their own country then they may as well be an American colony,' he said. 'Why is it that a Czech can see that better than we can?'

'We were almost a colony under the Austro–Hungarian Empire,'

I told him. 'Even for a Czech the national language was German, a foreign language. It would be a shame if Australians gave up their own culture so easily.'

The Rolands were setting out croquet hoops on the lawn. 'I can't abide that mindless game,' Philip said. 'Shall we take a turn about the garden?'

There was a path, wide enough for two, through the garden. We would not be out of the view of the other guests, so it did not seem improper to accept Philip's invitation. I walked next to him past the azaleas and oleanders, aware that our arms brushed against each other when the path pinched around a curve.

'I told my father about my plans to study children's medicine,' he said.

'How did he respond?'

'He would be happier if I pursued general surgery, but at least children's medicine is superior to psychiatry.'

'Why does he have such a poor opinion of psychiatry?' I asked. 'It is healing the mind.'

Philip stopped in his tracks and looked back to the group playing croquet. 'It's not just my father,' he said. 'It's the opinion most people have. Even Beatrice would prefer it if I dealt with matrons' dizzy spells and old men's gout, and she's not usually conservative.'

I thought of the lie my family had told about Emilie having been bitten by a diseased dog. 'People are ashamed of the mentally ill,' I said.

Philip turned to me. 'You don't think that way, do you? You understand. You visited Klára every day and gave your real name.'

'Don't most relatives give their real names?'

'No.'

We walked on and the path curved around the edge of the garden, turning back in the direction of the summerhouse.

'I'll miss you when I go to Europe,' Philip said. 'It's so easy talking with you.'

I sensed feelings were changing between us, and shrank back. Something was not right. Philip was engaged to Beatrice but seemed happier speaking with me.

'Beatrice will listen to you,' I told him. 'She'll understand if you make her.'

Philip shrugged. 'Beatrice's conversations are one-sided and a bit like my father's,' he said.

The bitterness in his voice surprised me. Wasn't he in love with Beatrice? Perhaps he was frustrated because she was difficult to pin down. I did get the impression she had left him in limbo a few too many times.

Beatrice saw us returning to the summerhouse and called out. 'Come and join the game, Adéla. I know Philip made you walk around the garden with him to avoid it. He does it every time.'

After a few rounds of hitting balls with mallets, three o'clock arrived and I excused myself to go and meet Klára after school at the Vegetarian Café. While Beatrice went to arrange for the chauffeur to take me to the city, Frederick approached me.

'I hope I didn't offend you,' he said. 'Beatrice gets me hot under the collar. She does it on purpose.'

'Not at all,' I assured him, although he had made me feel foolish.

'Officially, I distribute films,' he said, running his hand over his slick hair. 'But unofficially I scout for talent. I produced several films back in the States. If you bring me your script we can talk about it.'

'Thank you,' I said, quite sure that unless I felt like making a mindless romance or a comedy, Frederick Rockcliffe was the last person I would approach to produce my picture.

'Car's ready!' Beatrice called from the house.

The gathering walked to the front steps with me to bid me farewell. I was conscious that Philip lingered in the background. The chauffeur drove the car up to the front steps. There was a sudden 'pop' and then a hissing sound. Steam poured from the bonnet. The chauffeur climbed out and scratched his head. 'The engine's overheated, Miss Beatrice.'

Beatrice rolled her eyes. 'Again? That's twice this week. I'm sorry, Adéla.'

'I can take a taxi,' I told her.

'Nonsense,' said Beatrice, wrapping her arm around me. 'Philip will drive you to town. He has to go in that direction this afternoon anyhow.'

'I don't want to impose.'

'You won't be,' Beatrice assured me. Then, leaning her head close to mine, she whispered, 'It will be my way of apologising for inflicting that crass American on you. He's a friend of Robert's. It's the only reason I invited him.'

Philip left the top of his Talbot down so we could enjoy the afternoon sunshine. The roar of the engine and the wind rushing by our ears limited our communication to smiles and nods. In a way it was better. I did not want to talk about Beatrice.

Philip turned the car into George Street and pulled up outside the Vegetarian Café. He craned his neck to look at the Gothic script sign and the pictures of smiling sheep and cows that adorned the windows. 'Here?' he asked.

I nodded.

'I'm impressed by people who live by their convictions,' he said.

I expected that he would keep the engine running while he climbed out to open the door for me, but he pulled the car to the kerb and turned the engine off.

'You must think I'm a brute for how I spoke about Beatrice,' he said. 'As you can see, she's a terrific person and she's certainly taken a shine to you.'

'Please don't apologise,' I told him. 'There's no need.'

Philip glanced at me and smiled. 'You see, my mother and Mrs Fahey were best friends,' he said. 'After Beatrice was born they always said that she and I would get married when we grew up. Nobody questioned it, least of all me or Beatrice. I think that's why I never bought a female mud-figure. I never thought of there being other women.'

He turned and fixed his eyes on me. I was aware that his hand inched closer to mine and I was sure he was going to clasp it and take me in his arms. But the spell was broken by Klára's arrival.

'Doctor Page!' she cried, hoisting her books higher under her arm. 'Are you joining us for afternoon tea?'

'Hello!' said Philip, opening his door and stepping around the car and onto the footpath to greet Klára. 'No, I'm not going to impose on your time with your sister. I was dropping Adéla off. We were at a luncheon together.'

Philip opened the door for me. He searched my face when I got out but I looked away. Everything was different from how it had been just an hour ago. Philip had feelings for me beyond those of a friend, and I was drawn to him too. I had gone to Beatrice's luncheon expecting to have a good time, not for everything to be pulled off balance.

'My class is giving our first concert next month,' Klára told Philip. 'I will be playing the Grieg Piano Concerto. Do you think you will be able to come?'

'Klára,' I said, 'Doctor Page is very busy and that concert is during the day —'

'I'd be delighted,' Philip said, cutting me off before I had a chance to finish. He looked from Klára to me. 'I'll ask Robert and Freddy if they want to join me.'

I blushed to the roots of my hair. Klára noticed, which made my cheeks burn more. Philip wished us well and climbed back into his car and started the engine.

He waved one more time before driving off. I was overcome by a sense of pleasure mixed with foreboding. I felt myself drawing closer to Philip even as he moved away.

TWELVE

Production for Peter's film commenced with a tight shooting schedule of three weeks. Peter had to secure his main actor between theatrical roles and also make the most of daylight hours as the days were growing shorter. It was a relief to have a distraction from thinking about Philip. We did not have a telephone at the house so he had sent a note asking to see me. Several times a day I relived the pleasure of Philip's hand lingering near mine and the idea that he had intended to embrace me. But after the pleasure came pain. I did not want to cause Philip and Beatrice suffering by coming between them. I did not believe it was possible to build my happiness on someone else's misery. So I did not answer the note. How could I? Beatrice was my friend.

I arrived at Peter's studio in Surry Hills for the first day of shooting, and realised I was going to have my work cut out for me.

The studio was on the top floor of a house in a street that had been condemned for demolition. The walls were lopsided and the veranda sagged, as if the dwelling knew its fate and was resigned to it. There was a brewery next door with a foundation stone marked 1851. The broken windows and chains across the doors suggested that it was condemned as well.

I climbed the narrow stairs to the third floor. Strains of Ravel's *Pavane for a Dead Princess* wafted through the door. I knocked and Peter opened it. The studio was large but crowded: canvases were stacked against each other; columns of phonograph records were piled against bookshelves crammed with not only books but crockery, photographs, candle stubs and beer bottles. On one shelf there was a set of stoneware mugs shaped into the faces of the British royal family. The floor was barely visible for the newspapers that lay strewn on it, as well as the brushes and paint tins. In the middle of the space a light dangled from the ceiling with bits of paper pinned to its shade. The air reeked of mould and nitrate of cellulose — the latter, I guessed, emanating from stored films. I had heard that if you put a match to a single frame of film you could blow your hand off. The studio was a bomb waiting to explode.

'Come, meet the actors,' said Peter, directing me towards the end of the studio where Hugh was sitting with two men and a woman. We passed the light with the bits of paper stuck to it and I saw that they were lists: shopping lists, exercise lists, aims-for-the-year lists. There was even a preproduction to-do list. For someone whose studio was so disorganised, Peter was obsessed with lists. I caught a glimpse of the items on the preproduction list: 'Meet with Adéla to discuss storyline'; 'Send crew location schedule'. Those things had never happened and I realised there was a difference between writing things down and doing them.

'This is Leslie Norris,' said Peter, introducing the oldest actor first.

'What a pleasure!' said Leslie, giving a flourish with his hand. His theatrical voice rattled my eardrums. He had a tic at the corner of his mouth and I avoided looking at his face, afraid that I would inadvertently adopt it.

Peter turned to the woman, who sniffed and screwed up her eyes, before looking in the direction of the other man, who he introduced as Sonny Sutton. Sonny resembled a weather-beaten Rudolph Valentino and the hand he used to push back his hair was blistered. 'Welcome to the set,' he said. His voice was as soft as Leslie's was loud.

I thanked the men for their welcome and glanced at the woman. Peter introduced her as Valerie Houson. She sniffed again. I thought she had a cold, until I smiled and she responded by pinching her lips together. I realised that the likely answer to anything I asked Valerie would be a sniff. Her face was caked in powder and she reeked of Coty perfume. I was the only other female in the room and I sensed that Valerie did not like the competition.

With the introductions out of the way, we followed Peter up a flight of rusty stairs to the flat roof of the building where a sitting room had been set up, with chintz lounges and maritime pictures on the walls. Stretched over the ceiling of the set was a layer of muslin. It billowed in the breeze like a wispy cloud. A faint whiff of hops drifted on the air.

Hugh saw me looking at the cover. 'The muslin diffuses the sunlight,' he explained. 'In Hollywood they use klieg lights. Here we use nature.'

'Does it give a different effect?' I asked.

'It's cheaper.' Hugh's expression was harsh but I sensed laughter under his breath.

'You're going to have to be tight with the schedule,' he told me, opening his camera case and setting up the tripod. I was mesmerised by the way he cradled the camera in his arm while balancing on one leg. 'Peter bought his film from a director who's going out of business. But he could only get 9000 feet to shoot this feature, and based on what Peter's done with his other films we're going to need nearly all of that which means we can't do too many takes.'

'What if I see a problem with the scene?'

'You can make a suggestion,' said Hugh, locking the camera onto the tripod. 'But it's Peter's call to do a retake.' He peered into the lens and tilted the camera upwards.

It seemed as though we were going to do a lot of single takes, so I assumed my next task was to make sure the scenes ran on time. 'I didn't receive a copy of the script,' I said. 'Do you have a spare one I could use?'

He lifted his head. 'Peter doesn't use a script,' he said. 'He explains what he wants his actors to do as he goes along.'

His mouth twitched and I felt an undercurrent of humour ripple beneath his tough exterior. I was seeing a different view of him here behind his camera. In the wide world, I had been his enemy: another person trying to extend him sympathy. But on the film set we were colleagues. Just as Esther sometimes gave me glimpses of the carefree girl she used to be, so I was discovering touches of Hugh that belonged to his former life. There was something else that was different about him that day too.

'Where's Giallo?' I asked. 'I thought you two were inseparable.'

'We usually are,' said Hugh, studying the scaffolding that was constructed around the set. 'But he can't stand Valerie. He keeps telling her to bugger off.'

'You taught him that?' I laughed. I found myself warming to Hugh despite his gruff manner.

When the actors were in costume, Peter asked if I could help Leslie with his make-up. I did not have much experience with cosmetics and found I enjoyed powdering Leslie's face and creating ghoulish circles under his eyes. Leslie checked the result in the mirror.

'You've made both sides of my face symmetrical,' he said. 'Not many people can do that.'

With Leslie's face close to mine, every time he spoke the bones in my ears jangled. I wondered how Klára would have coped with his penetrating voice.

We waited for Valerie who was applying her own make-up. She rubbed rouge on her cheeks and darkened her eyelids and brows before adding another layer of powder. Sonny came and sat next to me. Valerie followed his path in the mirror and a scowl creased her forehead.

'So you're from Europe?' Sonny asked. 'Adéla. It's a beautiful name.'

Valerie patted her face violently. A cloud of powder floated around her like dust in a windstorm. Peter and Hugh, who were discussing camera angles, glanced in her direction.

'Thank you for the compliment,' I told Sonny. 'I like your name too. It suits an Australian. The country has so much sunshine.'

'I'm ready now!' announced Valerie, knocking over her stool when she stood up. She leapt onto the set. 'You'd better hurry, Sonny,' she said. 'Time is money.'

My heart jumped to my throat when Hugh pulled himself up onto the scaffolding and scrambled across it to check the perspectives he wanted. He was dangerously close to the side of the building. If he fell, it was a long drop.

Leslie turned to where I was looking and followed Hugh's perilous trail with me.

'The wound he sustained in France wasn't serious,' Leslie whispered. 'But gangrene set in. They took his leg off here in Sydney after he'd languished in veterans' hospitals for months. Peter said a couple of times Hugh has gone missing and he's found him lingering outside Sydney Hospital, as if waiting for his leg to come back.'

The picture of Hugh standing outside the place where his life had been shattered tore at my heart. I wished there was some way he could find happiness again.

Once the camera had been set, Peter asked me to drop the needle on the gramophone. I did as he asked and Pachelbel's Canon in D floated on the air. He shouted instructions to Sonny and Valerie. 'That's right, Valerie,' he said. 'Yawn and stretch and climb into bed.'

Peter did not give me much guidance on my role as a script girl. I tried to keep my eye on the action but I could not help admiring Hugh's camera technique. He had an extraordinarily steady hand to crank the camera as evenly as he did. After the first take, I realised watching him was more engaging than the picture we were filming. The story was about a newly married couple who move into a house where a man was murdered ten years before. The ghost returns to demand revenge. A series of events leads to the murderer being found and brought to justice, the ghost departing in peace and the young couple being able to sleep at night undisturbed. I inwardly scoffed, not only at the predictability of the plot but the ludicrousness of it. There was no justice for murder victims. Mother was proof of that.

By the end of the first week of filming, I was so bored that Klára had to wake me up in the mornings by whistling in my ear. Sonny, I discovered, was not an actor but a stablehand from Royal Randwick Racecourse who Peter had talked into being in the film because of his good looks. To describe Sonny's acting as wooden would have been understating the fact. The way he moved his head and legs gave the impression that the rotation of his joints was a third that of ordinary people. He would have been perfect if we were making a horror picture about a stiff Egyptian mummy that had lain in its sarcophagus for thousands of years. Leslie was the opposite. He pulled grotesque faces and used flamboyant gestures to perform the simplest of actions. Whether he had to open a door or peer through a window, he rose on his toes or fell to his knees according to the emotion. Valerie, however, was the worst of all. She wore the same sour expression for everything from shock to ecstasy. 'Smile, Valerie,' Peter called out. 'Laugh with relief and hug Sonny.' Valerie responded to Peter's direction by feebly performing the actions required. He could have elicited more emotional depth from a cardboard doll.

I took still shots for the film's publicity and wondered how Peter had convinced investors to put money into such an unartistic and disorganised venture. Even the title was uninspiring: *The Ghost of Spooky Hill.* And this was Peter's third picture! Had the first two been any better?

Hugh's camera work, on the other hand, was brilliant. He could not do anything about the non-existent script and stilted acting, but the way he shot the picture transformed it. He filmed everything with a hint of slow motion, which gave the picture a surreal atmosphere that was not there on set. 'Most films are taken at sixteen frames per second,' he explained to me. 'But I'm cranking the camera at twenty-two to create an eerie mood.'

'Won't that use up more film?' I asked.

Hugh looked impressed by my question. 'I've already accounted for that. I shot Peter's last film this way.'

A few days later, when Hugh and I were waiting for Peter to give the actors their directions for the scene we were about to shoot, Hugh asked me if I wanted to look through his camera.

'What do you think of the composition?' he asked me.

Peter had a habit of placing his actors in a straight line and having them face towards the front of the set rather than each other. The way Hugh had composed the shot, setting the characters against the rear wall, they looked as if they were in a police line-up. Instead of being static, as Peter would have left it, the shot was atmospheric. I was puzzled why a talented cameraman like Hugh was working on this film.

I told him that I liked the shot and why. 'Not everyone would have picked that up, you know,' he said. 'You have a keen eye.'

Klára resorted to splashing cold water on my face the morning of the final day of shooting. I only had another eight hours to go, but the thought of spending them on a slow and badly performed endeavour was excruciating. Even Peter had appeared to be running out of steam the last few days, and he was supposed to motivate us. Besides that, the weather was turning colder and staying in bed was more enticing.

After some blowing in my ear and bed-rocking from Klára, I managed to wake up in time to catch the tram to Surry Hills. I was surprised when I arrived at the set to see everyone there except Peter.

'He wants you to direct today,' said Hugh.

'Me?'

Valerie sniffed and patted her hair.

'Peter's got the measles and Leslie starts on his new production tomorrow. We have three more scenes to go,' Hugh said.

It would have been more logical to have shot all the scenes performed on the set in one go. But for some reason — perhaps because he did not have a script — Peter had filmed everything in chronological order. We had filmed scenes inside the house, then gone to Macquarie Lighthouse for the cliff scenes and Rose Bay for some flashbacks. Now we were back at the set with the weather threatening rain.

'All right,' I said. 'I'll see what I can do.'

Valerie sniffed, Sonny stomped around, and Leslie pranced as if he were performing in a children's pantomime. I talked them through their performances before we shot each scene. Then I did something Peter had not: I made the actors rehearse.

'It leads to unnatural performances,' sniffed Valerie. It was the first sentence she had directed at me since we had been working on the picture.

I wanted to answer that she could not give a natural performance if she tried, but I needed her cooperation. So I coaxed, coddled and flattered her. Her acting turned out the same, but Sonny's and Leslie's performances improved.

'Good,' said Hugh at the end of the last take. 'You could direct a film of your own, you know.'

'I would love to,' I confided. 'But I'm not sure where I would find the money.'

'Finding money isn't my forte,' Hugh said, packing up his camera. 'But if you get it and need someone to film your picture, let me know.'

Although Hugh's manner was abrupt, his compliment meant a lot to me. My toes tingled at the thought of making a picture with a cameraman of his calibre. I had a vision of us creating something as legendary as DW Griffith's *Broken Blossoms*.

'That wouldn't be disloyal to Peter, would it?' I asked.

Hugh shook his head. 'I think this will be Peter's last film. I've seen the signs.' He must have noticed my confusion because he added, 'Peter changes his mind about what he wants to do every two or three years. First it was painting, then dog breeding and now it's making pictures. I wouldn't be surprised if tomorrow he takes up the piano and decides to compose music.'

'How does he afford it?'

A wry look came to Hugh's eyes. 'His family lives in Roseville. They back him.'

I thought of the messy studio downstairs and the camp bed Peter slept on. Was he acting the part of the poor artist?

At the end of the day's shooting we had a tea party with lamingtons. Hugh put a jazz record on the gramophone. Sonny clasped Valerie in his arms for the quickstep. She danced as she acted; stiffly. But she seemed to be enjoying herself. Her high-pitched laugh startled me; I had become accustomed to her gloomy temperament.

My mind drifted to Philip. I wondered what he was doing. He had not tried to contact me again. Perhaps he had seen the folly of it.

'You get along well with Hugh,' Leslie said to me. 'I've never seen him be friendly to a woman before. He hates them.'

I remembered the hostile way Hugh had stared at me at the Vegetarian Café and marvelled myself at how his attitude towards me had changed. 'Why?' I asked.

Leslie took a sip of tea. 'He used to be a champion tennis player, you know. He didn't want to go and fight. He thought it was a useless war that had nothing to do with this country. But his fiancée's mother handed him a white feather. Then, when he ended up without a leg, she suggested his fiancée marry someone else.'

* * *

The day of Klára's concert, my heart raced all morning. Was Philip still coming to the concert as he had promised Klára? I knew it was best if he stayed away, but I longed to see him. I was pacing the floor in the parlour when Uncle Ota came home. His hours at the cinema were erratic and he often took a nap at home before lunch. It was only when he walked into the room and I saw the frown on his face that I realised something was wrong.

'I've received a letter from Doctor Holub,' he said, reaching into his pocket and unfolding a piece of paper.

I stared at the letter in Uncle Ota's hand. 'What did he say?'

'Miloš has left for America.'

I sank down onto the couch. It was two years since Klára and I had arrived in Australia. 'He's looking for us, isn't he?'

Uncle Ota bit his lip. 'Miloš has told clients it's a business trip to find suppliers of oak wood, but we can guess its real purpose. Doctor Holub says Miloš has appeared in public with his mistress. Perhaps she won't marry him unless he secures a fortune.'

My skin prickled. Mother had bought Miloš a partnership in a successful firm but it was not enough for paní Beňová. 'Secure a fortune': what a euphemism, I thought. It meant to get rid of us.

'We are not there,' I said. 'What do you think will happen when he can't find us?'

'America is a vast land. Even if you were there, it would be like looking for a needle in a haystack. Whatever he hopes to achieve, it has given us time.'

'Did Doctor Holub say anything about Aunt Josephine?' I asked.

A smile softened the strained look on Uncle Ota's face. 'Yes,' he said. 'He has included a note from her.'

He handed me a piece of blue paper. My eyes filled with tears when I recognised my aunt's handwriting. She wrote that she thought of us every day and that she would soon be visiting Mariánské Lázně, a spa town, and would write to us properly from there.

'I wish I could tell her what I am doing with my photography,' I said.

Uncle Ota placed his hand on my wrist. 'We will find a way to do that,' he promised.

Uncle Ota and I agreed to keep the content of Doctor Holub's letter to ourselves. There was no need to alarm the others, especially Klára, who was looking forward to performing that afternoon. She twirled in front of the mirror in the sapphire gown Ranjana and I had made her until she was dizzy. When she walked out onto the stage in it, with an orchid corsage and her hair softly waved, she was breathtaking. Klára did not look like my little sister any more, she was too sophisticated. In the past year she had grown willowy — all arms and legs and a long torso. I recalled the previous night when we were in the kitchen together preparing dinner. Uncle Ota was in the habit of stacking the plates on the top shelf, which I could not reach. 'Where's the stool?' I had asked, looking under the bench. I turned to see Klára on her tiptoes taking down the plates for me.

I listened to Klára play and willed myself not to look around the auditorium for Philip. I thought of the first time I had heard the concerto in Prague. Father had taken us to the concert hall before he left for the war. The hall was different from the Conservatorium's auditorium with its stark white walls and green chairs. I closed my eyes and remembered the feast of Art Nouveau trimmings, the stained-glass windows and the sculptures. I imagined sinking into its velvet chairs and the warmth of the chandeliers dangling from the ornate ceiling. If Father had not been killed, Miloš would never have come into our lives and we would all still be together. The thought made me sad and I opened my eyes and turned my attention back to the performance. The Grieg Concerto suited Klára's style. The structure was simple and repetitive but Klára and her classmates played each movement with such passion it was difficult to believe that the oldest of them was only sixteen. When they finished the final movement with ease, the audience stood up and filled the auditorium with the sound of applause. I forgot myself and looked in the direction of the dress circle. Philip was sitting there with Robert and Frederick. Beatrice was not with them.

I barely heard Mendelssohn's violin concerto or Berlioz's *Symphonie Fantastisque* after that.

At the party given afterwards, I trembled when Philip approached us with Robert and Frederick. My heart thumped so loudly I was surprised nobody else seemed to hear it.

'Miss Rose, you were marvellous,' Robert gushed to Klára. 'The strongest artist in a program of fine artists. What a gift to our country that you have come here!'

Klára blushed with the praise. 'Thank you very much.'

I introduced Klára to Robert and explained to her that he was a guest lecturer at the Conservatorium of Music. I was aware of Philip's eyes on me.

'My orchestrion has finally arrived,' said Robert. 'I would very much like to have you both to an afternoon tea to christen it.'

'We would be honoured,' I told him.

I could not bring myself to look in Philip's direction, although I felt him lingering next to Robert. I turned away and caught Frederick eyeing my new dress, a pink chiffon gown with a layered skirt.

'I like the way the waistline is higher than the current fashion,' he said, circling me. 'You look like a ballerina. It's a flattering style for a petite woman.'

I smiled, but thought that Frederick had a funny way of giving a woman a compliment. He was like a mechanic looking over a car.

Ranjana and Uncle Ota, who had been talking with Klára's teacher, joined us. No sooner had I introduced them to Robert than a waiter weaved his way around the room ringing a bell.

'Time for us to leave,' said Robert.

'But it's early,' said Frederick, inspecting his watch. 'Who can listen to stirring music then just go back to the office?'

'Exactly,' agreed Robert. 'But they need the hall for the Conservatorium students to practise.'

Frederick turned to Uncle Ota. 'Would you and your family care to stroll around the Botanic Gardens with us. The weather is magnificent.'

Ranjana glanced at Uncle Ota. Frederick's effort to be cordial surprised her. But it was hard to look past the red pockets and lapels of his suit.

'My wife and I must get to the cinema for the evening session,' Uncle Ota told him. 'But please accompany Klára and Adéla for an hour or so.'

'We'd be delighted,' said Robert.

The afternoon was sunny with a gentle breeze rising up from the harbour. The gravel of the path crunched beneath our feet. We walked towards the teahouse where Robert had suggested we celebrate Klára's performance with vanilla ice-cream.

'That's exactly what we should do,' Philip said, his eyes briefly meeting mine. 'Klára has done more than triumph in music. She has triumphed in life!'

The table in the café was small and everyone apologised to each other when we bumped knees while taking our seats. Robert and Klára shared stories about Indian musical instruments. Klára told the men about Uncle Ota's collection, including a string instrument called a sarangi on which she and Uncle Ota had somehow worked out how to play a Bulgarian folk dance.

Philip was sitting so near to me that I could feel the warmth of his body penetrating the air between us. His fingers lingered near my teacup. I experienced everything with a heightened consciousness: the smoothness of the ice-cream, the raspberry scent of the tea, the polished wooden table under my wrist. In all the pangs I had suffered thinking about Philip, I could never have imagined the sweetness of being together.

After the ice-cream, we continued our walk through the Gardens along the path to the ponds. A child ran past, chasing a ball that was gathering momentum as it rushed down the hill towards the water. Frederick and Robert sped after it, with Klára, her concert dress hitched up to her knees, after them. Philip slipped his arm through mine. 'Come,' he said.

I hardly noticed where he was leading me until we stood in a grove of trees sheltered from the sight of the others. He grabbed my hands and we clung to each other like two frightened children. His eyes searched my face. The breeze blew through the trees and rustled my dress and hair. Philip threw his arms around my waist and his lips swept over my face in search of mine. I felt delirious, as if I were sinking into a dream. But I woke from it with a start.

'No, stop!' I said, pushing him away. 'Beatrice. You're engaged now.'

Philip's eyes flickered. 'Perhaps now that she has finally agreed, it's me who's not sure.'

I swallowed. 'Why do you say that?'

'When I'm with you, I feel things I don't with her. I'm engaged to the wrong woman.'

Since that day in the car, whenever I thought about Philip I tried to imagine that Beatrice was his sister. I was happiest when I could abandon myself to such fantasies. But fantasies could not become real.

'Am I frightening you, Adéla?' Philip asked, his voice unsteady. 'Or do you feel it too?'

If it was love he was feeling, then my heart was burning with it. I saw now that the flame had been ignited the first time I had met him in his cramped office and had grown steadily ever since. Now it was like a forest fire, in danger of engulfing everything.

'Yes,' I stammered. 'I love you. I love everything about you. But I don't want you to break off your engagement. Not unless you are sure.'

'I am sure,' he said, stepping towards me.

I rejected his embrace. 'No, don't see me for a month,' I told him. 'Be only with Beatrice. If you still feel the same way then I will see you, but not before then.'

I heard the excited voices of Klára and the others returning from the pond. I rushed out of the grove to meet them. The boy was on Robert's shoulders, his rescued ball in his hands. Frederick was helping Klára, whose shoes were slipping on the grass, back up the hill.

Philip brushed his fingers down my back, then moved a step away.

Frederick drove us home, along with Robert, because Philip had to return to Broughton Hall for the evening rounds. Once we were in the house, I wanted nothing more than to take off my dress and disappear under the bedcovers. I was about to run up the stairs when Klára put her hand on my arm. She was too astute not to have guessed the cause of my distraction.

'You're in love with Doctor Page, aren't you?' she said.

'God help me,' I told her. 'He is engaged to his childhood sweetheart. She is a wonderful person. I don't want to hurt her. I don't know what to do.'

Klára took a step towards me. There was love in her eyes but I did not feel I deserved it.

'I can't blame Philip for falling in love with you,' she said. 'Who couldn't? And you are well suited.'

'But Beatrice?'

Klára looked away and nodded. She was at as much of a loss as I was about the answer to that problem.

Uncle Ota screened *The Ghost of Spooky Hill* at Tilly's Cinema. The audience booed it so much that it only ran for two nights. The curtains and the tablecloth on the set kept flapping, and in one climactic scene I was caught in the frame with the slate in my hand. The redeeming points were that Peter did not seem to mind the audience's reaction and that Hugh's cinematography was outstanding. If Hugh could get a start on one quality film, then he would have a magnificent career ahead of him. But there were few professional directors willing to give a one-legged cameraman a chance.

One day I received a note from Hugh asking me to meet him at the Vegetarian Café the following afternoon. When I arrived he was sitting in his usual booth with Giallo on his shoulder.

'Hello, pretty!' said Giallo, lifting his claw to scratch his head.

'Where did he learn that?' I asked Hugh. 'Is that what you say to him?'

'No,' said Hugh, almost smiling. 'He just knows what I'm thinking.'

I laughed, pleased to see Hugh was in a good mood. I was not so vain as to think he was flirting with me. I was sure I was the only woman he could say that sort of thing to because he felt safe with me.

We ordered cold milk and cheese sandwiches. When they arrived, Hugh spread his hands on the table. 'I've got good news for you,' he said. 'Yet another Australian production company has gone to the wall and I managed to persuade the assistant director to give me some end-of-reel pieces of film. I've got about six or seven minutes' worth. Enough for a decent short film. I can shoot something for you if you come up with a tight script.'

'Truly?' I asked, almost jumping out of my seat with joy. 'You want to work with me?'

I was over the moon that Hugh had remembered the conversation we'd had about making a picture together. He seemed as pleased as I was by the unexpected windfall.

'The only problem will be the developing and editing,' he said. 'That can be expensive.'

'I can probably cover the development for a short film,' I told him. 'And my aunt can do the editing if you show her how.'

Hugh raised his eyebrows.

'Quite often the films we get at the cinema are damaged. Ranjana has to cut and splice all the time,' I told him. 'She's good at it.'

'Well then, you just need actors now.'

'Oh, I have those,' I said. 'I think it's time you met my family.'

My good fortune in finding a talented cameraman and a supply of film was a welcome distraction from thinking about Philip.

I had told him not to see me for a month but found myself fretting that I had not heard from him. Perhaps he had forgotten me and was busy planning his wedding. That would be better for everybody, but the idea vexed me so much that one afternoon, on my way to the cinema, I did not look where I was going and was almost run over by a tram. In the end I decided the only solution was not to allow myself to think about Philip at all.

I sat with Esther's old typewriter under the silver gum and wrote a short film about a picnic where a boy sees a bunyip but nobody believes him. Uncle Ota and Klára agreed to act in the picture, while Esther took on the role of script girl and Ranjana offered to help with the catering. The boy was to be played by Mr Tilly's nephew, Ben.

It took us two days to make the film. Uncle Ota was a natural actor, but Klára stole the show. In one scene she was sitting on the beach with Ben. She had not noticed that the camera was rolling and she was telling him about Mister Rudolf. Her animated facial expressions and Ben's delight were magic. When Klára glanced at the camera and saw that Hugh was filming, she brought her hand to her cheek and smiled. Her face lit up with an incandescent beauty.

'You were right,' said Hugh, when we took a short meal break before moving the camera. 'Your family are actors.'

Everyone sat down on a picnic blanket to eat the sandwiches that Ranjana had prepared. I noticed that Esther was sneaking glances in Hugh's direction. There were tears in her eyes. Hugh and Esther's fiancé would have been about the same age. Her pity would irritate Hugh if he became aware of it. I diverted his attention to Giallo, who had moved himself to Thomas's shoulder.

'Rather good,' Thomas said to Giallo, pointing at the harbour. He was starting to speak in short phrases and in a mix of Czech and formal English.

'Hiccup!' Giallo cackled.

'Hiccup!' agreed Thomas.

Ranjana burst into laughter. 'God help us! My son is being taught to speak by a bird!'

'Oh well,' said Uncle Ota. 'Not everyone can boast of a child fluent in English, Czech, Marwari and Cockatoo!'

Raymond Longford's film *The Blue Mountains Mystery* was scheduled to screen at Tilly's Cinema in September. Uncle Ota suggested that we premiere my film as a short teaser before it. But in order to get it on the program, we had to edit it quickly.

Ranjana, Hugh and I sat up after the last picture session each night for a week to cut and splice the film in the projection room. I'd had no idea that a six-minute picture could be so time-consuming, and now understood why the editing of a feature film sometimes took months.

'It's three o'clock in the morning,' I said during one session, looking at my watch.

Hugh had a part-time job in a studio the following day so I told him to go home. There were only the final intertitles to be added and Ranjana and I could finish the edit in the morning. When we returned home, Ranjana's eyes were drooping with exhaustion.

'Would you like a cup of tea?' I asked her.

She shook her head. 'I'm going to check on Thomas then go to bed,' she said.

I was physically tired but my brain was racing. I was hungry too. I walked into the kitchen and switched on the light. I jumped when I saw Esther sitting there.

'It was the war, wasn't it?' she asked, pushing back her hair. 'That's how he lost his leg.'

It was four in the morning. Esther was usually in bed by ten. She had been waiting up for me.

I told her what I knew of Hugh's story. When I reached the part about being found outside Sydney Hospital, she rubbed her thumbs together but said nothing.

The following morning, Ranjana and I rose early to complete the editing before the first morning session. Esther came with us to catch up on the book-keeping. It was a chilly morning and I wound my scarf over my head while we waited for the tram.

'It wouldn't have made any difference to me if Louis had come home without his legs,' Esther suddenly announced. 'I still would have loved him.'

The tram arrived and we double-checked the bags we were carrying to make sure we left nothing behind. Esther slipped the strap of her satchel over her shoulder. I blinked. There was the butterfly resting on her arm. Esther's eyes met mine. I turned away, not wanting to upset her all over again about not being able to see the butterfly.

Trying not to think of Philip was like trying to unlearn to ride a bicycle. I could go a few hours without dwelling on our situation, but the postman's whistle always triggered my thoughts in his direction. It was wrong to pine for Philip but I secretly hoped that he would send me a letter.

Then a month to the day that we had talked in the Botanic Gardens, Philip appeared on our doorstep wearing a pair of plus fours and a vest over a white shirt.

'I promised to take Adéla to the National Park to photograph the rock formations,' he explained to a surprised Uncle Ota. 'Has she forgotten?'

'Indeed, I think she has,' said Uncle Ota, inviting Philip into the house. Klára, who was finishing her breakfast before leaving for school, sent me a glance.

'Adéla,' said Uncle Ota, 'you'd better hurry and get ready. The National Park is a few hours' drive away.'

I was as embarrassed as if I had actually forgotten the arrangement, although we had never made such plans. Philip grinned at me. Klára followed me to the bedroom.

'Bring a swimming costume,' Philip called after me. 'The lagoon is sheltered. It should be quite warm today.'

I quickly changed into a loose dress while Klára packed a towel, sunhat and swimsuit into a bag. Who went swimming in winter? But I did not think too much about that. Philip's appearance had answered the question that had been hanging over me for a month.

'I don't know what to do,' I said to Klára.

'Yes, you do,' she replied. She took my hand. 'Listen to your heart. Philip is a good person and you are too. Neither of you will do anything reckless. But you have to do what is honest — even if someone else won't like it.'

Philip's car rattled along the dirt track into the park. I stared up at the towering gum trees. 'I'll take you to Wattamolla beach,' he said, smiling. 'It's my favourite spot in the park.'

The menthol scent of the gums and the smell of damp earth were intoxicating. I glanced at Philip. He looked fresh and carefree. Had he told Beatrice? Had she accepted his decision gracefully? My heart leapt with hope as each mile passed. Philip reached across the seat and squeezed my hand. A thrill of joy ran through me.

He brought the car to a stop and we strolled along a track past banksias and cabbage tree palms to a clearing. I could see a sandy beach and the ocean below us. The beach was deserted except for a lone fisherman.

'Put your swimming costume on,' said Philip, turning his back to me and tugging off his vest and shirt. He undid his belt and slipped his trousers and underwear down his legs and kicked them off. I blushed at the sight of his buttocks, more athletic than I had expected from a doctor. He pulled on his swimming trunks and I realised, out of modesty, he had intended for me to turn my back to his while we changed. I spun around and undid my dress and stockings, pulling my costume up my legs and over my shoulders. When I turned back, Philip had already climbed out on the rock ledge. He beckoned me to follow him and offered his hand. I took it and inched after him on the slippery rocks to the cascading waterfall.

'It's safe,' he told me. 'We can jump from here into the lagoon. Ready?'

I flew with him into the air and plunged into the lagoon. The freezing water sent goose bumps over my skin. I broke the surface and looked for Philip. He surfaced a second later, pushing his hair from his face and swimming towards me.

'Bracing?' he said.

'Not at all,' I laughed. 'I've swum in colder. I'm a Czech, you know.'

I saw that he was not the same Doctor Page of Broughton Hall. Droplets of water shone on his sun-kissed skin. He swam towards the sandbank and I followed him.

'Wait here,' he said, when we emerged from the water. 'I'll go back and get our things.'

I watched him scramble up the slope to retrieve our clothes and bags. He returned and spread out a blanket for us to sit on. The sun warmed us and the sound of the water lapping against the rocks made me sleepy.

'So what have you been doing with yourself this past month?' he asked.

I told him about the bunyip picture.

He leaned back on his elbows. 'I should like to see it,' he said. 'I can tell from your photographs that you're talented. Do you like it here in Australia?'

I cast my eyes over the rugged cliffs and the cascading waterfall. Klára was not the only one of us sensitive to the appeal of natural beauty. 'Very much,' I said. 'It is spectacular.'

'I was brought up to think of England as "home",' Philip said. 'My children's books were filled with hedgehogs and badgers. But when I arrived in London for my studies I longed for gum trees, kangaroos and beaches.'

We laughed. Then I remembered Prague. The cobblestoned streets and the markets. My thoughts darkened.

'Does it bother you,' Philip asked, 'to think that your mother's killer may never be brought to justice?'

'It did at first,' I told him. 'But if I keep thinking of it, I will go mad. I concentrate on what I can do, and that is to help Klára through music school and safely to the age of twenty-one.'

Philip nodded and looked out to the ocean. His face twitched. 'My mother was in our house in Bowral,' he said. 'Father and I were out riding when a flame jumped out of the fireplace and started to burn the floor. The house was a pioneers' home and was ablaze within minutes. The servants managed to escape and formed a chain to the dam to try and save it, but Mother was trapped in her room on the top floor. My father and I saw the flames from two miles away. We galloped home but everything was gone except a staircase and the chimney. For months afterwards I imagined my mother's screams in my sleep.'

A seagull squawked overhead and we looked up at the blue sky and the clouds moving across it. There was nothing we could say to each other about our mothers' deaths. But we knew that the other one understood. I felt that I had known Philip all my life, and our conversations were simply to fill in the details.

'Is that why you became a psychiatrist?' I asked eventually. 'To help people with bad memories?'

The torment disappeared from Philip's face. He smiled. 'My father would be dismayed if he knew that he inspired me to study psychiatry. He wasn't always so serious. He became nervous after Mother's death and now clings to familiar things, fearful that they will change.'

'Life changes all the time, doesn't it?' I said. 'You have to adapt yourself to it.'

Philip took my hand. My skin tingled with his touch. It seemed the most natural thing in the world to be sitting in this beautiful place and holding his hand.

'Does Beatrice know?' I asked.

He shook his head. 'Helen has an inoperable tumour. Beatrice doesn't quite believe it. It's going to be hard for her. She and her mother are very close. We will have to be patient. I don't like to sneak around behind her back any more than you do, but I have to pick my timing.'

'Then you are sure?' I asked him. 'About us.'

Philip clasped my hand tighter and pressed it against his chest. 'I love you, Adéla.'

The disappointment I had felt that he had not yet told Beatrice disappeared with those words. Tears filled my eyes.

Philip looked down the beach. The fisherman had gone. 'Come,' he said, helping me to my feet.

He picked up the picnic blanket and moved it to a shady spot set back in the trees. When he had spread it out, we lay down and he pulled me to him and kissed me on the lips. His mouth was warm and velvety. His kisses swept down my neck. I stared up at the glimmering trees. I was a virgin and could never have imagined the ripples of pleasure his kisses sent through me. I ran my palms over his smooth, damp skin and felt the shiver of his muscles.

Philip knelt back and we fell silent, with only the sound of the rolling ocean and the birds about us. I wanted him to kiss me again and lifted myself towards him. But my hand caught the edge of my costume and the strap slipped down and exposed my breast. I was too mortified to think about covering myself up.

Philip lifted his hand to my breast and brushed his fingers over the nipple. My shame turned to desire. He withdrew his hand quickly. I wanted him to touch my breast again and kiss it the same way he had kissed my face. But he tugged my costume back over my shoulder.

'I want you more than anything in the world,' he said, his voice trembling. 'But we must wait for the right time. I want our love to be special.'

I sat up and he pressed his cheek to mine. His hair smelt of the ocean.

'We must marry first,' he said. 'I want to give you a child. I want it all to be perfect.'

'Yes,' I said.

Everything was perfect. Almost.

THIRTEEN

I awoke the next morning with the sun making lacework on my arms through the curtains. I wanted to lie like that for hours, relishing the memory of the previous day with Philip. But Esther's voice at the door brought me to my senses.

'A note came for you,' she said. 'It was delivered by a chauffeur.'

I clambered out of bed, expecting something from Philip. I was discomforted to receive a message from Beatrice.

> *Dear Adéla,*
> *It has been too long since I saw my lovely friend.*
> *I am sorry I have been out of touch, but my wedding*
> *plans and trip to Europe have been on hold as*
> *Mother's health has taken a turn for the worse. I*
> *miss my walks through the city with her. We seemed*
> *to discover so many curiosities that it was my*
> *greatest pleasure. I wondered if you might*

accompany me one day in her place? Soon? I miss
your smiling face.
   Your friend,
   Beatrice

The tone of the letter suggested that Beatrice was being brave. She sounded as though she needed a friend. I remembered Edith had not come to the luncheon because she was staying in the country. I was not the right person to comfort Beatrice, but what could I do? She needed someone. I called her from the cinema and arranged to meet her in the city in the afternoon.

'How good of you to come!' said Beatrice, rising from her bench in Hyde Park where we had agreed to meet.

She was drawn in the face but her eyes were as full of life as ever. She launched into a review of the book she had been reading while waiting for me. 'It's about four young people at turning points in their lives,' she explained. 'In some ways it's horribly depressing because the two women subjugate themselves to the men, but it's also ripping good reading.'

Beatrice and I linked arms and headed towards the stores. She was in a better state of mind than I had been expecting.

'I am very sorry to hear your mother is unwell,' I told her.

'It breaks my heart that I can't do anything for her,' she said. 'Old Doctor Page came this morning and gave her a dose of morphine to ease the pain.'

I lowered my eyes. What could I say?

Beatrice nudged me. 'Don't cry for us, Adéla. You have a tranquillity about you that is cheering. Besides, it's not all bad news. Philip might hurry up and set a date for our wedding.'

My pulse quickened. I wondered if she would feel it through my arm. I had hoped that Beatrice and I could avoid the subject of Philip.

We strolled along Elizabeth Street and a dress in a shop window caught Beatrice's eye.

'Look at that glorious dress!' she cried, pointing to a coral beaded sheath. 'Isn't it lovely?'

The dress was pretty but unsuitable for Beatrice. The colour would clash with her red hair and the style would accentuate her lack of a figure.

'Should I buy it?' she asked.

The dress on the other mannequin in the window was a raspberry colour that would set off Beatrice's hair. The wide V-shape of the neckline would give her a bust. A 'flattened' chest was the fashion, but only worked on women with breasts to begin with. I sensed that Beatrice was looking to lift her spirits with a new dress rather than having her heart set on the coral one so I said, 'Both these dresses are nice. Why don't you try them on and then decide which looks best?'

Beatrice grabbed my arm. 'Good idea!'

For a few moments, while we lost ourselves in trying on sumptuous dresses, I could almost put aside the fact that Beatrice was the obstacle to my being with Philip. I tried on a silk chiffon gown, the rose colour of which flattered my hair and eyes. The shop's prices were too high for me but I decided I would choose a style I liked and make something similar for the premiere of my bunyip picture. Ranjana was a skilful beader and we could decorate the dress together.

'That dress is lovely on you,' said Beatrice, stopping to admire me. 'You're like a little doll.' Sadness flickered across her face.

'What is it, Beatrice?'

'You remind me of my friend. Margaret,' she said, sitting down in a chair by the mirror. 'She died in Egypt. We were nurses together in the war.'

'I didn't know you were a nurse,' I said.

Beatrice grimaced and ran her hand through her unruly hair.

I was in awe of Beatrice. She had more courage than I had imagined. I wondered what Philip saw in me that he did not find in her. She had travelled and served in the war. I had not done anything significant.

'Well, come on then,' Beatrice said, slapping her knees and drawing herself out of her melancholy. 'Let's get this dress.'

After Beatrice had purchased the raspberry dress, we ate lunch at a restaurant in Market Street before making our way to Chinatown. Beatrice steered me away from the headless ducks on hooks and crabs in tanks in the food stores and led me to a street lined with curiosity shops. 'This is the place I love best,' she said. 'It's a treasure chest.'

We entered a shop piled with brocade cushion covers, drawstring handbags, embroidered slippers, parasols and lanterns. Beatrice stopped to admire a green cheongsam on a hanger.

'Tell me about Egypt,' I said.

She bowed her head and leaned against a hatstand. 'Philip was stationed in Egypt as a medical officer,' she said, looking back at me. 'I went there to join him. I don't think any of us were prepared for the carnage. One day the ambulance I was driving to the hospital was shelled. Margaret was killed and I was shredded with shrapnel. When they got me to the hospital no one expected me to survive. "I promise to live if you will marry me," I said to Philip, before they put me under.'

'So he promised?' I asked, trying to mask the tremble in my voice.

Beatrice smiled dreamily. 'I've been running around the world looking for excitement, but that's because I knew when the time was right I would settle down with Philip. When Mrs Page died, it was like losing my own mother. Even when we were children, she always said, "You'll take care of my Philip if anything happens to me, Beatrice, won't you?"' Her face turned serious. 'I will never break that promise. Never.'

We were silent for a moment, weighing up the gravity of her vow.

'Is that why you joined up with the nurses when Philip was posted to Egypt?' I asked.

Beatrice nodded. Her voice dropped to a whisper and she said, 'Lately, Philip has been looking distracted. I'm afraid I've kept him waiting too long ... I'm afraid that there's somebody else.'

A sickening feeling twisted my stomach. I clutched a row of shirts to hold myself upright.

'Dear God, Adéla!' said Beatrice, grabbing my arm. 'You're as white as a sheet. Here, let me help you.'

'It's the lack of air,' I said, tugging at my collar.

It was not the air, it was the guilt. Only the day before I had kissed Beatrice's fiancé on a secluded beach.

'It is stuffy in here,' agreed Beatrice, leading me to the door.

In the next street was a French café, its blue tablecloths and baskets of bread incongruous with the calligraphy of the signs of the stores next to it and the smell of bamboo and rotten fish that permeated the air. We sat down at a table near the window. Beatrice ordered some water and a pot of tea. Despite the mildness of the weather I shivered.

'Maybe you've got influenza?' said Beatrice. 'Let me get you a taxi.'

'No, truly, I'm fine, Beatrice. It was just in there. In that shop.'

I hoped that she might change the subject from Philip. I tried to distract her with questions about her travels in England and on the Continent, but each answer returned in some way to him.

'I gave myself to Philip in Egypt,' she said.

The blood drained from my face. I should have been embarrassed at such a shared intimacy but instead I was hurt. I thought about how Philip had restrained himself with me. 'I want you more than anything in the world,' he had said. I was shocked that he had been intimate with Beatrice. The only solace was that Philip and Beatrice had become lovers before he had met me. A sensation I could not explain passed over me. I glimpsed something inside of Beatrice that I had not noticed before; as if another person existed behind her freckles and energetic manner. But the feeling soon faded and everything seemed normal again.

After an hour had passed, I deemed that I had been polite enough and excused myself. I wanted to get away from Beatrice. I felt cold-blooded knowing that Philip was in love with me, and not her. I told Beatrice that I had to help Uncle Ota at the cinema.

'Goodbye, Adéla,' she said, kissing my cheek. 'I'm glad you could come out with me today.'

'Goodbye, Beatrice,' I replied.

She made no reference to seeing me again. The oddness of that only occurred to me as I walked to the tram stop. She seemed innocent of the nature of my relationship with Philip, yet I had the distinct feeling that I had been given a warning.

When I arrived home, the sun had disappeared behind the clouds and the world looked grey. I wanted to run upstairs and collapse onto my bed. But when I approached the gate I found Uncle Ota on the front veranda with Frederick Rockcliffe. They both had a glass of beer in front of them and leant back in their chairs, looking relaxed.

What is he doing here? I thought. Frederick's boisterous manner was the last thing I needed.

Frederick jumped to his feet when he saw me.

'Mr Rockcliffe came by this afternoon to have his photograph taken by you,' Uncle Ota explained. 'I found out that he works for Galaxy Pictures so I decided to get a better deal for our cinema. He likes the idea of a night a week devoted to Australian films.'

Frederick pulled out a chair for me. We had never discussed taking his photograph and I was irritated that he had turned up without an appointment. But I did not want an argument. All I wanted was to find a way to extricate myself from the conversation so I could be alone.

'That's wonderful.' I sat down and tried not to stare at Frederick's purple bow tie. I did not believe what he had told Uncle Ota about approving of a night dedicated to local films. From the discussion at Beatrice's luncheon, I knew that Frederick represented an American company with American interests.

Klára walked out of the house with a tray of assorted nuts. Despite my effort to put a polite smile on my face she could tell something was wrong. She cocked her eyebrow as if to say, Are you all right? I answered her by lowering my eyes in a way that conveyed: We will talk about it later.

'Do you mind if I practise in the front room, Uncle Ota?' Klára asked. 'I don't want to disturb you and Mr Rockcliffe. But I have a piano examination tomorrow.'

I hoped Frederick would take the request as a prompt to leave. Instead, he answered as if the question had been directed to him. 'Not at all, Miss Rose. I'd be enchanted to hear you play again.'

Klára blushed with delight and returned to the house.

'Mr Rockcliffe has been telling me about opportunities to build cinemas on the south coast,' Uncle Ota said. 'The pictures are increasing in popularity but there aren't enough cinemas. They are watching picture shows in sheep fields and School of Arts halls.'

'This is apart from my interests with Galaxy Pictures,' said Frederick.

I wondered why he felt he had to explain that to me. What he did or did not do in accordance with Galaxy Pictures was no concern of mine.

Uncle Ota and Frederick spoke about opportunities in country towns but all I could hear were Beatrice's words in my head: 'Philip has been looking distracted. I'm afraid that there's somebody else.'

Frederick gestured towards the plate of nuts but I had no appetite. The sound of Klára's piano playing drifted on the air.

'What is that music?' he asked.

'The *Ritual Fire Dance* by Manuel de Falla,' I answered.

'Manuel de Falla,' Frederick repeated, shaping his vowels to imitate my pronunciation of the Spanish composer's name. 'It had some queer buzzing notes at the beginning, like a swarm of bees gathering to attack.'

I was amused by Frederick's description of the music. He was the one who had not wanted to go back to work after the Grieg Concerto because he had found it stirring. He did not use the terms someone familiar with classical music might, but I liked the fact that his responses, although raw, were sincere.

'It is from a ballet called *Love, the Magician*. There are gypsies and witchcraft,' I explained. 'A young woman is haunted by the jealous ghost of her deceased husband. The *Ritual Fire Dance* is to get rid of him.'

Frederick was taken aback. 'She tries to get rid of him?'

'He was cruel. She has a handsome young lover.'

Frederick ran his thumb over his knuckles. I had the impression that he was absorbing the information for use at a later date. He turned to Uncle Ota.

'You have talented nieces,' he said. 'A pianist and a photographer.'

I wondered where Frederick had gotten the idea of me taking his photograph. Had he seen some of my work at a socialite's house or had Philip shown him the portrait I had taken of him and his father? But to ask him might start another train of conversation, and I wanted to avoid that.

The aroma of Ranjana cooking dinner wafted from the house: turmeric, garlic and cinnamon. They were scents that never floated from the other houses on our street. For one tense moment I thought Uncle Ota might invite Frederick to stay to dinner, although I could not imagine him picking his way through vegetable kofta and *sag paneer*.

'If you come Thursday morning, I can take your photograph then,' I told Frederick, praying that he would take the hint from my voice that I was tired and he should go.

To my relief, he stood up. 'It will be a pleasure to be photographed by you, Miss Rose.'

We saw Frederick to the gate and watched him climb into his car. He waved after he started the engine. 'See you Thursday!'

I watched the car turn the corner and regretted the brusqueness with which I had spoken to him. He was brash but somehow polite, and despite the garishness of his suits he was not unattractive. It probably was not easy to be an

American in a culture that did not appreciate people speaking their minds.

I told Uncle Ota that I was not feeling well and asked Ranjana to excuse me from dinner. My bed was the most welcome spectacle of the evening. I pressed my face into the pillow and cried all the tears that I had been holding back. I felt cursed that I had met Philip when Beatrice was engaged to him. I turned over and stared at the ceiling. Laughter burst up from the dining room and I heard Thomas asking where I was. I could have been in Japan the way I felt; I was so removed from everyone else.

I longed to open my heart to Klára, but exhaustion got the better of me and I fell asleep before dinner was over and she came upstairs. I awoke at one o'clock in the morning with Klára asleep beside me. I watched her peaceful face, unable to make up my mind about whether I should wake her or not. Then I remembered that she had a piano examination and did not want to disturb her.

I slipped out of bed and padded down the hall to the upstairs sitting room. Uncle Ota had left the porch light on. In the glow of the lamp I saw Louis's ghost by the gate again. Just as before, he was wearing his military uniform and peering into the house. We are both on the outside of life, looking in now, I thought.

'So your uncle is a collector?' Frederick asked, when he arrived to have his picture taken. He was standing near the shelf with the African masks.

'My uncle gathered those pieces on his travels,' I told him. 'And now we have our own museum. That red and black mask is from the Congo. The tribal chiefs wear such masks when making sacrifices to their ancestors.'

Frederick picked up the resin mask and studied its carvings. I could not help but smile: Frederick was wearing a red and black checked suit. He replaced the mask on its hook and moved on to the bookshelves, which sagged under the weight of our collective library. He ran his fingers along the plays by Shaw and Ibsen and the volumes of Nietzsche.

'"The man of knowledge must be able to not only love his enemies but also to hate his friends,"' he said, quoting the German philosopher. He turned to me. 'Have you read all these?'

'My uncle read them on his voyages but I am familiar with them too,' I told him. 'And you, Frederick, do you read?'

I realised that I had called him Frederick instead of Mr Rockcliffe. I had picked up the habit of using Christian names from the Vegetarian Café and Beatrice. But he did not seem to mind.

A smile came to his face and he shook his head. 'I don't have the luxury of time to read books. But I make sure I keep the company of those who do.'

I remembered a conversation between my father and mother that I had overheard as a child. Father had described an acquaintance of theirs as a 'self-made' man. Gentlemen were supposed to despise men who had made their own money, but my father clearly admired him, just as Aunt Josephine respected women who earned their own living. Frederick Rockcliffe was a young man determined to lift himself up in the world.

I decided that his portrait should be in sharp focus and taken from below. There were two spaces in the parlour where I photographed those clients who did not wish to have their picture taken at home. The first was a corner with an armchair upholstered in pink brocade and a still life in a gold frame above it. That was where most society ladies chose to be photographed. The other space was against a stark white wall. It was there that I planned to photograph Frederick.

'Why not against the bookshelf,' he asked, when I showed him where I wanted him to sit.

His suit would clash with the décor so I wanted to keep the background simple. But I gave him a more diplomatic explanation. 'This portrait should be about you, not books — especially as you don't read them. Pretending to be something you are not doesn't show confidence.'

I knew that I had hit the right note when he smiled. He wanted to look powerful, not silly. My photograph would help him achieve that — and one day I would speak to him about his suits.

Frederick sat on the stool against the wall. 'Your uncle invited me to the premiere of your film,' he said. 'He gave it a glowing review and I trust his judgement. I can get it distributed for you.'

'It's only a short,' I told him.

'Cinemas need those as well, you know.'

I mulled over Frederick's offer while adjusting my camera. I wanted to make pictures and perhaps he could help me. But as the session continued, I decided working with him might be too difficult. He would not strike the simplest pose without questioning why he should do it. I asked him to turn his body while facing the camera and we ended up in a half-hour argument over it.

'It looks dishonest,' he said. 'Like I'm about to run away rather than fight something head-on.'

I appreciated that Frederick was aware of what he wanted but not his manner of getting it. He wore me out. I was adjusting the lights when he quoted Nietzsche again: '"No price is too high to pay for the privilege of owning yourself."'

I stood up and looked at him. 'Pardon?'

'That's my motto. Own yourself.'

The photographs I had taken would make Frederick look like his own man. It was interesting that we should have the same end in mind when our approaches to achieving it were so different.

'I think you'll be happy with the result,' I told him.

'I know I will,' he said, to my surprise. 'You know what you're doing.'

'When would you like to see the prints, Frederick?' I could not believe I had just called him by his Christian name again.

'For God's sake, call me Freddy,' he grinned. 'You sound like my mother when you call me Frederick.'

'Then you must call me Adéla,' I told him.

I was not comfortable to be on personal terms with Freddy, but there was nothing I could do about it. It was my own fault.

He reached into his pocket and pulled out a cigarette. 'I can drop by this Saturday and take you and Klára to the party.'

'What party?'

'Have you forgotten already? The one Robert is holding in honour of his orchestrion.'

In Prague, afternoon teas were intimate affairs with no more than a handful of guests gathered around a table spread with cakes and sandwiches. When Klára and I arrived with Freddy at Robert's house in Lindfield, 'intimate' did not describe the number of people spilling out onto the verandas of the shingle-roofed mansion, or standing on the lawn and tennis court. From the number of Packards, Bugattis and Delages parked outside the fence there must have been at least fifty guests. We stopped at the gate and I looked for Philip but could not see him. I had been unsettled by my conversation with Beatrice. Which one of us did he truly love?

'Welcome!' said Robert, rushing down the path towards us and opening the gate. 'Come in.'

Robert's garden reflected his elegant and quirky personality. The house was framed by a massive lilly-pilly tree. In its branches sat two red and green king parrots. The oak trees, although leafless because of winter, flickered shade across the lawn and the path to the house was bordered by lavender in bloom. The path was geometrically tiled with an emu silhouette motif. The theme continued at the end of it where a giant statue of the bird formed an archway with its legs. The air was fresh and without a trace of salt. The soil gave off a rich aroma, different from the rocky ground at Watsons Bay.

Freddy was called to join the game of croquet that was taking place on the lawn.

'Go on, be a gentleman,' Robert told him. 'I'll take care of Klára and Adéla.'

'I'm sorry,' Freddy said to us.

'An apology is not needed,' Klára replied.

I sensed Freddy's reluctance to leave us and wondered why. The players were young women. Perhaps he was more interested in Robert's orchestrion than I had assumed.

'Come and meet my mother and sister,' said Robert, guiding us towards the house. 'They are terribly shy. They encourage my parties but always disappear somewhere on their own. I'm sure they will find you non-threatening conversationalists.'

Mother would have loved this house, I thought: the polished jarrah floors, the winged chairs, the cream embossed wallpaper and tiled fireplaces. The interior had elements of an English house in its ceiling roses and picture rails, but it was light and airy and had a calming effect on the soul.

Robert directed us to the sitting room where two women with high foreheads and immaculately set hair were drinking tea from Royal Doulton cups.

'Mother, Mary, I'd like you to meet my friends,' Robert said. 'Miss Adéla and Miss Klára Rose.'

If Robert had not warned me that his mother and sister were shy, I might have been intimidated by the two stiff-postured women who looked back at us.

'Robert tells me that your aunt is an Indian,' Mrs Swan said.

'That is right,' I replied. I wondered if Mrs Swan was about to express her disapproval and worried about how I should respond. I liked Robert and did not want to embarrass him, but I was not going to have Ranjana belittled either.

Mrs Swan surprised me when she said, 'My late husband was stationed in India when we were first married. Some of my happiest memories are of Bombay.'

She was not comfortable with meeting new people, I could see that from the way her chin trembled when she spoke. But I was impressed by her graciousness.

Mary was not dashing like her brother, but had gentle eyes. 'And you are a pianist?' she said to Klára. 'Robert must show you his music room.'

'We are on our way there now,' Robert told her.

'Very well, you had better hurry. Do not leave the other guests alone too long, my dear,' his mother instructed him.

I sensed that Mrs Swan and Mary had shared all the conversation they felt comfortable with and were politely dismissing us.

Klára and I followed Robert down a corridor lined with paintings of thoroughbred horses until we came to a set of double doors.

Robert opened them and ushered us into a space the size of an ocean liner's dining suite. In the middle of the room was a Mason & Hamlin grand piano and a harpsichord. Musical instruments from around the world hung on hooks on the walls. I recognised a few instantly: gongs, gamelans, bagpipes and balalaikas. A long wooden flute ornately painted with a dot pattern lay on a shelf. I had seen something like it before. I remembered the documentary Doctor Parker had screened at one of our Tuesday nights. It was a didgeridoo. The main attraction in the room was not the orchestrion, which had been set up in one corner, but the pipe organ that took up an entire wall.

Klára rushed towards the instrument. 'Do you play?' she asked Robert.

'It's my passion,' he said. 'It's like having a full orchestra at my fingertips.'

Klára stood on her tiptoes and glanced from Robert to the organ. She was longing to hear him play but did not want to be rude by asking.

'What sort of music do you like?' I asked Robert, trying another tack.

He stepped up to the instrument and brushed his finger over the lower keyboard. 'Anything really. Sometimes traditional church music and other times I lose hours playing Broadway hits.'

The sinews in Klára's neck were stretched taut. 'You have to use your eyes, hands, feet and ears all at once, don't you?' she asked.

Robert sat on the stool. 'It's like a hike, a dance and a swim in a rough ocean made at the same time,' he said.

He poised his hands over the keys and began to play. Klára and I stepped back. I recognised Pachelbel's Canon in D major. I had heard the pipe organ played in church before but in Robert's music room the sound was colossal. The clamour of the party outside evaporated with each clear note. I imagined conversations coming to a stop and heads turning in the direction of the house as one by one the guests became awestruck by the music. The floor vibrated under our feet and the tambourines, castanets and cymbals on the walls rattled and jingled. I pictured Mrs Swan's Royal Doulton tea set tinkling to the pulse of the music. Robert tossed his head and pressed his lips together and played with boundless energy. I was so entranced by the richness of the music that I hardly noticed Klára take my hand until she squeezed it so tightly she crushed my fingers.

Robert played the final chord then lifted his hands from the keyboard, pausing a moment before turning to face us. I was about to compliment him on his wonderful recital when a familiar voice called out.

'There you are! I've been looking for you. But I only had to follow the music.'

I turned to see Beatrice and Philip in the doorway. Beatrice was wearing a sea-green dress with silk piping around the neckline. She looked stunning. Philip appeared relaxed in a white suit. Beatrice's engagement ring was still on her finger. Philip tried to catch my eye, but I averted my gaze.

Beatrice rushed forward to kiss me and to greet Klára. 'So here is the little sister at last,' she said, embracing her. 'Though not so little, she is almost as tall as me.'

'How's Aunt Helen?' Robert asked Beatrice.

Beatrice's smile faltered. 'She's a little better this morning, thank you. I didn't want to leave her but she insisted that she only needed her nurse today.'

Freddy arrived at the door and told us that afternoon tea had been laid out on the tables. 'You're fools if you linger,' he said. 'It's a feast.'

'Better go then,' said Robert with a laugh. 'The cooks have been at it since yesterday.'

We followed Robert out onto the veranda where long tables had been set with cucumber and watercress sandwiches, scones with jam and cream, strawberries dipped in chocolate, as well as every kind of cake imaginable. Klára lingered near Robert, fascinated by his knowledge of music. I was as astounded when I overheard him say that he was the only musical member of his family. 'My father was keen on sport. The Swans have always been athletes. I'm a kind of aberration.'

Beatrice recognised the women from the croquet game and showed them her ring. Philip stood by her side. I took the opportunity to escape into the garden. He still loves her, I told myself, feeling the ache in my heart.

I strode across the lawn behind the cypress hedge and towards the tennis courts. The further away I moved from the party, the more relieved I felt. The garden had three tiers. The lowest was natural bushland, but on the second was a maze. I was drawn to it out of curiosity and a desire to disappear.

'To find your way in and out of a maze, all you have to do is brush your fingers along the left-hand side of the hedge,' Father had explained to me once when we walked through a maze at a summer party in Mělník.

I reached out and let my fingertips glide over the velvety leaves. A sense of calm fell over me as I progressed along the path moving in lines towards the centre. Statues and urns marked the pilgrimage. I arrived at the centre and found a pond with carp swimming in it and a stone bench.

I sat down and closed my eyes, turning my face to the sun. The throbbing in my heart quietened and I experienced fleeting seconds of peace.

I heard footsteps on the gravel and opened my eyes.

'Adéla?'

Philip stood before me. I thought I must be dreaming and reached out to touch his sleeve to see if he was real. He had beads of sweat on his upper lip. Did people perspire in dreams?

He sat down next to me. From the look in his eyes I could have imagined that he was in love with me. I could have told myself that he had followed me through the maze at the risk of being seen because he wanted to kiss me. But I refused to believe any of these things. I did not want to be hurt again.

'Adéla,' he said, touching my hand.

I snatched it away. 'Don't!' I said, standing up and moving towards the pond. 'You're engaged. To Beatrice.'

'I'm going to break off our engagement,' he said, following me. 'Today. After Beatrice and I leave. I wanted to tell her this morning, so that she wouldn't show off her ring, but she was running late and it couldn't be helped.'

'Beatrice says you became lovers during the war and that she gave herself to you. But you told me that we should wait.'

Philip was quiet, then said: 'The war ... it changed everything. We were young but we didn't know if we would be alive the next day. We did a lot of things without prudence, without thinking through the consequences properly.' He looked at me and smiled. 'It is better to wait, Adéla, believe me. Love is sacred.' He rubbed his hands. 'If I had waited, things would be less complicated now with Beatrice.'

'You expected to marry her, I suppose. You didn't think that would change.'

Philip nodded sadly. 'Yes, there was that too.'

'Beatrice said that you grew up together,' I said. 'That you promised to marry her when she nearly died.'

Philip shook his head. 'Beatrice says a lot of things, some of which aren't quite true. I've come to understand that she sees me as a warm, comfortable blanket rather than her life's partner. She's different when she's in Europe. She's more independent. She hardly writes to me when she's there. And when she does it's no more than a page of hurried prose.'

A voice called out: 'Philip!'

We jumped back from each other before we realised that the cry came from far away. Someone was calling from the house. It was a woman's voice but it was not Beatrice.

'She will be heartbroken just the same,' I said. 'And your father. He adores her.'

'Yes, he does,' said Philip, sitting down on the bench. 'And Beatrice will be hurt and embarrassed too. But after a while they will see it's for the best. Beatrice deserves someone who loves her with as much passion as I love you. Not a man who feels affection for her as a brother does for a sister.'

The stillness of the maze was peaceful. It was as if everything had stopped for us. Perhaps the guests had moved inside to hear Robert's orchestrion. I hoped whoever it was who had called out Philip's name had given up looking for him.

'What will you do?' I asked, sitting down beside Philip.

He squeezed my hand. 'It will be all right, Adéla. Please don't worry. Beatrice will be upset for a while. But a few months of unhappiness is better than a lifetime of lies.'

I pressed my head against his chest. It felt right to be with him.

'Happy?' he asked me.

'Yes.'

He leaned over and kissed me. I ran my fingers through his hair.

'Philip!'

The voice we had heard earlier called again. Only this time it was closer and more urgent.

'Philip!' Another voice joined in with the first. And then another. It sounded as though several people were looking for him.

Philip stood up and reached out his hand to me, helping me up. He brushed his fingers under my chin and kissed me again.

'I'd better go,' he said. 'It won't be right to be seen together until Beatrice has been told.'

Before leaving the maze, Philip turned to me once more and smiled. 'It's all going to be fine, Adéla. Don't worry. Promise?'

'I promise.'

I watched Philip disappear behind the hedge. A few minutes later the voices that had been calling greeted him. 'Come quickly to the house!' one of them said.

I sat back down on the bench and fixed my hair. Philip was right. We were not trying to hurt anybody. We only wanted to be honest and to do what was right. I stood up and walked through the maze, drunk with happiness, desire and sunshine. I stepped back out onto the path and gave a start when I saw Freddy waiting by the cypress pines, smoking a cigarette. He looked at me with appraising eyes. 'All the guests are leaving. I'm taking you and Klára home.'

'Leaving?' I asked, wondering why he was staring at me so harshly. Did he know I had been in the maze with Philip? 'But it is still early.'

Freddy did not answer. I realised the strap of my slip was showing under my sleeve and I tugged it back over my shoulder.

'What has happened?' I asked.

Freddy threw his cigarette on the gravel and stamped it out. 'A message came from the Fahey house. Beatrice's mother has died. Beatrice went home half an hour ago. Philip's just left to join her.'

FOURTEEN

Mrs Fahey's funeral rekindled my grief at my own mother's death. I was hesitant to take Klára with me, but she insisted. I was glad in the end she came, because when we arrived at the church the number of mourners was overwhelming. The Fahey family might have been small but they had many friends.

Mrs Fahey's coffin was lifted from the horse-drawn hearse and carried into the church by the pallbearers: Philip and his father, Robert and Alfred.

Beatrice stood at the entrance to the church looking dazed. Florence put her arm around her. When the coffin passed and I saw 'Mummy' on the ribbon of the wreath, I almost broke down. I knew how losing a mother changed you. My life was divided into two parts: life with Mother, and life without.

The mourners followed the coffin into the church. Beatrice stumbled and I stretched forward to help Florence hold her upright. 'Thank you,' Beatrice said, her tears spilling onto my hand. There was no colour in her face and her red eyebrows stood out as if they were floating in the air by themselves.

In the church, I bowed my head and prayed for guidance. I had not spoken to Philip since the afternoon tea. But I trusted in his promise that he would find the best course for us. I knew that he had not told Beatrice yet because of the changed circumstances and accepted I would have to be patient a while longer in order to do the right thing by Beatrice.

Outside the church, Klára and I waited with the mourners to give Beatrice our condolences. She was sitting in a chair with Philip and Florence by her side.

'I'm so sorry, Beatrice,' I told her.

She looked at me with tear-stained eyes. 'I know you understand what I'm feeling.'

'I do,' I said, patting her hand.

'It was good of you to come,' Florence said. 'To give us support. Beatrice is fond of you, Adéla. She thinks of you as a sister.'

'Oh dear Aunty, I do,' Beatrice said. Her lips trembled like an old woman's. 'That's exactly how I think of Adéla. I've only known her a short time but I would trust her with my life.'

I could not look at Philip when Beatrice said those words. I kissed her cheek and moved on to let the next mourner greet the family.

Klára must have sensed what I was thinking. She grabbed my arm and squeezed it.

'I feel like a thief about to rob a helpless victim,' I told Klára when we were out of earshot.

'Beatrice is not helpless,' said Klára. 'It is only unfortunate timing. Everthing will be all right.'

Afterwards, at the wake, Philip and I snatched a moment away from the others in the hall when I was heading towards the lavatory and he was rushing to the kitchen to request more hot water for the tea.

'Are you all right?' he asked me.

I nodded. 'And you?'

He stroked his temple. 'Yes, I think so. The situation is more awkward than I had anticipated. I have to help Beatrice through this time.'

'I understand.'

'I'm disappointed that I won't make the premiere of your picture. I hope you'll give me a private screening?'

'I will.'

Philip reached out to touch my cheek then quickly pulled away. Doctor Page Senior was standing in the doorway.

'Good day, Miss Rose,' Doctor Page said to me. He glanced at Philip and raised his eyebrows. 'The guests are waiting for the hot water.'

'Excuse me, Adéla,' Philip said. 'Thank you for your condolences to our family. They are much appreciated.'

He spoke formally in front of his father, but I caught the love in his eyes. The look was going to have to sustain me during our temporary separation.

After Philip left, Doctor Page turned to me. 'I hope you have been keeping well, Miss Rose,' he said. 'How is your portrait work progressing?'

I told him about Frederick Rockcliffe's portrait and other recent commissions, mindful to thank him for giving me a start to my career. I felt that he was scrutinising me and I did not know if he had seen Philip reach for me or not. His face was stern and I was not sure if his grim expression was caused by anger — or simply by grief.

* * *

After the funeral, I occupied myself by going to the cinema and meeting Hugh and Peter at the Vegetarian Café. I enlarged Freddy's portrait, as he requested, so he could hang it in his office. I had used the light to downplay his suit and bring to prominence his chin and brow. He looked commanding. I was keen to see his reaction to it, and at the same time I was not enthusiastic to see him after Robert's afternoon tea. I sent the portrait special delivery to the Galaxy Pictures office. It was the first time I had not delivered a portrait in person. I usually liked to see the subject's initial reaction.

My twenty-first birthday arrived, and Ranjana baked a vanilla cake with pink icing. Mother used to make vanilla cakes for our birthdays. After a round of 'Happy Birthday', Ranjana placed a slice in front of me. It tasted exactly the same as Mother's cakes had.

'Josephine sent the recipe,' said Uncle Ota, handing me an envelope and a small box. 'Happy Birthday, Adélka.'

I opened the envelope and saw it contained a letter from Aunt Josephine.

'Excuse me one moment,' I told the others, before stepping out into the garden to read what Aunt Josephine had written.

> *My beautiful Adélka,*
>
> *It is too difficult to believe that the baby who arrived in such a hurry one summer morning is now a young woman. How I wish I could share this important birthday with you, but in a way we are all together. Before leaving for Mariánské Lázně, I visited the bank and took these diamond earrings from your mother's jewellery collection for you. I know she would have wanted you to have them. While there I remembered*

her special recipe book and went to the blue house to
see if I could find it. Indeed I did and was thrilled when
I came across her birthday cake recipe, which I then
sent to Ota and your aunt. How proud your mother
would have been of you. How proud I am of you.

When I return to Prague, I will arrange for Doctor
Holub to send some money to you. We will wire it to
you from Austria so it can't be traced ...

Aunt Josephine wrote about Mariánské Lázně but did not
mention Miloš. She described her hotel set in the hills above the
town and how Frip was pampered by the staff. Although Aunt
Josephine said nothing of it, I feared that she was not well. Why
was she visiting a spa? I wished I could be there with her.

I opened the box. Inside, tucked into a piece of silk, were two
drop earrings. I admired the pretty fleur-de-lis tops and the
sparkling diamonds. I shut my eyes and saw Mother wearing the
earrings while she danced with Father at a Christmas ball that I
had been allowed to attend when I was a child. Mother's off-the-
shoulder gown had been trimmed in lace, bows and flowers. I did
not let the memory linger further than that. I did not want to
think of Miloš or how he was progressing in America. No doubt
the fact that I was now twenty-one was spurring him to greater
efforts to find us.

The night of the premiere of *The Bunyip* Philip sent me a
bouquet of pastel roses along with a card:

I'm thinking of you, darling.
My love always,
Philip

Beatrice was in mourning for three months and it would be improper of Philip to attend festivities while they were still officially engaged. I was disappointed not to be able to share my birthday or this important milestone with the man I loved, but I did my best to rally my spirits. Uncle Ota was providing the champagne and the cocktail sandwiches at his own expense and had gone to a lot of trouble for me. Raymond Longford's feature film had already screened at the major release theatres and there was no need to hold a premiere for a short. But Uncle Ota wanted to bolster my courage. 'You've got talent,' he told me. 'Let's get you off to a good start.'

I stood by the entrance with him, greeting the guests as they arrived. There was quite a crowd, including former colleagues of Uncle Ota's from the museum, guests and past speakers from our Tuesday night gatherings, as well as the regular cinema patrons. Mr Tilly and his wife came with Ben. Klára placed herself beside me. She looked beautiful in the blue dress she had worn for her concert. I was happy to see how far she had come since her illness. She was my stronghold now.

'I didn't realise how many people we knew,' she whispered to me.

Robert and Freddy arrived together. Robert looked elegant but Freddy was dressed in a yellow tuxedo with blue shoes. I remembered my promise to myself to talk to him about his dress style.

Robert could not take his eyes off Klára. She looked older than her age but was just a week shy of fourteen. She would not be interested in him.

Other guests were waiting, so Robert and Freddy wished us the best before moving inside. 'I've been looking forward to seeing your picture all week,' Freddy told me.

Peter arrived with Hugh, who had Giallo on his shoulder.

'Giallo's been to the pictures before,' Peter assured Uncle Ota. 'If he poops on anything it will be Hugh.'

'Will he talk during the picture?' Klára asked with a cheeky smile. She scratched Giallo's head, which he obligingly bent towards her.

'Only during intermission,' Hugh replied.

Uncle Ota glanced at his watch and told us to take our seats in the cinema. I saw Ranjana sneaking up the fire escape to reach the projection room without anyone seeing her. I felt sympathy for the charade she had to maintain. I had one of my own.

After the audience had sung the national anthem and we had been entertained by a comedian waltzing with his pet pig, the lights lowered and my film appeared on the screen. I listened with relief to the audience sighing and laughing in the right places. Esther, who was sitting between me and Hugh, gave a start when the bunyip appeared. It was amusing as she had fashioned the costume herself, from one of Uncle Ota's tribal masks and a blanket.

'The audience is enraptured,' Uncle Ota whispered. 'Congratulations.'

But my little effort was overshadowed by the feature film, *The Blue Mountains Mystery*. The cameraman, Arthur Higgins, captured the grand beauty of the setting in a way never seen before. It was as if the mountains had risen up before our eyes to dazzle us with their majesty.

Afterwards, the guests mingled in the foyer while Klára played the piano with two of her classmates joining her on violin and clarinet. Hugh, who was not comfortable with crowds, left immediately after the session, and Uncle Ota, Ranjana and Esther were occupied with the catering. I stood by the fountain and surveyed the room. I spotted Peter in the crowd, but before I could reach him I was intercepted by Freddy.

'I'd like to see what you can do with a bit of money,' he said. 'That wasn't a bad effort.'

'Thank you.'

Freddy scratched his head and signalled to a waiter carrying a tray of champagne glasses. 'I received my portrait and all the compliments that went with it. How come you didn't bring it yourself?'

'I would have,' I lied. 'But I have been busy.'

The waiter brought over the tray of glasses and Freddy took two, handing one to me. 'Have you seen Philip lately?'

I was taken aback by his question. I had not forgotten how he had looked at me when I had emerged from the maze. But I had done nothing wrong. Freddy could judge me all he liked.

'No,' I said, firmly. 'Beatrice is still in mourning.'

Freddy cocked his head. 'Beatrice,' he sighed. 'Now there's someone who has more to her than meets the eye.'

My curiosity was aroused. I was about to ask him what he meant when Uncle Ota signalled to me to move to the front of the room to give a speech.

'I'll catch up with you later,' Freddy said.

But afterwards, when I looked for him, Freddy was gone and I had lost my chance to find out more about Beatrice.

Two days after the premiere Philip sent me a note asking me to meet him in the garden of Broughton Hall. Now it begins, I thought. Now my happiness with Philip starts.

'You both deserve all the joy in the world,' Klára said, when I told her where I was going.

The day was unusually humid. I stepped off the tram and the sun disappeared behind the clouds and the sky threatened rain. I had dressed in a floral skirt and blouse and had curled my hair especially for the occasion. But the listless air turned my locks frizzy and my blouse stuck to my back. I reached the path to the garden and the sky suddenly opened. Rain splattered down and splashed mud onto my shoes and stockings.

I hurried past the pine trees and tropical ferns to the summerhouse where Philip had said he would wait. I passed a fig tree and the summerhouse came into view. Philip was standing with his back to me. I was filled with such love that I forgot my clothes were soaking wet and my curls were falling into straggly ringlets around my face.

Thunder cracked. A wind that came from nowhere whipped against my face. The heat dissipated from my skin and goose bumps rose on its surface.

Philip turned when he heard my step behind him. His eyes were pinched and had no lustre to them. The expression on his face was one of such sorrow that I instantly stiffened.

'Good God,' he said, tugging off his jacket and wrapping it around me. 'You must be frozen.'

His concern for me did nothing to quell the terror rising in my heart. A man in love with a woman does not look at her that way unless he has terrible news. Scenarios raced through my mind: Beatrice had refused to break off the engagement; she had threatened suicide; Philip had realised he was in love with her, not me.

'What is it?' I asked.

Philip drew me to the centre of the summerhouse but the position gave us little protection from the rain, which blew horizontally.

Tears welled in his eyes. 'Beatrice is going to have a baby,' he said.

I swallowed but I could not get rid of the lump in my throat. Beatrice could not be pregnant even though Philip had just told me so. No, I refused to believe it. Nothing as awful as that could have happened to us. Philip fumbled for my hand.

'Are you sure?' I asked.

'My father examined her.'

My legs turned leaden. I wanted to make for the bench to sit down but could not move.

Philip buried his face in his hands. 'It's like some terrible nightmare,' he said. 'Until my father said that Beatrice wanted lots of babies, I wasn't sure that she wanted any. We were careful.' He looked at me with tear-stained eyes. 'After Wattamolla beach ... well, I made excuses to Beatrice and during her mourning I told her that it was better to abstain. But it was too late. It must have happened in that month you and I agreed not to see each other.'

The shock of the truth dawned on me and the joy of a few minutes before extinguished. If Beatrice was pregnant, Philip was going to have to marry her. He had no choice. He would have to be father to her child. The future I had pictured for us rolled away like a film spinning off a reel.

I shook my head. 'No.'

Philip placed his hands on my shoulders. He was trembling. 'I wanted it to be you. I wanted to have children with you.'

Yes, I had wanted that too, but I was not pregnant. It was Beatrice who was going to be mother to Philip's children. I moved away from him. He was not the same man. He was going to be someone else's husband. I was going to be shut out, like a tramp looking in the window of a cosy home.

'Well, now she is pregnant, maybe she will settle down,' I said.

Philip grabbed my arm. 'Don't say that! I wanted to marry you!'

I found myself imagining terrible things. Perhaps Beatrice would miscarry; it was still early. Or perhaps she would die in childbirth. But if any of those things happened I should hate myself, and it would not bring happiness to Philip or me. No, the hand of fate had given us its verdict.

I sank down to the floor and Philip knelt down and put his arms around me. Tears burned the back of my throat but I was too shocked to cry. I felt tired. I wished I could fall asleep, to have some reprieve from the torment in my heart.

'What will you do?' I asked Philip. 'I don't think ... I don't think I could bear to see you with Beatrice.'

He shuddered and held me closer. His heart was racing. He did not answer at once, but after a few moments he stroked my hair then said, 'I will take Beatrice to London. She wanted to live in Europe and I will work at the hospital there.'

He lifted my face in his hands and kissed me. I realised that he was saying goodbye. But I could not withdraw my heart now that I had given it. I would love him forever even if I never saw him again.

The rain calmed for a moment. A ray of light shone through the clouds but disappeared when the skies grew darker still. I wished that we could be frozen in our embrace and stay that way forever. But when the day began to fade, the futility of lingering became apparent. There was no future for us now.

Philip helped me to my feet. 'I will never forget you, Adéla.'

I nodded, my heart too full to answer him. I took off his jacket and held it out for him. 'Keep it,' he said.

He turned and ran down the steps of the summerhouse. I watched him rush past the pond and over the bridge. Before he disappeared into the grove he stopped and turned back to me. Then, an instant later, he was lost from my sight.

I wanted to sink to my knees, but I somehow remained upright, standing in the summerhouse with my dreams in tatters around me. I had no home in Prague to go to and Philip was to marry someone else. The rain fell harder and the wind grew fiercer, blowing the droplets in my face. But I did not turn away.

'Goodbye, Philip. I won't forget you either,' I whispered.

FIFTEEN

Philip and Beatrice married and left for England a few weeks after that miserable day in the garden at Broughton Hall. As Beatrice was just out of mourning, and because she knew she was pregnant, the wedding was a small family affair and I was relieved not to be invited. For Philip's sake, and to quell any doubts that may arise, I sent a Belgian lace tablecloth as a wedding gift.

The day the ship departed it was as if my life had been washed away and I was left with only a faint imprint. I was sure my love for Philip would not die but what about his for me? Would I meet him in the street one day and receive only a friendly smile or a platonic kiss? It would be better that way and yet ... I could not bear to imagine it.

'He will return one day,' I told Klára. 'His father is here, and Beatrice's aunt and uncle are too.'

'Don't worry about the future,' she said. 'Think about how you can find happiness now.'

Uncle Ota kept his eye on me, although I did my best to hide my broken heart. I had never told him or Ranjana about my feelings for Philip, but they had guessed. Ranjana showed her sympathy by yelling at me whenever she found me slouching about the house. 'Get off your posterior, young lady, and help Esther with the garden! I don't want to look at your long face!' It sounded cruel, but she meant well. She did not want me to shut down and stop moving. Esther had done that and we knew the results too well.

Uncle Ota was softer. 'Adéla, come with me into the garden,' he said to me one day. I sat next to him on the bench under the Japanese maple.

'I know you're sad and that you won't tell us why,' he said. 'I remember how life wounds the young.'

I rested my head against his shoulder. He stroked my hair and continued. 'Long before I met Ranjana there was somebody … somebody I loved very much. But circumstances were against us and we had to part.'

He stumbled on the word 'circumstances' and I was sure that he had meant to say 'people'. I knew he was talking about Aunt Emilie but who were the 'people' he referred to?

'I'm not going to give you platitudes about time healing all wounds. It doesn't. Life leaves its scars. But it's not without its beauty and order either. I'll never forget the woman I gave my youthful heart to and lost tragically, but I am deeply happy with Ranjana. Sometimes your true companion turns up in a surprising place. Mine did. I found her on a funeral pyre.'

I had to smile. You're not the scoundrel who ruined Emilie's life, I thought, snuggling closer to him. I would have asked Uncle Ota about what happened all those years ago, for at that moment I sensed he was strong enough to remember it. But I was not strong enough to hear it. I was in too much pain myself to bear another's sorrow. But one day I would ask him for the story … when we were both ready.

Summer passed slowly and I did nothing more than clean the house, work in the garden and take a few portraits. I tried not to think of Philip and Beatrice in England together. In March the following year, Freddy sent a note that he would like to see us. The last I had heard of him was the night of the premiere and I thought it strange that Freddy should ask beforehand what day and time was convenient for us: I had assumed if he wanted to see someone then he simply showed up. He arrived at the appointed time in a new car: an Opel Sportwagen with a red trim. He brushed off his orange suit and followed us into the house.

'There's an old cinema for sale in Thirroul,' he told us, when we sat down in the parlour with a glass of Ranjana's lemonade. 'Thirroul is the untapped entertainment centre of the south coast. It draws crowds in summer as a resort and has a railway and colliery too. It's a golden opportunity.'

'What are you proposing?' asked Uncle Ota.

'As a representative of Galaxy Pictures, I can't be seen to be investing in the local industry,' Freddy answered, with a smile in my direction. 'I make a lot of money for the company but no one becomes rich working for somebody else, do they?'

Freddy looked from me to Uncle Ota. 'I want you to go buy that place for me then work the same magic you did with Tilly's Cinema. If you do that, I won't just appoint you its manager, I will make you my partner.'

Uncle Ota was not one to turn down a challenge. I could see his mind ticking over. He had transformed Tilly's Cinema into a successful business, but it had not made him wealthy. It occurred to me that he and Freddy would make a good team. Uncle Ota had the imagination and flair; Freddy had the nerve and the financial shrewdness.

'All right,' Uncle Ota said. 'I'll look it over and tell you what I think.'

Freddy shook his head.

'Surely you want me to inspect it before you buy it?' said Uncle Ota. 'What if it's a wreck? How do you know it will work?'

'I don't care *if* it will work,' Freddy answered. 'I want you to go there and *make* it work.'

Uncle Ota considered the matter for a few moments before answering. 'I'd have to live there with my wife and son while I was setting it up,' he said.

'I'll pay your rent,' said Freddy, rising from his chair. 'Think about it and give me a call tomorrow morning. Before ten.'

I showed Freddy to the door.

'Good afternoon, Adéla,' he said, taking his coat and hat from me. 'I'm still receiving compliments on the portrait you took.'

'I'm glad,' I said.

'Do you like jazz?' he asked.

'I don't know. I haven't listened to it much.'

Freddy raised his eyebrows. 'What century are you living in? There are a couple of good places in this city. I'll take you there some time. Bring Klára and Robert, and Esther if she wants to come too. Then you and I can discuss that funny little film of yours.'

Freddy honked the horn of his Sportwagen before pulling out from the kerb. Our neighbours looked out their windows to see what was going on. The McManus children from two doors away chased the car down the street.

I smiled. Freddy was abrasive but he had cheered me up too. His social and business personas were the same: pushy. But I had a sense that he did things other people were afraid to do, and I admired him for that.

I returned to the parlour to find Uncle Ota making notes on the borders of the newspaper.

'So you will move to the south coast?' I asked him.

'I'll talk to Ranjana about it,' he said. Then, looking at me, he smiled. 'Would you like to come too?'

'Why are you refusing to go?' Klára asked me when she heard about Freddy's offer. 'You need a change from Sydney for a while.'

'Who is going to look after you?' I said.

'I am fourteen years old, Adélka, and Esther is here. We can come down on the weekends. Thirroul is not so far away.'

She was right, but Uncle Ota had received word from Doctor Holub that Miloš had returned to Prague. He had married paní Beňová. Uncle Ota thought that meant that they had given up on pursuing us. But he had never seen paní Beňová's covetous eyes as Mother had described them in her letter to Aunt Josephine. Nor had he been witness to her single-minded ambition as I had. I could not believe she had married Miloš without being sure that she would one day reside in our town house and country manor. No, she must be more confident than ever of gaining them. But why?

'Adélka, you could take photographs of the seaside towns,' Klára said, waking me from my dream. 'I have heard the coast is ruggedly beautiful.'

'No,' I said, shaking my head. 'I am not leaving you.'

Klára's jaw set, the way it used to as a child when she was determined to get her way. But her calm voice was that of an adult. 'Philip is in London studying to be a children's doctor. Beatrice is his wife. What about *your* dreams, Adélka? I am not going to let you waste your life over things you can't change. I am not going to watch you despair until you end up in hospital like I did.'

Beatrice had once described me as her friend but we could never have shared the bond I had with Klára. It hurt to hear the truth, but my sister's words had been spoken with love. I would be of no use to anyone if I did not pick up my spirits again. In my present state, I could not protect her. I would have to trust Esther for that.

Uncle Ota trained another manager for Tilly's Cinema, and took Ranjana, Thomas and me to Thirroul with him in June. The train rattled through miles of untouched bushland. The angular rocks with ferns in the crevices, the giant gums and their massive limbs, and the cabbage tree palms were different from any forest I had seen in Europe. The dappled light and the golden flowers of the undergrowth presented a photograph worth taking at every bend in the tracks. The train burst from the bush and we saw endless bays and undulating hills rolling out before us. Dozens of bungalows, with plumes of smoke rising from their chimneys, dotted the landscape. On the inland side, mountains towered over the train line and the fields.

The book I had been reading fell from my lap. I thought of Philip. It was strange, considering the way Beatrice had treated me as though I were her bosom friend, that she had not written to me since her arrival in London or informed me of the birth of her child. It saved me from being a hypocrite, but it was disconcerting too. I could not help but think that she knew about Philip and me. Perhaps Freddy had told her? Or Philip himself? Perhaps she had simply guessed.

By the time the train stopped at the station in Thirroul, the weather had changed and it was drizzling with rain. Uncle Ota pulled the directions to the house Freddy had rented for us from his pocket and squinted against the droplets slipping from his hat into his eyes. The skies opened and rain splashed down with Pacific fury. There was no taxi or bus service available. We left our luggage with the stationmaster, to be collected later, and walked down the sandy road in the direction of the coast. The sea was hissing and rumbling but I could not see it. Everything was a waterfall of rain and I was soaked through to the skin. Our shoes filled with water and squelched when we ran.

We found ourselves dripping and muddy on the doorstep of a weatherboard bungalow. Uncle Ota searched for the key under a flowerpot, as our landlady had instructed, and found it. We were relieved to see there was a provision of dry wood and coal in the hallway to light a fire.

'We'd better get dried off,' Ranjana said, hoisting Thomas on her hip. 'We don't want to come down with pneumonia.'

The house was cosy with cottage windows and hardwood floors covered with braided rugs. A veranda with curved eaves protected it from the worst of the weather. We started the fire in the sitting room and I noticed that we had a view out to sea. Although the rain had stopped, flashes of lightning darted across the swollen ocean.

The following morning, while we were preparing breakfast, there was a knock at the door. Uncle Ota answered it to find our landlady holding a pail of milk. 'It's from the dairy,' she explained, passing the pail to Uncle Ota. 'Mr Rockcliffe wrote to say there was a little boy here and that I should deliver fresh milk every morning.'

Uncle Ota reached into his pocket for some coins to pay the woman, but she shook her head. 'It's all been fixed up.'

When Uncle Ota returned to the kitchen, he placed the milk on the bench and scooped out a cup for Thomas.

'It's still warm,' said Thomas, licking his lips. 'Delicious.'

Ranjana picked up a cloth and wiped his mouth. 'You be sure to thank Mr Rockcliffe when you see him next.'

'I will,' promised Thomas.

After breakfast we walked to the town to inspect the cinema. The rain had left puddles on the unfinished road and Ranjana had to tug Thomas to stop him jumping in them.

'Thomas!' she scolded. 'Not in your best clothes.'

Thomas giggled. When the next puddle appeared he did his best to jump into that too.

'Well, better a boisterous boy than one who can't walk or jump at all,' said Uncle Ota. 'We have to count our blessings.'

Buggies and motor cars were pulled up in the town's streets. People scurried in and out of stores, carrying bread, potatoes, saddles and other household and farm necessities to their vehicles. A woman cradling a baby stopped when she saw us, as did a man in an oilskin coat. At first I thought we might have stood out as city dwellers because of my bobbed hair and Uncle Ota's two-toned shoes, but I realised that they were looking at Ranjana. I shivered when I remembered that awful day when we were attacked on our way to the cinema. But the stares here were more curious than hostile, and when we said 'Good morning' our greetings were mostly returned.

'Ah, here you are,' said Mr Garret, the real estate agent, when we walked into his office. He had been eating fried eggs and reached for his handkerchief to wipe his mouth. 'I'll get the key. The cinema is down the street.'

He pulled a sheet of paper from the stack of files on his desk and disappeared into the back room, returning a few moments later with his coat and hat. 'The cinema hasn't been used in a while but it has a roof,' he laughed, stroking his sideburns. 'The old one didn't. Weather like yesterday's used to send us scurrying to get out of the place.'

'The School of Arts has a roof though, doesn't it?' Uncle Ota asked.

'Yes, it does,' Mr Garret agreed. 'They screen a few sessions a week and are talking about putting in new seats. But they won't be able to compete with a purpose-built cinema like the one you want to open.'

'Won't that upset the committee?' asked Ranjana.

Mr Garret was taken aback, as if he hadn't been expecting her to speak English. 'Business is business,' he replied, addressing his answer to Uncle Ota. 'And the School of Arts doesn't have the seating capacity to fulfil the town's true picture-attendance potential.'

When we saw the cinema we did not know whether to laugh or gasp. It was nothing more than patched iron and weatherboard walls and a warped roof. A faded sign hung above the doorway: *The Royal Picture Palace*. I thought Mr Garret opened the doors gingerly, afraid that if he pushed too hard they would twist off their hinges. The interior was as dilapidated as the exterior. The matchboard and fibro walls must have made the cinema a cold place to sit in winter and an oven to endure in summer. The air stank of a mix of salt and cow manure. The seats were planks resting on bricks.

'There isn't a biograph box. You will need to build one to pass the fire regulations,' Mr Garret said. He sounded as if he were making a decorating suggestion rather than pointing out a major fault with the building.

Uncle Ota tapped his knuckles against a pillar. The lattice ceiling shook and we dodged the falling dust. The pillars blocked the view and I wondered what they were doing there because there was no gallery to support.

'This building has to come down,' observed Uncle Ota, poking at a rust patch in the wall. He turned to Mr Garret. 'We are going to have to start from scratch, which is a bigger investment than I was intending.'

Mr Garret lifted his chin. 'But when it is done ... just imagine the crowds it will attract ... the profits. What do you think?'

'What do I think?' replied Uncle Ota, raising his eyebrows. Two mice poked their heads out of the lattice and scampered down a wire and into a hole in the floor. Uncle Ota's face broke into a smile. 'I think it might work.'

Uncle Ota wrote to Freddy with an estimate of what he thought building a picture palace would cost.

> We have potential competition from Wollongong
> Theatres who have made enquiries into leasing land. If
> we want to make a go of this, we had better get it
> right from the start. We should look at about 1800
> seats with at least 300 of those in a well-appointed
> dress circle. If we want to maximise potential then we
> need décor at least as good as you would find in
> Wollongong, though my suggestion is that we do
> better with sprung seats and a magnificent foyer to
> keep up the novelty of a luxurious theatre. These
> people are proud. They do not want to be second to
> any major centre and we can do well by catering to
> that. We also need the latest equipment. I have
> checked with suppliers and it looks as if we will need
> a minimum of around 10,000 pounds.

Uncle Ota grinned when he wrote in the figure. He was throwing down the gauntlet to Freddy, testing his nerve.

Uncle Ota waited for a reply by mail, but instead opened the door one day to find Freddy pulling up at the gate.

'Thirroul is too good a township to lose to a competitor, and if Southern Pictures build a reputation here, then other places could be conquered,' Freddy said, before he had even taken off his hat to greet Ranjana and myself.

Uncle Ota invited him into the sitting room. Ranjana set about making tea. 'Can you obtain the capital quickly?' Uncle Ota asked.

'I've already done it,' said Freddy. 'I mortgaged my house. I want you to do whatever is necessary to build the best, most impressive cinema on the south coast.'

Freddy stayed for lunch. I was curious to see how he would react to eating the korma curry and lentils Ranjana had prepared, but he ploughed through his food with a voracious appetite.

'Now, Mrs Rose,' he said to Ranjana, 'I want you to source the best equipment for your projection room. And I want you to stop hiding. You are a talented projectionist. Let people know who you are.'

Ranjana rolled her eyes. 'That's easier said than done —'

'Only in one's mind,' said Freddy, cutting Ranjana off. 'That's the problem with black people in my country. They struggle to be second-class whites. They should use what is unique about them. White people couldn't have invented jazz.'

It was the first time I had ever seen Ranjana lost for words.

'The projection room will need to be fireproofed, and isolated from the rest of the cinema in case of an emergency,' Freddy said, before glancing at his watch and standing up. 'I'm sorry, I can't stay. It's been delightful.'

'No!' cried out Thomas.

We turned to look at him.

'I haven't said "Thank you, Mr Rockcliffe" yet,' he protested.

'What for?' Freddy asked him.

'For the milk,' Thomas said.

Freddy gave him a salute. 'You are welcome, young man!'

He was like a storm that crashed through the sky but cleared the air. Freddy took significant risks in anticipation of large rewards. I found him inspiring.

I walked Freddy to his car.

'Are you all right down here?' he asked me. 'Is there anything you'd like from Sydney?'

I shook my head. 'Thank you, but I have everything I need.'

He pursed his lips. 'Did you bring your typewriter? Are you working on something new?'

'No.'

Freddy did not say anything. He reached forward and brushed a leaf off his windscreen. There was a question on the tip of my tongue that I wanted to ask. I had been waiting to ask it but had kept losing my nerve.

'Freddy ... have you heard from Philip and Beatrice?'

'No,' he said.

'Don't you find that strange? Klára says they haven't written to Robert either.'

Freddy turned to me. 'Do you know what the difference is between civilisations that survive and those that perish, Adéla?'

I could not see what his question had to do with our conversation and did not answer.

Freddy started the engine. 'Civilisations that survive deal with their present and their future. Those that perish cling to their past.'

Freddy sent me a wave before speeding off down the road. I bit my lip, holding back my indignant tears. I was sure now that Freddy had known I was in love with Philip and had been insensitive enough to make light of it. I would be cordial, for Uncle Ota's sake, but I would never ask another thing of Freddy Rockcliffe I promised myself.

A week later the postal truck delivered a package to me. 'It's heavy,' said Uncle Ota, lifting it onto the dining table. I cut the string and opened the package to find a new Imperial typewriter inside. Freddy had not included a letter, only a poem with the writer unacknowledged:

> *I had one dream left*
> *One bullet in the barrel*
> *I stared down the beast at my door*
> *Ready to pursue that dream with the desperation*
> *Of someone with nothing left to lose.*

The poem lacked rhythm and structure and I had a suspicion that Freddy had written it himself. But I did not laugh at it. I appreciated the sentiment. Perhaps Freddy realised he had hurt me and was sorry. He was abrupt but he motivated people. I had given thought to what he had said about clinging to the past. I rolled a piece of paper into the typewriter and composed a thankyou note.

The next day, I set up the typewriter on the dining room table and listed ideas for a script. I was ready to take some risks myself to realise my dream of making pictures.

I typed the first three pages effortlessly, but as I was winding on the paper for the fourth page I looked out of the window and noticed the fig tree in our neighbour's garden. I suddenly remembered Philip's face on the day we had parted in Broughton Hall's garden — and froze.

Uncle Ota wasted no time setting about the construction of the Cascade Picture Palace. Two months after he had seen the site, the old building had been demolished and the foundations for the new one put in place. While Uncle Ota consulted architects over granolite stairways and stained-glass windows, Ranjana set about sourcing an Ernemann cinematograph and a Crompton 10 hp motor convertor. She had a superior knowledge of her craft compared to most projectionists and was tired of the stares and the second-class treatment that suppliers dealt out to her.

'I am renouncing my position as a "token Australian",' she proclaimed one morning. She swapped her western clothes for saris and her pearls for a bindi. But instead of the traditional cotton and silk saris, Ranjana made hers from western fabrics. One day, when she and I had to travel to Sydney to source Axminster carpets, she donned a sari of linen patterned with giant maple leaves. The coalminers and their wives waiting on the platform could not take their eyes off her. If she had hoped to discourage people staring at her, the outfit had the opposite effect. But Ranjana, who had insisted that we buy first-class tickets, acted as if the attention was homage. She lifted her chin like an exotic maharani leaving her palace in Jaipur. Her performance worked. I expected the guard to stop us entering the carriage and to tell us that dark people were not allowed to travel first-class. Instead, he dusted off our seats with his handkerchief before allowing us to sit down.

'Thank you,' Ranjana said, like a true sovereign. Then, turning to me, she whispered, 'Freddy was right.'

I thought of the day Freddy had come to our house in Watsons Bay to have his picture taken and how he had quoted

Nietzsche: 'No price is too high to pay for the privilege of owning yourself.'

Perhaps there was more to Freddy than met the eye.

While the cinema was being built, we screened three sessions a week at the School of Arts to become familiar with our audience. The locals loved everything from serious documentaries to frivolous comedies. Thirroul truly was a potential goldmine.

I missed Klára and was happy when she and Esther stayed with us on weekends. The scenery around Thirroul was breathtaking and Klára was enamoured of it. I accompanied her on walks in the bush because I wanted to spend time with her. But Klára had inherited Uncle Ota's adventurous spirit while I was timid.

'Aren't there snakes in the bush?' I asked her. The weather had turned warmer and I had heard that snakes came out of hibernation in spring.

'Plenty,' Klára replied. 'Tigers, browns, copperheads and red-bellied black snakes. The tigers are the most deadly.'

'Doesn't that worry you?' I asked, watching her scramble up the slope ahead of me.

Klára turned to face me. 'They can't move faster than you or I can walk. If they sense the vibration of your footsteps approaching from a distance, they will move away. So we will proceed through the undergrowth slowly and make up for lost time on the established tracks.'

'And should one of us get bitten?' I asked.

Klára patted the satchel she wore on her hip alongside her water bottle and compass. 'We will cauterise the wound and apply a tourniquet.'

'How do you know so much about snakes?' I asked her.

'Robert told me. He had a pet diamond python when he was a child, and is fascinated by reptiles.'

'Robert Swan? Where did you see him?'

'He is a patron of the Conservatorium of Music and occasionally comes to the high school's performances too. He and Freddy took Esther and me to see a jazz band.'

I stopped in my tracks. Robert seemed a decent young man, but Klára was fifteen and still at school. But Klára had said that Esther had accompanied her when she went out with Robert and Freddy so I did not believe they were trying to lead her astray.

'Do you like Robert?' I asked.

Klára glanced at her feet. 'I am not sure,' she said. 'I enjoy talking with him so much that I never want our conversations to end. He knows a lot about so many things and he is passionate about music.'

She is in love with him, I thought. It would have been foolish not to see how well suited Klára and Robert were to each other. But since she had been born, it had always been her and me. I was not prepared for Klára to share her secrets with someone else. Perhaps I wanted her to remain a child. But that was ridiculous. One day she would marry and have children of her own, as I had hoped to do with Philip. But I did not want to think of those things now. I changed the subject to the shape of the clouds floating overhead.

'That is definitely a sailboat,' I said, indicating a cumulus cloud.

'No,' said Klára. 'I see a set of scales.'

One day Klára and I were taking our morning walk, and had progressed a short way along the path, when Klára stopped and pointed at something. My gaze followed the line from her finger to the branch she was looking at. I heard the familiar 'koo-koo-ka-ka-kook' call of the kookaburra before I saw it. We had a shared fascination for the squat birds with the mask over their eyes. There was a family of them that sat on our washing line in Watsons Bay in the early evenings. The kookaburra swooped to another branch and we continued on our way, Klára a short distance ahead of me. She pushed aside a fern with her walking stick then dropped to her knees in the leaf litter. Thinking that my worst fears had come to pass and she had been bitten by a snake, I rushed towards her. But there was no snake. Klára was running her fingers through the fur of an animal, about the size of a cat, lying on its side. There was a wound to the head near the ear and a trickle of blood oozing from its mouth.

'It's a possum,' Klára said, turning the animal over. From that angle I could see that the creature had a pretty face with eyes framed by kohl-like markings. 'They shoot them for their fur,' she said, studying the gum tree above us. 'This one must have fallen where they couldn't find it.'

I touched the possum's fur. It was soft and dense and would be appealing to coat makers. The body was cold but not stiff. It must have been killed at dawn. The death of the possum affected us and we remained silent until something in its stomach moved. My first thought was maggots and I was appalled when Klára pushed her fingers into the white belly fur. Two skinny legs with clawed feet appeared then disappeared again. Klára lifted a flap of skin and eased something out. I remembered that some Australian animals had pouches.

'It's a female and she has a joey,' Klára said. The creature that appeared in her hand looked nothing like its mother. The eyes were still closed and it had a head like a bald puppy. Its ribs were showing through its fragile skin. 'It is still warm,' she said, holding the creature towards me. 'You take it. Your skin is warmer than mine.'

I tugged the cotton scarf from around my neck and formed it into a truss. Klára placed the animal in it and I tucked it down the front of my blouse, securing the ends of the strap to my camisole and holding the animal against my chest. I felt it wriggle then settle against my flesh.

'It is so small and has hardly any fur. Will it live without its mother?' I asked.

'I don't know,' she said. 'Let's see what Uncle Ota says.' She gathered up her satchel and we picked up our sticks before running in the direction of home.

Uncle Ota examined the joey and pointed to a slit in its tummy. 'It's a girl. See, she's already got a tiny pouch of her own.'

Ranjana appeared with one of Thomas's woollen caps. 'Shall we wrap her in this? It looks like a pouch.'

Thomas was proud that his hat was being employed in the joey's cause, and watched me tuck the scarf and possum into the pouch before placing them on a warm water bottle in a small hatbox, provided by Esther, with holes in the lid.

'What are we going to feed it?' he asked.

Uncle Ota averted his gaze. He was thinking the same thing I was: that the unformed creature was not going to live more than a few hours. But I could still feel the tingle on my skin where the joey had lain against me and prayed that she would.

Ranjana had taken to the joey as much as Thomas had and was full of suggestions. 'They give orphaned kittens Carnation milk and vitamin drops,' she said. 'Perhaps we can try that. And egg yolk might be good.'

Uncle Ota looked as if he was wrestling with his conscience. But something made him decide to get into the spirit of things. 'All right,' he said, sitting up. 'What shall we call our little orphan?'

'Angel,' Thomas replied.

'Angel is a good name,' agreed Esther. 'We all need an angel.'

Ranjana rummaged through the cupboards and found a can of Carnation milk. She pierced it, added some vitamin drops and poured the creamy mixture into a jug, diluting it with warm water from the kettle before handing the mixture to me.

'Indeed, we all need an angel sometimes,' said Uncle Ota, giving me a knowing smile. 'Now let's hope our little one lives.'

SIXTEEN

Opening night for the Cascade Picture Palace was set for 18 December. The auditorium had been built with a sloping floor so that every seat had an unhampered view. There was a dress circle, finished in Russian red with gold trimmings and chandeliers that could be dimmed or brightened on demand. But when the beginning of the month came around, there were many jobs still uncompleted. The columns of the proscenium were not finished and only half the fresco had been painted. We had plasterers and painters working day and night. The stage was designed so that it could be converted from a film screen to a traditional platform for cabaret acts, but the mechanism for closing the curtain jammed when it was halfway down. Freddy sent technicians from Sydney to iron out the glitches.

I was supervising them one morning when Uncle Ota rushed into the auditorium and called out my name.

'I am over here,' I answered from the second row of seats.

Uncle Ota shook his head. 'I'm going deaf with all the noise. Come with me, I need to speak to you about the program for opening night.'

I stepped over the canvas that had been laid across the floor to protect it. 'I will be back here in half an hour,' I told him. 'I have to go home to feed Angel.'

'Ah, Angel,' said Uncle Ota, with a smile and a nod. 'Of course.'

The first night we had Angel, Klára and I did not sleep. Her cries for her mother were pitiful and we had to change the water bottle every three hours to keep her warm. Klára and Esther returned to Sydney on Sunday afternoon, and Angel was left in my care. Despite my efforts to encourage her to eat, she would not take any food. Her weight dropped half an ounce. By the third day, it was clear from her laboured breathing that Angel was ailing.

'The little thing is like an orphaned child,' lamented Ranjana. 'She wants the smell of her mother.'

'Her mouth opening is not very wide,' Uncle Ota observed. 'And she can probably only drink small amounts at a time.'

Ranjana found a baby bottle and some teats that had belonged to Thomas. She took a fine piece of rubber tubing and pushed it into the opening of the teat. I tested the temperature of the milk mixture and gently inserted the tube into Angel's mouth.

She began to drink.

I fed her every two hours, through the day and night, for the next week. Ranjana offered to help but Angel would not accept food from her, nor even from Klára who came down the following weekend. As the baby possum began to put on weight, I took on the glowing but dishevelled look of a new mother.

'It's just like when I had Tommy,' Ranjana laughed.

I toileted Angel and rubbed her body with a dab of lanolin. One day when I opened the pouch I found her gazing back at me with shining eyes.

In the moment the little creature looked at me, my relationship with nature changed. I had always loved the beauty of trees and forests but I became interested in all the lives around me, no matter how small: the magpie on its nest; the kangaroo grazing at the edge of the bush; the fish that kissed my legs when I waded in the shallows. I felt a sense of lightness and ease that I had not experienced in months. Happiness bubbled up inside me when I came across another living creature. Even when I found a brown snake sleeping in the woodshed, I did not ask our landlady's husband to kill it, as I might have done in the past. I shut the door loosely and put a note on the handle: *Snake in residence.*

'The Buddhists have a saying that whenever you help another living being to thrive, you will find that the real healing has taken place in yourself,' Klára told me.

I thought about Klára's words when I fed Angel her first solid food: the new tips of gum leaves. I tickled her ears. The other brushtail possums I had seen walking along the fence at night had pointed ears, but one of Angel's ears was flat. It was her special quirk.

Klára finished school for the year and she and Esther stayed for the holidays so Klára could rehearse with the cinema orchestra for opening night. Hugh, Giallo and Peter arrived from Sydney on the train the day before the event. Uncle Ota and I met them at the station.

'The ticket collector wasn't going to let us on the train with our feathered friend here,' said Peter, pointing to Giallo. 'We almost didn't make it.'

'Oh, silly people,' I said, putting my finger out so Giallo could shake hands with me using his claw.

'It's all right,' said Hugh. 'I played the crippled soldier. I lost a leg for this country, I reckon they can let me ride a train with my bird.'

Hugh sounded bitter. I decided to introduce him to Freddy. They had met briefly at my premiere but Hugh had not stayed for the party. Ranjana and Freddy were instant cures for self-pity: Ranjana would kick you in the pants, and Freddy would walk right over you if you did not get up soon enough.

When we arrived at the house we found Esther had baked an orange cake for our guests. She was wearing the emerald green dress she kept for formal occasions. She placed the cake on the dining table and went about setting out the teapot and cups and saucers with care. She served everyone but made a special point of asking Hugh how he liked his tea.

'Sugar for sweetness? Milk to make it smooth?' She held the jug over one of the rose-patterned china cups we saved for special occasions.

'Just milk, thank you,' Hugh said, without looking at her.

Esther was not perturbed by his aloof manner. She moved to Uncle Ota's gramophone and dropped the needle. 'Un bel di vedremo' from Puccini's *Madame Butterfly* filled the room.

She knows how he likes his tea, I thought. Esther had made a cup for Hugh almost every hour when we were working on *The Bunyip*. He asked her to stop because he was going to the toilet all the time.

I glanced at Klára. She shrugged her shoulders, not able to understand Esther's diligent attention to Hugh either.

* * *

On the night of the premiere, I weighed Angel. She had tripled her weight and was covered in dense fuzz. Klára and Thomas clapped their hands with delight.

'She looks like a pom-pom,' observed Thomas, stroking Angel's fur when I held her out to him. I pinned her pouch to the side of a parrot cage and left her to munch on the grevillea blossoms Thomas had collected with Klára.

The whole town turned up for the opening of the Cascade Picture Palace. I was proud when I heard the guests chattering in the auditorium before the show. The excitement in the air was palpable. As well as Beaumont Smith's picture *The Prehistoric Hayseeds*, there were chorus lines, comedians and an opera singer on the program. The local beauty queen cut the ribbon and the president of Bulli Shire Council gave a speech commending us on building a cinema in Thirroul. Klára, beautiful in a saffron yellow dress encrusted with sequins, performed Tchaikovsky's Piano Concerto No 1. Robert, who had come to the premiere, could not take his eyes off her.

At the party afterwards, we lowered the lights and a dance band played in the foyer. I knew that Freddy was coming but I had not seen him all evening. I was making my way past the dance floor when someone tapped me on the shoulder. I turned to see a well-built man with dark hair standing behind me. I assumed that he wanted to dance. In a strange way, I felt it would be disloyal to Philip to dance with another man, but the gentleman was a guest. He was dressed in a formal evening suit with a white tie and textured silk lapels. I took the hand he offered to guide me to the dance floor and caught a glimpse of the smart braid-covered buttons of his jacket.

'You look swell,' the man said, leading me into the light of the dance floor.

I recognised the voice and blinked. 'Freddy!'

'Yeah, what?' he said.

'Your suit!'

He glanced down at his jacket. 'Klára chose it for me. You know, I wanted to blend in a bit. I have to play it low-key. There are a couple of people from Galaxy Pictures here and I don't want them knowing I own the place.'

'You look nice,' I told him.

The band started up a foxtrot and Freddy led me around the floor. His hold was a touch too firm, but he was a big man and I barely reached his chest, so we had a strength disparity anyway. We glided past couples and I thought of Beatrice and Philip.

'So what have you been doing down here? Any writing?' Freddy asked me.

'I have tried,' I said. 'But nothing comes out.'

'Maybe you're trying too hard. The bunyip idea worked. You need to take a story like that and make it longer.'

I did not want to tell Freddy that I was finding it difficult to write because I was thinking about Philip. But somehow he saw through me.

'I know you were in love with Philip Page, but Beatrice had the claim on him and that's the past now,' he said.

I was astounded by his brazenness. 'You don't mince words.'

'Mincing words is a waste of time. If you respect someone, you tell them the truth.'

The shock of the truth in what Freddy said unsettled me. Klára had said the same thing and Uncle Ota had hinted at it. They were all right: if I was to move forward I had to put Philip behind me. But whenever I thought of him, I wanted to hold on to the memory a little longer and that was what was keeping me trapped.

'I thought you didn't approve,' I said. 'Of Philip and me.'

Freddy's brow wrinkled. 'I was jealous. Philip was lucky.'

The band played a quickstep and Freddy spun me around. Perhaps he thought Philip was lucky to have had two women in love with him. I remembered Robert saying once that Freddy was lonely. His parents had passed away and his only family was an old aunt who lived in New York.

'What have you been doing if you haven't been writing?' Freddy asked when the band took a break. 'Taking photographs?'

Apart from helping Uncle Ota with the cinema and bushwalking with Klára, I had not done much at all. I told him about Angel and how Klára and I had saved her life.

'That's nice,' said Freddy, leading me off the dance floor. 'You raised a possum. Are you going to make it into a collar or something?'

After believing that Freddy might be more sensitive than he appeared, my hopes were dashed. The suit has changed but not the man, I thought.

I awoke the next morning with an idea for a film, and jotted down the seeds of the story before getting out of bed. My conversation with Freddy had sparked something, because every morning after that when I woke up I knew what was going to happen in the next scene I had to write. The story was about a society girl engaged to a wealthy man. They have an argument one day and to make amends the man takes the woman shopping and tells her that she can have anything she wants. She decides on a coat made of possum fur. But each time the woman wears the coat she is struck by bad luck. She wants to show off her coat to her girlfriends at a restaurant but is stung by a bee on the eyelid before she leaves home. She wears it to visit her parents and her father chokes — nearly fatally — on a pea. She wears the coat to a society function and her fiancé trips and breaks his ankle. The woman, however, cannot see that her bad luck is related to the purchase of the coat.

After breakfast I typed out the scene I had imagined in the morning. As the script grew, I reviewed the pages with a sense of excitement: *I* wanted to know what would happen next.

The couple's wedding is to take place in a church on the south coast. But the woman wears the coat to the rehearsal and the church burns down. At a party in the couple's honour, the woman overhears a young man, a friend of her father's, tell another guest that the possum is known in Aboriginal legends as a curious, sometimes mischievous, but always kind animal. He jokes that these are not traits of the woman, who was rude to him on a previous occasion. 'She's wearing the wrong coat. She should be wearing skunk.'

When I reached the end of the story, however, I became stuck. Then one evening when I was feeding Angel gum leaves and pieces of apple, an idea came to me. I scribbled it down in the margins of the newspaper I used to line her cage.

While driving home one evening, the woman's fiancé — drunk and cantankerous — hits a possum on the road. He wants to drive on but the woman, burned by what she overheard about herself, insists that they stop to check whether it is alive or dead. The possum is still alive and has a joey in her pouch. The fiancé suggests that they run over the possum again, but the woman says that she might just be in shock. She wraps the possum in the only warm thing she has — the coat — and takes her home. While holding the possum in her lap the woman runs her fingers through the animal's fur and then looks at her coat. It dawns on her what it is made of.

The next morning the possum is alert — she was only suffering concussion — and at dusk the woman takes her to the forest near where they found her and lets her go. The woman realises her coat has blood on it, but rather than get it cleaned she buries it. Then she tells her fiancé that their engagement is off. She finds the young man from the party of the previous night and tells him that she did not like what he said about her but he was right. The man looks at her differently and the audience is left with the impression of a possible relationship for them in the future.

Klára was the first person to read the script. 'The sense of magic reminds me of Prague,' she said. 'But the story feels Australian too.'

I sent it to Hugh, knowing that if there was a fault with the script he would have no qualms about pointing it out. *The story never lags, which is important*, he wrote in reply. *But it is a fantasy and bitter-sweet. Australian audiences usually want realism and a straightforward ending. But that does not mean you cannot take a chance; it only means you will have to find a producer willing to take that chance with you. In terms of the camera work, this picture could be visually stunning. But we cannot use leftover stock for this one, Adéla. You are going to need to raise about three thousand pounds.*

Hugh was right. Most Australian films were about station life and bushrangers. There might not be an audience for my picture — and three thousand pounds was a lot of money.

From my photography work, I managed to keep Klára and myself. The funds Aunt Josephine had sent amounted to one thousand pounds and I wanted to save the money for emergencies that might arise. I was not going to be able to make the picture without investors. I was hesitant to approach Freddy because the subject matter would go over his head and I needed a producer who could sympathise with my vision. Uncle Ota gave me the idea of approaching local businesses to see if they would invest in return for advertising. But it was obvious from the polite smiles and the offers of cups of tea I received that none of the businessmen I met with took me seriously. The most I was offered was two hundred pounds and an invitation to dinner. Part of me wanted to retreat, and have Uncle Ota or Hugh stand in my place when asking for money. But Aunt Josephine had instilled in me the belief that women were capable of anything, as long as they had faith in themselves. So I had faith, but it still did not bring me any money.

Half a year passed before I progressed further with the script. The Cascade Picture Palace was turning into a successful venture and Uncle Ota planned to put a manager in charge of the cinema and move to Balgownie to create another picture palace there with Freddy's backing. Ranjana and Thomas would go with him. It was time for me to return to Sydney to be with Klára. She was entering her senior years at the Conservatorium High School and needed my support.

Esther had proved a dedicated chaperone to Klára, but it was clear to me that my sister's feelings for Robert had become serious. She spoke with undisguised enthusiasm about all the things they did together: attending lectures at the Theosophical Society; sketching the bowerbirds in Robert's garden; rowing boats in the National Park. I could not leave Esther in charge of my sister forever. Klára was blossoming into a lovely woman but she could be wilful too and I wanted to make sure nothing distracted her from her studies. In truth, I was also jealous. As Robert and Klára's mutual adoration grew, I felt my own part in my sister's life diminishing and I wanted to be at the centre of it again.

I had not been successful in attracting investors for my picture and was on the verge of giving up on the idea when I saw a film that was to change everything. On my last night in Thirroul, Uncle Ota screened Fritz Lang's *Siegfried*. My breath was taken away by the retelling of the Nordic fable. It was simply too beautiful for words. I lay awake that night remembering the magnificent sets and costumes. A picture like that would cost more than three thousand pounds. I rolled over and turned on the light. Perhaps I had set my sights too low? But there was only one person I could go to who I knew could provide the kind of finance I needed to make my film into a masterpiece: Freddy.

The following day, I returned to Sydney with Angel in a cat basket. We had become inseparable. I looked forward to dusk when she woke up to munch the native leaves and blossoms Thomas and I collected. When she was a baby, she would climb out of her cage and sit on my back, as if I were her wild mother. But once she emerged from her pouch and moved into the hollow branch I had hung in her cage, she began to outgrow her home.

At Esther's house, Klára and I put Angel in an aviary in our room, with some branches for her to climb and a hatbox with a hole cut in it for her to sleep inside. I left the door open at night so she was free to wander the house. But in the morning there would be broken dishes on the floor and droppings on the carpet. No one complained about cleaning up after her because we all loved Angel, but she was a wild animal, not a cat that could be house-trained. The unsuitability of keeping her as a pet was dawning on us. To curb some of her habits, I tied a rope from the end of my bed through the window and out to a tree in the back garden. In this way, Angel could wander from the bedroom to sit in the tree to eat her fruit and do her droppings.

For the first three nights, we found Angel back and asleep in her hatbox in the morning. But after the fourth night, she did not return. Klára and I searched nearby gardens and parks for her.

We left corn out at night, and found in the morning that it had been nibbled, but whether the raider had been Angel or another possum, or a flying fox, we did not know.

'You will see her again,' Klára reassured me. 'She has probably found some other possums to play with.'

Each night I looked out my window in vain. There was no sign of our Angel. 'What if a cat has caught her?' I lamented. 'Or a dog?' I shuddered when I remembered that greyhound trainers used possums as bait.

Angel was born to be wild, Uncle Ota wrote to me. *She has gone to do what is natural to her. She will be there somewhere around, you will see.*

I tried to take comfort in his words, but I felt the loss of my animal friend.

The empty space left by Angel motivated me to send my script to Freddy. He replied by telegram: *Come straight away.*

I was ready to throw myself into work.

SEVENTEEN

Hugh and I went to see Freddy at his home in Cremorne. He did not bring Giallo. 'He would compete for attention,' he said.

We entered Freddy's driveway and found ourselves on an estate that was the opposite in every way to the shade-dappled gardens and genteel features of the houses around it. Freddy's house was a two-storey mansion with a bell-cast roof and Moorish arched windows, minarets and towers. It might have been attractive if it was softened by a leafy garden, but it stood solitary in the middle of an expanse of lawn. Perhaps the architect had advised Freddy that it would appear imposing that way, but it looked like a mausoleum. The atmosphere of domination extended to the parterre garden. The trees and shrubs had been sculptured into cones, corkscrews and pyramids. No plant had been left untouched. It was as if Freddy thought that the flowing shapes of nature should be subjugated. The garden was lifeless too: there was not a bird to be seen anywhere.

I hesitated at the door and glanced back at the garden. Was Freddy the right person to produce a film about nature? I sighed. What choice did I have? I nodded to Hugh who turned the ringer.

A maid with a long nose and black hair greeted us at the door. 'Mr Rockcliffe is in his study,' she said in a Spanish accent. 'Come this way, please.'

We followed her down a hallway with a Gobelin tapestry on one wall and a suit of armour against the other. The maid knocked on a door and opened it. 'Mr Rockcliffe, your visitors are here.'

'Come in,' said Freddy, rising from his desk.

I walked into the room and stopped in my tracks. Freddy was wearing a blue checked suit with a mustard-coloured shirt but that was not what shocked me. Spread-eagled on the floor was a polar bear skin. I had seen tiger, zebra and wolf skins in the houses of people I had photographed but I had never seen a pelt like this one. The head was still intact and the mournful glass eyes stared at me. A rope was twisted around the animal's muzzle and extended to its outstretched paws, as if it had just been trapped and was looking death in the face.

'Christ!' muttered Hugh when he came in behind me.

'You like it?' asked Freddy, signalling to his maid to prepare tea. 'The first director I made a film with gave it to me.'

A fire burned in the fireplace and the room was stiflingly hot. It had been cold outside but now my head boiled under my cloche hat. I patted my neck with my handkerchief.

'Please, sit down,' Freddy said, indicating two wing-backed chairs.

Hugh and I edged our way around the rug, not able to bring ourselves to step on that unfortunate animal.

The maid brought the tea. I was glad for the excuse to look at my cup instead of the rug or Freddy's suit. Maybe he does these things on purpose, I told myself. To unsettle people.

Freddy sat back in his chair and folded his hands behind his head. 'I've read your script, Adéla,' he said. 'And, boy, do you have some work to do. It's full of flaws.'

'What flaws?' I asked.

'Well to start with, the assumption that people might care about a possum the same way they care about a dog. Don't you know that Australians slaughtered five million possums last trapping season? Why the hell should they care if one of them gets hit by a car? Or if a dozen of them are turned into a coat for some society lady to wear?'

I knew possums were hunted for their fur but the number that were being slaughtered left me speechless. I thought of Angel's innocent eyes. She was more beautiful than any dog or cat. How could people kill animals like her?

'What about a native bear then?' Hugh suggested. 'People seem to like them.'

Freddy scratched his chin. 'One of Australia's national symbols? Just as many of them are killed in a season. I think you two have been hanging around the Vegetarian Café too long. Children might think those animals are cute but their parents couldn't care less.'

He waved a box of cigars in front of Hugh, who declined, and took one himself.

I was on the verge of tears. My script did not have a flaw: the whole premise was wrong. I stared at the rope around the polar bear's muzzle. I did not blame Freddy. He was only speaking the truth. Who was going to take a story about a possum seriously? I lived in a much kinder world with Uncle Ota, Ranjana and

Klára. Even my burly cameraman would not hurt a lamb — let alone eat one. But why did Freddy call us here if he was only going to scoff at the script?

'If the story is so out of touch with what people think, why did you want to see us?' I asked him. 'Are you trying to humiliate us?'

Freddy's eyes opened with surprise. 'Why?' he asked. 'Because this is so different from the pictures that are being produced here it's refreshing. I'm excited about it — and believe me, that's rare.'

I was too stunned to take in immediately what Freddy had said. A moment ago I had been ready to leave.

He laughed and shook his head. 'You artists are all the same — too sensitive! I tell you there are flaws in your script and you think I'm saying the whole thing is trash. What you need to do is get your idea across not to other nature-minded people like yourself but to kangaroo-shooting, meat-eating, leather-wearing men like me. You find a joey in a pouch, you save it; I find one in an animal I've shot and I toss it in the bush to die. You have to stand in my shoes and make me see things differently. You haven't achieved that yet with this draft. I didn't shed a tear.'

I saw my relationship to Freddy in a different light. He ruffled my feathers, but it made me stronger. 'What do you suggest?' I asked him. I was ready to do whatever it took to make my script work. I knew that if I did not listen to Freddy's advice, the picture — even if made — would be ridiculed and forgotten.

Freddy took a puff of his cigar and blew a smoke ring in the air before answering. 'What you have to do is make your main character see the world as most people do, then have something happen that changes that perception. Why should she care about some animal's life when she has concerns enough in her own? What's important to her is how she looks and how she is perceived. Is she fashionable enough? If millions of animals are being killed each day, what does it matter if she harms just one?'

I tried to put myself in the position that Freddy was describing. I had been a vegetarian for so many years now that it was difficult for me to see the moral difference between killing an animal and killing a person. But church ministers, loving mothers, policemen and schoolteachers killed and ate animals every day. It was the heartstrings of the indifferent I had to reach, and I was not sure how I could do that.

'You need to plot nature calling out to this heroine long before the possum gets hit,' Freddy explained. 'Perhaps she goes on a hunt with her friends and sees a mother fox and her cubs ripped apart by dogs. Maybe she has to turn away — or feels compelled to look. You have to plant these things from the beginning of the story.'

When Freddy saw that I was absorbing his words, he turned to the next flaw in the script.

'Why does the story have to be set on the south coast?' he asked Hugh.

'The scenery is lush,' Hugh said. 'The way this picture will look is important.'

I suddenly was not sure why it had to be set down south, apart from the fact that I was living there when I wrote the script.

'No more lush than you'll find in Ku-ring-gai Chase, which is closer. If we go south we'll have to accommodate the whole cast there. And, if they work in the theatre, we'll have to pay them for missing a season. If we film in Sydney they can still work at the theatre in the evenings.'

'Yes, that's true,' Hugh said.

It was my turn next. 'Adéla, you mentioned in your letter that it would be necessary to use Waverley Film Studios for the indoor sets. Was there any particular reason?'

I had never forgotten the premiere of *The Ghost of Spooky Hill* and the way the curtains on the set constantly moved in the breeze and how the actors' hair became more windblown as a scene progressed.

'I don't want to shoot interior scenes on an exterior set,' I said. 'Even if it means we have to pay for klieg lights.'

'Wanting klieg lights is understandable,' said Freddy. 'After all, if we want to get this film sold overseas we can't have the technical standards laughed at. But why do we have to build sets in a studio? Surely if it's a socialite's house we're trying to evoke, we can find someone to lend us their home for the day in return for a location fee. Why don't I ask Robert if we can use his place?'

I was exhausted. But I was excited too. *In the Dark* was not going to be some two-bit production. Hugh actually smiled when Freddy told him that we were going to buy a new Bell & Howell camera.

'Thank you,' I said to Freddy when the meeting was over. 'I am looking forward to working with you.' I was surprised to find that I meant it.

He pointed to the scarf around my neck. 'Beautiful fabric. Silk?'

'Yes,' I answered, fingering the scarf Mother had given me.

'Silk indeed,' said Freddy, an amused expression on his face. 'Any idea how it's made?'

I had thought my hard work was over when I had finished my script, but it was only beginning. To find the answer to Freddy's question about my scarf, I asked Uncle Ota how silk was made and was appalled to learn that silkworms were boiled alive to obtain minute amounts of cloth.

It was something of a shock to me to realise that I could be just as indifferent and uncaring about another creature's suffering as people who ate meat. How could I judge them when I found myself justifying that silkworms were only insects that did not feel anything, and if they were not killed for silk they would be eaten by birds anyway. But inside I knew I was making rationalisations to defend one thing: I did not want to give up my beautiful scarf. I looked pretty in it. Freddy, in his perceptive way, had given me an insight into how women justified their fur coats.

A picture that did not touch people's hearts was a pointless one to make. Freddy told Robert what I was doing and he invited me to meet a friend of his mother's who had formed a group to discourage women from buying hats with lyrebird feathers.

'When I was growing up, those beautiful birds were everywhere,' the woman told me. 'My grandchildren may never see one.'

The woman gave me the idea of questioning the other patrons at the Vegetarian Café. What motivations did they have for not harming animals? 'Why did you stop eating meat?' I asked.

Many of them said it was because they believed eating flesh caused all sorts of diseases. Most, however, spoke of 'the rights of animals'. One man told me that he grew up on a farm where he'd had a pet piglet. When the pig became a sow she was sent off to the butcher. 'Molly looked into my eyes when they loaded her on the cart. She knew what was going to happen to her. I had betrayed my childhood friend.'

I spent hours in the State Library, poring over parliamentary notes on the bills that had been passed to protect wildlife and the arguments against them: *I entertain no sort of doubt that instead of bringing in a bill to protect native animals it would have been far better in the interests of the settlers generally to bring in a bill to exterminate the whole lot of them.* The farmers of the coastal districts where I had found Angel demanded that possums be systematically eradicated: *They are not only a nuisance about gardens but they get underneath the iron roofs.* But every so often a voice would speak up in defence of the 'useless brutes': *This bill has not been submitted for the protection of native animals, or in order to prevent their extinction, but to foster and keep up the trade in skins.* I found letters to editors written by members of the Wildlife Preservation Society of Australia that touched my heart: *It's a wicked thing to shoot such beautiful animals. We must take pride in our unique fauna if we are to have any sort of pride in our unique nation and not send them to the brink of extinction. We must educate our children to love and cherish these creatures as they should love and cherish this country.* I began to see that I was not so alone in my thinking, although like-minded individuals were in the minority. *What is the use of these animals?* one letter said. *They are of no use ... I hope any bill to protect them will be thrown out because they are a nuisance.*

Despite my bond with Angel, I changed the animal in my script from a possum to a native bear. The message was more important than the species. Possums were accused of all sorts of crimes against crops while native bears were seen as benign. They looked like people too, I thought, with their flat facial features. Lying back with its arms and legs spread out, a native bear almost resembled a child.

Imelda, the beautiful artist's model at the café, turned out to be called Mabel. She gave me some invaluable insight.

'I've been a vegetarian nearly all my life,' she told me. 'I would never harm an animal.'

When I asked her why, she lifted her skirt and pulled off her boot. Half her foot was missing. 'I was going to be a dancer but no chance of that after what happened. When the artists paint me they drape satin over my feet.'

I stared at the injury, expecting a story about a shark bite.

'I was seven years old when I put my foot in a steel-jaw trap. My father used them to catch rabbits and foxes but half the time we got wallabies and roos. I'd been having a fantasy about fairies living up on the mountain so I'd snuck out of the house when my sisters weren't watching. It was two days before they found me, not having expected me to have gone so far. They dredged the dams and searched the wells, but I was up there on the mountain in agony, burning in the sun during the day and freezing during the cold, lonely night. My struggles to relieve the pain broke my bones and tore open my flesh. When they found me I was covered in bulldog ants.'

The image of a little girl with her foot shattered in a trap left me speechless. Mabel looked me in the eye. 'I know the crushing grip of those traps, the ravens circling overhead ready to peck out my eyes. Who could subject an animal to that?'

I went home that day knowing what I had to do with my script. The leading lady was not going to tell her fiancé to stop when they hit the native bear with their car. She was not going to pick it up and wrap it in her expensive fur coat. Klára might have done something like that, but the average woman would no sooner think to help the bear than she would to nurse a sick rat. The woman would have a flicker of conscience but nothing more. Then one night after she has a fight with her fiancé she walks away from him. Down the road she is run over by a carload of drunk party-goers. They stop for a moment to see what they have struck. The woman cries out for help, but when they see a person lying on the road, they get back in their car and drive on, frightened of the consequences. The woman is left on the road all night with only her fur coat for comfort. As she lies there she remembers the native bear in its agony throes.

I sent the new script to Freddy. He arrived the following day at our house. 'Now we're talking,' he said with a grin. 'Now we have something powerful. It will either soar or sink. Let's see which one.'

Once the script was ready we auditioned actors. Hugh and I did the first rounds and Freddy joined us for the final selection. The auditions took place in Freddy's drawing room, which was as macabre as his study. A stag's head hung above the mantelpiece and a stuffed owl perched in the corner. But instead of being oblivious to my discomfort this time, Freddy seemed embarrassed.

'They were my father's,' he said, looking at the trophies as if seeing them for the first time. 'He was a keen hunter.'

I arrived the next day prepared to ask Freddy if we could move to another room, but the stag and owl were gone. In their place were a tasteful still life and a watercolour painting of a rosella.

'They are beautiful,' I told Freddy.

He tugged his collar and smiled. 'We are influencing each other.'

The two actors we chose to play the male leads, Andy Dale and Don Stanford, had been on stage since they were children. The role of our female lead proved more difficult to fill. We auditioned actresses and models before settling on a ballet dancer named

Dolly Blackwood. Rather than mouth lines and pull faces, Dolly walked about touching things: running her finger along the marble fireplace; stroking the chairs; gazing at her reflection in a mirror. There was something mysterious about her that was right for the part. Freddy described her as 'an Australian Louise Brooks'.

During the first day of rehearsals, Hugh filmed some of the key scenes. When we viewed the rushes the following morning my blood turned cold. Dolly was luminescent but Dale and Don were grotesque. Everything about them was out of proportion and twisted. We tried again the following day, but the result was the same.

I woke up that night unable to breathe. What made you think you could direct a film? I asked myself. My only experience at being a director was finishing off Peter's half-hearted attempt at a picture and directing my family in *The Bunyip*. This time I had two famous names in my production and finance from not only Freddy but investors such as Farmer's department store. I thought of the disaster looming when everyone realised that I did not know what I was doing. Then I remembered Aunt Josephine's faith in me and decided to act like a professional, and not like a child bursting into tears at the first sign of difficulty.

I wrote to Raymond Longford, who Mr Tilly had put me in touch with when I first became interested in making pictures. I told him that I admired his work and asked if he would meet with me and give me some advice on film technique. I waited for a reply, but nothing came. I grew desperate and lost more sleep. Then two days before we were scheduled to start filming, I received a note from him inviting me to afternoon tea.

We agreed to meet at a teahouse in Neutral Bay. I recognised Mr Longford as soon as I stepped into the room with its lace curtains and velveteen chairs. He was sitting by the fireplace, a copy of the morning newspaper in his hands. He was exactly like the picture I had seen of him in *Everyone's*: smooth ivory skin and a mouth that looked on the brink of a smile. When he stood up to greet me he towered above everything and had to bend to avoid hitting his head on the light-shade that dangled above the table. The soft eyes framed by peaked eyebrows conveyed a great sadness. I did not have to ask why.

'Lottie would have liked to be here to meet you,' Mr Longford said, pulling out my chair for me. 'She enjoys the company of intelligent women with talent. But she's busy reviewing some of the scenes for our next film.'

Mr Longford was in denial. I had heard from Hugh, who was friends with his cameraman, that Mr Longford's partner, Lottie Lyell, was too sick to do anything any more and that *Fisher's Ghost*, which had been released the previous year, was probably the last great Longford–Lyell collaboration. She was in the final throes of consumption.

'If I had half Miss Lyell's talent, I should be blessed indeed,' I told Mr Longford.

Tears welled in his eyes and he turned his head to signal to the waiter, who alleviated further awkwardness by bringing a tray of tea and sponge cakes to the table.

'Now, what is it that I can do for you?' Mr Longford asked me.

I told him that I was making my first feature picture and I was experiencing trouble with the actors. What I wanted them to be on screen was not happening in the rushes. I had chosen Mr Longford over other directors because I hoped he would have more respect for a female director due to his partnership with Lottie Lyell.

Mr Longford listened to me thoughtfully. 'The technique the actors need for the stage and what is required for film are quite different things,' he said. 'It sounds as if your actors are projecting themselves too much. You mustn't make them run over and over their parts, as a theatre director might do. They mustn't be conscious of acting. Rather they must live their parts and *be* the characters rather than *act* them. If you want your actor to convey that he loves a woman, let his gaze follow her out of the room rather than have him make dramatic gestures. That's why *The Sentimental Bloke* was praised so highly. Everyone appreciated the naturalness of the actors.'

I considered his advice and realised that he had pinpointed the problem. He also told me that I should treat the whole cast as if they were stars. 'Every performance counts towards the whole.'

When the waiter offered us more tea we both gladly accepted. I was happy to see that Mr Longford was enjoying talking to me as much as I was him.

'But you know, Miss Rose,' he said, rearranging the napkin on his lap, 'the greatest problem you will face with your film is not the acting nor your age nor your sex. No, the biggest challenge facing you is that you are making a film about Australia. Have you heard of the Combine?'

I shook my head and Mr Longford explained that the Combine referred to the merger of two companies: Australasian Films, which dominated production and distribution, and Union Theatres, which controlled eighty per cent of Sydney's cinemas. 'If it were not for the efforts of the Combine to crush the Australian film industry, we would be well ahead of the Americans.'

Mr Longford must have noticed my surprise for he was quick to continue. 'Make no mistake: the Combine acts in the American industry's interest,' he said. 'It is much cheaper to import films than to make them. Before the war Australian productions were quite crude, but when Lottie and I started making pictures like *The Fatal Wedding* and *Margaret Catchpole* for small sums and earning profits here and in England, we were perceived as a threat.'

I listened with interest while Mr Longford went on to explain that the Combine had sabotaged *The Silence of Dean Maitland* by refusing it a release at premiere theatres.

'I had to go to an independent exhibitor,' he said. 'The Combine then threatened to cut off their supply of films if they screened any more Australian productions.'

I was even more appalled at the financial problems faced by local producers. 'Because Union Theatres wouldn't exhibit *The Sentimental Bloke*, I was offered the lowest price possible by Hoyts' city theatre,' Mr Longford said. 'After one week of screening the film three times a day to full houses, they made a fortune and I got thirty pounds.'

I glanced at the palm trees outside the window. The sky was growing dark. A waiter lit the fire and stoked up the flames. It was unbelievable to me that the finest director in Australia was having so much trouble getting his films exhibited and was living a borderline existence when his films themselves were making profits. I reviewed my position. When I had asked Freddy about distribution, he had told me to concentrate on making the best film possible and that he would take care of the rest.

'And *Fisher's Ghost*?' I asked. 'How did that do?'

Mr Longford's thin lips broke into a smile. 'Same story,' he said. 'Lottie and I made it for one thousand pounds. It played to full houses and made everyone else a fortune. Our production company went broke.'

'But you managed to get it distributed?'

'Not through the Combine,' answered Mr Longford. 'Stuart Doyle of Union Theatres said it was "gruesome".'

'I thought it was atmospheric,' I told him. 'Compared to a lot of American films, I would hardly have called it gruesome.'

Mr Longford put down his cup. 'It probably wasn't Mr Doyle anyway but his friend, Frederick Rockcliffe, who had that opinion. It's well known that Rockcliffe has a low opinion of Australian directors.'

The mention of Freddy's name fell like an iron on my head. If what Mr Longford said was true, why was Freddy supporting me? I almost admitted to Mr Longford who was producing my picture, but I hesitated. I liked Mr Longford and thought he was a great artist. But there were other Australian directors producing good work too, and Beaumont Smith could get his films exhibited. Yet when Mr Longford spoke, one would have thought he and Lottie Lyell were the only Australian directors of any note. In all my conversations with Freddy, he had seemed supportive of the idea of local production. He had only expressed a dislike of character studies and stories of down-and-outs, which was the genre Mr Longford specialised in. Was it possible that this was not about a large firm trying to crush an artist, but rather a clash of personalities? Mr Longford had presence but he also had an ego. And so did Freddy.

After another round of tea, the subject of our conversation changed from films to my homeland.

'One would hardly detect an accent although there is something exotic about you, Miss Rose,' said Mr Longford. 'And yet, most encouragingly, I find you more passionately Australian than most Australians.'

I thanked him for what I considered a great compliment. Yes, I did feel passionately about my new homeland and its natural beauty. My mind drifted to Ranjana. She spoke with a perfect

British accent but until she adopted her sari again she had not been accepted.

It was dark outside when Mr Longford and I agreed that we should head to our homes. Mr Longford helped me with my coat and walked me to the wharf. Before I boarded the ferry, he tipped his hat to me and said, 'You are very young, Miss Rose. You have so much to learn and so much ahead of you. I envy you ... and in some ways I pity you too.'

I waved to him as the ferry chugged off, leaving a wake of white foam in the black water. The next time I would see him, Lottie Lyell would be dead and his career in pictures would be over. Mr Longford's words were an omen, even though I did not know it then.

EIGHTEEN

When I told Klára and Robert that Raymond Longford had made Lottie Lyell and Arthur Tauchert mingle with the poor of Woolloomooloo to prepare them for *The Sentimental Bloke*, Robert suggested that the actors of *In the Dark* live in his house while we were filming. 'They should look as though they belong here,' he said.

Freddy agreed when I repeated Robert's suggestion to him. 'The picture will be more convincing if the actors look natural in their surroundings. It should be the most normal thing in the world to them that someone else will clear a table after them or pick up their clothes.'

He bought Dolly a tailored dress to rehearse in, rather than the blouse and skirt she had been wearing.

'It's not very comfortable,' she complained.

'Society women are never comfortable,' Freddy told her. 'But they always look smart.'

Andy and Don spent their breaks playing tennis with Robert,

and finished their day by investigating the labels on the bottles above the bar.

During one lunch break I noticed that Esther, who was organising the catering, had set her hair in waves. She looked beautiful. Robert and Freddy complimented her but Hugh said nothing. Esther stared at Hugh longer than necessary each time she passed a plate or piece of cutlery in his direction, but Hugh looked straight through her.

She is besotted with him, I sighed. In the years we had lived with Esther, she had ceased to be our landlady. We were more like a family, and Esther, who had been an only child, often said she felt she was living with her sisters and brothers. I had been unlucky in love, but that did not mean I couldn't hope for the best for those I cared about. So what about Hugh? Was he oblivious to Esther's interest or was he only shy?

One afternoon, while Hugh and I were having a production meeting, Esther snuck into the room with a tray of tea and biscuits. She placed it on the table beside us without a word and crept out the door again. Hugh did not even look up. I could not stand it any longer.

'Hugh, I want to talk to you about Esther,' I said.

'Who?' he asked, continuing to make notes on his script.

'Esther!' I repeated.

Giallo jumped from Hugh's shoulder onto the table. 'Esther!' he squawked.

Hugh glanced up. 'Oh, Esther,' he said. 'Yes?'

'She likes you … she likes you a lot. As a man.'

Hugh stared at me with such incomprehension that at first it was comical. Then his eyes darkened. 'I don't want any woman's sympathy. I know she lost her fiancé in the war and he was a hero and all that. Well, I'm not him.'

'I don't think she thinks you are,' I said. 'You remind her of him, but of course she knows you are someone different.'

Hugh turned back to his script and did not answer.

'Don't you even think she's nice, Hugh?'

'I don't think anything at all,' he said, slamming the script on the table. Hugh had a gruff manner at the best of times but I had never seen him lose his temper. It took me a few seconds to recover.

'What are you angry about?' I asked him. 'I'm only trying to help. Do you want to be alone all your life?'

Hugh turned his back to me and muttered, 'Yes, well, I don't say anything about you and Freddy.'

'What did you say?' I asked, not sure if I had heard correctly. Was Hugh jealous that Freddy had become so involved in the picture?

'I'm here to make a picture with you,' Hugh replied. 'Not to have my life interfered with. Can we get back to work?'

I felt my face redden. Hugh had never spoken to me like that. We had always been equals. 'Four eyes are better than two' was our motto. He had reprimanded me as if I were a schoolgirl because I had pointed out Esther's interest. She was a lovely person and he would be lucky to have her.

'I'm the director of this film,' I reminded him. 'Be careful how you speak to me.'

Hugh did not respond to the rebuke. A chilly silence hung between us while he returned to writing on his script. He glanced up and noticed the tea tray. 'Here,' he said, pulling it towards us and pouring me a cup. 'Let's say no more on the subject and concentrate on the picture. Agreed?'

My anger softened when I heard his conciliatory tone. 'Agreed,' I answered. I was glad that the goodwill was restored between us, but when I looked at the freshly baked biscuits on the tray I could not help feeling sorry for Esther.

A few days after we finished filming, Uncle Ota wrote to say that he would be returning to Sydney with Ranjana and Thomas. Uncle Ota had found a manager for the Balgownie cinema and Freddy had invited my uncle to become his partner. The two men intended to make an offer on Mr Tilly's cinema, which Uncle Ota would manage himself in order to be with us. I was thrilled by the news. I had missed Uncle Ota and Ranjana and especially Thomas. The house was not the same without his cheerful chatter.

The same night, another friend returned.

I was in the kitchen thinking about ideas for a new script, when I heard a bump on the roof. The house had been silent until then except for the occasional creak of its walls. I listened. Footsteps scurried along the roof then came to a halt. A cat, I told myself. The steps were too heavy for a rat or a mouse.

Something jumped into the tree outside the window. The leaves rustled and two eyes glistened in the dark. A possum with one flat ear peered through the foliage.

'Angel!'

I grabbed an apple from the fruit bowl and rushed outside. The possum was twice as big as the Angel I remembered but she did not run away when I approached her.

'Angel,' I murmured. 'Where have you been?'

I bit off a piece of apple and passed it to her. She clasped it in her paws and chewed it noisily. Something moved in her belly. A crimson nose and whiskers appeared and sniffed the air. Then a tiny head with pointed ears and bright eyes emerged from the pouch.

'You've got a joey!' I cried.

I sat on the back steps and watched Angel and her baby. The joey crawled out of Angel's pouch and onto her back. It nibbled the soft tips of leaves while Angel crunched on the mature ones. I filled Angel in on everything that had happened since her disappearance.

'And you inspired my first picture ... although I had to change your character to a native bear.'

When dawn broke, the joey crawled headfirst into Angel's pouch. Angel gave me a look before climbing up the silver gum tree and disappearing into a hollow.

'Welcome home,' I said.

With Ranjana back in Sydney, I had someone I trusted to do the editing of *In the Dark*. But while the filming of the picture had been a cooperative effort, the editing did not go smoothly.

'Cut that,' Freddy told Ranjana, after she had played a scene of a car moving along a country road. It was a beautifully composed sequence with the interplay of light and shade.

'No,' said Hugh. 'You have to leave that. It builds up atmosphere.'

'It builds up nothing,' said Freddy. 'Cut it.'

'It is visually stunning,' I said in Hugh's defence.

'It's boring,' said Freddy. 'It slows the story down.'

We all liked working with each other but never held back our opinions. Hugh and I were digging in our heels. Ranjana adjusted her tartan sari and rolled her eyes.

'Look!' she said. 'I will play the previous scene then I want you to cover your eyes, and open them again when I tell you. That way you'll see what the picture looks like without the car.' We did as she suggested and saw that Freddy was right. Hugh and I were thinking artistically, but the way Freddy wanted the picture edited made it jump from the screen. I realised I had to see the difference between what had seemed like a brilliant idea at the time and what worked.

I nodded to Freddy and he smiled at me. It amused me to think that I had once found him annoying. He was dressing more elegantly these days, and, after Klára had told him that I thought his garden was sterile, he had employed a new gardener, Rex, to make it leafier.

The day we finished the last intertitle, I arrived home in the afternoon to find Uncle Ota sitting in the parlour by himself. The sight of his wet cheeks stopped me in my tracks. I had never seen my uncle cry before.

'What is it?' I asked, my stomach clenching with fear that something had happened to Klára, Esther or Thomas. Ranjana, I knew, was safe. I had just left her at the cinema.

Then my eye fell to the letter in Uncle Ota's hand. I recognised Doctor Holub's handwriting.

'Aunt Josephine?' I asked. 'Has something happened to Aunt Josephine?'

Uncle Ota tried to say something but he could not. I took the letter from him and my gaze settled on the words:

> *It all happened within a matter of days. I assure you*
> *that your dear sister did not suffer long. We buried*
> *her with a picture of you and one of your nieces*
> *with their mother and father. Frip is an old fellow*
> *now but he is well taken care of by my wife.*
> *Although he misses his mistress, he has my four*
> *daughters to dote on him so he does quite well in his*
> *new home ...*

My eyes blurred. I could read no more.

Uncle Ota looked at me. 'Influenza. There is a bout of it sweeping Europe again.'

I threw my arms around Uncle Ota and wept. Memories of Aunt Josephine and Frip visiting us in Prague flooded back to me. Miloš had not murdered Aunt Josephine, as I had once feared he might, but he had robbed us of time with her. I remembered her letter from Mariánské Lázně. She had sounded unwell then. Undoubtedly dealing with Miloš had weakened her health and left her susceptible.

'I thought I would see her again,' Uncle Ota told me, taking my hands in his trembling ones. 'She wasn't old. There was still time. I thought when Klára was twenty-one I would pay her a visit.'

A cloud fell over our household after the news of Aunt Josephine's death. Klára and Uncle Ota retreated into quiet moods, but somehow I could not. Aunt Josephine had encouraged me to be an independent woman, and I was sure the best way to honour her was to continue to work on my career. I imagined if she had known that I was soon to be one of only a handful of female directors, she would have been proud. I could not stop now, no matter how sad and lifeless I felt.

Aunt Josephine had left her house to Uncle Ota to be managed for him by Doctor Holub. She had also left Klára and me five thousand pounds each, kept in safekeeping with Doctor Holub until we returned to Prague. Five thousand pounds was the budget for *In the Dark*. It seemed almost symbolic.

In the Dark was bought by Union Theatres for distribution. Freddy gave me the news when he turned up one evening in his new Bugatti sports car. He had invited me to the Wentworth Hotel 'to celebrate something special', although I suspected he was trying to cheer me up.

'That's wonderful news, Freddy,' I said, when he opened the car door for me.

'Wonderful news?' Freddy mimicked, with a smirk. 'You are hard to please. Here,' he said, reaching into his pocket. 'Look at what Stuart Doyle had to say about you.'

He took out a sheet of paper and unfolded it. It was an article from *Everyone's* reporting an address Mr Doyle had made to prove Australasian Films' support for local pictures:

> *Miss Rose's film is exactly what distributors and exhibitors want. The kind of film that is capable of finding favour in all parts of the world. She has created a story that shows Australia in its glory without lapsing into clichés about bush life. We have sold the film to Britain and there are other countries interested in it as well, including the United States ...*

'The film has already been sold to Britain?' I asked.

Freddy shut the car door and climbed into the driver's seat. 'Sure has. They're expecting it to make good returns too.'

I read the article again. Established directors would have been thrilled at the news, but my mind drifted to Philip. I felt oddly disappointed, as if my life were a surrogate dream and what I most wanted was out of reach and always would be. I often hoped that Robert might say something about Philip and Beatrice's life in London, but he was silent on the subject. Klára wanted to ask him but I begged her not to. I knew it would be intruding on her blossoming relationship.

At the Wentworth Hotel ballroom the maitre d' led us to a table next to the dance floor. I had not been to a fine restaurant in years and my eyes drank in the beaded gowns and diamonds

326 • BELINDA ALEXANDRA

that sparkled on the women around us. A waiter appeared at our table to take our order. I chose the vegetable stew, the only non-meat dish on the main menu apart from the bread. I was surprised that Freddy ordered it too when he could have chosen the roast lamb or beef Wellington.

When the waiter left, Freddy turned to me. 'Dolly Blackwood will be the next big star.'

'I know,' I said. 'I want to use her for my next film.'

'You won't,' he said, taking a sip of champagne. 'As soon as the Hollywood studios see her they'll snap her up.'

'But we discovered her,' I said.

'Indeed,' said Freddy, with a smile. '*We* did.'

Something about the way Freddy had emphasised 'we' embarrassed both of us. We fell into an awkward silence. We had never been self-conscious around each other before. There was something odd about him that night, apart from him ordering the vegetable stew. There was a nervous look in his eyes and he kept fidgeting with his collar.

Freddy never seemed to be concerned by anything. To protect his job with Galaxy Pictures he had given the production credits on *In the Dark* to Robert, who acted as his frontman for business transactions relating to the picture.

'Aren't you afraid of losing your job if you are found out?' I had asked Freddy. It was apparent from his lavish lifestyle that he was paid a lot of money.

'I only worry about things when they happen,' he said.

So what was on his mind now? Was there a problem with the picture he was not telling me about?

The waiter brought our food and the band started up. The music was loud and I was grateful for it as an excuse not to speak to Freddy until the dessert arrived.

'Pêche Melba,' he said, looking at the plate in front of him. 'That brings back memories. That's the dessert we ate at Beatrice's luncheon the first time I met you.'

'So it is,' I said.

'I asked you what kind of pictures you wanted to make and when you told me you liked Fritz Lang I said that you'd never make any money.' Freddy dabbed his lips with his napkin and laughed. 'You must have thought I was rude.'

'You still are,' I ribbed him. 'I have just become used to it.'

After dessert, Freddy asked if I would like to dance. The band was playing a quickstep. Freddy was light on his toes. We danced well together, despite our difference in size.

The music stopped and I expected Freddy to lead me back to the table. But he stood there, holding me in his arms. Then, with a suddenness that startled me, he lifted my hand to his lips and kissed it. 'Adéla, will you marry me?'

I stared at him, not able to believe I had heard those words from Freddy. Was he drunk? No, I had only seen him sip one glass of champagne and one of brandy.

'I've known for a long time that you're the woman for me,' he said.

My mind struggled to take in what was happening. I was fond of Freddy but I had never thought of him romantically.

He pulled me closer to him. 'Look at your face,' he said, and smiled. 'I couldn't have shocked you more, could I? Have you never thought of marrying me?'

I thought back over the past months. It became clear that Freddy's change in dress style, the disappearance of the dead animals from his house, and his remodelled garden had all been leading up to his proposal to me. But I had not seen it.

The band played a waltz and couples returned to the floor. Freddy was looking at me waiting for an answer. I was too unravelled to give one. A frown came to his face.

'How insensitive of me,' he said, shaking his head. 'I should have waited longer for you to grieve for your aunt.'

He is the eternal optimist, I thought. I had never given him any reason to think that I was in love with him, but he was confident that to receive he simply had to ask.

'It's not that,' I told him. 'I don't see myself getting over my aunt's death but we still have to live.'

I wanted to tell him the truth. Hadn't he said himself that mincing words showed a lack of respect? I was about to explain that I could not forget my past, that I was still in love with Philip and always would be, when he threw back his head and laughed.

'Oh, I understand,' he said, pulling me towards him again. 'I'm used to American gals. I'd forgotten how traditional you European ladies are. I should have asked your uncle first, is that it? Well, my darling, I'll do that tomorrow and then you can say "yes". All right?'

The evening had taken a strange turn, but at least I had been given a reprieve.

Freddy took me home after midnight when the household, including Klára, was already asleep. I washed my face and hands, brushed my hair and cleaned my teeth, but when I climbed into bed I was still wide awake. I realised that I would not be able to wait until the morning to tell somebody what had happened. I shook Klára's shoulder.

'Freddy?' she said, sitting up and turning on the light when I told her what had passed. 'Freddy asked you to marry him?'

'Shh!' I said. 'I'm not ready for the whole household to know.'

Klára beamed from ear to ear. 'I like Freddy. He would —' She must have noticed the uncertainty on my face because she stopped herself. 'What is it?' she asked.

I could not find the words to answer her. In the end I did not have to.

'Adélka, because you can't be with Philip does not mean you can't be happy,' she said. 'He loved you so much, but he was already involved with Beatrice when he met you. He would be heartbroken if because of him you never married or experienced the joy of having children of your own.'

I climbed out of bed and looked out the window. Robert would propose to Klára as soon as she finished her studies, I was sure of it. I would be alone, like Esther and Hugh, longing for a past that could never be lived again. What Uncle Ota had said about Emilie came back to me: 'I'm not going to give you any platitudes about time healing all wounds … I will never forget the woman I gave my youthful heart to and lost tragically, but I am deeply happy with Ranjana. Sometimes your true companion turns up in a surprising place.'

Was Freddy my true companion turning up in a surprising place? I had enjoyed arriving on the set of *In the Dark* every morning and seeing him there because I benefited from the challenges he was always throwing me. If I had become a good director, it was due to him. Freddy was intelligent and full of life. I thought of his house in Cremorne and the changes he had made to it — and himself — to please me. I was looking at a life that I had not envisaged until this moment. But to enter it, to even consider it, I would have to forget Philip.

'Freddy is going to ask Uncle Ota's permission tomorrow,' I told Klára.

'Uncle Ota will say "yes" if that is what you want. He likes Freddy. He has always said so.'

I rested my head against the cool window glass. Freddy had held me in his arms when he proposed to me. I had felt safe in his embrace. It was like being wrapped in a warm coat on a windy day.

'Freddy makes you laugh,' Klára said. 'He will make you happy. I am sure of it. Are you going to say yes?'

I trembled with the trepidation of someone turning away from one path and committing themselves solely to another. Aunt Josephine had been against marriage because she saw it as the end of a woman's independence. But things would be different with Freddy. He supported my career. I could have the best of both worlds.

'Yes,' I told her. 'Yes, I am.'

I clenched my fists, knowing that my life was about to change as surely as my name. Freddy was a wonderful person, and the more I knew of him the more I liked him. Philip's face flashed into my mind but I turned my thoughts away from past memories. I would think only of Freddy from now on.

'Mrs Adéla Rockcliffe,' I whispered.

'Mrs Frederick Rockcliffe,' Klára corrected me.

'Mrs Frederick Rockcliffe,' I repeated.

I had made my decision.

NINETEEN

———————

Freddy and I married in October that year, on a day so windy that when we stood on the steps of St Peter's Church in Watsons Bay, waiting for Uncle Ota to take our photograph, the skirt of my gold lace dress billowed about my legs like a seabird about to take flight. Klára, in a dress of china blue, and Ranjana, in a matching sari pinned in place with coronets of imitation pearls, flanked me on either side to hold my dress down by clutching the skirt between their fingers. Thomas stood in front of me with an orchid from my bouquet in his buttonhole. I smiled when Uncle Ota showed me the picture. The five of us looked as if we were standing at the helm of a ship, our faces to the wind and our fortune waiting on a distant horizon.

Freddy and I married in the sacristy, not at the altar, because of our different faiths. When we emerged from the room behind the altar, Uncle Ota, Hugh and Robert burst into applause and Thomas danced a jig out of happiness. The priest reminded them that they were in the house of God, not a cinema.

Freddy had wanted a society wedding with hundreds of guests and part of the church steps cordoned off for the press. I had forbidden it. 'We can have that sort of thing for the premiere of *In the Dark*,' I told him, 'but not for our marriage.'

The night before the wedding, I woke with a start. Klára was shivering so violently that the bed frame was rattling. I turned on the light. Her face was flushed and strands of her hair stuck to her forehead in wet stripes.

'Have you caught a chill?' I asked, pulling the covers over her.

Klára rubbed her neck. 'Just night shivers,' she said. 'I get them sometimes.'

I had never noticed Klára shivering at night before and we had shared the same bed nearly all our lives. The pallor of her complexion worried me. I had been caught up in my wedding preparations and realised that I had neglected my sister.

'Do you want a cup of Horlicks?' I asked her.

She shook her head. 'Go back to sleep, Adélka. It is your wedding day tomorrow.'

Klára's trembling subsided and she drifted off to sleep holding my hand. I watched her for an hour. Klára had suffered night terrors as a child and often dreamed of monsters under the bed. There had been many nights in Prague when I had held her hand until her mind settled and she could sleep. Had she had a nightmare and not wanted to tell me? Perhaps, for all her support regarding my union with Freddy, Klára was apprehensive. I had been glad when everyone agreed that after Freddy and I returned from our honeymoon, Klára should come and live with us in Cremorne. 'We will miss you both,' Ranjana told me. 'But Klára would be lost without you.'

'I will always watch over you, Klára,' I whispered. 'I promised Mother that.'

I put my head on my pillow but my mind was on edge. It would be useless to try to fall asleep now. I pulled on my dressing gown and tiptoed down the stairs. Perhaps seeing Angel and her joey, Cherub, would calm me. I slipped out the back door, intending to sit in the garden and watch them for a while. I moved towards the steps and bumped into someone. I stifled a scream as I realised that the figure in the coat and nightcap was Uncle Ota.

'Can't sleep either?' he asked, smiling at me.

I shook my head and sat down next to him. He put his arm around me. We gazed at the full moon with the clouds moving by it before Uncle Ota whispered:

> *A fair girl at the rim of land*
> *Watches the evening's rosy phases;*
> *Under the oak-tree by the strand*
> *Far out across the lakes she gazes.*

The poem 'May' again. What was the connection between that sad tale and Mother, Uncle Ota and Aunt Emilie? I looked up into Uncle Ota's face. Kissed by the moonlight it was a young man's countenance.

'Mother cried when you wrote of your marriage to Ranjana,' I told him. 'But after your second letter she said that your wife sounded delightful and suited to you. She was glad that you were happy.'

Uncle Ota turned to me. Something passed in his eyes. A memory? He held his hands to his chin as if he were praying. 'Your mother and I made a mistake,' he said after a while. 'We thought we had all the time in the world. We thought that because we were young, we and everyone around us would live forever.'

'You loved Emilie, didn't you?' I asked him.

He nodded. 'I told you that your father and I first saw your mother and aunt at the opera, didn't I? That is true. But I fell in love with Emilie when our family was invited to paní Navrátilová's soirée and Emilie read Karel Hynek Mácha's "May".'

'"May" is a tragic poem.'

'So is life. I should have seen it as a warning. But I only heard her voice. I fell in love with it.'

I saw Angel make her way down the trunk of the silver gum. Cherub, who was now independent, followed her. They looked at me, wondering what treat I had brought them. But they would have to wait. I wanted to hear Uncle Ota's story. I was ready for it now.

'I had journeyed through Italy and France by then,' Uncle Ota said. 'Adventure was in my blood. Emilie was fascinated by the idea of seeing the world but ...'

Angel scampered across the grass and into the lilly-pilly beside me. Cherub watched from her position on a branch. Angel hung by her tail and swept her paw at my hair. I gently pushed her away and she climbed onto the orange tree and bit into one of the young fruits.

'But what?' I asked Uncle Ota.

'But your mother didn't want her sister to go away. So she worked your family against me.'

I was stung by his words. It was not how I pictured Mother: Always gracious and warm. Always so lovely. How could she have done such a thing?

'Yet ... she married Father,' I said. 'Did she turn him against you too?'

Uncle Ota sighed. 'He convinced me to go away rather than destroy the bond of the two sisters.'

'And you did,' I said, at last understanding Mother's strained expression when Aunt Josephine read Uncle Ota's letters to us. 'It destroyed Emilie.'

Mother loved Emilie. Whatever she did, it would have been motivated by that. But how misguided she must have realised she had been. I thought of how Mother had acted when Uncle Ota asked after her in his letter. It was as if she had been relieved of a burden. Uncle Ota was an honourable man, he would have taken care of Emilie. She must have regretted her interference bitterly.

'Emilie was heartbroken,' said Uncle Ota. 'But what destroyed her was her misdirected rebellion. She threw herself into the arms of a rogue and when he was finished with her she had no reputation and nothing left to live for.'

'Mother wrote you a letter,' I told him. 'Miloš destroyed it before I could send it to you. She quoted "May".'

The thoughtful expression returned to Uncle Ota's face.

'I think she was writing to you to ask for your forgiveness,' I said. 'But you had already granted it, hadn't you?'

A tear glistened in Uncle Ota's eye. 'I hated your mother for a long time. First of all for separating Emilie and me, then for allowing her sister to become involved with that man. But when Antonín was killed in the war, I couldn't hate her any more. Your mother had suffered enough. I wanted to write to my brother's daughters. I wanted to know you.' Uncle Ota smiled and touched my cheek. 'I'm glad I did.'

'Mother entrusted us to you.'

'It was the highest compliment she could have paid me,' said Uncle Ota, folding his arms over his knees and resting his chin on them.

'Are you still sad over Emilie?' I asked.

He nodded. 'Always, Adélka. I love Ranjana. I love Thomas. But I'll never forget Emilie.'

As I'll never forget Philip, I thought. But I will cherish Freddy.

The following day at the wedding lunch, my attention constantly drifted to Klára and Robert. Klára never took her eyes off Robert and he maintained contact with her, whether it was his arm around her shoulders or his hand to her elbow. He was loveable and well suited to my sister. It was confronting to me to admit that I saw him as a threat too. Klára's life had become a whirl of tea parties, theatre openings, lunches, dances and concerts. Robert was one of those people who could sleep two hours and then get up and do it all again the next day. But could Klára keep the pace? I remembered her shivering the previous night. What if she became sick again?

I understood the position my young mother had been in regarding Emilie. Mother had thought that she was protecting her sister. I shuddered: but what terrible consequences! One day I would have to let Klára go into the protective arms of Robert. Meanwhile, I would watch over my sister as vigilantly as Angel watched over Cherub.

Freddy and I honeymooned at the Hydro Majestic Hotel in a room that overlooked the Jamieson Valley. The morning after our first night there, while Freddy savoured an extended sleep in bed, I stared out the window. My eyes drifted past the hotel's lawns and potted shrubs to the magnificent blue forest. Everywhere I saw magic: in the cloud formations, the valleys walled in by perpendicular rock, the sheer sandstone cliffs, the cascading waterfalls, and the dells and gullies. It was the forest of my ideal picture.

Freddy sighed and rolled over. The previous night I had emerged from the bathroom to find him lounging on the bed in his dressing gown. There was a red rose on my pillow and champagne in an ice bucket on the side table. We'd had a wonderful wedding and when Freddy and I had danced the bridal waltz, it was as though I was bathed in a sublime light. But one look at Freddy's come-hither eyes and apprehension gripped me.

'Just a moment,' I told him, disappearing into the bathroom again.

I shut the door and leaned against it. I shuddered at the thought of Freddy lying on the bed so expectantly. It seemed ... *abnormal*. Memories flooded back of the day Philip had taken me to Wattamolla beach. We had come together naturally. Tears welled in my eyes. This is a terrible mistake, I thought. It was not the physical act that frightened me, for Freddy and I had already discussed that — he would take precautions so that I would not become pregnant for at least two years. 'You ought to make another picture first,' he had said. 'Otherwise you might resent children, and I want you to be happy.' It was the idea of emotional intimacy with him that suddenly was so abhorrent.

I sat on the edge of the bath. 'I can't do this,' I said, breathing in gulps of air. 'I can't be Freddy's wife.'

I tried to calm my thinking and envisioned us remaining friends and not consummating our marriage. That would be grounds for divorce, I remembered. But perhaps Freddy would not divorce me. He could have a string of beautiful starlets to amuse him and I would look on benevolently, like a queen blessing the king's consorts. The fog in my mind cleared and I shook my head. No, queens tolerated those arrangements because they were tired of having children. I wanted children. Maybe not immediately, but I did want them.

I raised myself from the bath and splashed cold water on my face. I turned to the door. Everything seemed quiet on the other side. Maybe Freddy had fallen asleep? Perhaps I could delay this awful moment until later?

'Adéla,' Freddy called.

I bit my lip. He was not asleep. I would have to face him now.

'Yes?' I called back.

'Are you all right?'

I put my hand to the door and drew a breath before opening it. Freddy had switched off the lamps and lit candles on the mantelpiece. The glow of the flames sent beams of golden light flickering around the room. There was a bracing smell too: witchhazel and sandalwood; Freddy's aftershave. The knot gripped my stomach again.

Freddy looked up at me. 'You're beautiful,' he said, holding out his hand. I crossed the rug on the balls of my feet and took his fingers in mine. He tugged me onto the bed.

'Nervous?' he asked.

I nodded.

He gathered me into his arms. 'I won't hurt you,' he said.

My heart ached: Freddy, usually so brash and clumsy outside of the bedroom, was sensitive and caring in it. I did not deserve him but I would do my best to make him happy. I reached up to put my arm around his back but somehow managed to bring my elbow up so that I struck him in the eye. He pressed the heel of his palm to his head and collapsed onto the pillow. I had a pointy elbow and I had hit him in the eye socket. It must have been agony.

'Freddy!' I cried. 'I'm so sorry!'

Freddy lifted his hand. The flesh around his eye was red and swollen. It might even be black tomorrow.

Freddy's shoulders began to shake. I thought he was crying, but then the boom of his laugh echoed around the room. I had always liked his laugh. It was from the heart.

'I had no idea you were so violent,' he said. 'I'll have to keep my place with you.'

The humour of the moment caught me and I laughed too. Before I knew what I was doing I leaned forward and kissed Freddy's eyelid. I nestled my cheek against his shoulder and he slipped his arms around me. My breath caught with surprise as desire lifted me up then gently dropped me down again like a wave on the ocean. Freddy rolled over to face me and kissed my forehead. I brushed away the lock of hair that had fallen across his face. The paralysing fear that had held me captive only a few minutes ago vanished. I laughed again. Freddy pushed open my dressing gown and ran his fingertips across my stomach and hips. 'Lovely, beautiful, exquisite,' he whispered. I slid my hands over his chest. Everywhere Freddy touched me tingled to life. He continued his explorations down my legs and up my torso to my breasts, stroking me until I ached with yearning. He eased himself into me, checking my face for signs of discomfort. There was no pain, only pleasure so intense that I could not recall anything like it.

'What are you looking at?' Freddy asked.

My mind returned from the recollections of our wedding night to the morning sun glistening on the valley. Freddy was awake and propped up on his elbow. I was relieved that his eye had not turned black.

'If we made a picture here, we would not need a studio to "stylise" nature,' I said.

Freddy reached for his dressing gown and joined me at the window.

'This is the place I want to make my next picture,' I told him. 'I love it.'

Freddy wrapped his arms around me and kissed my cheek. 'And I love you.'

I returned his embrace before looking towards the valley. I want to live here one day, I thought. Then I would wake up to this magic every morning.

In the Dark premiered at the Lyric Wintergarden Theatre on 8 December 1925. The same night Robert and Klára announced their engagement.

'We're not trying to steal your limelight, Adéla,' Robert announced in his speech to our family, who had gathered for a celebration at our home before leaving for the theatre. 'We only wanted our engagement to be announced on a day when wonderful things were happening.'

Klára looked radiant in her buttercup yellow dress. Who could deny such a charming person her happiness?

I turned to Freddy and clutched his hand.

'You know the old saying, darling,' he whispered. 'Don't think of it as losing a sister. Think of it as gaining a brother-in-law.'

At least I am seeing more of Klára these days, I thought. Not only was she living with us, but Freddy and I went with Robert and her to the same parties and functions.

Freddy had invited the reviewers of the *Sydney Mail*, the *Daily Telegraph* and *Everyone's* magazine to the screening, along with Jack Lang, the Premier of New South Wales, and the musical star Gladys Moncrieff. I had watched the finished version of the picture many times, but now it had its first public audience I found my heart racing. Would they be drawn into the story? Would they be moved by the sad scenes and chuckle at the light-hearted ones?

Or would they laugh in all the wrong places? I was still nervous about the theme. Perhaps some people would be offended. I sat on the edge of my seat, my fingers numb from clenching them.

'Relax,' said Freddy, prising my hand from the chair arm and squeezing it in his own. 'You've done all you can to make a great film. The rest is out of your control.'

The lights lowered. When the picture came on, I could not watch it or look at the people around me. I dropped my gaze to my lap. But halfway through the screening I heard sobbing and looked up to see Klára and Esther crying. The native bear had just died. They had seen the picture before the screening so they knew that it was going to happen. Their reaction gave me courage to lift my eyes and look at the audience. All eyes were on the screen. Gladys Moncrieff's mouth was gaping open. Not one person fidgeted or spoke until the lights came back on. When they did, the applause from the audience was deafening. I had captured their hearts and I was elated.

'Stand up!' said Freddy, pulling me out of my seat. 'Receive the acclaim.'

'Bravo, Mrs Rockcliffe!' someone called from the crowd. Other voices soon joined him. 'Well done! What a picture!'

When it was my turn to give a speech I emphasised that I could only take part of the praise. The magnificent camerawork was Hugh's, the acting was a credit to the stars, and, of course, the story would not have come together without Freddy.

'You should be very proud of your wife,' I overheard the Premier tell Freddy at the reception party afterwards. 'She has made a great Australian film.'

'We made a great Australian film,' I mouthed to Freddy. '*We* did.'

*　　*　　*

In the midst of our good fortune and happiness, Klára and I could forget that we were still fugitives. We felt almost normal. But I knew something had happened with Miloš when I received a call from Uncle Ota in February the following year.

'Adéla, you must come to my office right away.'

When I arrived, Esther quickly ushered me into Uncle Ota's office and shut the door behind her when she left. There were circles under Uncle Ota's eyes as if he had not had any sleep.

'What is it?' I asked him. 'Another letter from Prague?'

He nodded gravely. 'Doctor Holub has written that Miloš was involved in an extortion attempt on a client. Rather than report him to the police, the firm convinced him to retire from his partnership.'

I sat down and clenched my fists. 'Mother spent a fortune buying Miloš that partnership and the company was very profitable,' I told Uncle Ota. 'If he had applied himself, he would be wealthy now. I had hoped something like that might happen and he would leave us alone.'

Uncle Ota pinched his chin. 'Not wealthy enough for his extravagant wife it seems. Here, listen to this,' he said, reading the letter out to me.

'... I am afraid pan Dolezal is now so desperate for funds and in such debt that he is becoming careless. He arrived at my office two days ago and demanded to know where his stepdaughters were. The change in his cool, calculated demeanour was unnerving. I have employed a guard to accompany me to and from the office each day, and am convinced that your nieces are in greater danger than ever before ...'

I shivered and pulled at my sleeve cuffs.

'You and Klára have been carefree here,' Uncle Ota said. 'You have lived lives of liberty. Now I must insist that you be careful.'

I nodded in agreement.

'If there is one comfort,' he said, 'it is that Miloš does not have any idea where you are. And that Doctor Holub will not tell him.'

Thomas was old enough now for Klára to teach him to play the piano. I was delighted to have my cousin staying with us one night a week for his lesson.

Seeing Freddy and Thomas together gave me an idea of the kind of father my husband would make. One of the changes I had made to our garden was to have a pond built at the bottom of it. To me, the pond was an oasis for frogs and birds, and was dappled with colourful water lilies and flowering marsh plants. But to Thomas, the pond was a lake. One morning, I awoke later than usual and stepped out onto the balcony to see Freddy and Thomas poised near the edge of it. Thomas was holding the toy boat Freddy had ordered from America. It was a Bermuda sloop with brass fittings and a mainsail and jibs. The scale of the boat matched Thomas in size, but my little cousin held it securely in his arms. He was dressed in a sea jacket and cap. I stifled my laughter when I saw the brightly coloured handkerchief Freddy had knotted at his throat. The morning was still and I caught their voices across the water.

'We'll be under way as soon as the ebb is set,' growled Freddy in an affected seaman's accent.

'Aye aye, skipper,' answered Thomas.

Freddy lifted his nose. 'Smell that sea air. It brings the sense of adventure to boil in my blood, it does.'

'Aye aye, skipper,' Thomas said again.

Freddy asked Thomas if he was ready to pull away from the port and my cousin nodded his assent. Freddy grabbed the back of his sea jacket so Thomas would not fall into the pond.

Thomas launched the sloop and clapped with delight when it glided across the pond without listing. Freddy laughed.

The boat floated into the middle of the pond and wedged in the lilies. Thomas was crestfallen. Freddy searched around for a branch to push the boat free. But our trees were still young and not large enough to produce branches of any significance. He spotted a rake Rex had left against the gate and grabbed it. But no matter where he stood on the edge of the pond, the boat was always just out of reach.

'It's all right, Freddy,' Thomas told him, the disappointment in his voice palpable. 'Maybe a breeze will loosen it later.'

Freddy scratched his chin, thinking something over. Then he undid his belt and took off his pants, hung them over an azalea shrub and waded out to the middle of the pond where the water came up his chest. I was almost too scared to look. Freddy hated beaches or any natural environment without marble tiles and gold fittings.

Thomas jumped up and down at the edge of the pond and called out with glee. Freddy managed to grab the sailing boat and pushed it back to where Thomas was waiting.

'I have another plan, my hearty first mate,' Freddy said, hoisting himself out of the pond and squeezing the green water out of his cotton leggings.

'What?' asked Thomas. His face was full of admiration for his oversized playmate.

Freddy extracted a piece of slime from his waistband and grimaced. 'Before we set sail into the blue yonder again, we'll tie a piece of string to the bow,' he said.

Thomas was able to read complex pieces of music but his hand span was small and Klára forbade him from playing them until he was older so as not to damage his tendons. Instead, she drilled him in correct posture and hand technique with simple pieces. He absorbed his lessons with only the occasional lapse of concentration.

'Klárinka, if spiders use their webs to catch insects, how come they don't get caught in their own webs?' Thomas asked her one time. I enjoyed watching Klára teach Thomas, so I sat in on their lessons and sewed while Thomas played.

'They can get caught in their own webs,' Klára answered him, marking the fingering for the scales in his notebook. 'They are only smarter than most insects and watch where they are going.'

Thomas thought over her answer. 'Just like people,' he said. 'Mummy told me that a person should never set a trap for another lest they get caught in it themselves.'

After the piano lessons, if Freddy was working late, Klára, Thomas and I would have supper together with Thomas selecting the food. Usually he made good choices: roast pumpkin or spinach on toast, vanilla custard or poached pears. But one evening he requested whipped chocolate cream with porridge. Klára and I went to bed queasy.

On another occasion, after Klára and Thomas had completed their lesson, they decided to make a card for Uncle Ota's upcoming birthday. I listened to their chatter about the design and what colours to use while I read the newspaper. They were undecided about whether the card should be trimmed in silver or gold foil.

'What do you think, Adélka?' Thomas asked me.

'Both,' I answered, flipping over the page. I caught my breath when I saw a photograph of Philip.

'Two-toned?' said Klára. 'What a good idea. Do you think …?'

I did not hear the rest of her question. I picked up the paper and rushed to my room, locking the door behind me. I sank to my knees and stared at the picture again. *Doctor Philip Page, back from London, has opened his own practice in Edgecliff*, the caption read.

The article below it said that Philip had written several important papers on the child's mind and physical health and was an advocate for progressive treatments for illnesses such as infantile paralysis and chickenpox. There was no mention of Beatrice or a child or anything else about him that I longed to know. It had once struck me as strange that Beatrice had never written to me or sent me a thankyou note for the wedding present, but then I stopped thinking about it. I ran my finger over Philip's face. The luminous eyes were the same but the innocence in them was gone. He had taken on something of his father's commanding figure.

After that, I lived a tormented existence. I loved Freddy but I found myself seeking out Philip. Whenever I caught the tram, I took a window seat and stared at the people on the footpath. My eyes would search for him in every man. I even thought about going to see Doctor Page Senior on some flimsy excuse to find out about Philip, but wisdom warned me against it.

One day, I was overwhelmed by a desire to see Philip and caught the tram to Edgecliff. I had found out the address of his practice and had carried it around in my pocket for days. The tram stop was at the corner of the street. I alighted, my legs trembling beneath me. I crept past a white picket fence covered in clematis to a gate with a red lantern.

Doctor Philip Page: Children's Specialist the brass plate read. My heart leapt. Philip had achieved his dream.

I put my hand on the gate, unsure whether to proceed or not. What was the wild hope in my heart? What did I expect from seeing Philip? To look in his eyes and see that he still loved me? Well, even if he did, our love could never be.

The door to the surgery opened and woke me from my dream. A nurse came out with a boy walking on crutches. 'Can I help you?' she asked. Somehow the coolness of her tone brought the foolishness of what I was doing to light.

'No. Thank you,' I said, turning and hurrying away.

After that, I promised myself never to go near Philip's surgery again.

The following morning, Klára slept in while Freddy and I took breakfast on the terrace. The upset of the day before had given me an appetite and my mouth watered at the sight of scrambled eggs and fresh toast and butter.

I sat down and the maid, Regina, filled my teacup. I took a grapefruit half and sprinkled sugar on it. As I did so I caught Freddy's eye. He had a smug look on his face.

'What is it?' I asked.

'I've been reading my correspondence this morning,' he said. 'And the film exchanges have confirmed what I already knew about *In the Dark*.' He paused and smiled at me. 'You're a success, darling. *In the Dark* has been sold not only into the United States but into France and Germany too.'

I dropped the grapefruit. Freddy had named the largest film markets in the world besides Britain and Australia. I could not think of anything to say. I was not so foolish as to think that my first attempt at a feature film was as brilliant as Lang's *Siegfried* but I had exceeded my own expectations.

'That's wonderful, Freddy ... I couldn't have done it without you.'

Despite having given me such astounding news, Freddy seemed to be keeping something back. 'You're teasing me,' I said. 'Come on, out with it. There's more, isn't there?'

'Hmm,' he said, picking up a slice of toast and buttering it.

'Come on, Freddy,' I begged. 'This is too much tension for the morning.'

He threw back his head and laughed. 'All right then,' he said. 'I'll tell you. I sold your bunyip film as a short to go with the feature.'

'Truly?' I said, straightening my back and trying to hide my annoyance. Freddy was obviously pleased with himself and I did not wish to deflate him. But I had not expected my amateur film to go anywhere beyond its screening in Australia. It was unpolished in comparison with *In the Dark*. After all, I had made it with scraps of film and for less than two hundred pounds. I was not ashamed of it, but I had not wanted it to be sent out to the wider world.

'The German distributor sent it out through the European market,' beamed Freddy. 'And guess what? It's been sold into Czechoslovakia! It's going to be shown in your home country, my dear.'

A chill froze my bones while my mind raced to recall details. For *In the Dark* I had used my married name, Adéla Rockcliffe, for the director's credit. But the bunyip film? My God! Klára had been the star!

Czechoslovakia and Australia were so geographically and culturally distant that I had never expected my films to be shown in my old country. What a fool I had been to put myself out in the public arena. I should have been content to stay hidden!

I leapt up and sent the milk jug over the table. 'You have to stop it from being shown! You have to buy it back!'

Freddy had been expecting me to be pleased and was bewildered by my outburst. 'Why?' he asked.

'Because my stepfather might see it. Then he will know where we are.'

Freddy reddened under the strength of my retort but he still could not comprehend what had warranted it. 'What does it matter if he knows where you are?'

I had never told him the reason why Klára and I had fled Prague, not even after we were married. I wanted to forget what had happened. I was also afraid of Freddy's bullheadedness. If I told him the full story, he was likely to go to Prague and finish Miloš off. He would either end up getting himself killed or hanged for killing a man with no evidence.

'Because my stepfather murdered my mother and wants to get rid of me and Klára. We came here to hide from him,' I said.

Freddy was dumbstruck. His eyes fixed on my face then he said, 'I thought you left Prague because your mother died. I thought you had nowhere else to go so came to stay with your uncle and aunt.'

I pressed my face into my hands. It had been wonderful to feel safe in Australia and now that was ruined. I looked up at Freddy. His eyes blazed with anger.

'I'm your husband,' he snapped. 'You're supposed to tell me everything. How come you couldn't tell me that?'

Freddy had never spoken to me so harshly. I was too overcome by remorse at my own folly to say anything further. We sat in silence for a while, neither of us looking in the direction of the other. Finally, Freddy stood up.

'I'll send a telegram to Germany now,' he said.

Freddy bought *The Bunyip* back from the exchange but it had already been screening at a cinema in Prague. What were the chances that Miloš had seen it? When Mother was alive he had always said that the cinema was for the lower classes. But things had changed rapidly since then. Almost everybody went to the pictures these days. All we could do was wait for further news from Doctor Holub.

* * *

On Ranjana and Uncle Ota's wedding anniversary, Klára, Esther and I decided to take Thomas to Bondi beach for the day. Not only because we wanted to play on the sand with him, but also because we felt that Uncle Ota and Ranjana needed time together. Klára, who considered herself an expert on romance, convinced us that the flirtatious looks Uncle Ota and Ranjana once exchanged had ceased and that they treated each other like comfortable old armchairs. 'It is exhaustion,' she said with such authority that I was convinced by her argument. 'They have worked hard and they have supported us. They need a day to themselves.'

We agreed to give Ranjana and Uncle Ota time alone together. After all, they had a very romantic beginning: not many men could claim to have snatched their wife from a burning bier and fallen in love with her the moment their eyes met. While Ranjana and Uncle Ota were in bed, we made them a breakfast of freshly baked rolls. 'What's that wonderful smell?' I heard Uncle Ota ask Ranjana from the bedroom. We put camellias in a vase in the centre of the table and checked that the plates and silverware were set out correctly on the lace cloth. When we heard Uncle Ota and Ranjana coming down the stairs, we snatched up our coats and fled before they could see us. Klára stuck our note to the back of the front door:

> *Happy Anniversary, Ota and Ranjana! We will be back at five. Love from your nieces, Klára and Adéla, your friend Esther, and your adoring and adorable son, Thomas.*
>
> *PS Freddy and Robert are watching over the cinema today.*

Freddy was giving me driving lessons, but I was not confident enough to take passengers yet, so we caught the tram to Bondi beach. Although it was late autumn, the weather was mild and the sun shone brightly on the sea. Thomas, who normally would not have hesitated to take off his shoes and run through the sand, dragged his feet. Klára tried to entice him to build a sandcastle with her. Such an invitation usually sent Thomas into a mind spin of intricate plans for moats and turrets decorated with shells and necklaces of seaweed. He sat down with Klára to help her mould the structure but after only a few minutes his hands flopped listlessly to his sides and I could see that his heart was not in it.

'I'm tired,' he said, looking at us with drooping eyes.

It was the first inkling that something was wrong. Thomas was normally enthusiastic about everything. While some children would count to a hundred if pushed, Thomas would count to one thousand — if you let him.

'Let's get some tea and cake,' Esther suggested. 'It's too windy for sandcastles anyway.'

Although most of the teahouses were closed in preparation for the winter, we found one whose interior smelled alluringly of vanilla, hot chocolate and cinnamon buns. Thomas stared at the bread and butter pudding that was placed in front of him.

'You're not hungry?' Klára asked him.

Thomas shook his head. 'I feel hot.'

Esther pressed her palm to his brow. 'He has a fever,' she said. 'We'd best get him home.'

Thomas fell asleep on my lap as soon as we boarded the tram and I carried him, wrapped in my coat, all the way from the stop to the house. Ranjana and Uncle Ota were sitting in the parlour when we arrived.

'Did you tire Tommy out?' Uncle Ota said, laughing. His face was glowing and he looked more relaxed than he had in years. I felt awful for what we were about to tell him.

Ranjana knew straightaway that something was wrong. She pressed her cheek against Thomas's forehead then took him from me.

Uncle Ota's smile collapsed.

'He has a fever,' Ranjana told him. 'Quickly, go get the doctor.'

I helped Ranjana put Thomas in bed while Klára prepared a bowl of water and a washcloth for a compress. Uncle Ota returned with the message that the local doctor was delivering a breech baby but he would come to us first thing in the morning. 'He said we must keep the fever down.'

When Freddy came by to pick me and Klára up, I told him that we would be staying. The three of us collapsed on the sofa but could not sleep. I stared out the window, hoping to see Angel and Cherub, my bearers of good luck, but they did not appear.

Thomas's fever subsided in the early hours of the morning. He was asleep and he did not stir when each of us leaned over to stroke his face. Ranjana wanted to lie in the chair next to him, but Uncle Ota said she would be better with a proper rest in bed.

In the morning, I checked on Thomas and found him staring at the ceiling. When he saw me, he began to cry. 'Adélka, I can't move my leg.'

I tugged back the sheet and saw that he had one of his legs tucked up behind the knee of the other.

'You have a cramp, that's all,' I reassured him. 'You have slept on your leg and cut off the circulation.'

I straightened his crooked leg. The flesh felt cold. 'There,' I said. 'Can you feel pins and needles?'

He shook his head. 'I can't feel anything.'

'You sleep,' I told him, kissing his forehead. 'Sleep cures all.'

Thomas closed his eyes with the trust that only a child can place in an adult. When the others arose, I assured them all was well and that Thomas was sleeping. I did my best to quell the panic that was rising in my own chest. There was no point causing a commotion, which would only frighten Thomas, when the doctor was due to arrive at any moment. Klára was not fooled. I saw her staring at my quivering hands as I went about cooking the eggs for breakfast.

When the doctor arrived, he examined Thomas's leg then listened to his pulse and chest. His grave expression did not bring us any comfort.

'I will send for an ambulance,' the doctor announced, returning his stethoscope to his bag. 'We'd best get him to the Children's Hospital without delay.'

Ranjana's mouth dropped open and the colour drained from her face. 'What is it?'

The doctor grimaced. I sensed this was a devastating prognosis he had delivered too many times to too many anxious parents. 'Poliomyelitis.'

The word pierced me like a knife. Infantile paralysis. *The crippler*. It was the most sinister disease because it was fond of children.

Ranjana's face contorted with disbelief. 'How could Thomas have contracted polio?'

The doctor shook his head. 'We don't know exactly how the germ is spread. But we do know that the disease is quite common in affluent families. You haven't done anything wrong by your son.'

The ambulance arrived and Ranjana was allowed to accompany Thomas in it. The rest of us travelled behind in Freddy's car. The horse carts and pedestrians seemed to be moving in slow motion around us. My mind whirred with images of withered, shrunken limbs and wheelchairs. No, not Thomas, I prayed.

Thomas was admitted as a critical case. Because of the gravity of his illness, he was put under the care of a specialist and we were allowed to keep a bedside vigil. The specialist, a wiry man with a wrinkled brow and round metal glasses, examined Thomas's reflexes and breathing. 'Polio is like a landslide,' he explained to us. 'We can only watch and wait for when and where it will stop. It might only affect his left leg, but tomorrow it might be both and the next day his arms.'

We all let out a gasp. Uncle Ota turned grey in the face. 'Surely not!' he cried.

'Consider it a mercy if it is only his limbs,' warned the specialist. 'If the paralysis travels to his chest he will have to be put in an iron lung.'

The next few days were a nightmare as a fiend racked Thomas's body. Sometimes he would be awake and coherent and other times he would sleep for hours. The hospital was a parade of futures ruined by poliomyelitis. Children were pushed around in wheelchairs by nurses, while others stumbled along in leg braces or using walkers. Outside the physiotherapy department we saw a boy of no more than fourteen who had developed shoulders out of proportion to the rest of his body from using crutches. But the worst cases were the children in the iron lungs. I passed the respirator room on the way to the ladies' lavatory and caught a glimpse of tiny faces poking out from the boxes, gasping for air. I overheard a mother tell the doctor on duty, 'She says she can't swallow.'

'I am truly sorry,' the doctor replied. 'The polio has reached her brain.'

I rushed into the ladies' room, stood in a cubicle with my hands over my face and wept.

When I returned to the ward, Robert was there with the others. I was glad that he had come to give Klára support.

Freddy noticed I had been crying and put his arm around my waist. 'I'll always be here for you and your family, Adéla. Always,' he said.

I buried my face in his chest. Freddy had become my best friend and the person I most relied on. I could not imagine life without him.

When the worst of the danger for Thomas passed he was transferred to the general ward for rehabilitation. He could not move his leg from the hip down, and yet we were grateful for this as only people can be who have been given an expectation of outcomes ranging from bad to worse. The specialist decided that Thomas's leg would be put in a calliper to prevent his muscles from twisting and becoming deformed.

Uncle Ota and Freddy brought Thomas home from the hospital a few weeks later. The nurses had taught him to walk using crutches and he did it skilfully. But when the car door opened and Thomas limped down the path with a three-legged hobble, I thought Ranjana was the strongest woman in the world not to break down. She threw her arms around Thomas. 'I'm so glad you are home,' she said, covering his face in kisses. But I knew what she had witnessed was as devastating for her as it was for us. Thomas had always been a boy who ran and jumped for joy.

The person who most quickly reconciled himself to Thomas's disability was Thomas himself. Once the illness and pain had passed, he was again his laughing, cheeky self. Esther understood this better than anyone. One afternoon, I stopped by the house and found her and Thomas in the backyard together. Esther was helping him sketch out a hopscotch pattern on the path.

'Won't it be too difficult for Thomas?' I whispered to her. 'What if he hurts himself?'

She straightened up and looked at me. 'You've got to stop undermining his confidence and help him lead as normal a life as possible.'

Thomas smiled. 'Don't be concerned, Adélka. Hopping is something I've learned to excel at.'

His response sent Esther into giggles. I had to laugh too.

When Hugh heard that Thomas was home, he and Giallo became frequent visitors. It was moving to see the three of them together. It must have been painful for Hugh to watch Thomas adjust to his disability, but he did not show it. I appreciated that he was willing to come out of himself to try to encourage Thomas and to show his support for us.

One afternoon, after Hugh had played with Thomas in the garden he came to the parlour to talk to me. Esther walked in with a duster. When she saw Hugh, she retreated.

The dejected look in her eyes saddened me. I had intended to speak to her about Hugh's lack of interest but she had worked it out herself. Ever since Freddy's and my wedding, where Hugh had ignored her to the point of coldness, Esther returned to wearing drab clothes and hardly saying a word to anyone except us.

When it was time for Hugh to leave, I walked him to the front gate. Esther was in the garden watering the azaleas. Hugh lifted his hat to her but she did not see him. The blue and black butterfly was resting on her shoulder.

'Do you see the butterfly on Esther?' I whispered to Hugh.

He stared at Esther and I realised that he did not.

'Call me whenever you need me to look after Thomas,' he said.

'I will,' I replied, then gave a gasp of surprise when I saw that the butterfly had landed on his chest. Giallo noticed and cocked his head. But Hugh was puzzled by my reaction. I watched him hobble down the street and turn the corner before looking back to Esther.

I had no idea what to make of what had just happened.

Despite his optimistic attitude to his illness, Thomas suffered a setback the following month. The hamstring in his damaged leg contracted and he was in constant pain. He could no longer straighten his leg.

'We are going to have to operate,' the specialist told us.

After the operation, Thomas's leg was in plaster from his hip to his ankle and he was subjected to the excruciating post-operative treatment of having wedges driven behind his knees to keep his hamstrings stretched. One day, I turned up at Watsons Bay to find Ranjana crying.

'If it was me who was suffering, I could take it,' she wept. 'But how can I just look on when my child endures such pain?'

Thomas had been treated by the hospital's best specialist but even he was saying he had done all that could be done and Thomas would have to accept life as a cripple. I thought back to the article I had seen on Philip. He was an advocate of progressive treatments for infantile paralysis. An idea grew in my mind. Perhaps there was someone else who could help us.

TWENTY

Philip's rooms in Edgecliff were different from those of the specialist who had treated Thomas at the hospital. There were the graduation certificates on the walls of the reception area from the University of London, but instead of leather-bound volumes and *objets d'art* on the shelves there were teddy bears and rag dolls. I half-smiled when I saw the collection of mud-men that filled a cabinet of their own. A girl with a patch over one eye and a boy with his arm in a sling were playing with a train set on the floor. I helped Thomas to the couch then approached the nurse, who wrote down his details on a card. Behind her was a framed motto:

Your sickness can affect your personality
or
Your personality can affect your sickness

I had told Ranjana, who was working at the cinema that day, that I was taking Thomas to a new specialist. There was no reason why I could not have told my family that I was taking him to Philip. Even Freddy would not have stopped me where Thomas's welfare was concerned. I had come for Thomas's sake but I wanted to see Philip alone. I hoped that in seeing him again I would be able to put the memories to rest and give my heart wholly to Freddy. But as much as I tried to push the memories away, they kept floating up. I saw Philip in his cramped office at Broughton Hall and remembered the taste of his warm, salty skin when he had kissed me on Wattamolla beach.

Once the nurse had taken Thomas's details, I returned to the couch. Thomas had joined in playing trains with the boy and girl on the rug. I glanced at the children's mothers. One was absorbed in a magazine, but the other was watching them play. Thomas wound up the engine and sent it for a turn around the tracks. It made the distance before coming off the rails. The mother cheered for him. When Thomas had been in hospital I was sure someone would object to the presence of a dark child in the ward. But no one did. Perhaps suffering made people more generous.

Philip was running late and a tinge of apprehension fell over me. What would he say when he saw us? I had given the nurse my married name.

The door to the doctor's office opened and a boy with a club foot stepped out with his mother. The pair were smiling as if they had just shared a joke. Then Philip came out to call in his next patient. He saw me and stopped in his tracks. I was equally stunned. Philip was no longer the fresh-faced young man I had known when he was a medical officer at Broughton Hall. His shoulders were broad and straight. His hair was brushed up from his forehead in a cowlick. The whimsical smile lit up when he saw us but the eyes above it looked sadder and the roses in his cheeks had vanished.

Philip stepped towards us. He gaped at me before remembering himself, and placed his hand on Thomas's shoulder. 'You've had a bad case of polio, I see,' he said. 'I'll have a look at Mary's eye and John's arm and then I'll examine your leg, Thomas.'

Philip's eyes sought mine and I saw it there in his face. He loved me. He had never stopped loving me. I faltered, embarrassed, and averted my gaze.

Thomas's turn came and Philip invited us into his office. I willed him to look at me again so I could confirm what I had seen in his face had been love, but he avoided my scrutiny. He sat Thomas on the bench to examine his leg. I glanced at his desk for a picture of Beatrice or their child, but there was none. I thought it strange because I expected Philip to be a devoted father. Where had he been all these years and what had he been doing? Did he enjoy working with children? I wanted to ask these questions but my tongue was stuck in my throat and Philip addressed his comments to Thomas rather than me.

'I try to match the treatment to the child,' he told him. 'What is right for you may not be right for another child and vice versa. You've been treated conservatively with splints and braces but I'm going to concentrate now on more intensive therapy for you.'

Thomas, who looked like a little man in his tweed suit and tie, answered, 'I did see some children getting massages at the hospital. I thought a massage might be nice.'

Philip did not laugh at Thomas. He looked him in the eye and answered, 'I am in correspondence with a nurse who has had success with massage on polio sufferers in the Outback. But at the same time, we need to be careful, Thomas. Too much stimulation can sometimes cause more damage.'

Thomas held Philip's gaze and nodded. It occurred to me that it was unusual for someone to speak *to* him. Most people looked over his head: firstly, because he was a child, and secondly, because he was dark.

'When I grow up, I want to be a doctor like you,' Thomas told Philip. 'I want to be kind to children.'

After examining Thomas and writing out a program of treatment, Philip showed us to the door. Thomas manoeuvered himself out ahead of me with his crutch and Philip touched my arm. I lifted my eyes to his face. The rise in my blood was met by an opposing emotion: the need to run away. I took Thomas's free arm and helped him out of the office. Philip had prescribed a three-month program but it would have to be Ranjana or Esther who brought Thomas to Edgecliff for the treatments. For I had come looking for the truth and had found it. My feelings for Philip, and his for me, were unchanged.

When I returned home, Freddy was not there. Some executives from Galaxy Pictures were in Sydney on business and their meeting with him must have been running late. Klára was staying the night with Uncle Ota and Ranjana. It was Regina's night off but she had left a pot of pumpkin soup on the stove and a loaf of bread. Outside, a drizzly rain was falling and there was a chill in the air.

I ran a bath and soaked in the tub, trying to calm my racing heart. Nerves I had thought were dead had come back to life.

I dressed in a white blouse and black skirt and sprinkled my hair with rosewater. I put on every piece of jewellery Freddy had given me: the gold wedding band with its diamonds and cutwork highlights; the ruby engagement ring; the rose gold pendant and earrings he had bought for our first anniversary; the sapphire and diamond bracelet he had given me when *In the Dark* was released in the United States.

I returned to the kitchen and stared at the soup on the stove, wondering if Freddy had eaten yet. I took out a tin of wafers and laid them on a plate, topping them with a spread of cheese and olive halves. Freddy liked to have a mint julep waiting for him when he came home. I heard his car in the driveway. Freddy parked in the garage and ran through the rain. I held the front door open for him.

'You're a lovely sight,' he said, taking the towel I offered and pressing it to his face.

'Here, let me take your coat, it's wet,' I said. 'Have you eaten?'

'We didn't have time.' He looked into the sitting room where I had laid out the canapés.

'I thought you might want to relax before dinner,' I told him.

Freddy sank into a chair and accepted the julep from me. It was not unusual for me to spoil him when he came home. Seeing him smile gave me pleasure. But it was not pleasure I was looking for that evening and Freddy knew me well enough to sense it.

'What's wrong?' he asked, when I sat down next to him.

'I took Thomas to a children's specialist today. It's our old friend Doctor Philip Page. He's back from England.'

Freddy did not say anything and I wondered if he had heard me. He sat motionless for a few moments staring at his hands. I cursed myself. I had tried to sound casual but had blurted everything out too quickly.

'Will you be going to see him again?' Freddy asked me.

It was difficult to tell from his calm tone what he was thinking.

'I don't think so,' I answered, rubbing my forehead. 'Ranjana or Esther will probably take Thomas to his appointments.'

Freddy lit a cigarette and blew a stream of smoke into the air.

'Philip is considered the best children's doctor in Sydney,' I said. 'He is confident that he can have Thomas walking normally again — or at least without a crutch.'

Freddy leaned back into his chair, thinking something over. He doted on Thomas, so I knew that Philip's assurance would please him. But there were lines across his brow. 'And how is Philip?' he asked.

I picked up a wafer. Freddy and I were skirting around what we most wanted to say.

'We didn't have much time for personal chat,' I answered. 'We talked mainly about Thomas, but he seems well. A little older.'

Freddy stubbed out his cigarette and glanced towards the kitchen. 'What's for dinner?'

I was relieved and yet disappointed that the strained conversation had ended. I was relieved because I had told Freddy that I had seen Philip. Yet there was so much more I had to confess. But my husband was not like my sister. I could not tell him everything without hurting him. My father had always been fond of the saying 'Better a lie that heals than a truth that wounds.'

During dinner Freddy and I talked about trivial day-to-day things. I told him about the hydrangeas I had planted in the garden and he told me that one of the executives at Galaxy Pictures in Hollywood had written to ask him if the picture director Adéla Rockcliffe was his wife.

'Freddy, they may not like you being married to an Australian director,' I told him.

'Well,' said Freddy with a smile, 'at least while they are grumbling about that, they haven't noticed the local cinemas I've acquired with your uncle's help.'

After dinner, we carried the plates to the kitchen and Freddy rested his hand on my hip. The silence that fell between us weighed on me but seemed not to bother him. He was usually like the Weimaraner Aunt Josephine had owned before Frip. The dog wanted to be the only living creature around Aunt Josephine and used to push everyone else away with his head. If a man struck up a conversation with me at the cinema or a party, Freddy would be at my side in an instant. But when it came to Philip reappearing in my life, he was surprisingly unconcerned.

Freddy returned to the sitting room and lay on the sofa. It was a habit of his to take a nap after dinner. I sat next to him and he pulled me closer, pressing my face to his chest.

'If you want to go to see Philip about Thomas's treatment, you can, you know,' he said. 'I want Thomas to get better and will pay whatever it costs to make sure he does. I don't want you to think I don't trust you. The past is the past, Adéla. We are husband and wife now.'

I thought back to my visit to Philip's office that day. Philip must have seen that my surname was Rockcliffe and yet he had not been surprised. He had not even mentioned it.

'Freddy, have you seen Philip since he returned from England?' I asked, pushing him away so I could look at his face.

Freddy's head dropped then snapped up again. My nerves were on tenterhooks and he was nodding off to sleep! 'It was only fair that I told him that we were married before he tried to find you,' Freddy mumbled. 'His union with Beatrice is a disaster. She's still in England.'

'Beatrice is still in England?'

Freddy yawned. 'They're estranged. Beatrice won't give him a divorce although I don't think they've had a day of happiness together since they married.'

I could not believe what I was hearing. I thought of the day Beatrice had asked me to go for a walk with her in the city and how she had told me she adored Philip and that he was her childhood friend, her confidant, and her reason for living. Philip had described himself as Beatrice's warm, comfortable blanket. But it seemed she had discarded him the moment they married.

'Freddy, you once said that there was more to Beatrice than meets the eye. What did you mean by that?'

Freddy did not answer. I thought he was thinking over the question. I waited a few minutes then turned to him. His chest was rising and falling in a slow, steady rhythm.

'Oh my God,' I said. 'I am in torment and you are asleep.'

Freddy's confidence that I would not be unfaithful to him was as unnerving to me as my fear that I would be if I saw Philip again. I had made Thomas promise not to tell Ranjana and Uncle Ota that we had visited Philip until I had a chance to explain it to them. The following morning I went to see them at the cinema.

'Philip!' said Ranjana. 'He thinks that he can help Thomas?'

'If anyone can, I'm sure he can,' said Uncle Ota. 'Thank you so much, Adélka, for thinking of it. It's the best news we have had in months.'

Ranjana and Uncle Ota's reaction added to the commotion in my head. When I explained to Ranjana that she and Esther would need to take Thomas to Philip's rooms themselves, she did not bat an eye.

'Oh course,' she said, hugging me. 'I understand that you are busy with Klára's wedding plans.'

Uncle Ota and Ranjana took it for granted that now I was married to Freddy, my feelings for Philip had changed.

The one person who would have understood my confusion was Klára. But she had conflicts of her own.

Klára and Robert were to be married in the Swans' garden. It should have been simple enough but, ironically for such a shy person, Mrs Swan had her heart set on a large society wedding. She and Klára had agreed on a pure white dress trimmed with Brussels lace but disagreed on everything else.

'She is a lovely lady but when it came to the wedding I had no idea that she would be so obstinate,' Klára complained to me one afternoon. 'I want a bouquet of lilies of the valley in memory of Mother and she insists on calla lilies with bows. When I told her I wanted to follow our family tradition of a rosemary wreath around my veil she did not speak to me for two days. It is as if she expects me to just forget where I came from.'

We were sitting together on the terrace, a basket of fruit between us. I eyed the juicy strawberries and nectarines and wondered why Klára and Robert were intent on having their wedding before Christmas. They were causing everyone more anxiety. Klára had her graduation to think about too. She was going to perform in front of a public audience. The wedding date had been set for the following year but for some reason she and Robert had changed their minds.

'Why don't you leave the wedding arrangements to me,' I told her. 'I will take the place of Mother in making something lovely for you. And I will handle Mrs Swan too. What about Mary? Is she all right?'

'Mary is being a darling,' said Klára. 'She wants to make our cake.'

'That's lovely,' I said. 'What kind?'

Klára's mouth twisted to a wry smile. 'The six-tiered kind.'

We both laughed. A magpie landed in the leaf litter and regarded us with its dark eyes.

'I think magpies are magical birds,' I said. 'Their black and white feathers are plain compared to the beautifully plumed lorikeets and rosellas. But when you look at a magpie — one on one — they transform: their personality shines through.'

'Has Uncle Ota told you about Angel?' Klára asked me.

'Yes,' I said. 'She has another joey. She is a busy mother.'

A change came over Klára's face.

'Is there something you want to tell me?' I asked her.

Klára tilted her head back so the filtered sunlight danced over her skin. 'You are going to be an aunty,' she said.

I sat up. 'What?'

'The baby is coming in June.'

I was too stunned to speak. I loved Klára and was happy for her, but this was too much at once. She was getting married, graduating and having a baby all in less than a year. She had assured me that she had been well since the night before my wedding when she'd had the attack of chills, but she was still pale. I wondered how she had fallen pregnant when I had been watching her so closely. Freddy and I went almost everywhere that Klára and Robert did, and she had been living in my house.

Klára was not an immodest girl and she blushed deeply. It was not the done thing to get pregnant before one was married.

'Are you disappointed with me?' she asked.

I stood up and put my arm around her shoulders. I could not judge her because the same thing could well have happened to me and Philip all those years ago, and at least she and Robert were officially engaged. 'Not at all. I am very proud of you.'

Klára pressed her cheek to mine. 'I am so lucky you are my sister,' she said.

*   *   *

Ranjana called me each week to report on Thomas's progress. Philip had given him a cyclical course of hot baths, physiotherapy and rest. From the way she spoke from the first day of his treatment, it was clear she thought that Philip was a miracle worker.

'Already, I can see an improvement,' she said. 'And Thomas told me on the way home that the pain is gone.'

I could not have been happier for Thomas. I loved him and I was sure that Philip would help him as he had promised. But Ranjana had no idea how she was unsettling me.

To avoid thinking about Philip, I locked myself away in the morning room every day and worked on a new script until Freddy came home in the evenings. Freddy had told me that the success of *In the Dark* would attract more investors for this next film. I wanted to pull all the stops out now and produce something not only visually stunning but remarkable in every way. I wanted my next picture to be a masterpiece.

When I had completed the first draft, I asked Hugh to meet me at the Vegetarian Café so I could run my idea by him before talking to Freddy. My husband was the best judge of whether a story was appealing or not but I wanted to talk to another artist first.

Hugh and Giallo were already in the café when I arrived. No sooner had I sat down and ordered a chicory coffee than Hugh begged me to tell him about the script.

'I don't want to give you tickets on yourself, Adéla,' he said, 'but I've been itching to work with you again.'

I was flattered because since finishing *In the Dark* Hugh had shot a feature film in Tasmania with a Hollywood director and had worked on documentaries in the Outback.

'I am slow,' I said with a smile. 'I am not exactly what you call "prolific".'

Hugh shrugged and Giallo went up and down with the movement. 'Art takes time. So what is the new story about?'

I put aside my cup. 'It is about a ten-year-old boy who has been crippled by polio and is convalescing in a rest home,' I began. 'The boy had been athletic and is despairing of life because the doctors have told him that he will never walk again. In the garden of the home there is a bevy of peafowl. One day, when the boy is out in the sunshine on his own in his wheelchair, a peacock with beautiful plumage catches his eye. The boy calls to the peacock and is surprised when the bird turns into a man in fine clothes and a crown of emeralds. The man tells the boy that he is a prince and was born in a faraway place called the Emerald Valley where humans and animals live together in harmony.'

I checked that I was not boring Hugh. Freddy said I should learn to summarise my ideas in two sentences but it was impossible for me to do. I either had to give the full explanation or none at all. I was pleased to see Hugh was pursing his lips, which I knew was a sign he was thinking about how the story would develop visually.

I continued. 'One day, an evil spirit from another valley, the Valley of Darkness, stole away the princess that was promised to him in marriage and turned him into a peacock. For one hour a day, the prince can regain his human form but this has not proved sufficiently long for him to travel to the Valley of Darkness to save his princess. He asks the boy if he will help him. The boy doesn't think he can, but in the prince's presence he finds that his wheelchair turns out to be a flying carriage. The prince and the boy have adventures together and eventually save the princess. When they triumph, the boy is given a special celebration in his honour in the Emerald Valley.'

370 • BELINDA ALEXANDRA

I paused to see if what I had said so far had made any impact.

Hugh shifted in his seat. 'How does it end?' he asked. 'Are you going to tell me or make me wait?'

'I will tell you,' I said, with a triumphant smile. 'The boy later awakens to find himself in his wheelchair in the convalescent home's garden. The nurses think he has been sleeping but the adventures the boy shared with the prince are real to him. Although he now accepts that he will never walk again, the boy has a new vision: he will find a way to do good in the world and make his life count for something.'

If Hugh had burst forth with a flurry of words in response to the script, it would have been out of character. I searched his face for the signs I knew from working with him that told me when he thought something was good. I was pleased to see him tap his fingers on the table, twitch his mouth, and cock his head. He was itching to work with me all right.

'When do we start?' he asked.

'I have to discuss it with Freddy first. Early in the new year if we can.'

Hugh and I stayed at the café for another hour and talked about Thomas. I knew that Hugh had been spending some time at the house, and I appreciated his care for my cousin but worried about the effect his visits might be having on Esther. The last time I saw her she was looking even dowdier than when I had first met her.

'You believe in ghosts, don't you?' Hugh asked me.

I nodded. 'I see them. Not often, but often enough to know they are there.'

'There's one that lingers around Esther's house,' he said.

My spine tingled. Hugh was the least superstitious person I knew. 'Did you see … something?'

He hissed out a breath. 'I thought that was all hocus-pocus, but I've seen him three times now. A young bloke in military uniform.'

I did not respond. I did not want to prompt him.

Hugh looked at me. 'The first time, I spoke to him. "G'day, mate!" I said. That was before I realised I could see right through him.'

'Did he say anything back?' I asked.

Hugh shook his head. 'He just stared at me as if he wanted something.' He glanced at his hands then back at me. 'What do you think he wants?'

I hesitated, wondering what I should tell him. I thought if I said it was Louis looking out for Esther that it might only alienate Hugh from her further. Speaking to ghosts sometimes sent them away, and I did not want to encourage him to try any more conversations.

'He is just watching over things,' I said. 'He is probably someone who lived in the street or visited it often.'

Hugh shook his head. 'Poor bugger. And I thought I was unlucky losing my leg.'

My heart lightened with Hugh's words. It was the first time he had sounded grateful rather than bitter. I wondered what had changed him. Perhaps it was looking after Thomas. I remembered what Klára had told me about how helping another living being brought healing to oneself. But how was it Hugh could see Louis and yet not see the butterfly?

After wishing Hugh goodbye, I walked down George Street towards Circular Quay to catch the ferry. It was Freddy's birthday and he was coming home early so we could go to a restaurant for dinner. I glanced at my watch. I was running late and would have to hurry. I had only walked a short distance when someone called out to me.

'Adéla, is that you?'

I turned around. Philip was standing on the opposite side of the street. The wind was ruffling his hair. His teal-blue coat matched his eyes.

My heart thumped in my chest. Philip crossed the street and walked towards me. There was no recrimination in his face and I guessed he knew why I had not gone back with Thomas to his rooms.

'Thank you for all you have done,' I said.

My words were sincere. I would be grateful to Philip forever for what he had done for Klára and now Thomas. But my compliment was a defence too; I did not want the conversation to turn to us.

'Where are you headed?' Philip asked me.

I nodded towards the Quay.

'That's right, you live in Cremorne now. Can I walk with you?'

I caught my breath, then answered, 'Of course.'

We headed in the direction of the Quay. The sun was setting and the breeze from the harbour was cold. Yet I felt warmth emanating from Philip's body as he walked beside me, just as it had the day he sat beside me in the teahouse at the Botanic Gardens.

'How's Freddy?' he asked. 'Still working for Galaxy Pictures?'

'Yes,' I said.

'Life has taken us in strange directions, hasn't it, Adéla?'

I stopped and turned to him. I could not bear the sadness in his eyes. What had happened with Beatrice? She had him and now she had rejected him. Why had she not left him to me in the first place? We could have been so happy together.

'Freddy told me Beatrice did not come back with you,' I said, lowering my eyes. 'I am sorry. You of all people deserve to be happy.'

'Do I?' Philip asked quietly.

'Why, yes,' I said. 'You do so much good work for the sick. You should be with someone who cherishes you.'

What I had told him was heartfelt but I had to be careful not to mislead him. I was a married woman and I could do nothing more for him than offer my sympathy.

Philip flinched but said nothing. We strode on to the Quay. The Cremorne ferry was already in port and passengers were heading up the gangway. There would be another ferry in half an hour. I wished I could miss this one and spend more time with Philip but I was already late. And I knew the truth: if I did not get on that ferry, I would betray Freddy's trust. For when I stood next to Philip I felt things that I had never experienced so ardently for my husband: my skin was tingling with life and I was dizzy with desire. I longed for Philip to take me in his arms and kiss me. But he and I were honourable people. Honour was what we clung to when everything else in our lives fell apart. That was why he had married Beatrice although he did not love her. Why he did not leave her for me.

Philip must have sensed my hesitation to board the ferry. His breathing was shallow and his eyes were steady on me. I only had to weaken for a moment and we would both be lost to our passion. There were a few passengers left to board. A boy was helping an old lady up the ramp, sparing us a few more minutes.

'You still love me, don't you, Adéla?' Philip asked.

I nodded. I could not bring myself to look in his eyes. I twisted the wedding ring on my finger.

'But you love Freddy too, don't you?'

'Beatrice did you a terrible wrong,' I said, my voice a whisper.

'All aboard for the ferry to Cremorne,' called out the deckhand. A lady carrying a child pushed through the gate and shouted to the deckhand to wait a moment. We still had a few seconds' grace.

Philip and I looked into each other's eyes.

'Lady, are you coming or not?' the deckhand called out to me.

'You'd better go,' Philip said.

I turned in the direction of the gangway. My heart felt as if it was being torn to shreds. My legs trembled when I stepped onto the ramp. My body was so heavy that if I had slipped into the water I would have sunk like a weight.

I glanced over my shoulder at Philip. His face was contorted with pain. I longed to relieve his agony, but I could not without hurting Freddy.

'Come on, love,' said the deckhand, untying the rope. 'You've kept everyone waiting.'

I cried out when the deckhand pushed the gangway onto the wharf and a strip of churning water separated me from Philip. For one moment, I thought I might climb on the railing and throw myself into Philip's arms. But a second later it was too late. The ferry lurched and moved from the wharf. Then, suddenly, the boat swerved to the dock and Philip's face was only a few yards from mine. 'I love you, Adéla,' he said. 'But I will never hurt you or Freddy. You let me go once because you wanted to do the right thing by Beatrice.'

'Where is your child?' I asked him. 'Is he with Beatrice in England?'

Tears came to Philip's eyes. 'There was no baby,' he said. 'It was a lie. A lie Beatrice told to get me to marry her quickly and to keep me away from you.'

The last of his words faded as the ferry gathered speed and pulled away into the evening. I could not move from the railing. I clung to it while Philip shrank into a tiny figure on the edge of the dock. We watched each other until the ferry passed Fort Denison and we were lost from each other's view.

TWENTY-ONE

P hilip's revelation left me stunned. I muddled through Freddy's
birthday dinner, lifting my champagne glass and
complimenting the band, all the while with Philip's voice in my
head: 'There was no baby. It was a lie. A lie Beatrice told to get me
to marry her quickly and to keep me away from you.'

The following morning I went to the sewing room where I
kept my photographic equipment and pulled out a copy of the
print I had taken of Beatrice. I stared at her pale eyes, the white
skin with its galaxy of freckles, the mass of hair. I had a different
impression of her now. Gone was the image of the breezy girl
who gathered people to her bosom. She was manipulative and
cunning. I put the print down and stared out to the garden where
the builders were working on the summerhouse and fernery that
were my birthday present to Freddy. Beatrice had a way of
clinging to people. We had all felt sorry for her because her
mother was dying. I remembered what she had said about not
having many female friends. I no longer wondered why.

I thought about waking Klára but decided against it. Her wedding plans were tiring her out and her graduation performance was to take place the week after she and Robert returned from their honeymoon. The head of the school had not been pleased by the proposed interruption to Klára's studies but had given her leave, not wanting to lose her altogether. Klára had not started to show her pregnancy but she had been plagued by morning sickness. I decided to leave her alone to rest. But there was someone I could talk to and that was my future brother-in-law.

'Klára's all right, isn't she?' Robert asked, when I telephoned him. 'There's no problem?'

The relief in his voice when I told him there was nothing wrong with Klára endeared him to me. There had been a time when I had doubted that he would take care of my sister properly, but I no longer did. 'No, everything is fine,' I assured him. 'It's Beatrice I want to talk to you about.'

Robert paused for a moment. 'Then come this morning,' he said. 'I will be waiting for you.'

Freddy had already left for the office and Rex would be required to chauffeur Klára to school. If I wanted to see Robert that morning I would have to drive myself. I opened the garage door to access the shiny Bentley Freddy had bought me. On another morning I might have smiled when I remembered those driving lessons on Sunday afternoons with my husband. The Bentley had a trumpet horn mounted on the outside of the cabin right next to the handbrake. Every time I went to release the handbrake, I would toot the horn by mistake instead so that each trip began with a cheerful 'honk' and ended with one too, which would send Freddy and me into peals of laughter.

I was greeted at the Swan residence by a maid who showed me into the drawing room where Robert was waiting.

'I distanced myself from Beatrice after she wrote to me from England,' Robert said as soon as the maid had left. 'I knew she was good at getting her way, but when she congratulated herself on having "snared" Philip with a good bit of "trickery" I could no longer respect her. I knew she could be calculating but that was the icing on the cake. She's changed.'

I remembered what Philip had said about Beatrice being different when she was in Europe.

Robert took a sip of tea. 'Freddy figured Beatrice out long ago,' he said. 'That's why she didn't like him. She knew he could see through her. He once tried to tell me that Beatrice wasn't virtuous and I wouldn't listen. Well, now it's Philip who suffers.'

'His father must have lied to him about the pregnancy,' I said. 'Philip said that he had confirmed it.'

Robert nodded. 'That's the worst of it, I think. It's caused a rift between the father and son. But Doctor Page Senior was set on Philip marrying Beatrice. Poor old fellow. He didn't know her any better than we did.'

I thought about what Philip had told me about his mother's and Mrs Fahey's pact. I imagined when Philip found out that he had been 'tricked' he could not play the doting husband Beatrice expected him to be.

Robert studied me. 'You and Philip were in love, weren't you?' he said, without a hint of disapproval.

'Did Klára tell you?'

Robert shook his head. 'Klára and you keep your secrets and that's fine by me. If you asked her never to speak of it, then she never would. I'm sorry about what happened to Philip, but I can't say I regret you marrying Freddy. You and Freddy have been good for each other. You've brought each other to life.'

It was nearly ten o'clock and Robert was giving a guest lecture on Indonesian instruments at the Conservatorium of Music at eleven. I told him I should leave. He called the maid to collect my coat. When she returned she also gave me a bag of flower bulbs. 'Mrs Swan said I was to give these to you,' she said.

'My mother knows that tomorrow is your gardening day,' explained Robert. 'Klára told her.'

'Wednesday is Rex's day off,' I said. 'I like to potter around the garden by myself, planning what plants to add and which ones to move or replace. It helps me work out problems with my script.'

Robert walked me to the car. 'I'm grateful to you, Adéla,' he said. 'You've been kind to me and you've managed to get my mother and sister on side about the wedding arrangements. You've made life smoother for us where a lot of sisters would have made it harder.'

Robert's words reminded me of Mother and Emilie. 'I am glad to help you,' I said, slipping my hand into his.

Robert leaned over and kissed me on the cheek. 'We will be brother and sister soon, you know.'

I returned home with a heavy heart. The workmen had finished the summerhouse and were planting the ferns. The garden had transformed since I had come to live with Freddy. Rex and I had gotten rid of the formalities better suited to Europe with its bleak winters. This garden was alive with glossy-leafed camellias and lilly-pillys in their natural forms, tree ferns and borders of gardenias, boronias, native daisies and agapanthus. Rainbow lorikeets and honey-eaters bounced on the bottlebrush and grevillea blossoms while ducks splashed in the pond. Gum saplings stood in the corners of the garden where they would one day be trees. I had not seen any possums or flying foxes yet, but they would come in time, when the trees grew.

'You and Freddy have been good for each other. You've brought each other to life,' Robert had said.

I opened the door to the house, glad to be alone for the day. I called to Regina and asked her to make me some tea. Her eyes shifted to the drawing room door, which was shut. I flung it open and was struck by the splashes of colour that jumped at me. On every table and sideboard were bouquets of flowers: roses, dahlias, lilies, irises, gerberas and sunflowers.

Regina handed me an envelope, smiled and fled. I looked at the envelope then opened it.

> *Darling,*
> *Thank you for my lovely birthday dinner last night.*
> *You were tired when we returned home and you*
> *forgot to hide your script. I found it on the hall table*
> *along with your purse. I couldn't resist reading it.*
> *What a story! My dearest, you've exceeded yourself. I*
> *can't wait to work on* The Emerald Valley *with you.*
> *Love always,*
> *Your Freddy*

I sank down on the sofa, overwhelmed by everything. The flowers filled the room with a heady, intoxicating fragrance. I closed my eyes and squeezed away the tears. I could not give in to them. If I did, I may never get off that sofa again.

If Mrs Swan had set her heart on a traditional Anglo-Saxon wedding, even one not performed in a church, she should not have let her son marry into our family. Uncle Ota emerged from the house in a morning suit with trousers with turn-ups, white gloves and a carnation in his buttonhole. Klára was lovely in a lace dress with the hemline longer at the back and a veil with a rosemary headdress. Ranjana followed in a shell-pink sari and Mary and I glided after her in matching beaded dresses with handkerchief skirts.

We walked down a green carpet bordered by pots of petunias and past the guests to the summerhouse, which was decorated with roses. Robert, who was standing next to Freddy, beamed at his beautiful bride. But the traditional English wedding ended there. Before the couple made their vows, Ranjana tied a cloth from Klára's waist to Robert's shoulder to symbolise the marital bond and Uncle Ota placed a stone on the floor of the summerhouse for Klára and Robert to rest their right feet on. Both of these were Indian traditions to bless the couple. At the reception afterwards, the bridal waltz gave way to a polka that brought the rest of the wedding party onto the floor. Mrs Swan nearly fainted at the sight of her guests snubbing tradition. Hugh and I plied her with champagne. Freddy twirled by and swept her into his arms, spinning her around the floor until she took on the blush of a young girl.

'I like Europeans,' I heard her tell him. 'They are so … lively.'

I turned to see Esther with Thomas. He had trouble bending his knee but could move well enough with Esther's help and no longer needed a crutch.

At the dinner afterwards, Freddy read out the telegrams of the guests who had not been able to attend. He paused for a moment before reading the final one: 'Doctor Philip Page wishes Mr and Mrs Swan every happiness for their future life together.'

'Dreadful business, that Doctor Page,' I heard an elderly society matron say to her companion during the supper.

'But isn't he the best children's doctor in Sydney?' enquired her companion.

The society matron sniggered. 'Indeed, you may go to his rooms for treatment ... but no decent family would have him in their home. They say his wife has got up to all sorts of things in London and that she is even living with another woman.'

'Good gracious,' exclaimed her companion. 'The Pages used to be such a respectable family.'

I felt Philip's humiliation as keenly as if the woman had been talking about me. I glanced at Klára and Robert, so happy in their love. Our family would be proud to have Philip in our homes if not for the complication of my feelings for him. All he had ever wanted to do was help people and now he was seen as an unsuitable guest — neither an eligible bachelor nor a decently married man. I found myself hating Beatrice for what she had done to him. Not only had she blighted his hopes for a happy married life and children, but she had exposed him to public shame. If what the woman had said was true, he had grounds for divorce. But the press loved nothing more than a scandal, and he was probably afraid to drag his family's name any further into the mud.

When it was time for Klára and Robert to leave, the guests lined up like a royal guard along the green carpet. Each one of us held a candle. I felt as if a piece of glass had lodged itself in the pit of my stomach. The thought that my sister, so much a part of me, would no longer live under the same roof was a separation I had put out of my mind while I had planned her wedding. I realised how ill prepared I was for it. It had been difficult enough to get used to sleeping in different rooms when I married Freddy and Klára came to live with us.

Don't cry, I told myself. Don't spoil the moment. The more I tried to control myself, the faster the tears filled my eyes.

Who could be more in tune with Klára or me than we were with each other?

Klára stepped in front of me. In the candlelight I saw the conflict of happiness and anxiety that waged in her eyes. When she glanced at Robert it was with adoration. But when she looked at me, her mouth trembled.

'We must buy a place where we can all live together like we did at Watsons Bay,' she whispered.

'Klára ...' I began but could not finish. How could I admonish my sister and tell her that we were married women now and must start families of our own with our husbands? It was taking all my strength not to cling to her.

After Klára and Robert had left, Freddy drove me to Cremorne Point and we sat together in the car with the top down and gazed at the stars. He sensed my sadness and so did not talk about the wedding.

'I've been thinking about *The Emerald Valley*,' he said. 'There is really only one place to make it: the Blue Mountains.'

I turned to him. I had written the picture with the Blue Mountains in mind but Freddy and Hugh had been scouting locations closer to Sydney for the bushland scenes. The Blue Mountains were only eighty miles away but the roads were rough and it would not be an easy journey. It also meant we would have to pay our actors more because they would be far away from the theatres.

'Truly?' I asked Freddy. 'What about the costs?'

'Hang the costs,' he said.

Freddy could not have known how happy he had made me.

To distract myself from missing Klára and thinking about Philip, I persuaded Freddy to take me to Tilly's Cinema every night, even if it meant seeing some pictures several times. Uncle Ota invited Charles Chauvel to speak about his new film after the screening one evening. We had enjoyed his first one, *The Moth of Moonbi*, and were keen to hear what he had to say.

Greenhide was a well-constructed film so I was surprised when Chauvel told the audience that he'd had to travel around the Outback towns of Queensland to get it screened because the major theatres would not show it. 'And even in the Outback I had to pay the showmen to take off their American film for the night and do all the publicity myself,' he told us.

Chauvel was not only the writer and director of his films but the business manager, producer, publicist and distributor! I appreciated how easy Freddy made directing pictures for me.

'If it goes on like this, the local film industry will be dead in a year,' I told Freddy, after we had returned home and were sitting in the kitchen drinking our nightly glass of buttermilk before bed.

Freddy cocked an eyebrow. 'What are you being so pessimistic about? Australasian Films have built a new studio, and have spent over one hundred thousand pounds on equipment.'

Uncle Ota had told me about the new studio. Australasian Films were not intending to produce Australian films; rather they wanted to make American-style films in Australia where costs were cheaper. They had employed an American director, Norman Dawn, to head the production of *For the Term of His Natural Life*. The story was based on a classic Australian novel but the stars were American and the production sounded as if it were going to be a Hollywood extravaganza. The budget was a staggering forty thousand pounds. As for Australasian Films suddenly investing in the local industry, perhaps that had something to do with the fact that the Combine and American film interests in Australia were about to be investigated.

'Aren't you worried about the Royal Commission, Freddy?' I asked. 'They are going to call you and other American distributors to answer for your practices.'

'Ah,' said Freddy, 'but I supported one of this country's finest directors. And I helped her uncle keep local cinemas in Australian hands. I even protected him from getting blacklisted when he screened Australian films in preference to American ones.'

'Yes, darling,' I said, 'but that was on the sly. That's not what Galaxy Pictures did and certainly not what you were sent here to do. You were encouraged to shut the local industry down to leave it open to American products. Who are you going to represent when they call you before the Commission? Hollywood or Southern Pictures?'

'I'll decide on the day depending which way the wind is blowing,' said Freddy, downing the last dregs of his milk and placing his glass on the table. Then, seeing the look of disdain on my face, he laughed and added, 'If *The Emerald Valley* turns out the way I expect, I won't be working for Galaxy Pictures. I'll be working for you.'

The previous week, Freddy and I had seen the McDonagh Sisters' picture *Those Who Love*. The story had been beautifully characterised, acted and plotted. Those clever Australian sisters had made the film for less than one thousand pounds and it had been sold into Britain. The budget for *The Emerald Valley* was ten thousand pounds, an amount most Australian directors could only dream of.

I kissed Freddy's cheek. I did not have an excuse for not making the best film possible. I should be more like my husband, I thought, and not let depressing talk about the local industry get to me.

* * *

Klára and Robert returned from their honeymoon at Hepburn Springs in the middle of December. Klára was showing a bump and had put on weight around her face.

'It was the pancakes we ate for breakfast each morning,' she said, pushing back her cloud of dark hair and running her palms over her belly.

'I think you're having twins,' said Ranjana, working with me to let out Klára's yellow dress for her graduation performance, which was to take place at the end of the week. Klára was too pale for someone who had just returned from a spa resort. She also had a persistent cough.

'It's just a tickle in the back of my throat,' she assured me.

She promised me she would see the Swan family's physician as soon as her concert was out of the way. 'It was Doctor Fitzgerald who confirmed my pregnancy,' she told me. 'He is very kind and capable.'

The week of Klára's graduation concert, I was plagued by disturbing dreams. Emilie was in them. Sometimes she was leaning over my bed and in other dreams she was in the music room in our house in Prague. It seemed as if she wanted to say something to me, but I was afraid to hear what it was and made myself disappear from the dreams before she could speak. But then, the night before the concert, I saw a restless ocean that I knew was the sea between me and Prague. I woke with a start. Dreams of bodies of water were bad luck. They foreshadowed death.

I entered the Conservatorium's concert hall along with the Rose and Swan families and Freddy, Hugh and Esther, and imagined how proud Mother would have been at this moment. Despite being so far from the musical culture of Europe, Klára had applied herself and was graduating from music school. It was

ambitious for her and her class orchestra to have chosen
Beethoven's Piano Concerto No 5 for their graduation piece. It
was grand in scale and nature. But their rehearsals in the past
week, despite Klára having been away, had been flawless. My
only concern was how peaked Klára looked when I had helped
her dress for the evening. The head of the school, Alfred Steel,
put her pallor down to nerves when he saw her, but I worried
that it was her pregnancy. Madame Henri, the school's French
teacher, who was sitting in the wings with the purpose of
soothing flustered nerves, told Klára to lie down in the dressing
room and rest before her performance.

'You can sit here in the wings when she plays,' she said to me.

While a quartet played Mozart's String Quartet in G Major, I
looked around at the audience and studied their faces. Everyone
was enraptured. The Handel solos that followed were note
perfect and so sublimely performed that my toes tingled. But all
the while I clenched and unclenched my hands waiting for Klára.
If she could make it through this performance, then she would be
able to rest at home until the baby was born.

When Klára's part in the program drew near, I slipped out of
our row and crept to the wings as Madame Henri had suggested.
Klára was there, waiting with the orchestra. I was pleased to see
that the colour had returned to her face and there was no sign of
her cough. I was also satisfied that my skilful draping of the
fabric across her belly hid the fact that she was pregnant.

Klára had told me that any performance nerves she
experienced disappeared the moment her hands touched the
keyboard, so I almost jumped for joy when she played her
cadenzas in the first movement vibrantly and passionately. The
notes she produced on the piano sparkled with energy. The
orchestra was well matched to her and the clarity of the flutes

and oboes made me think of an ice palace in a wintry kingdom. I could see in my mind the light sparkling from the icicles and feel the stillness of the chilly air.

The shift to the lyrical second movement brought soothing and tender music to my ears. I peered through the curtains at Klára who always managed to astound me with her ability to contrast the dramatic and the calm. I dropped the curtain again and closed my eyes.

There was no break between the second and third movements and I almost pinched myself in anticipation of the majestic ending. Then I noticed a blurring of the notes. It was so slight that I only picked it up because I had heard Klára rehearse the piece so many times. I opened my eyes again and peered through the curtain. Klára had picked up her mistake and was playing the movement as flawlessly as before. But I was startled to see her bathed in perspiration. She had a damp patch in the small of her back and the wisps of hair about her ears were wet. Klára was one of those cool-fleshed individuals who rarely perspired, unlike me who became flushed at the drop of a hat. Was she becoming fatigued? Had she lost her nerve? Despite her dishevelled appearance, Klára completed her quiet 'conversation' with the timpani before the orchestra rejoined with her for the stirring conclusion.

When Klára lifted her hands from the keyboard the audience could not hold back their enthusiasm. They jumped to their feet to give her an ovation. Klára returned their adoration by standing up and performing a slight curtsey.

She turned to me and I gasped. Her face was grey. My God, I thought. She's going to faint.

Klára staggered to the wings before she swooned. I caught her in my arms. She was much taller than me and it took all my strength not to topple over. I helped her to a chair. Madame Henri was quickly by our side. 'I'll get some water,' she said.

I brushed Klára's hair from her face. The audience was still clapping, waiting for her to reappear on stage.

'Klára,' I said, holding her close to me. 'What is it?'

She turned to me and the terror I saw in her eyes chilled me.

'Is it the baby?' I asked, placing my hand on her stomach.

Klára shook her head. 'I saw him. He was sitting in the audience.'

'Who?' I asked.

Klára's pale lips trembled. It was a struggle for her to speak and her voice came out as a whisper. 'Miloš.'

TWENTY-TWO

The morning after the concert, Robert, his mother and sister, Freddy and I sat in the drawing room of the Swan residence waiting for Doctor Fitzgerald to arrive to examine Klára. Uncle Ota, Ranjana, Hugh and Esther waited at Watsons Bay for the doctor's prognosis. While Klára slept upstairs, Robert tapped his fingers on the arm of his chair and I tried to sort my thoughts. It was nearly six years since Klára and I had seen Miloš. Klára had told me it had been only her determination not to show she recognised him that kept her performing under his gaze. But had she really seen him — or had she imagined him? I had not found him in the audience when I looked around, and Klára had been under enormous strain. I remembered Philip instructing Ranjana to make Klára's life as tranquil as possible after her time at Broughton Hall. I prayed that Klára was not suffering a relapse and that her tired mind had simply been mistaken. The other alternative — that Miloš had come all the way to Australia — was too horrifying to contemplate.

Doctor Fitzgerald arrived in the manner of a country practitioner. We heard the 'clop' of horse's hooves and rushed out the front door to greet the black-clad doctor who was driving a horse and buggy.

'Good morning,' he said, alighting from the carriage and pulling a leather case from the seat. From the mass of silver hair that sprang from his head when he lifted his hat, I put the doctor's age to be around sixty. But he was solidly built and his pale skin was smooth.

Doctor Fitzgerald greeted Klára with a smile when he and I entered her room but she returned his salutation coolly. I was surprised because she had spoken highly of the doctor before.

Doctor Fitzgerald waited a moment then cleared his throat. 'You've not been well, Mrs Swan,' he said. 'I'm sorry to hear that.'

Klára raised her eyebrows and turned to me. Her pupils were dilated and I could see the veins under her skin. She did not look like herself. I glanced to the doctor. Perhaps my worst fears were realised: the condition that had sent her to Broughton Hall had returned. Had she not once been convinced she had seen Miloš on the ship that had brought us to Sydney?

Doctor Fitzgerald checked Klára's pulse and temperature. I sat in a chair by the window, listening to his requests for her to breathe deeply and to cough into a cloth. I tried to read between the lines to understand what he was thinking, but his manner was jolly and professional although I could see in his eyes there was something wrong.

My fears mounted when afterwards Doctor Fitzgerald requested to speak to me and Robert in the drawing room. 'Mrs Swan's pregnancy seems to be progressing normally but she is nervous about something,' he said. 'What worries me most, however, is that cough. Has she had it long?'

I told him I had only noticed Klára's coughing fits recently.

Doctor Fitzgerald nodded. 'A skin test may or may not be an indication,' he said. 'And she's not coughing up blood — but it could be consumptive.'

It was the second shock I'd had in less than twenty-four hours. I sank into a chair. Consumption? It was the wasting disease that had killed Lottie Lyell.

I turned to Robert, who was deathly pale, then back to Doctor Fitzgerald. 'Is my sister going to die?' I asked.

Doctor Fitzgerald pursed his lips. 'I believe whatever is ailing her hasn't quite taken hold yet. It might improve with rest, fresh air and good food.'

'But most consumptives die, don't they?' said Robert, clutching the back of a chair. 'And the baby …?'

Doctor Fitzgerald shook his head. 'Some patients have a mild case throughout their life, while a small number are cured spontaneously. I believe your wife and child are safe for now — as long as Mrs Swan experiences no upheavals or upsets.'

No upheavals or upsets? I thought. *She thinks she's seen Miloš!*

Robert's hands trembled while he watched Doctor Fitzgerald write out a care regimen for Klára. After the doctor had left, we informed the others about the nature of Klára's illness. Later, Freddy and I sat on the veranda watching the sky darken and threaten rain. Was Klára going to die? Was she going to lose her baby? With these questions on my mind, I could almost forget her claim to have seen Miloš.

Uncle Ota wrote to Doctor Holub asking if he knew Miloš's whereabouts. During the anxious time while we waited for a reply, the women of Klára's old and new families banded together to nurse her back to health. Christmas and other engagements were forgotten while Ranjana, Mrs Swan, Mary, Esther and I went about our tasks. We opened and closed windows to allow Klára the benefits of fresh air without giving her a chill; ran steam baths; supervised meals; performed body rubs; and ordered the household staff to change and boil the linen daily. Klára's illness had one disguised blessing: it brought us together. Mrs Swan and Ranjana became close friends. I would often find them drinking tea together on the veranda and sharing stories of India. Esther and I formed a bond with Mary, who proved to be a good organiser. She wrote a schedule so that Klára always had someone with her.

It was with relief that we received Doctor Holub's response to our enquiry:

> *Pan Dolezal has moved to Vienna with his wife. I employed a contact to check that he was in Austria on the date you mentioned. Indeed he was, so the person paní Swan saw could not have been her stepfather ...*

'Thank God for that,' I said, when I had finished reading the letter. Doctor Holub had confirmed what I had suspected: Klára's ill health and nervous state had fooled her to believe she had seen Miloš.

'At least now I can stop living in fear of Miloš hiding in every nook and cranny and devote myself to seeing Klára get better,' I told Robert.

I went to Klára's room to tell her the reassuring news. While I climbed the stairs I thought about how I would express it to her. I wanted to explain that her mistake could have been made by anyone who was not feeling well and to avoid any hint that her mind was unsound.

When I entered the room, Klára was sitting in bed with her hands clasped around her knees, looking out the window.

'Klára,' I said, moving towards the bed. 'We have received a letter from Doctor Holub.'

Klára changed her position slightly but said nothing. I read her the letter. 'You see, the man in the audience, whoever he was, was not Miloš.'

'Yes,' she murmured. 'That is what I heard you and Robert saying downstairs. The sitting room is beneath me and your voices carried.'

I moved closer to her. 'Klára, if Miloš were intending to murder us why would he have turned up at your concert and made himself obvious?'

'He had disguised himself with a moustache and a wig.'

'If he was disguised, how do you know it was Miloš?'

Klára sighed. 'Very well, I will accept your reassurances that I was mistaken and do whatever you wish.' She sounded so faint and desolate that I had a sense that rather than being reassured, as I had intended, she was questioning the stability of her own mind.

When I returned downstairs Robert and Freddy were in the drawing room. Robert stood up. 'How is she?'

I could see in his eyes that he was pleading with me to give him some glimmer of hope that Klára had improved if not in body then at least in spirit. I sank into the nearest chair. Robert's gaze followed me. Freddy reached over and patted my knee. I laid my hand on top of his.

'We called Philip Page,' Robert said. 'He's coming to see Klára now.'

The implication of Robert's announcement barely registered with me. Klára was sick. She needed the best help possible.

Philip arrived a short while afterwards, appearing at the same time as Uncle Ota, here to receive an update on Klára's health. Philip glanced at me when the maid showed him into the drawing room, then turned to Robert. 'Where is she?'

Mary and I had moved Klára to the sitting room upstairs. For Philip to examine Klára in her bedroom without a female member of the family in attendance would be unseemly, yet I feared that the presence of one of us would inhibit her in telling him everything. The men were looking in my direction; it seemed it had fallen on me to take Philip to Klára.

'This way,' I said, indicating the stairs. I walked up them ahead of him and my eyes met his in the mirror at the top of the landing. Our faces coloured. Were we to spend the rest of our lives like this: yearning for each other, but always having to turn away?

Philip spoke with Klára for an hour. When he returned downstairs, the Swans, Uncle Ota, Freddy and I were waiting for him.

'The death of Klára's mother was harrowing, to say the least,' he told us. 'Now that she's married and having her first child without her mother present, it may be bringing up those memories for her.' Philip did not look at me when he spoke, but I was aware that his body was turned in my direction. He paused, then added, 'That doesn't mean we shouldn't take her claim seriously. But Robert has told me that the matter of the stepfather's whereabouts has been confirmed. My advice would be to keep doing what you have been and to make sure Klára — and, I might add, Adéla, for Klára is equally concerned about her — are not left alone. When the stepfather does not appear, she will calm down and turn her mind to other things.'

'It's an unsatisfactory situation,' said Freddy. 'There are two men and a woman in Europe who killed my wife's and sister-in-law's mother. An attempt was made on their lives as well. Until that man and his accomplices are brought to justice, how can either woman have peace?'

'You are quite right,' said Philip. 'Part of the problem for Klára is that the matter is unresolved. Her mother's killer is still at large, no matter his geographical location.'

Uncle Ota and I exchanged a glance. 'We will wait until Klára is twenty-one,' Uncle Ota said. 'Then we will change the benefactors in the will. After that we will see what we can do about Miloš and his accomplices.'

Philip came to see Klára every day for the next fortnight. Sometimes he stayed for lunch at Mrs Swan's request, but most often he would excuse himself by saying that he had patients to see. There was something unspoken between us and, while it remained unsaid, it hung heavily in the air whenever we passed each other in the corridor or on the stairs.

Each time Philip left, I had a sense that precious moments had slipped away. I was surprised that no one guessed the turmoil in my heart. Except Klára.

One day, after Philip had left, I went to take her lunch and found her dressed and reading by the window. I wondered if Klára was angry at me for not believing she had seen Miloš, but that afternoon, with the gentle autumn sun on her face, she looked better than she had in weeks. She smiled at me.

'Have you finished rewriting your script?' she asked.

I put the tray on the side table and sat down next to her. 'I have a few scenes left to complete. Freddy says we can shoot it in the Blue Mountains even though it will escalate the budget.'

Klára threw back her head and laughed. 'That man loves you, Adéla. He'd do anything for you.'

'I love Freddy too,' I said.

Klára caught the pain in my voice. 'What is it?'

I was cautious in how I worded the story of Philip and the lie Beatrice had told him. I'd had time to process the revelation but it was the first Klára had heard of the story. She was too shocked to speak for a few moments. Then she shook her head.

'There was something about Beatrice that I did not trust from the beginning,' she said. 'She was too … too buoyant all the time. But I didn't say anything. I wondered if I were jealous.' A pained look pinched her brow while she gathered her thoughts. 'And now you?' she said, looking at me with pity in her eyes. 'You still love Philip, don't you?'

There was no need for me to reply. There were no answers. What could be said to help the situation? Truly, nothing at all.

During one of Philip's visits, I was alone with Klára in the house, except for the maids who were cleaning the windows. After speaking with Klára, Philip entered the sitting room where I was trying to concentrate on a novel.

'I've done all I can for Klára,' he told me. 'She needs to stand on her own feet now if she is to get better. Doctor Fitzgerald will be able to take her through to her delivery.'

The thought that this could be the last time I would see Philip brought me to my feet. 'But Klára trusts you,' I said. 'After all she has been through …'

Philip turned away. 'I've told Klára and she understands. She only asked that I explain it to you.'

His hands were trembling. I hesitated before speaking, then I took the risk.

'I accept that we cannot be together as man and wife but I can't accept not having you in my life at all. Can't we even be friends?'

Philip flinched. 'What good will that do, Adéla,' he said, 'when seeing you is painful to me? I don't want to visit you for cups of tea. I want to care for you. I want to be there when you need me — not as a doctor but as your lover and husband.'

Philip had expressed the desires I harboured in my own heart. If I took a step closer to him our safeguards would collapse. I thought of that dreadful moment in Broughton Hall's garden when we had looked into each other's eyes, knowing that we would have to walk away from each other for good.

'Don't you see, Adéla?' Philip pleaded. 'I can't love you unless I give you up. You did that for me once, remember?'

'I was wrong,' I said. 'Look where it left you.'

'But Freddy is a good man, isn't he? He loves you and is honest with you?'

I drew a breath, dazed by pain. When I was with Freddy, I loved him with all my heart. But when I was with Philip, my soul was full of longing. Philip was right. It was impossible for us to be friends.

'How did this happen?' I asked him. 'How did I find you and then lose you?'

Philip moved forward and took me in his arms. My body leapt to life when he pressed his lips to mine. I thought back to the day on Wattamolla beach; I wanted Philip as much now as I had then.

He pulled away. The withdrawal of his touch was like being plunged into cold water. 'I'd better leave,' he said, and rushed out into the hall.

The maids were still occupied with the windows so Philip fetched his coat himself from the closet and walked to the door. When he reached it, he turned and gave me one last look that said 'farewell'.

The sound of the door closing was as sad as the first thud of soil on a coffin. He has gone for good this time, I thought. I reached up and touched my lips. They were warm from when Philip had kissed me.

I walked into the garden and wandered down to the maze. I sat on the bench at its centre, my eyes fixed on the pond, and tried to think but it was too painful. 'It must be this way,' I told myself. My heart would not believe it. But I could not be with Philip without going behind the backs of the people who loved me. That, of course, was impossible.

When I returned to the house, I found that Mrs Swan and Mary were home.

'Adéla, you are looking tired,' Mrs Swan told me. 'We don't want you to fall sick as well. Why don't you take tomorrow off? That's your gardening day, isn't it?'

'I haven't gardened for a while,' I said, feeling self-conscious that everyone seemed to know how I spent my Wednesdays. 'I have been too worried about Klára.'

'She's so much better now, and Mary and I can watch her tomorrow. You can come on Thursday with Esther. It won't help Klára if you become ill too.'

I was grateful for Mrs Swan's kindness. The truth was, I was exhausted and I needed time alone.

'Potter around the garden, relax,' Freddy told me, stooping to kiss my forehead before leaving for the office the following day. 'You've been under enormous strain.'

'I will,' I said, stretching up on my tiptoes to return his kiss.

It was Rex's day off and Regina had gone to the markets. I luxuriated in the peacefulness of the house over a cup of tea before changing into a skirt and cotton blouse. I wanted to plant the bulbs Mrs Swan had given me before they dried out and repot some cyclamens.

Rex kept my gardening tools in a shed behind the garage. My feet crunched on the gravel drive as I made my way towards it. The sun was behind a cloud but the day was mild and I was looking forward to spending a few hours amongst the trees and flowers. I was surprised to find that the door to the shed was open. I peered inside. The garden tools were on their nails and the pots were neatly stacked. I had hoped a possum had found its way in to make a nest on one of the shelves: I missed Angel and Cherub. But no such fortune.

Perhaps the wind last night blew the door open, I thought.

I went to the cupboard and took out a smock and searched around the shelf for my gardening gloves. I was surprised to find that they were tucked into each other in a ball, the way that Freddy liked his socks rolled. I never did that to my gloves. I always brushed them down after use and laid them out flat. I put the gloves in my pocket, picked up a trowel, hand-spade and bucket and headed for the beds at the end of the garden.

I set down my tools on the grass and played with the gloves in my pocket while I inspected the flowerbeds for weeds. The cold had kept most of them at bay but there were places where the grass was growing into the bed. I pulled the gloves out of my pocket and my fingers tingled. I had a sense that someone was watching me. I glanced around but there was no one there.

'Mother?' I said, for I smelled the distinct fragrance of lily of the valley and I knew there were none in the garden. The strangest sensation crept over me. It was one of enveloping peace and paralysing terror. But no sooner had the feeling come than it departed and I sensed that I was alone in the garden again.

A ghost had stood by me, of that I was certain. I was usually able to see them, but the sensation I had experienced left no doubt in my mind that I had been given a warning. I thought of Klára and wondered if something was wrong. I looked at the gloves in my hand. There was a lump in one of them, about the size of a walnut. I stared at it and was sure that it moved. Had a mouse gotten into my gloves?

I began to untuck them but my spine tingled and I threw them on the ground. I picked up my trowel and spade and prised them apart. At first nothing happened and the lump in the gloves remained where it was. I was about to pick them up again when two black legs emerged. A pair of fangs followed then more legs and I found myself looking at a large black spider. I was not an arachnophobe — I admired the webs the golden orb weavers made in the garden and the stripes of the St Andrew's Cross spiders that hung in the lilly-pillies; I did not even mind the hairy huntsman spider that ran across the garage doors whenever I opened them. But I knew about this spider. Rex had warned me. 'The funnel-web is the deadliest spider in the world, Mrs Rockcliffe,' he had said. 'One bite and you'll be gone in a few hours.' The paper had reported a woman dying of a funnel-web bite last summer. It had crawled into her washing basket.

I barely felt my legs as I stepped back from the flowerbed then turned and ran to the house.

'But, darling, we've seen those spiders here before. The north shore is their habitat,' said Freddy that evening, passing me a glass of brandy. 'It's all very nice to have a garden with native birds and animals but the spiders think they're welcome too.'

'You don't understand,' I said. 'It was tucked into my glove. And the door to the shed had been left open.'

402 • BELINDA ALEXANDRA

'Maybe Regina used your gloves to cut some vegetables from the patch. Those spiders are known to climb into people's galoshes and shoes.'

'Then how did it get inside my gloves? They were balled up like a trap, and it must have been done recently otherwise the spider would have starved.'

Freddy sat down on the windowsill and folded his arms, thinking. 'I've heard that they do crawl around a lot, you know, when they're mating and after the rain.'

'That's in summer, Freddy. And it hasn't rained for weeks. Someone put it there.'

'Who in our house would put a deadly spider in your gloves? Adéla? Rex? Regina?'

Freddy held my gaze. A shadow passed over his face and he stood up and paced the floor before sitting down next to me and taking my hand.

'Your stepfather is in Austria. That's already been confirmed.'

'I know,' I said, a tremor in my voice. I was beginning to see how astray my imagination was leading me.

Freddy squeezed my fingers. 'Poor darling,' he said, kissing my hand. 'You're exhausted.'

At the end of May, Mrs Swan's mother, who lived in the southern highlands, suffered a turn. Mrs Swan and Mary planned to travel there to look after her and needed Robert to accompany them. With Klára so close to term, and with it still unconfirmed whether she had consumption or not, it was decided that she had best stay in Sydney. So it was with great reluctance that Robert left her to travel with his mother and sister.

'I'll call you every day,' he assured her. 'And I'll be back before the baby is born. Grandmother has these turns occasionally, but always pulls through. She's as strong as an ox.'

Klára had convinced herself that Miloš was in Europe, but I saw the apprehensive look in her eyes. 'We will never leave each other alone,' I promised her.

While the Swans were away, Klára stayed with me and Freddy. If there had not been a question mark over her health, then having my sister back with me would have been perfect. One morning, Freddy, Klára and I breakfasted together on the terrace before Freddy left for work.

'The garden is so lush now,' said Klára, admiring the camellias with their red flowers, the white-blossomed paperbarks and the blueberry ashes that had shot up in height in the last month. Lights had been installed around the garden and pond so that we could have parties in the summer.

My eye fell to a lilly-pilly that was dappled with new crimson leaves. I recognised it as one of Freddy's tortured topiaries; I'd had Rex plant it in the ground and it was growing into a handsome tree. It's been set free, I thought. I remembered what Robert had said about me and Freddy being good for each other, and I realised that Philip had set me free too.

'I'd better be going,' said Freddy, taking one last sip of tea and leaning across the table to kiss me. 'I have clients to visit this morning and then I'm going to drop by Tilly's Cinema to discuss another venture with your uncle.'

I wished Freddy well and turned back to my breakfast. A feeling I could not understand gripped me. I stood up and rushed out to the hall. He was gathering his coat and hat from Regina and he turned to me and smiled. 'What is it?'

I rushed forward and flung my arms around his neck. 'I forgot to return your kiss,' I told him, and pressed my lips to his.

* * *

That evening, before dinner, Klára played the piano in the drawing room. It was unusual for us to be in there; we usually spent our evenings in the sitting room. But she had an urge to play music and I was happy to indulge her.

'It is just as well I am so tall and have long arms,' she said, with a smile. 'Otherwise I would not be able to reach the keys.'

I remembered Ranjana's prediction that Klára was carrying twins. Despite her illness, Klára had put on weight. She was no longer lanky, she had a full chest and her face was round like a peach.

I heard the telephone ring. A few minutes later, Regina appeared to say that Freddy wished to speak with me. Our normally healthy maid looked peaked in the face.

'Adéla, is that you?' Freddy said when I picked up the receiver. He sounded flustered.

'What's wrong?' I asked.

'There's been a fire at the cinema. They've just managed to put the flames out now.'

'My God! Uncle Ota? Ranjana?'

'Nobody was hurt, but the projection room and our film supply is gone. The police are here. They want to make a report.'

'Do they think it was deliberate?'

'We don't know yet. Apparently there have been extortion attempts on cinemas lately. But I think it was an accident. It was only the projection room. If it was extortion surely the office would have been set alight as well.'

Freddy was right. It was not unusual for films to catch on fire. That was why Uncle Ota had installed safety equipment in the projection and storage rooms.

'Listen,' said Freddy, 'Ota, Ranjana and I are trying to sort out the mess and the police won't let us go until they've made their report. Esther is at Watsons Bay looking after Thomas. Are you and Klára all right there? I've called Robert. He's already on his way back to Sydney. He'll be there first thing in the morning.'

I looked into the drawing room. Klára was still sitting at the piano reading some music. 'Yes, we are fine.'

'Hopefully we can wrap all this up in a few hours,' said Freddy. 'But don't wait up for me.'

I rang off and went to find Regina. I told her Freddy would be delayed, so not to keep his dinner.

'Very good, madam,' she said in a hoarse voice.

'Are you unwell?' I asked her.

Regina looked embarrassed. 'I have stomach pains,' she said. 'A pedlar came to the door with cream buns this afternoon. I should not have purchased them. The cream must have turned sour.'

'Go to bed,' I told her. 'I can serve the dinner myself. Doctor Fitzgerald is coming tomorrow to visit my sister. I will ask him to examine you too.'

'Thank you very much, madam,' said Regina. 'Goodnight.'

I watched Regina walk up the stairs to her room. When I returned to the drawing room, I found Klára asleep on the sofa. I picked up a blanket and spread it over her. Klára's pregnancy had made her a heavy sleeper and I knew I had no hope of rousing her to send her to bed. I had not drawn the curtains yet and I stopped to admire the moonlight on the garden. The news of the fire had unsettled me, and I would not be able to sleep until Freddy came home. I selected a book from the library and settled next to Klára by the dying fire.

Just after eleven o'clock a breeze rose up and whistled around the walls and rattled the doors. I heard a bang upstairs that sounded as if it might be coming from Freddy's and my bedroom. I wondered if Regina had left a window open. I laid my book on the table. The house lights went out. It was not uncommon for us to lose power if there was a strong wind and the wires crossed each other. I would leave it to Rex to fix the problem when he arrived in the morning. I groped around for the oil lamp we kept on the bureau and found it. Then I felt along the mantelpiece for a match to light it.

Klára sighed and rolled over, tugging the blanket over her face. I shut the door behind me. She would have to stay there for the night. I did not want her stumbling about in the dark.

The lamp cast only a small circle of light but it was enough to find my way upstairs. I put my hand to the banister and listened for the banging window again, but heard nothing. Regina must have risen and closed it. I reached the landing, pushed open the door to our bedroom and lifted the lamp towards the window. It was shut, with the latch fastened, but the script notes I had left on the side table were scattered about the floor.

I held the lamp higher and gasped. The drawers to my dressing table had been upturned and the contents strewn about the room. A sickening feeling clenched my stomach. A fire? A thief? All in one night?

I rushed into the hallway. Regina's room was on the same level as our bedrooms but further along. I decided to fetch her, then wake Klára, put them both in the car and drive to Esther's house. If the window was locked, the thief may still be somewhere in the house. I crept in the direction of Regina's room. Suddenly the door to Klára's room flew open and a figure stepped out. In the lamplight I saw that the intruder was holding the gold and diamond chain Robert had given Klára as a wedding present. He turned in my direction.

'Take whatever you want,' I told him. 'Take it all. I won't stop you. I won't look at your face. Just take it all and go!'

The intruder hesitated a moment and then his laugh shattered the silence of the house. I knew that laugh. I lifted the lamp higher and my blood chilled when I saw this figure's pale hair and skin. I was looking at a ghost.

'Just like you to think that I want your cheap jewels,' Miloš sneered.

I staggered backwards, my heart thumping in my chest. I stared at my stepfather, not able to believe my eyes.

'Regina!' I called, my voice weak. 'Regina! Lock your door and call the police!'

Miloš laughed again. 'I don't think your Spanish maid will be waking up tonight,' he said.

The lamp wobbled in my hand and I almost dropped it. Miloš stepped forward, yanked it from me and placed it on the hall table. I caught sight of the knife in his hand. The truth dawned on me. He intended to kill us and make it look like a robbery.

He grabbed my wrist and twisted it so painfully that I dropped to my knees. I caught a glimpse of his face. The thin-fleshed forehead was the same but his eyes had a strange glint to them. He did not look like the cool, calculating man I had known in Prague. My mind raced to make sense of the situation. How could Miloš be here when Doctor Holub had assured us that he was in Austria?

'Where is your sister?' he asked, pressing the knife against my back.

I was determined not to look in the direction of the drawing room. I struggled against Miloš's grip and he slapped me in the face. The sting awoke me to my senses. Miloš had not found Klára so far and Freddy would be home soon. If Miloš had looked through the drawing room window any time in the last few hours, he would have assumed only I was sitting there. He could kill me right now, but waste another hour searching for Klára. Our house was large and had twelve bedrooms altogether. Time was what Miloš did not have and what I needed to gain. My stepfather was physically stronger than me but I had not forgotten his weakness: his incessant need to boast.

'They will know it is you,' I baited him. 'The person who has the most to gain is always the first one suspected.'

'Oh?' replied Miloš. 'In a city where extortion, kidnapping, robbery and the murder of rich wives is rife? Besides, everyone thinks I am in Austria.'

'Klára saw you at her concert.'

Miloš laughed. 'And you proved her mistaken.'

A chill passed over me. Miloš must have been eavesdropping on our family to know that. I remembered the spider. Had he been in the house before?

He dragged me to the staircase. I was sure he was going to throw me down the stairs, but his desire to show off got the better of him.

'What fools you people are,' he said. 'I learned the trick from you. Weren't you supposed to be in America? My wife has a cousin who owes us a favour. He travelled to Vienna with her and is posing as me. Who in Austria would be any wiser? When I am finished here, we will simply move back to Prague. After all, by that time we will have a house waiting for us there and money will no longer be a problem. Now, where is your sister?'

I shivered. This was not the remote man I had known, conniving to get what he wanted. He was taking pleasure in what he was doing. My terror gave way to a sense of sadness. It is over, I thought. Klára and I are going to die here. The child she cradled in her belly would never see the light. I remembered my sudden urge to kiss Freddy that morning. I must have known I was bidding him farewell.

And then my grief gave way to anger. I would not let Miloš harm my sister.

With the sense of surrealness I had felt when I kicked the man with the broken glass to save Uncle Ota, I jerked my elbow back into Miloš's ribs. He let go of me and fell back. From the 'crack' of air he spat out, I realised I had winded him. I raced down the stairs with one thought in my mind: I had to get Miloš to chase me. I had to get him away from Klára.

I reached the bottom of the staircase and turned in the direction of the kitchen. I heard Miloš's footsteps in pursuit. I opened the door to the sitting room, which was empty and dark, and screamed out: 'Klára! Come with me!' I ran into the kitchen, slammed the door behind me and locked it. My shaking hands struggled with the catch of the door to the garden. I heard Miloš coming down the hall. I turned the catch and rushed out into the darkness just as I heard him hurl himself against the kitchen door. It was not a sturdy lock and I knew he would soon be through and after me. I launched myself at the camellias, making as much noise as I could. Branches scratched at my face, 'Klára, quick, this way!' I shouted.

'You won't get far!' I heard Miloš say. 'You stupid bitches!'

I dropped to my stomach and hid behind a rock near the pond. My plan had worked: Miloš thought Klára was with me. Through the blades of the reeds, I saw him standing on the kitchen step and holding up the lamp. There was a dark streak down the side of his face: blood. He must have knocked his head when he fell backwards. Klára would wake up with the commotion. I had to keep him pursuing me. I picked up a stone and threw it as hard as

I could in the opposite direction. It thudded against the fence. Miloš turned towards the sound and I realised that he could not see anything beyond his lantern.

I am safe, I thought. For the moment.

Then, like a flash of lightning, the garden lights came on. So the wires had not crossed at all; Miloš had tampered with the fuse box. I pressed myself low into the ground. Freddy, come home, I prayed, knowing that under the lights my hiding place would soon be discovered.

I lifted my eyes to see where Miloš was now. A blow crashed down on the back of my head. I lay dazed in the mud for a few seconds, then touched my head and felt a warm, sticky trickle. Blood. From the corner of my eye, I saw Miloš's leg near my face. He grabbed my hair and pulled my head up, but at the same time dropped the knife. It fell into the pond with a splash. As he reached for it I bit his arm as hard as I could. He hit me across my face again, then grabbed me by the shoulders.

'It will give me more pleasure to kill you with my bare hands,' he said coldly. 'Out of the three of you, you were always the one I hated most.'

He was so calm. It was more terrifying than if he had raved at me like a lunatic. Yet surely he had lost his mind? Greed had driven him mad. I opened my mouth to scream but produced only a gasp. Miloš gripped my head and pushed my face into the water. I tried not to inhale, but could not stop myself. I swallowed mouthfuls of mud. I reached behind my head and struggled with his hands, taking in more water in doing so. Something was pressing down on my back. His knee?

I am going to die, I thought. How will I ever tell Freddy now how much I love him?'

Stabbing pains jabbed my lungs and there was a rushing sound in my ears. My hands lost their strength and everything began to turn black. Then, suddenly, whatever it was on my back lightened. My head rose to the surface. I pushed myself out of the pond, coughing up water so violently that the back of my throat felt raw. My hair was strung over my face like seaweed and my eyes itched from the mud. There was a dark shape moving in front of me. I heard male voices, shouting. I wiped my face with my wet blouse and saw that the dark shape was Freddy. He was beating Miloš back with a shovel. Klára was there too. I remembered the knife, and searched for it in the water, but could not find it.

Freddy pushed Miloš backwards. He fell into a flowerbed, crushing some daisies. Freddy rushed towards him with the shovel. I saw something glint in the light and my breath caught in my throat when I realised what it was.

'Freddy!' I screamed.

Freddy's eyes fell to the knife just as Miloš drove it into his chest. I screamed again at the top of my voice. I found my legs and sprang up, lunging towards Freddy. He fell on his back. The knife had been thrust so deeply into him that I could only see the handle amongst the blood oozing around the wound.

I dropped to my knees beside him and threw my arms around his neck. 'I love you! Don't leave me!'

I heard a sound and looked up. Miloš was staggering towards us. There was a thud. His head split open, straight down the middle, like an overripe plum. He collapsed and I saw Klára standing behind him with a block of wood in her hands. With her white dress and round stomach, tears streaming down her cheeks, she looked like a Greek goddess. My heavily pregnant sister had killed the beast.

The light in Freddy's eyes was fading. 'Adéla,' he said, and I felt all the love he had for me in the way he said my name.

'Don't go, please,' I wept.

Freddy tried to lift himself onto his elbows, but gasped. He collapsed back into my arms and listed to one side as if he had fallen into a deep sleep. But I knew he was gone.

The wind died down and the garden fell silent. There was not a splash in the pond or the click of a beetle to be heard. It was as if the whole of nature was standing still, out of respect.

TWENTY-THREE

I was too numb to remember much of Freddy's funeral. I recall only snippets of things: Klára reading Psalm 23; Thomas reciting a poem. The coffin was decorated in wildflowers from our garden and Giallo clawed down Hugh's sleeve to nibble at the grevilleas on the wreath. Freddy would have laughed at the bird's irreverence on such a solemn occasion.

When they lowered Freddy's coffin into the ground, I understood that the life I had shared with the man I had known and loved had ended forever.

Philip was amongst the mourners, but I barely saw him through the blur of my tears. I had been foolish to pine after another man when the love of my life had been right there by my side. But I had realised it too late.

After the wake, I rested on my bed, and reached across the space where Freddy used to lie. I wondered if the sense I had of him still being there was what Hugh had felt after the amputation. Since his death, I had often dreamed of Freddy. We would be having breakfast on the terrace, or driving to a restaurant, and I would be happy in his presence. Then I would wake up and remember the terrible night that had brought our happiness to an end.

'You must come and live with us,' Klára said to me. 'I cannot bear to think of you alone in that house.'

I could not bear it either. I agreed to move in with the Swans, not because I wanted to but because I was lost for alternatives. Whenever my family tried to comfort me, I shied away. 'Please' and 'Thank you' were all I could stand to exchange with other human beings. I was lonely in a way I had never been lonely before. Klára and I had faced Mother's death and our exile together. Our family had tackled Thomas's illness as a united force. But this ... this dark hole of grief for Freddy ... I had to face it alone.

Klára's twins were born on 1 July. Robert and I both wept when Doctor Fitzgerald pronounced them healthy. After what had occurred in the past month, as well as Klára's illness, we had been worried. Even more astounding was Klára's rapid recovery from her confinement.

'I have two babies and Adéla to take care of now,' she told the Swans. 'I am not lying about like some invalid.'

'Pregnancy can be taxing on the body,' Doctor Fitzgerald explained to us, puzzled himself at Klára's vitality. 'But sometimes it does strengthen the lungs. Perhaps that's what has happened here. I no longer see symptoms of consumption.'

Regina, who had recovered well from the sedative Miloš had put in the cream buns but not quite as well from the shock of waking to learn of Freddy's death, was appointed nursemaid. She spoke to the twins in Spanish, much to Mrs Swan's horror and Klára and Robert's delight.

Despite my grief, I was struck by the beauty of the two girls lying in their cradle side by side.

'We are going to call them Marta and Emilie,' Klára told me.

Klára did not know the full story of our mother and her sister and I wondered if I should tell her before she made any announcements. But I decided against it. Marta and Emilie were in heaven together now. Why shouldn't those babies carry their names? It was a chance to make things new.

While some things were resolved, others were not. Miloš was buried in a pauper's grave. Doctor Holub wrote to us that paní Beňová plunged into a life of poverty and ill repute after learning of Miloš's death. Doctor Holub took it upon himself to visit Doctor Hoffmann and accuse him of his crime but found the doctor a broken man. His son and wife were killed in a train accident several years before. 'Revenge is for God,' my Father always said. Perhaps he had been right.

Klára and I had lived in fear of Miloš so long that it was difficult to adjust to the idea that he could no longer harm us. But we could not be free of him entirely; he had taken precious Freddy with him.

Four months after Freddy's death, Philip came to see me. Thomas had visited that afternoon and we had sailed the sloop on the Swans' pond.

'When I sail this boat, I feel that Freddy is with me,' Thomas said.

I stared at him in wonder, then kissed the top of his head. My heart was too full to speak.

After Uncle Ota had taken Thomas home, I retired to my room to begin a task I had been dreading: unpacking the box of photographs I had brought from Cremorne. I picked up the wedding photograph of everyone standing outside the church and I ran my fingertip over Freddy's beaming smile.

'Did I make you happy?' I asked him.

A maid knocked on the door and told me that I had a visitor. My heart did not flutter when I saw Philip in the drawing room. It merely ached.

Neither of us could bring ourselves to speak at first.

'I didn't come sooner because ...' he began, but could not finish. He looked at me with his blue eyes. 'If there is anything I can do to help you, Adéla, please tell me. I can't stand the thought of you suffering.'

The maid walked in with tea, although I had not asked for it. She must have assumed Philip had come to see me about Klára. When she had finished laying out the cups and teapot and left with the tray, I turned to Philip. He was looking towards the window as if something fascinating was happening outside. But the view only revealed that the sky was darkening to a sapphire blue.

'Your happiness is everything to me,' he said. 'Even when you found it with another man.'

'There is no happiness now,' I told him.

'No.'

We fell silent again, not looking at each other. Something lingered in the air between us. I knew what it was: a question.

'You were right to walk away,' I said, my heart beating painfully in my chest. 'It would have been unthinkable to have hurt Freddy.'

I choked back a sob and sank into a chair. Speaking of Freddy in the past tense was agony. It reminded me that I would never be able to touch him again or hear his laugh. There had been many times in the past when I had imagined myself in Philip's arms, comforted by the strength of them and the feel of my cheek resting against his firm chest. But now that Freddy was gone, I saw those feelings had been only illusions.

'It is too late for us now,' I whispered.

'No!' Philip said. He paced the floor. 'I didn't come for that. You must grieve and I am still married. But who can say what will happen in the future, Adéla ... maybe things will be different for us then.'

For a moment a flicker of feeling lit the numbness. I found myself pitying Philip, but pity was not what he wanted. All tenderness, all thoughts of laughter and happiness, had drained from me. The world had disintegrated and it could never be put right. How could it while I had loved Philip when I should have been loving Freddy?

Philip's eyes were intent on me and I saw the hurt and fear in them.

'Can you see nothing in the future for us?' he asked.

The daylight in the room faded and Philip switched on a lamp. There were no words I could use to explain how my love for him had died. We'd had a chance, long ago, and we had lost it. All that had remained was the dream and now that was gone too. I imagined Emilie cutting off her fingers. Her action no longer seemed insane. Perhaps if I could cut out my heart, I could go on living.

Philip covered his face with his hands. 'Don't let him win, Adéla. Your stepfather might be dead but he is still hurting you.'

'I am sorry,' I said. 'It is not your fault. Nobody can help me.'

Philip moved towards me, touched my shoulder then walked to the door. 'I'm the one who is sorry,' he said. 'You and Freddy were happy together.'

I realised then that he had understood.

I accompanied Philip to the front door and watched him walk down the steps to his car. He paused for a moment to look about him. The night sounds of the garden — crickets, frogs, beetles — had come to life in a chorus. He put his hand to the driver's door then turned back to me.

'I'm going to help develop an aerial medical service in the Outback,' he said. 'I'm giving up my practice here in Sydney for a while. My father will watch over it for me.'

So Philip and his father had reconciled? At least there was some light for one of us.

Philip started the car engine and disappeared down the drive and through the gates. The last of my hopes went with him.

One day, Hugh asked me to meet him at the Vegetarian Café. The place belonged to a time in my life when I was wide-eyed and innocent. I was not that way any more.

On my way up George Street, I saw a gentleman walking towards me. He lifted his hat and I recognised Alfred Steel, Klára's former teacher at the Conservatorium High School.

'I was sorry to hear about your husband,' Mr Steel told me.

I thanked him for his sympathy and quickly changed the subject to Klára. 'She told me she has been offered a teaching post with the school.'

I saw that Mr Steel was looking at me with a questioning smile. He seemed to be deliberating whether he should ask me something or not. Some people had a grotesque curiosity about Freddy's death, which was the reason why I had stopped attending social occasions outside of my family. I was about to excuse myself in order to avoid another painful inquisition when he suddenly said to me, 'Klára's not really a teacher. She's a performer, wouldn't you say? Performing is in her blood.'

Mr Steel's statement was so different from what I had been thinking that it startled me. I looked at him, not comprehending his meaning.

He gave a short cough into his fist. 'She'll never fulfil that dream *here*. There are few avenues for performers beyond afternoon teas and weddings.'

The penny dropped. 'You mean, Mr Steel, that if she wants seriously to perform, she must return to Europe?'

He answered my question with a shy laugh. 'Of course, she would scold me if she knew I was telling you this ...'

'I am not going back to Europe,' said Klára, placing Emilie on my lap. 'I will be happy being a teacher.'

'And watch lesser performers go in your place?' I asked.

Klára pursed her lips and set about changing Marta's nappy. Emilie gurgled and grinned at me. The girls were identical in appearance but not in personality. Marta was a model baby who slept when she was supposed to sleep and ate everything she was offered. Not Emilie. Emilie wanted to see as much of the world in a day as she could, and fought against sleep or anything else that interrupted her view of life. Emilie and I had an affinity. When she cried in the night and would not settle, Klára brought her to me. As soon as I held her, Emilie's bunched-up face transformed into a smile.

'Why didn't you say something to me before?' I asked. 'I feel so selfish. Have you always wanted to return to Prague?'

Klára fastened Marta's nappy and glanced at me.

'I see,' I said, touching Emilie's tufts of hair. 'We did intend to return when we left, didn't we?'

I stood up and walked to the window. Emilie wrapped my finger in her palm. I looked out at the garden and the bushland beyond. When Klára and I had fled Prague, it had been with the idea of returning once Klára was twenty-one. I turned and stared at my sister's heart-shaped face and high cheekbones. She was still every inch a Czech. But I was not. I had become something else. When I thought of Prague, I felt only pain and sadness. Mother was not there and neither was Aunt Josephine. The fifth continent, with its strange trees and animals and siren-like birdsongs, was my home now. I could never imagine leaving the place where Freddy was buried. Suddenly, I understood why Klára was reluctant to go back to Europe now it was safe for her to do so. She knew that I could not go with her and she was afraid to leave me on my own.

'It would not be forever,' I said. 'Both you and Robert have your families here. You would return one day. And I would be waiting for you.'

Klára shrugged. 'Things might improve here,' she said. 'It is still a new country. There are new avenues for performance being developed all the time.'

I sat down next to her and perched Emilie on my knee. 'But not before you are past your prime years,' I said. 'Your time is now.'

I remembered the performances I had seen Klára play: the Grieg, Tchaikovsky and Beethoven concertos. My magnificent sister. I thought about Philip saying that he could not love me unless he gave me up. I did not want to be separated from Klára, my brother-in-law and my nieces, but I knew I could never be at peace with myself if I let Klára sacrifice herself because of me. If I was going to convince her to follow her dream, I would have to prove that I was strong enough to live without her — for a while at least.

*　　*　　*

A few days later, I was eating breakfast on the veranda when the maid brought me the newspaper. I could not bring myself to read the news any more, knowing that a few months ago the headlines had shouted the story of the film executive who had heroically lost his life defending his wife against an attacker. I reached to push the newspaper aside and as I did my eye fell to an advertisement on the back page:

> *Cottage for Sale*
> *Katoomba*
> *Views of the Blue Mountains*

There was a drawing of a house with gables and an L-shaped veranda. The Blue Mountains. I closed my eyes and remembered looking out to the Jamieson Valley from the bridal suite of the Hydro Majestic Hotel. For a moment, it felt as if Freddy was still with me, breakfasting beside me. Instead of the pain such memories usually caused, my fingers and toes tingled. I opened my eyes and tore out the advertisement. I hoped it was still for sale.

My father was fond of the saying 'He who is hopeless is capable of anything.' I bought the cottage without inspecting it, simply because my heart told me to do so.

'You're buying a house that you've never seen in a town that you've never visited?' Robert asked, astonished. 'Why?'

'I don't know,' I told him. 'I only know that I must go.'

My family and the Swans were in turmoil because of my decision but Klára understood.

'I don't want you to be away from me,' she told me one day when we were pushing the twins' pram around the garden, 'but I understand why you need to go. You are not running away. You are leaving to find something. To discover what your next step in life has to be.'

No one would ever understand me better than Klára.

'You'll telephone every week and write every day, won't you?' Uncle Ota made me promise, once he and Rajana had resigned themselves to the fact that all arguments about why I should not live alone in the mountains had been exhausted and that my mind was made up.

The cottage did not have a telephone and I did not intend to install one, but the township and the post office were only half an hour away on foot or a few minutes by car.

I arrived in the mountains in late February. My trip took longer than usual because of the bushfires. Springwood was gritty with smoke and the vegetation at the sides of the road looked dry and brittle from the rainless summer.

'If the wind changes direction the fires could sweep over Katoomba in a matter of hours,' the policeman at Springwood warned me when I asked for directions. But I was not afraid. I was not afraid of anything any more. The days since Freddy's death had dragged on, slow, tedious. Perhaps a bushfire would stir me into motion again.

A while later, as the sun was softening, I pulled the car up outside the cottage. The exterior of the house was much like the drawing I had seen in the newspaper and, although due for some fresh paint, it was in good repair. The garden needed tending because the flowers in the beds had shrivelled in the heat and no longer resembled anything but dried sticks. I had no idea what the interior of the house would be like except that it had three bedrooms, a small attic and a single-storey kitchen out the back.

It was with some curiosity and a lot of trepidation that I ventured down the path to the front door. There was a brass plate with the cottage's name engraved on it: *Silver Wattle*. A tingle ran down my spine when I read it. It was strange that neither the advertisement nor the real estate agent had mentioned the cottage had a name. It was the flower Uncle Ota and Ranjana had sent us to put on Mother's grave. But the cottage's name did not make me sad. It made me feel that Mother was with me.

I took out my key and opened the door. Like most cottages of its style, the front door opened straight into the sitting room where the first things that caught my eye were the brick fireplace and the built-in bookshelves. The polished jarrah floors and the cream wallpaper with a green vine motif gave the room a serene feeling, which complemented the view of the valley.

I inspected the rest of the cottage. It was compact with no more space than I needed: a small kitchen with an enamel stove and shining white sink; an icebox in the hall; a narrow dining room that could take five people at most. Aunt Josephine, who hated waste but loved simple elegance, would have adored it. It was not furnished, but the previous owner had left behind an armoire in the main bedroom that must have been too heavy to move. I ran my fingers over the carved roses then turned to inspect the room's wainscoting. I was lucky the house was as charming as the advertisement described because I could have easily been cheated.

I was suddenly tired. I had brought with me only the necessities and would have to buy a bed and a table and chairs. But that could wait. I spread the travelling blanket from the car on the floor and lay down on it with my purse as my pillow. The setting sun sent fiery pink beams of light about the room. The house was quiet except for a faint rustling in the ceiling. Despite my spartan bed, I closed my eyes and slept better than I had in months.

* * *

'You're not afraid here on your own?' the grocer asked when he made his delivery a few days later. 'You're the last house in the street and the one furthest from the other neighbours. I know Mrs Tupper at number six. I could ask her to look in on you.'

'Thank you,' I told him. 'But I am all right.'

I liked my neighbours and the people in the town. They were curious about me but did not intrude. When they saw Silver Wattle Cottage was occupied they brought me cakes and biscuits but did not ask me any questions.

I wrote away for catalogues to view furniture and unpacked the few books I had brought with me to put on the shelves. My hand fell on the script for *The Emerald Valley*. Why had I kept it, I wondered. That film would never be made now that Freddy was gone.

At night, I would close my eyes and listen to the wind in the trees. Every so often I heard the rustling in the ceiling that I had noticed during my first night in the house. I wondered if I had rats under the roof but the bags of flour and sugar in the kitchen cupboard were not raided.

When the weather turned cooler, I walked every day, beginning with short strolls along the cliffs or on the outskirts of the town to admire the gardens. Then I began to take the established tracks into the valleys. The fresh air and the massive tree ferns, cascading waterfalls, rippling creeks and the towering turpentines with their gnarled roots reawakened my love of nature. I took my father's camera out of its box and began photographing everything: the trees, the shrubs, the ferns, grasses, tiny mosses and fungi. I used my father's camera rather than my own because it made me feel that I was showing him the

Australian bush the same way he had taken me exploring in the forests around Doksy. Although I was aware I was breaking the rules of walking in groups of three and telling someone where I was going, my fascination with the landscape and the bellbirds and robins I found along my way lured me further off the tracks. My walks and photography comforted me.

But one day, after I had spent an hour photographing a lyrebird near a cascade, I turned and saw a solitary rock jutting out in front of me. The shape of it reminded me of the way Miloš had stuck out his chin when he tried to kill me. My heart beat faster and I was overcome by anger. I walked furiously along a creek for an hour. By the time my adrenaline was spent, the sun had faded and I just made it back to Katoomba before darkness fell. My walks with Klára in the bush near Thirroul had given me some skill in reading landforms but I was aware that the Blue Mountains had ensnared more than one dreamy walker. I considered finding a walking companion, perhaps a woman from the town, but dreaded the thought of another human intruding on the soothing sounds of water and birdsong. Instead I bought a compass and marked my trail with a pile of rocks at significant trees.

I set up a darkroom in the laundry shed and sent the pictures of my journeys to Uncle Ota.

'Your landscapes are stunning,' he wrote back. 'Your work has grown in depth. I can't believe you aren't using your professional camera.'

Klára updated me on the twins and family life in her letters. 'Uncle Ota showed me the beautiful photographs you took,' she said. 'But remember, the rock formations you so lovingly capture cannot replace intimacy with human beings.'

As I became more adventurous in my walks it was apparent that a dress was not the most suitable attire for scrambling through scrub and over slippery rocks. I approached the local dressmaker to sew me some pairs of loose trousers. Women had been wearing trousers to play sports for some years but they were still frowned upon socially. Coco Chanel had tried to make them acceptable for day and evening wear with little success.

'I suppose you are enamoured of all those Hollywood film stars too,' said the dressmaker, looking over her pince-nez. 'Everyone wants to be a "modern gal" these days. You are the fourth young lady this week who has asked me to make trousers for her.'

We both looked out the shop window in the direction of the King's Cinema. I had not seen a picture since Freddy's death. I could not bear the thought of sitting in the dark by myself.

Once my trousers were ready I set out early one morning for a walk. The valley was alive with flowers — boronias, drumsticks, waratahs, wattles and eucalypt blossoms. I wanted to photograph them. I had been walking for about an hour when I heard voices up ahead and came across three women sitting on a rock.

'Goodness gracious, are you lost too?' the eldest of them asked me. She was a plump woman of medium height with straight brown hair tucked into a bun at the nape of her neck. A drop of sweat trickled down her cheek and she took a lace handkerchief from her pocket to dab at it. The other two women were younger and slimmer, but their straight brown hair and button noses told me they were related.

'Where are you trying to get to?' I asked them.

'We want to walk the Federal Pass,' the first woman said. She took out her map and showed it to me. The Federal Pass was a well-known track that wound along the foot of the cliffs. I had walked it many times to photograph the rainforest. The women were only slightly off course but they had panicked and become disoriented. I glanced at their equipment. Each had a light rucksack, a water canister and sturdy shoes. They were not complete novices.

'You are not so far from the track,' I said. 'I can walk with you, if you don't mind me stopping to take photographs.'

The women rallied. 'Not at all,' they said. The first woman, who introduced herself as Grace Milson and her daughters as Heather Cotswold and Sophie Milson, told me that the Sydney Bushwalkers Club was not running anything that week in the mountains and the other clubs the women had approached did not accept female members. 'We only have a week in the mountains and we wanted to walk. It's so beautiful.'

We headed off in the direction of the track. I was surprised at myself for offering to guide them rather than just showing them how to correct their course. I thought I had grown wearisome of human company. Yet something about the women was refreshingly frank.

We came to an upward turn in the path where there was a ten-foot-high waratah standing up like a red-crowned queen amongst the green foliage. Her blood-red colour would be lost in the photograph but not her majesty. Drained of colour she would appear more mysterious.

'It's glorious,' said Sophie.

'Waratah is an Aboriginal word for "red-flowering tree",' I told the women. 'The botanical name, *Telopea*, means "seen from afar" and *speciosissima* means "most showy".' I was surprised at how much I had picked up from Ranjana's interest in botany and was flattered to see that the women were impressed.

They sat on a rock while I set up my shots. I was struck by their self-control. I had been concerned that they would chatter while I was concentrating and start asking me questions about whether I had lived in the mountains all my life or if I was married. It was a relief to find that once we were back on the trail none of them asked me anything personal, although they were fascinated by my photography.

'Do you pick your subjects instinctively or is there a lot of deliberation?' Heather asked me.

Although I gave them little information about myself, the women were open about their own lives. Before we had walked another half hour I had learned that Grace's husband was an orchard farmer in Dural and that she had lost two sons in the war and Heather had lost her husband. Sophie was not married and worked as a teacher.

Despite several photograph stops, we made good time on the track and stopped by a rock shelter to rest. Quite often on my walks I would come across a cave or an overhang decorated with the faded stencils of Aboriginal art. Since the white settlers had crossed the mountains the Aboriginal population had declined and there were only a few tribes left. Yet when I photographed the plant or animal life near a waterhole my skin often tingled and I sensed that ancient ghosts were watching me.

'I've always liked artists,' Grace said to me while Heather sketched the ferns into a notebook and Sophie gazed out at the view. 'They make us stop and think. You know, when we passed those wombat burrows, you spoke with such interest about those creatures and their habits that I felt swept up by your passion. My brother has a farm and shoots them. He says the cattle break their legs in their burrows, but you pointed out that wombats eat the grass the cattle don't and so stop those grasses taking over paddocks. Surely there must be a way to live in better harmony with our land and native animals?'

On the way back I mulled over Grace's words. It was unusual to hear a farmer's wife speak as she did. Since arriving in Australia I had been struck by the aggression with which people attacked the land and chopped down trees. Re-establishing harmony with nature had been my message in *In the Dark*, but I had no idea if my film had changed anyone's outlook. Was it possible a simple walk with someone could do more than a picture ever could?

When we arrived at Echo Point I asked Grace if she would like me to take a photograph of her and her daughters as a memento. She accepted my offer gratefully.

'Where are you staying?' I asked her. 'I can bring the photograph there in a couple of days.'

'We are at the Carrington,' she said. 'Please do come on Friday at three o'clock. We would very much like to have you as our guest for afternoon tea.'

The following Friday, at the agreed time, I climbed the stairs of the Carrington Hotel with my photograph satchel under my arm. The entrance of the hotel was a tiled piazza surrounded by Doric columns and topped with an Italianate balcony. There were two men sitting in wicker chairs and reading newspapers near the entrance. 'It's too shocking to believe,' one of them said. 'I would have thought with his connections he would have been untouchable.'

I had continued to make a deliberate effort to avoid reading or hearing about the news since coming to the mountains. I gave generously to charities to help the unemployed, but the stories of shanty towns springing up around Sydney and the evictions of people from their homes were too depressing to do any good to my already troubled mind. I understood that the two men were talking about another politician being toppled for failing to fix our struggling economy.

High tea was being served that day in the dining room. When the maitre d' led me past paintings and chandeliers to a long table at the end of the room, I was surprised to see not only Grace and her daughters waiting for me but several other ladies as well.

One of them, in a navy blue suit and matching hat, grabbed my arm before I had a chance to sit down. 'Mrs Milson told me all about your wonderful walk,' she said. 'I'm wondering if you could take my sister and me to Wentworth Falls next week? We went for a hike with my husband and brother-in-law when they were here on the weekend and it was more like a sports marathon. We didn't stop to admire anything.'

'I'd like to try camping out there in the bush,' said one young woman, with sunken eyes and skin as white as marble. The other women pressed similar requests upon me until Grace called them to order and reminded them that we had not even gotten around to introductions. I was unnerved. I had come to the mountains to be alone, not to become some sort of unofficial bushwalking guide for ladies.

The waiters brought us pots of tea, sandwiches, scones and cakes cut into bite-sized squares. It was only at that point that the gathering calmed down enough for me to notice the woman sitting at the opposite end of the table and smiling at me. She needed no introduction. I recognised her from her reddish-brown hair and the Scotch terrier who sat on her lap and the other one who lay by her feet on the floor.

'You and I are kindred spirits, Mrs Rockcliffe,' she said. 'I greatly admired your film *In the Dark*. Your picture and my paintings show people that what is achingly beautiful is also fragile. Perhaps in this way we might encourage our fellow citizens to preserve our native animals and bush. I have been waiting with anticipation for you to make another film. Now, when do you intend to do it?'

May Gibbs was the author of *Tales of Snugglepot and Cuddlepie*, Thomas's favourite book. He and I had pored over her books together, lost in the frolics of the Gumnut babies and Little Ragged Blossom. My eyes filled with tears, not only because her call to save something precious to Australia moved me but also because I realised how much I missed my family.

A week later, I was surprised to find a letter from Hugh waiting at the post office for me. Hugh had not written to me the whole time I had lived in the mountains. When I had told him about the cottage, he had said I was running away and that he was disappointed in me. I was anticipating another reprimand and was not let down.

> *You are the only one who thinks you are to*
> *blame for Freddy's death. The punishment is*
> *not worth the crime, if any 'crime' was committed.*
> *I hope being away for this long means you are*
> *getting better and are not going to torture*
> *yourself any more.*
>
> *Freddy was proud of you. Fiercely proud of you.*
> *You made him a happy man, although no amount of*
> *persuasion seems to make you able to see that.*
>
> *Now that he needs you, what have you done? You*
> *have run away to the mountains like a scared cat. It is*
> *now that you have deserted him and reneged on your*
> *wifely duties.*

I flinched. What did Hugh mean? How had I deserted Freddy?

> *As I am sure you are aware, the Royal Commission*
> *into the Australian picture industry is under way.*
> *Your uncle has been called as a witness, but not until*
> *next year, and no doubt you and I will be summoned*
> *some time in the future too. But it will be too late*
> *then. Freddy has been slandered by Australian*
> *producers and his reputation dragged through the*
> *press. He has been described as one of 'those cunning*
> *Yankees sent here to destroy the local industry'.*
> *Where were you to defend him? Where were you to*
> *say that your husband risked his career to set yours*
> *in motion?*

I gasped. Freddy? Dragged through the press? I shut my eyes as I relived Miloš thrusting the knife into Freddy's chest. I had been helpless to save him. Now the Royal Commission was killing him again.

'No!' I cried. 'Freddy did so much for this country!'

I turned to the next page, wondering if there could be any more terrible news. I had not read the paper in months and perhaps my family had been shielding me.

> *Do the right thing by Freddy, Adéla. Do what would*
> *have made him most proud. Make* The Emerald
> Valley. *You have everything ready that you need.*
> *Robert will act as producer and we will dedicate the*
> *film to Freddy. The opening credit will be 'To*
> *Frederick Rockcliffe, a great pioneer for the Australian*
> *film industry'.*

I remembered May Gibbs looking at me down the table at the Carrington. 'Your picture and my paintings show people that what is achingly beautiful is also fragile ... I have been waiting with anticipation for you to make another film. Now, when do you intend to do it?'

I returned to the cottage. I would do anything for Freddy. But did I have the strength to make *The Emerald Valley* without him?

It was dusk and I sat down at the dining table and watched the sun set over the valley. I remained in the stillness for an hour before I heard rustling in the ceiling above me. I looked up to see the light fitting tremble. Then, suddenly, the ceiling vent flew open and a dark brown mass tumbled onto the table, knocking over my saucer and cup. The mass formed into a creature with broad paws. It wriggled itself onto its legs and stared at me with bright eyes. The animal resembled Angel, only its ears were smaller and rounder and it had no facial markings. Its coat was a glossy dark brown and the scent it gave off was like a mix of eucalyptus leaves and bark. Neither the possum nor I moved for a few minutes. I noticed that it held one hind leg differently from its other limbs and then realised that its left foot was missing. It was a past injury that had healed over and I wondered what misfortune had befallen it: a cat, a fox, a steel-jaw trap?

'It is all right,' I said, slowly standing up and backing away from the table. 'I won't hurt you.'

The possum kept its eyes on me as I edged my way around the room to open the door to the back steps. I gave the door a shove then inched my way back to the other end of the room. The possum lifted its nose to sniff the air and then, with one final backward glance at me, leapt from the table and scrambled for the door. It flung itself onto the railing and from there into a nearby pine tree.

It has learnt to compensate for that missing foot, I thought. It was badly injured but it survived.

I walked into the kitchen to fetch the brush and pan and an idea struck me: I had to do the same thing as the possum. The injury would always be there but I must learn to live with it and move on.

I cleaned up the mess, then sat down again to write to Hugh. My heart fluttered with fear and expectation.

> *Yes, Hugh. We must make* The Emerald Valley. *When can you get here?*

TWENTY-FOUR

For the convalescent hospital in *The Emerald Valley*, Hugh and I found a homestead in Springwood with a magnificent garden of liquidambar, all in fresh leaf, white cedar, elms and pines. There was a bevy of peafowl wandering about, including a tame peacock who we nicknamed King George because of his regal manner.

As breathtakingly beautiful as the Blue Mountains were for a location, they brought complications. They were not mountains that you climbed to reach their peaks. Rather, you started at their peaks and climbed *down* into the valleys, sometimes at a descent of two thousand feet. It was only logical that if we went down into the valleys to shoot a scene, the return trip was going to be an upward climb with heavy camera equipment, props, costumes and supplies strapped to our backs.

I felt responsible for the safety of our ten-year-old star, Billy Sulman, who had played David Copperfield at the Theatre Royal, and his guardian aunt, May Sulman. The other actor in my care was our 'prince', James Blake, an unknown player who we had taken from a suburban theatre.

The rest of the cast and crew consisted of my family.

'We decided it was the only way we were going to see you,' said Uncle Ota, climbing out of the equipment truck that had been driven by Ranjana. I blinked when I saw Thomas. Gone was his chubby face; he now had cheekbones and a defined chin. His legs were like long tree limbs under his shorts. He bounded through the gate and down the path towards me. There was no trace of a limp in his stride. A twinge of regret pinched my heart when I remembered who was responsible for that miracle. But I had learnt to turn those memories away.

'You are a little man,' I said, hugging Thomas. 'You are not a baby any more!'

He pressed his cheek to me. 'I've missed you,' he said.

Klára, Robert, the twins and Esther arrived the following day in Robert's car. Emilie clapped her pudgy hands when she saw me.

'I'm looking forward to getting some sleep again now you are reunited,' said Klára, throwing her arms around my waist. She stood back a moment and glanced over me. A smile lit her face. 'You look well,' she said.

'Thank you for understanding,' I told her.

She took my hand and squeezed it. She was going to play the princess and Uncle Ota the doctor. Ranjana would be taking care of the continuity as well as supervising the rushes. Robert was to travel to and from locations to deliver supplies and courier the finished scenes to the development laboratory in Sydney. Esther had come along to babysit.

'We have to minimise low-priority items,' Robert instructed us. 'Everyone must share a tent, and we must limit our cutlery —

only two sets of knives, forks, spoons and plates are to be shared between the cast and crew.'

I wondered how Hugh was going to manage the steep descents along with his camera equipment. But for a man with one leg he was more agile than the rest of us and I remembered how I had seen him manoeuvre himself along the scaffolding for Peter's film.

As we would be departing from the established tracks for filming, we hired a bushman by the name of Jimmy Ferguson as our guide. Hugh and I found him at the pub in Blackheath. I remained near the door, as women were not welcome in that domain, while Hugh asked who was the best guide in the area.

'A lady by the name of Mrs Rockcliffe. Lives in Katoomba,' the publican answered. 'Bit of a loner but she'll take good care of you. That's what all the tourists say.'

From Hugh's silence, I imagined he was trying not to laugh. 'All right, who is the second-best guide in the area? We're going into rugged terrain.'

There was a murmur of voices. 'You want Jimmy Ferguson,' a man shouted. The other patrons mumbled their agreement. 'Knows the bush like the back of his hand.'

Hugh came out of the pub grinning. I was glad that he had taken the assumption about his disability so well. As for me being a guide, how had I developed a reputation so quickly? I could not have helped more than half-a-dozen people.

'Well, Mrs Rockcliffe,' Hugh laughed. 'If our picture doesn't work out you know what else you can do to amuse yourself.'

We found Jimmy Ferguson living in a house of rubble stones on the edge of a cliff with his Aboriginal wife, who came from the Dharug people. Jimmy was about sixty-five years old with grey hair and raw-looking skin.

The age of his ebony-complexioned wife was indiscernible. With her smooth skin and black hair she could have been thirty; but her missing teeth and rotund stomach made her look closer to sixty. Despite their rough-hewn appearances, it was clear from the way Jimmy and his wife spoke that they were intelligent people. After listening to our request, Jimmy scratched his beard and said that he would guide us if his wife — who answered to the name of Betty — could come along too.

'She's got superior bush skills and a sense of direction like an eagle. She can cook for you too. Save you lugging stuff up and down the mountains. She'll find it for you down there in the valleys.'

We needed someone to organise the catering because Esther was staying at my house to look after the children. But eating goannas, snakes and possums was not something we would do. I wanted to capture the rock wallabies on film, not on my plate.

'Ah, no worries, love,' Jimmy assured me. 'No animal need come to harm in the making of your picture. Betty knows where to find all the nectars, berries, fruits and tubers you could want, and her seed johnny cakes are the best around.'

On Tuesdays, we waited at the post office to receive Robert's telegram after the latest scenes had been developed. *Scene 11, Slate 4. Not good. Too dark and flat. Rest fine.*

Timing was important on location because the weather could change in an instant. Once in the Grose Valley, Klára complained that her make-up was melting. We used the sun for our lighting and close-ups involved catching its rays with a mirror and reflecting them into the actor's face. In her elaborate costume of tulle and sequins, Klára was uncomfortably hot. The rest of us were wilting also. Betty brought pannikins of water from the stream, but the drinks provided only temporary relief. Then, out of nowhere, a bracing wind began to blow and clouds loomed on the horizon. Streaks of lightning stabbed the sky. It was atmospheric and Hugh kept the camera rolling while Ranjana stood by his side holding an umbrella. I was torn between getting the shot and the safety of the cast and crew. Robert took over and moved the cast to a nearby cave, where he built a fire and Betty and Jimmy set about making billy tea. Robert was not as sharp as Freddy had been about what made a good story, but he was helpful in stepping in where he was needed.

I had worried about Hugh's ability to handle the terrain with one leg, but I should have been concerned about myself. In the film, the boy's wheelchair became a flying chariot. Hugh insisted we needed shots of the valley from the air.

A plane would not produce the floating effect Hugh was after so he contacted a mining company near the Ruined Castle to ask if we could use their flying fox cable mechanism to get a bird's eye view of the chasm. Hugh was as stubborn as a donkey; it was the only explanation I could give for how he managed to persuade the supervisor to let a one-legged man and a woman use one of the flying foxes when workmen were forbidden from travelling on them due to safety regulations. The only restriction the supervisor put on us was that the trip be taken in clear weather.

I was horrified by Hugh's suggestion that we risk our lives to get a 'once in a lifetime' shot of the valley. 'If one of the cables break, we are going to plummet to our deaths,' I told him.

'If the cables can carry shale, they can carry us,' he said, with such confidence I wondered if he had gone mad. And yet I must have been the one who had lost my sanity because in the end I did exactly what he told me to do.

'We'll put the director in first, then myself and the camera,' Hugh told the workmen who had been assigned to help us by operating the flying fox. I was glad that we had told the others they would not be needed for this scene and could have the day off. The workmen helped me into the open-topped crate, which was nothing more than some pieces of hardwood nailed together. Hugh positioned himself with his leg in the crate and straddled the side so as to get an uninterrupted view of the gorge. My job was to hold on to his belt to stop him from falling because he needed both his hands to operate the camera and keep it steady. I was also supposed to take notes of the shots by leaning my notebook against his back and writing with my free hand. I had no idea how I was going to do that with my fingers trembling so violently.

Once I was in position, I felt like a circus escape artist about to be lowered into a pool of crocodiles. There was no backing out now. My mouth was dry and it hurt to swallow. From this great height the valley was silent. A wedge-tailed eagle circled the sky. I shivered when I realised that it was eye-level with me.

'Hold on. Here she goes,' called one of the workers, releasing the brake while the other two gave us a push off from the station. The crate jerked down the rocky slope towards the edge of the cliff. This is not so bad, I told myself, gazing out at the magnificent stretch of green. I leaned over Hugh's shoulder and instructed him to film the tree tops.

While we travelled over the slope of the mountain, with the ground not too far from our feet, I felt calm enough to look at the station across the valley, where a handful of miners were waiting for us. I wished it were closer and prayed that it would not take us long to reach it. Then the crate passed over the edge of the plateau and the full expanse of the valley appeared below us. My stomach lurched with the sensation of falling. I tried to concentrate on note-taking but my hand dripped with sweat and smudged the letters.

'You all right?' Hugh called to me. I was glad he could not see my face. I took a gulp of air. This was not the place to panic. 'I am fine,' I answered.

'It's beautiful,' Hugh muttered. 'It's like a dream.'

1 ... 2 ... 3 ... 4 ... I counted in my head. I seized on the idea that if I kept counting in lots of one hundred it would only take ten lots before we reached the safety of the station. Then the unfathomable happened: the mechanism slowed down as we reached the halfway point. It creaked then came to a halt. The crate swung for a moment before stopping as well. I looked up. The pulley was stuck.

Hugh stopped filming and waved to the workers on the plateau. I could tell from their dumbfounded expressions that we were in trouble. What could anybody do to help us? We were dangling one thousand feet above the valley.

'Sit down and hold on,' Hugh told me. He secured the camera to the side of the crate with a piece of rope, grabbed the cable and stepped up onto the side of the crate. It dipped and the valley gaped below me. I clutched the sides but Hugh could not get the pulley unstuck fast enough and I began to slip. My vision turned white.

'Keep your eyes closed and hold tight!' Hugh shouted.

I found myself thinking about Freddy. 'Adéla, you can do it!' he would have said.

Hugh managed to get the pulley unstuck. The crate returned to its upright position and he inched us along the length of cable towards the station. A few minutes later I was lifted out of the crate by the miners and placed on firm ground.

It was over an hour before the strength returned to my legs and I was able to walk with the others to the tramway that would take us back to the top of the gorge. I did not utter a sound. The minutes of stark, cold fear on the flying fox had taken my voice away. Hugh held my hand and asked me if I was all right. I was surprised that he was unaffected by what had happened, and even less by what *could* have happened.

'It doesn't serve me to ask what could have happened,' Hugh said. 'I did that for years over my leg. We got the shot we wanted and both of us are still here, right?'

Hugh's words were not bravado. Once we were back at the mine, he laughed about the incident with the workers and shouted them beer and cigarettes.

As for me, whether we got the shot or not, I *was* affected by what had happened. I developed a terror of heights.

With the scenes at Springwood and Katoomba completed, we had only to film the final ones at Jenolan Caves, which we had chosen to represent our Valley of Darkness. The beauty of the caves was more spectacular than evil but with the right angles and filters, the cliff faces, cave openings and the surrounding bushland could be twisted into something menacing.

The first day of shooting, Hugh and I rose before dawn to film the wildlife for our Emerald Valley scenes. Ranjana was suffering a migraine and Esther came with us instead to take the continuity notes. I wondered how Esther felt about working with Hugh again. She behaved professionally if somewhat aloofly towards him. She has moved on, I thought. But whether that was good or bad, I did not know. I still thought she and Hugh would be good for each other.

The light was too dim for us to capture on film the ringtail possums scurrying to their dreys or the wombat who eyed us cautiously while rubbing himself against a tree. But when the sun broke the sky and the early morning light shimmered over the bush, we filmed rock wallabies bounding across a ridge; a flock of cockatoos swooping through the sky; and a family of kookaburras squatting together on a branch. In a fern gully we found a lyrebird scratching the scrub. He was a natural actor and broke into a song and dance, opening his magnificent feathered tail, the moment the camera started rolling. 'The lyrebird is an unsurpassed mimic,' Uncle Ota had once told me. 'He can imitate not only the sounds of a cockatoo or wren but also of a train whistle or a howling dog.' On our way back to the Blue Lake, Hugh found two koalas asleep in the fork of a gum tree and I directed him to film them from so many different angles that Esther was compelled to remind me that we had limited film stock.

We ate lunch with our actors and crew at Caves House before completing a battle scene at the Devil's Coach House. Then we trekked through the bush towards McKeown's Valley where we intended to film the final battle between the heroes and the evil spirits. We had left Jimmy and Betty behind at Caves House, with Ranjana and the children, to clean our camping and other equipment before we departed for Sydney the following day. We soon missed Betty's remedies when we found ourselves covered in welts from stinging nettles. Although there were clouds in the sky, the light remained consistent and the shooting of the first scenes went smoothly. I was struck by the silence of the valley. There was not a bird or an insect to be heard.

The manager of Caves House had lent us some of the staff as extras in return for a film credit, and we had managed to recruit local farmhands and a pastoral family. Although that amounted to only twenty people with which to create a battle scene, Hugh and I used them ingeniously. We shot the actors in wooded areas rather than open ones so that the trees became characters in themselves. For the first scenes, I had the 'good characters' move towards the right, with the intention of recostuming everyone as 'evil beings' and filming them moving towards the left. It was a trick Klára and I had observed in low-budget Westerns where the cowboys moved in one direction and the Indians, played by the same actors, moved in the other.

While the actors were changing their costumes, I sat down on my stool to make notes on the scene descriptions. Hugh passed me to adjust one of the light reflectors. A flash of gold shot up from the grass. My heart leapt to my throat. 'Snake!' I cried.

The reptile flattened its head aggressively. Hugh turned but was too late. The snake struck his shin then disappeared in the grass.

'Damn!' Hugh swore, grabbing his leg. Klára was at his side in an instant.

'Are you sure it was a snake?' she asked me.

I nodded.

'Look in the grass,' she instructed the rest of us. 'See what kind it was.'

While we were searching for the snake, Klára made Hugh sit down. 'Does it hurt?' she asked.

He shook his head. 'At first I thought I'd trodden on a stick and it had whipped me.'

Robert lifted Hugh's trouser leg to the place he had been bitten. I stopped to see what he was doing. I remembered when Klára and I used to walk in Thirroul she had told me that most snakebites through clothing resulted in scratches and not all bites injected venom. But I could see the two puncture marks from where I was standing, and that the wound was swollen. The snake had struck deeply.

'Let's hope it's a black,' whispered Uncle Ota, who was searching next to me. The black snake was venomous but not as deadly as the browns, copperheads, tigers and death adders. The snake I had seen had been gold.

I saw something slithering under a rock. I caught sight of the last part of its body. 'Stripes,' I said.

Klára and Robert tied Hugh's belt as a tourniquet around his leg. I could tell my description was bad news because Klára turned pale.

'A striped black snake then?' Esther piped up. She knelt down beside Hugh.

I shook my head. The snake I had seen was striped like a tiger. Black snakes had red or yellow bellies but no stripes — Klára had told me that years ago. Then something in Esther's eyes stopped me. The sign in Philip's reception room flashed into my mind: *Your sickness can affect your personality or your personality can affect your sickness.*

Hugh broke into a sweat. Drops of moisture dripped down his forehead and cheeks. I prayed it was shock and not the poison.

'God,' he said through gritted teeth. 'Am I going to die?'

'No!' Esther told him. 'But it would have been better if the snake had bitten your other leg.'

Despite the gravity of the situation, Hugh managed to grin.

Klára told Uncle Ota to make a fire and heat up his pocket knife. She was going to cauterise the wound. Then she turned to Hugh. 'You have got to stay still. You will be fine as long as you do what I tell you.'

Robert and Esther pushed down on Hugh's shoulders while Uncle Ota held his leg. Could the mind defeat a deadly poison, I wondered. Esther had lied about the colour of the snake to trick Hugh. I had not heard of anyone surviving a bite from a deadly snake, especially not so far from a hospital.

'Bloody hell!' Hugh screamed when Klára pressed the heated knife into the wound. The air stank of singed flesh. Hugh's speech was slurred and his eyes twitched. I fought back my tears. Surely he was not going to die!

'We have to get him back to the hotel,' Klára said. 'Jimmy will know what to do next.'

'But he can't walk,' said Esther. 'We need to make him a stretcher.'

I admired how Esther was taking control of things. I was the director of the picture but I had no idea what to do.

When we arrived back at Caves House an hour later, Hugh was unconscious. We carried him to his room where Jimmy looked at the wound. 'You've done all you can,' he said to us. 'It's up to God now.'

Betty disappeared into the bush to collect medicinal berries and mud to use as a poultice against infection. 'My people sit in the river before losing consciousness, but it's too late now,' she said.

Darkness was falling and there was no chance of travelling the treacherous winding road to fetch the nearest doctor. But as Jimmy had already told us, all that could be done for Hugh had been done. Esther stayed by Hugh's side, checking his pulse every quarter of an hour and listening to his breathing. She was watching for signs of respiratory paralysis as desperately as we had searched for them in Thomas when he struggled with polio. 'You'll make it, Hugh,' she kept telling him. 'You're strong.'

Sometimes his eyes would flutter open and I was sure he had heard what she said to him. I imagined Esther wished she could have been there for Louis when he was suffering on the battlefield.

A short while before dawn, I was shaken awake by Esther. It took me a moment to realise that I was lying in the armchair in my room and not the bed. Esther held a lamp near her face. She was pale and her pupils were dilated.

'Hugh?' I asked, sitting up. 'Is he dead?'

Esther shook her head. 'I think he's going to be all right.'

Although Hugh was well a few days later, I insisted we take him back to Sydney to rest. We only had the shots of the extras playing the evil beings to complete and we could return to the mountains for those. I was not worried about the cost. I was worried about Hugh. Robert and Klára invited Hugh to stay in Lindfield and I went with them. When she could see he was better, Esther withdrew her ministrations and let Klára and Mary take over Hugh's care.

One afternoon Robert, Esther and I were discussing the editing of the first part of *The Emerald Valley* in the Swans' sitting room while Hugh was resting on the veranda, when Peter arrived.

'I heard the news,' Peter said to Hugh when I showed him to the veranda. 'You are very lucky. Why didn't you have Giallo with you? He would have given the thing a run for its money.'

Robert and I sat down with Hugh and Peter while Esther joined Klára in the garden where she was playing with the twins.

'I think it is kookaburras you are thinking of,' I told him. 'Cockatoos don't eat snakes.'

It was nice to see Peter again and, even though it was spring, he still wore his cap and scarf.

'Not many people survive a tiger snake bite, my friend,' Peter said. 'Certainly not one as deep as the one you received.'

'We're not sure it was a tiger snake,' Robert told him. 'But it was something deadly. It was probably Hugh's build that saved him.'

Hugh, who had been quiet while we were speaking, shook his head. He gazed out to the garden where Esther was tickling Marta. 'No,' he said. 'It was something else.'

*   *   *

When the editing of *The Emerald Valley* was completed, I returned to the cottage to await Robert's news on distribution. The first thing I did on arriving home was to drag a ladder to the side of the house to see where my resident mountain possum was entering the roof. The air had summer in it and the garden was bursting with new shoots and flowers. I found a space near the eaves above one of the bedrooms and peered into the hole. I could make out the fur of the sleeping possum and the rise and fall of his rump as he breathed.

Because summer was hot in the mountains, I slept with all the windows in the house open. The possum, who I had named MP, liked the arrangement and sometimes I would hear rustling in the kitchen at night and find him sitting on the table working his way through the fruit bowl.

'MP! What are you doing?' I would scold him. 'Go and eat some gum leaves!'

MP would slow down his chewing and hold the piece of fruit in his front paws, responding to my lecture with an innocent stare. He must have sensed my soft spot for him because more than once I awoke at dawn to find him in bed with me, curled up against my leg.

'This has got to stop, MP,' I told him. 'You are not a cat! Go and find yourself a nice girl possum and have some babies.'

To help MP readjust to his life as a possum, I cut wood from the timber pile and made him a box with an opening in the front. I took some of his nesting material from the roof when he was out for the evening and put it in the box, then rubbed a slice of apple around the opening. The next morning I pulled out the ladder with the intention of securing the box in the pine tree near where MP exited the roof in the evenings. I wanted to place the box as high as possible so that he would be safe from cats and foxes, but once I got to the top of the ladder I froze, memories of my experience in the flying fox over the valley flooding back to me. I managed to steel myself enough to bind the box to the tree and secure it in place. Then I gingerly climbed down the ladder, my heart thumping.

'He had better use the box,' I said to myself. 'I don't think I have the courage to move it somewhere else.'

A few weeks later I received a telegram from Robert. I drove to Sydney full of expectation. I had asked him to secure the State Theatre for the premiere of *The Emerald Valley*. It would not be showing at Tilly's Cinema this time because, after the Royal Commission, Uncle Ota had retired from the industry. He had sold his cinemas on the south coast to Wollongong Theatres and Tilly's Cinema to Greater Union.

'All the fun in screening Australian films is gone,' Uncle Ota told me. 'It doesn't look as if the states are going to cede the powers the Commonwealth needs to implement the recommendations made by the Commission. Australian production is at its all-time lowest and no one is going to do a thing about it. But even if America doesn't finish the local industry off then sound-on-film will.'

During the editing of *The Emerald Valley*, Ranjana, Uncle Ota, Thomas, Hugh and I went to see *The Jazz Singer* at the Lyceum. The picture was billed as the first 'talking picture', but I had seen a few of those before. When we had been setting up the Cascade Picture Palace, another showman had sound discs to accompany his pictures. Ranjana and I were intrigued and visited his show one afternoon. Things started well enough with a music track and sound effects, but at the beginning of the second reel something must have jolted the needle and the picture and sound went out of synchronisation. For the rest of the picture, the sound effects did not match the images: a gun went off when a man sat down and a rooster crowed as a lady began to sing. The showman sweated over his projector, trying to get everything to match again, but he had lost his audience to laughter. Ranjana and I were in stitches all the way back home.

It was a Saturday night at the Lyceum and we were treated to an organ recital, a chorus line and a jazz band that played a few numbers from the picture. After the rendition of 'God Save the King' and a speech from the theatre manager saying that what we were about to see would change our lives, the lights dimmed and the screen lit up. At first it seemed that *The Jazz Singer* was like any other silent picture with a recorded soundtrack of music and sound effects, when all of a sudden the soundtrack ceased and the picture shifted to sound on set with Al Jolson singing. The audience went wild and clapped enthusiastically. That's it? I thought, shocked that Al Jolson's voice sounded scratchy and trebled, like a bleating sheep.

Afterwards, we stopped by the Vegetarian Café and discussed our impressions of the 'first talkie'.

'The camera work was poor,' said Uncle Ota. 'It looked static.'

'That's because they encase the camera in a booth and shoot through glass so it doesn't pick up background noise and the hum of the lights,' Hugh explained.

'I've heard that they hide the microphones in flower pots and telephones and that the actors can't move from the one spot,' said Ranjana.

'That is probably why I thought it resembled a radio play with pictures,' I said, sipping my camomile tea.

'Well, I was impressed,' said Hugh. 'I think sound-on-film is where the future of pictures lies.'

Rubbish, I thought. It is just another fad. Like flagpole sitting and dance marathons.

I arrived at Lindfield just after three in the afternoon and was happy to see that Robert had afternoon tea waiting for me. 'Hello!' he said and waved as soon as he saw me step out of the car.

He has good news for me, I thought, clenching my hands with excitement. He's got the big one!

The State Theatre was due to be completed in a few months. Just when the country's economic problems seemed to dragging down the mood of Sydney, with factories closing and the Australian picture industry on the brink of collapse, Stuart Doyle had stepped in bravely to build a 'Palace of Dreams'. I had read that when completed the theatre would be breathtaking. The interior was to be a fusion of Gothic, Italian and Art Deco styles with a Kohinor-cut crystal chandelier weighing over four tons. There would be paintings by William Dobell, Howard Ashton and Charles Wheeler in the dress circle gallery, and even the restrooms were to be lavishly decorated in different styles reflected by their names: Pompadour, Empire Builders, College, Futurist, Butterfly and Pioneers.

'Klára and Ranjana have gone shopping with the twins and Thomas,' Robert said, passing me a plate.

I folded my hands in front of me, waiting for Robert's good news. He sat down and looked at his palms for a minute then at me. My throat suddenly felt dry.

'I have approached Greater Union and Hoyts cinemas about the picture,' he said. 'But they won't touch it.'

My heart dropped to my feet. 'What do you mean?'

452 • BELINDA ALEXANDRA

Robert grimaced. 'Stuart Doyle said *The Emerald Valley* is the best film ever made in his lifetime and that you are the finest director but ...'

'But he won't distribute it?' My voice rose in pitch. 'Why? Is it something to do with Freddy?'

I would have been disappointed with a lesser theatre than the State, but now it looked as though there would be no major theatre at all.

Robert shook his head. 'No. It's because it's a silent. And nobody is buying silent pictures any more. The public have gone crazy over sound films. That's all they want. The silent picture industry is dead.'

I tried to take in what Robert said but it was too hard to believe. 'But it could not have just died overnight,' I said.

Robert pursed his lips. 'It has, Adéla. It's gone. For good.'

TWENTY-FIVE

The public flocked to the new pictures. They were an escape from the worries about the worsening economy and it was cheaper to see a light-hearted musical or comedy at the cinema than it was at the theatre.

The sound-on-film technology fascinated Hugh. He wanted me to see every new 'talkie' with him. 'There's merit in the technology,' he said. 'With the sound and film together on one strip, there's no problem with either getting out of synchronisation.'

'But the equipment is so expensive. How will we ever afford to remake *The Emerald Valley* as a sound film?'

'Australia will have to follow the Hollywood model,' he replied, bending so Giallo could transfer himself across his shoulder blades. 'We need to form into studios with continuous productions and contracted actors.'

My mind drifted to a friend of Mary's who had made a society drama and managed to get it premiered at the Prince Edward

Theatre. It had cost all of her inheritance of six thousand pounds and had not returned her a penny. Still, six thousand pounds had been enough to produce a picture with PJ Ramster as the director and Jessica Harcourt and Gaston Mervale as the leads. She would never have been able to do that if she'd had to do it with sound. I thought of all the homespun stories that had been made for under one thousand pounds. That would be impossible now.

'Out of all those glitzy Hollywood pictures you are so enthusiastic about, Hugh, can you name one that was directed by a woman?'

He thought for a moment then shook his head.

Our stories will be lost now, I thought. I knew that my picture-making days were over. I longed for beauty, I ached for it. I was sure that I would not discover it in pictures made by large studios with chauvinistic directors whose main concern was commerce, not art. I remembered the first time Klára and I had gone to the cinema with Uncle Ota and Ranjana. Felix the Cat coming to life before my eyes had been magic. What I was witnessing on the screen these days was not. The actors' voices dripped with evidence of elocution lessons and their performances were static. Instead of showing us the story, the producers saved on costs by having the actors tell it.

'I miss Charlie Chaplin and his funny little mimes,' Klára confided in me one day when we were walking with the twins. 'I enjoyed guessing what the actors were thinking. It was like reading a book: you filled in the gaps with your imagination. Now the comedies are one-liners that get used over again and all the thinking is done for you.'

'The technology will improve and the art with it,' Hugh assured me, when I relayed my conversation with Klára to him. 'Now everyone's enamoured with speaking but they'll find ways to make the camera move and then visual images will be important again.'

'I will try to keep an open mind to it,' I told him. 'But now I have one more favour to ask of you.'

Hugh stood back, eyes open wide, when I told him that *The Emerald Valley* would never be a sound film. I had made it for Freddy and I was not going to leave it to rot in some vault along with all the other silent films that had been made obsolete overnight.

'What are you intending to do?' he asked. 'The cinemas aren't going to screen it.'

'I am going to do what Australian directors have been doing for years, only Freddy protected me from it. I am taking *The Emerald Valley* on the road.'

'We need another person to help steady the equipment,' Hugh said when we were loading the truck for our trip down the south coast. Ranjana was going to drive and Hugh was to navigate. Uncle Ota and Esther were coming with me in the supply van. Thomas was staying in Sydney with Robert and Klára.

'So you want Uncle Ota to go with you?' I asked.

'No, you need a male with you in the van. I'm talking about Esther,' Hugh said.

I raised my eyebrows. The truck was heavy enough now. It was better for more people to travel in the van to avoid the truck getting bogged on muddy roads.

'I will be driving in front,' I said. 'You'll be able to see me. You will need someone stronger to help with the equipment.'

'But what if we get separated?' said Hugh. His voice was pleading. Ranjana cleared her throat noisily. I glanced in her direction. She rolled her eyes.

'Oh!' I said, the penny dropping. 'All right, Hugh. Esther can go with you.'

Uncle Ota and I climbed into the van while Ranjana started up the truck.

'Just as well you don't act in your films,' Uncle Ota said. 'You'd be terrible.'

I glanced back at Esther who was climbing into the equipment truck. Hugh offered her his hand to help her up. She accepted it cautiously. She had been hurt by his indifference so I did not blame her for her uncertainty.

The roads down south were rough to travel by motor vehicle. Many were nothing more than horse and cart runs. The tracks were often too narrow for the van and on the first day of our journey we became bogged twice. On the second day, we saw a farmer misjudge the depth of a river crossing. His truck sank like a weight, and it was only quick thinking on Uncle Ota's part to throw the driver a rope that saved him from being washed downstream. The time we lost saving the farmer meant we would not reach the town before dark so he invited us to camp on his property.

The moon was full, and in the firelight I saw Esther and Hugh exchange a glance when Hugh handed her a cup of tea. I envied them the joy of falling in love.

I remembered how Esther had been unsure of Hugh the day before when he had offered her his hand. People hurt others all the time, even when they loved them. Especially if they loved them. It was usually because they were in pain themselves. I closed my eyes and for the first time in a long time allowed myself to think about Philip. Since sound films had become important to the fate of *The Emerald Valley* I had taken up reading the newspaper again. One day I had seen an article about the Aerial Medical Service. A Presbyterian minister was trying to raise funds for a service to fly doctors to remote areas in the Outback when medical assistance was needed. I glanced at the picture. There was Philip standing next to the Reverend John Flynn. My heart had surged with pride. I was happy for him.

I opened my eyes again and looked at the stars. I remembered the night that Philip and his father came to our house in Watsons Bay with their telescope and how Philip had tricked me into believing he knew how I liked my tea.

'What are you smiling at?' Ranjana asked, rolling over. 'I can see your teeth glowing in the moonlight.'

'Nothing.' I had not realised I was smiling.

'Well, go to sleep,' she said. 'We have some more driving ahead of us and we have to make an early start.'

I tugged the blanket up around my neck and drifted off to sleep still thinking about Philip. He had found a fulfilling purpose but something in his expression in the photograph had made him seem lonely.

The first stop on our schedule was a town south-west of Thirroul where we had booked the School of Arts, a ramshackle building that had been erected at the turn of the century. The weather was hot and the sun beating down on the tin roof made me dizzy while I helped unpack the equipment and put out the seats. The hall could hold two hundred people and, as the town's regular showman had left the area to run theatres in Victoria, we expected a good turn-out. Sound pictures had not yet reached country New South Wales, so we were one step ahead of them. We put up posters in the town and handed out leaflets in the main street, but on opening night only three men and two women turned up and none of them would cross the threshold.

'We're not paying,' announced one of the party, a man with a sun-burned face. 'We've paid too much for rubbish before.'

Uncle Ota assured them that the picture we had to show was of the best quality, and even offered that they come in for free. If they did not like the film, he would not charge them. But the disgruntled five shook their heads and walked away.

'Why did they come at all if they weren't intending to see the picture?' asked Ranjana. 'Just to scoff?'

An unsuccessful first night did not bode well for the rest of our journey. We had paid for the School of Arts four nights in advance, intending to screen not only *The Emerald Valley* but *The Bunyip* and some other Australian silent films that we had hired. It did not help our spirits when we discovered the local pub owner, who had provided our accommodations, was charging us three times his normal rate.

'I can't trust you entertainer types,' he claimed, when Uncle Ota challenged him about the deception. 'You're always ready to skip town.'

We were wondering if we should give up the tour for lost when I had an idea. 'Why don't I replace the scenes in Watsons Bay in *The Bunyip* with scenes from here?' I said. 'People are vain. Surely they will turn up to look at themselves and where they live?'

The following day, we set out to capture the town on film. The baker and the grocer were obliging for the scenes outside their stores but the rest of the townspeople were unfriendly. I approached a group of men to ask them to act as extras but they turned their backs on me. The women gave me the same chilly reaction even when I turned on my charm.

'What a lovely dress,' I said, approaching a woman standing outside the post office. 'It will look nice in our film.'

The woman turned on her heel and walked into the post office without as much as a backward glance.

'We'll be in your film,' a voice said. I turned to see a group of boys standing behind me. The spokesperson looked about nine years old with sandy blond hair and a smudge of dirt on his nose. The rest of them were as motley, with unevenly buttoned shirts and their socks rolled down. Hugh suggested we film the boys playing cricket.

'Here,' Uncle Ota said afterwards, handing the boys tickets. 'Come to Saturday's matinée. For free.'

Uncle Ota hurried back to Thirroul to get the rushes developed. We were thrilled to see how well the town fitted in with the plot, even though we'd had to keep the scenes on the beach that had been shot in Watsons Bay and in one frame there was a glimpse of a ferry crossing the harbour.

The matinée was attended by the town's children who brought along their mothers and fathers. The audience applauded at every scene in *The Bunyip* and enjoyed the pictures we showed afterwards. Most of the parents returned for the Saturday evening session and we had to bring in extra seats. Even the group who had refused to enter the hall on our first night in town showed up.

'Children are the teachers of their parents,' Uncle Ota said to me when he saw the crowd lining up at the door.

The Emerald Valley was acclaimed by the crowd, who stood up to applaud and confirmed what we already knew. It could have been a hit. Afterwards, Hugh and I fielded questions from the audience about the theme of the film and how it was made. The audience's enthusiasm both buoyed and depressed me: it was wonderful to have the picture well received but it was sad to know that it had no chance of national distribution.

*   *   *

We continued our tour for two months, working our way down the coast through the towns of Unanderra, Wongawilli and Dapto all the way to Nowra, then back up the coast again through Gerringong and Kiama.

In Kiama, Hugh met me in the hallway of our hotel when I was on my way down to breakfast. We had finished late the previous night, but he looked refreshed. There was something else different about him. He was smiling. Not just smiling but beaming. I realised that he was a different person to the man I had first met at the Vegetarian Café. He had softened. But of course, I could not tell him that.

'Do you think we could stay here a few more days?' he asked me.

'Do you like Kiama so much? I thought you had to get back to Sydney?'

Hugh was suddenly shy and glanced at his hands.

'What is it?'

He blushed. 'Esther likes the church here. We want to get married.'

I grabbed his shoulder and nearly screamed for joy, but I checked myself. We had been warned by the management not to make too much noise in the mornings. My eyes filled with tears. 'Hugh!' I whispered. 'That's wonderful!'

Esther, Ranjana and Uncle Ota were already in the dining room when Hugh and I entered. Giallo was bouncing on Esther's shoulder.

'It looks like Hugh's best friend has taken to you too,' I told her.

Esther's face was the mirror of Hugh's. She was beaming too. It pleased me to see her so happy. Perhaps not every love story ended badly.

When Hugh told Ranjana and Uncle Ota the news, Ranjana became so excited that the manager rushed out of the kitchen to see what the commotion was about. But Ranjana sent him one of her queenly looks and he scurried away.

'You must give the others time to get here,' I told Esther. 'Klára, Robert and Thomas would not miss it for the world. And you must have a pretty dress, Esther. It will be my gift to you.'

Esther and Hugh were married in Saints Peter and Paul Church four days later. The church was restful, with translucent light filtering through the stained-glass windows and forming columns on the floor around the altar. The smell of sea salt drifted in the air and mixed with the scent of Esther's lily bouquet. She was beautiful in the antique white dress with a tan underslip that Klára had rushed from Sydney with and which Ranjana had altered overnight. Uncle Ota was best man and stood by Hugh with Giallo on his shoulder. Klára was matron of honour. Peter took time away from the opera he was writing to come.

As Hugh was a Catholic, there were no difficulties with their church marriage but I wondered if Esther was thinking about Louis and if her happiness was tinged with some sadness too. My thoughts drifted to Philip. Had I been wrong to turn him away? Perhaps all I had needed was time? Esther had loved Louis with all her heart but she was also able to love Hugh passionately. While the priest was talking, I noticed the blue and black butterfly on Esther's bouquet.

She glanced down and blinked. From the flush that rose on her neck I realised that she saw it too. The butterfly stayed during the wedding vows and exchange of rings and was still riding on the bouquet when Esther and Hugh left the church as man and wife.

Outside, Esther and Hugh posed by the front door for me to take their photograph. As I was about to depress the shutter, the butterfly took to the air and winged away towards the sun. Esther and I watched its path until it disappeared from sight.

'What are you two looking at?' asked Uncle Ota, shading his eyes. 'A gull?'

Esther turned to me and smiled, her hands trembling. I waited for the mist in her eyes to clear before I took the photograph.

Afterwards, when we sat down to the wedding lunch, Esther leaned over and touched my arm. 'I understand now,' she whispered. 'He was trying to tell me to be happy.'

When Stuart Doyle heard of the success we'd had on the south coast with *The Emerald Valley*, he recommended that Australasian Films distribute it even though it was a silent picture. Australian exhibitors were in a gridlock with American sound companies who wanted to gain a monopoly by enforcing expensive contracts on local operators. The Americans outpriced themselves and only the large venues could afford the equipment required to screen 'talkies'. The suburban theatres still needed silent films and would do so until Australia developed its own sound technology. It was a small window left to us to have *The Emerald Valley* screened nationally, but I seized the opportunity. There was no glamorous premiere or publicity; the film's success snowballed by word of mouth. Everywhere the picture was screened, Freddy's dignity was restored and he was recognised as one of the local industry's supporters.

Ironically, *The Emerald Valley* generated a profit for Australasian Films in America. *It seems there is still some nostalgic interest among the public for silent films*, Stuart Doyle wrote to Robert. *And, of course, the United States is a large domestic market.*

The Emerald Valley made more money for Australasian Films than did *For the Term of His Natural Life*, which also had found itself outmoded overnight. Because the production costs of our picture had been lower, the profit margin was much higher. *For the Term of His Natural Life*, the budget for which had blown out to sixty thousand pounds, made a loss.

Stuart Doyle offered Hugh a permanent job with the new Cinesound Studios. I told him to take it. The steady income would help him support his new family. Esther was pregnant.

On Freddy's birthday that year, I stayed with Uncle Ota and Ranjana, who had bought Esther's house from her after she had married Hugh, and drove to Waverley Cemetery in the afternoon to place flowers on Freddy's grave. It was something I had done every November since Freddy's death. The cloudy weather suited my mood on what had become the saddest day of the year. I shivered when I saw the cemetery gates. They reminded me of the first day I had seen them, when Freddy was laid in the earth and put away from me forever.

I bought irises from the flower seller, then took the path to Freddy's grave. I had been in too much pain after my husband's death to think of tombstones, so Klára and Robert had stepped in and organised everything, including the verses from Tennyson's poem for Freddy's epitaph. I placed the flowers on the grave and knelt to read the gold lettering:

I hold it true, whate'er befall;
I feel it when I sorrow most;
'Tis better to have loved and lost
Than never to have loved at all.

The words I had read so many times suddenly touched my soul. A ray of sunshine burst through the clouds and sparkled on the graves around me. The darkness that had settled on me for so long lifted and floated away. It was as if for that moment, Freddy had embraced me then let go. I felt as if he had told me that it was time to move forward.

I was returning from the path to the main gate when I noticed an old man shuffling ahead of me. I recognised him instantly. He did not look as formidable to me as he once had. I realised that he must have been visiting his wife's grave.

'Doctor Page,' I called.

Doctor Page Senior turned and squinted at me. I was almost expecting a reprimand for disturbing his peace and was relieved when he smiled.

'Mrs Rockcliffe,' he said, stepping towards me. 'I was sorry to hear about your loss. It is a while ago now?'

'Five years,' I told him.

Doctor Page studied my face. His eyes looked dazed with pain. I realised that he was sweating although the breeze from the ocean was cool. I reached out and took his arm. 'Shall I walk with you?' I asked him.

Tears filled his eyes and I remembered the day I had taken the photograph of him and Philip. Perhaps if I had seen Doctor Page before visiting Freddy's grave, I might not have greeted him and continued to harbour resentment for his collaboration with Beatrice's lie. But I was aware now that I was as fallible as anyone else. I had no cause to be self-righteous. When I stood before Freddy's grave, I had finally understood how lucky I had been to have loved him. I had loved him unexpectedly and imperfectly. But I had loved him just the same.

Before we reached the end of the path, Doctor Page stopped. I was worried that he might be feeling unwell. 'I am too old to hide the truth,' he said, his voice rising a tone. 'You and Philip were in love and I pushed you apart because I had my heart set on him marrying Beatrice.'

The force of the truth left us both breathless. Doctor Page had summed up the sorry tale. The cemetery was quiet, as if all the deceased who lay at rest in it were wondering what would happen next. Only the seagulls and the faint roll of the ocean assured me that I had not gone deaf.

'Beatrice deceived all of us,' I told him. 'But I am glad that you and Philip have been able to mend your relationship.'

Doctor Page continued to look at me. 'And you and Philip?' he asked. 'That could not be repaired?'

The pointedness of his question startled me. I shook my head. 'By the time Philip returned, I was already married.'

Doctor Page glanced back to the path.

'Is your car waiting for you?' I asked him.

He nodded and I saw the same Bentley that he had taken me in to meet Beatrice that first time was parked at the gate. The chauffeur opened the door and helped Doctor Page into the car. The old man offered to have his driver take me home, but I told him I had brought my own car.

He opened the window so he could say goodbye again before the car took off. 'Philip is taking leave in February,' he said. 'I wonder if you would like me to give him a message from you?'

The sense of light that had filled my heart at Freddy's grave burned even brighter. 'Tell him that Adéla says hello,' I said. 'Tell him to come and visit me some time. It would be nice to see an old friend.'

Doctor Page smiled and I knew that we had understood each other perfectly.

The time that Klára and I had spoken of arrived: the day she and Robert would leave with the twins for Europe. She had waited until she felt the twins were old enough to travel and — although she refused to say it — until she was sure that I could manage on my own. At twenty-three years of age, she was older than most serious performers embarking on their first tours, but I knew she would be well received.

'I still cannot convince you to come with us, can I?' she said on the morning of their departure.

I took her hand. 'Wherever you are, we will always be sisters. You will always be in my heart.'

Klára kissed my hand and pressed it to her chest. 'And you in mine.'

I remembered her wedding day and the gulf I had felt opening up between us. I could never have imagined myself living separately from my beloved sister and now I would have to learn to do so.

'What will you do?' Klára asked. 'Now that you will not be making pictures any more?'

'I will find something,' I said, and thought of the letter I had received recently from Myles Dunphy, the leader of the new conservationist movement.

Klára studied my face. She pushed a lock of hair off my forehead. 'It is amazing,' she said.

'What?'

'How much you have grown to look like Mother.'

Uncle Ota, Ranjana, Thomas and I were there to farewell Klára and her family at the dock. Mrs Swan and Mary were there too. Esther was too heavily pregnant to come, but she and Hugh had sent flowers. After the ship disappeared through the Heads, Uncle Ota and Ranjana suggested that I stay the night with them. I was grateful for the invitation. I had an empty feeling in the pit of my stomach.

After everyone else was in bed, I sat up and watched Angel. She was still in the garden, the matron of the local brushtail possums. Cherub and her other offspring had taken up residence in the bush across the road. I took out the letter Myles Dunphy had sent me and reread it several times.

> *Dear Mrs Rockcliffe,*
>
> *My breath was taken away by the picture you made in the Blue Mountains. It strikes me that you are a woman who will understand what I mean when I say that tree destruction is a kind of national complex and too much of the character of this country has been ruined in the name of progress. I wish our forefathers had been as sensitive to the balance of nature as you clearly are and had been more intelligent with their axe work. You may have heard by now of our campaign to save the blue gum forest in the Grose River Valley for the purposes of retaining this area of beauty for generations to come. I am writing to see if you will join us in our campaign and allow us to use your picture to raise public awareness of this issue. As we destroy our bushland, we destroy ourselves along with it.*

The following morning, I drove back to the mountains with a stronger sense of purpose than I had known for years.

I arrived just after dark to see MP sticking his head out of his box. I thought of the possum population I had seen in Watsons Bay the previous night. In all the time I had been in the Blue Mountains, I had never seen MP with another possum. Why had he never had a mate? I smiled when I realised he may have thought the same thing about me.

'You are not a young boy any more, MP,' I told him. 'Hurry up and make some babies.'

The following morning I drove to the post office to collect my mail, which had been held for me. There was so much that the postmistress gave it to me in a hessian sack to carry it to my car. When I arrived home, I sat on the veranda and sorted out the letters. There were dozens praising *The Emerald Valley*, and a few requests for me to take ladies on bushwalks, which reminded me of the day Hugh and I went to the pub at Blackheath and I had to laugh. Tour guide, indeed!

I sorted the post into three piles: personal letters from people I knew; letters from people I did not know; and bills. My eyes settled on an envelope marked AMS: the Aerial Medical Service.

My fingers trembled when I opened it. My vision blurred and I had to blink a few times before I could focus on the two sentences the letter contained:

Can I come and see you? Tell me when.

The following Saturday, I smoothed the skirt of my new dress and waited on the veranda for Philip to arrive. The dressmaker had sewn the lemon-yellow dress for me in haste because I had realised after years of wearing mostly trousers that I did not have any feminine clothes that were in fashion. I was consumed by a vanity I had not known in years. When I had risen that morning, I had stared at myself in the mirror, trying to guess what changes Philip might see in my appearance. I was almost thirty and the first flush of my youth was gone. The face that stared back at me was harder and the set of the mouth was a little grimmer than before. But I hoped not too much so.

An hour passed and still there was no car on the road and my hopes began to sink. What if Philip was not coming? What if there had been some emergency? I still did not have a telephone so I had no way of knowing. I could go to the post office to see if there was a telegram, but I might miss him on my way. I sat on my hands and bit my lip.

I was aware of a buzzing sound in the sky. I shaded my eyes to see a biplane heading in the direction of the house. The plane flew overhead with a roar then circled and returned, this time so low that my skirt flapped in its slipstream.

Does Philip own a Gipsy Moth, I wondered.

The pilot brought the plane in to land in the empty lot next to the cottage. I walked towards it, aware that I had to stand back until the propeller had stopped spinning.

The pilot lifted himself out of the cockpit. The figure seemed taller than I remembered Philip and for one moment I thought I might have a tourist wanting a guide on my hands. Then the pilot removed his goggles and my heart leapt when I saw Philip's face smiling at me. He had hardly changed since I had seen him last. His skin was slightly weathered and he looked more rugged, but his eyes were bright and alive.

'A plane!' I cried. 'Does it belong to the AMS?'

'No,' said Philip. 'We have Qantas pilots to transport us. This one's my own.'

There was a second cockpit in the plane and, rather than walk towards me, Philip went to it and pulled out a flying jacket.

'I'll take you up while the engine's still warm,' he said. 'The weather is perfect.'

My heart sank. I was excited to see Philip but the sick feeling that grabbed my stomach whenever I thought of that day in the flying fox returned to me. If I could not put up MP's box without becoming dizzy, how would I manage a flight in an aeroplane?

'Come on, Adéla,' Philip said, holding out a helmet and goggles. 'Suit up!'

I remembered the look in Philip's eyes when I had turned him away after Freddy's death. I cringed when I thought of the hurt I had inflicted. I had punished Philip because I was consumed by guilt. But Philip had done nothing wrong; all he had ever done was to try to help people, to love them honestly and to behave with dignity. Both Beatrice and I had let him down. I looked up at him. His eyes were full of warmth. What he was asking me to do now — to go up in the Gipsy Moth with him — was so much less than he had ever asked of me before. Surely I could manage such a simple thing to make him happy?

My knees trembled and my heart pounded while Philip helped me into the flying jacket and strapped me into the passenger seat. I tucked the skirt of my dress underneath me. Once I was actually in the plane, my fear got the better of me. 'Philip,' I pleaded. 'I am not sure I am up to this.'

Philip did not hear me. He strapped himself into the rear cockpit. Our helmets had earcups coupled to rubber tubing and there were mouthpieces. This was our means of communication. He taxied the plane to the end of the lot and turned into the wind. Then he opened the throttle and we commenced our take-off run. My stomach lurched and it took all my willpower not to be sick. The Moth headed straight for the edge of the cliff at full speed, and if it was not for the roar of the engine as we became airborne I would have deafened Philip with my scream.

The plane vibrated as it climbed into the sky under full power. 'Let's do a tour of the mountains,' Philip said through the speaker tube. I was too terrified to look over the side of the plane. It had been a warm day down on the ground, but up in the air the wind bit my cheeks and I could feel my lips cracking.

After a few minutes of flying over bushland we came to a valley and Philip put the nose of the Moth down so that we could take a closer look. I recognised that we were over the Grose Valley and I could see the majestic blue gum forest. My heart fluttered with excitement and for a moment I forgot my fear. It was a bigger picture of the wilderness than I had ever seen before. I was filled with awe.

The rest of the flight was a wonder to me. I could not have imagined the exquisite beauty of the mountains from the air. I found myself envying birds. They saw the world as if from heaven — the tree tops, the sparkling rivers and valleys. When Philip brought the plane in to land next to my cottage, the nervous woman who had climbed into it an hour earlier emerged transformed.

'So you like flying?' Philip asked, helping me out of the jacket.

I was so moved I was in tears. 'I loved it,' I told him. 'Thank you so much.'

Philip's eyes danced over my face. 'You haven't changed, Adéla. You have always been susceptible to beauty.'

I blushed and looked towards the house. 'Are you hungry?' I asked him.

After lunch, we strolled through my garden and I showed Philip my lavender and the box I had made for MP. We stopped near the maple tree I had planted in memory of my mother and father and looked out over the silent, sweeping valley. Philip reached out and took my hand. I clasped his fingers in mine and felt his grip tighten.

'When I saw *The Emerald Valley* I knew that you had healed. That you had found a new purpose,' he said, looking into my eyes.

He is going to kiss me, I thought. When I had received Philip's letter, I had made up my mind that, no matter what, I would not turn him away again. Now was our chance for happiness and, if he still loved me, I intended to take it.

But he turned and stared up at the sky.

'I have to hurry back now,' he said. 'I have some patients to see in Sydney tomorrow morning.'

'Are you back in Sydney?' I asked, my heart sinking. Philip had not come for love, he had come for companionship. I had once asked him if we could be friends and I would have to be happy with that. I was thankful that at least he was only going to Sydney and not somewhere as far away as Cloncurry.

'I've helped set up the structure of the medical service,' he said. 'Now it's time for me to return to my practice. But I will act as a relief doctor for the service from time to time.'

We walked back to Philip's plane and I listened with fascination while he told me about his trips from Cloncurry into the Northern Territory and emergency landings in the mining camps of Mount Isa; about remote places in the Cape York Peninsula and the starkness of the inland towns and their inhabitants' ability to endure the harshest conditions.

Philip zipped up his flying suit. 'Can I come again next Saturday?' he asked. 'I could take you over the Hawkesbury River.'

Joy tingled through me. 'You intend to come to the mountains again so soon?' I asked, unable to restrain a smile. 'Are you looking for a guide?'

The corners of Philip's mouth twitched in return. 'No. I'm looking for a navigator.'

'What would a navigator do?' I asked.

'She would keep an eye out for clearings devoid of tall trees, power lines or livestock in case there is a need for an emergency landing.'

'I think I could do that,' I laughed.

Philip strapped himself into the cockpit and waved. I watched the aeroplane lift into the sky and followed its path until it disappeared on the horizon.

A gust of wind blew up from the valley and I hurried back inside. The nights could turn bitter even in late summer in the mountains, and it would be cold enough tonight to build a fire. I opened the door of my cottage and found MP snuggled behind a cushion on the sofa. He was lying on his haunches in a half-moon shape with his tail between his legs and his head tucked onto his tummy. I gently prodded his rump but he was fast asleep.

'Well, you had better hurry up and find that girl as I've been telling you,' I said. 'I don't think I am going to be alone much longer.'

A few days later, I walked to town to post a letter to Klára. She would not receive it until she arrived in Prague, but I wanted to write to her anyway. I had deliberated over mentioning Philip, and decided not to for now. I had a superstitious notion that declaring my happiness prematurely invited bad luck. I had been in love with Philip and lost him to Beatrice. I had come to adore

Freddy and had lost him too. Happiness in my own heart was enough for now.

I stopped by the dressmaker's shop and caught my reflection in the glass window. In a trick of the light, I was doubled. Just outside my reflection was another image of me — slightly fuzzy at the outline and ethereal. I had been many people in my life: Adéla Ruzicková; Adéla Rose; Adéla Rockcliffe. Who was I going to be now?

I remembered my conversation with Myles Dunphy when I agreed to join him in the fight to save the blue gum forest. 'Opportunities are made, Mrs Rockcliffe,' he had said. 'They don't happen of themselves. I don't want to read about the achievements of people with verve. I want to be one of those people myself. It's not enough to be intelligent and thoughtful. You have to be bold.'

Those would have been Freddy's sentiments exactly.

Many people I loved were still with me. I had not lost Klára, Thomas or Hugh, although they had all had brushes with death. Uncle Ota, Ranjana, Esther, Robert and the twins were happy and well. Even MP, despite being without a foot, seemed to have managed to dodge predators.

'You have to be bold,' Myles Dunphy had said.

Perhaps it was time I was.

When Philip helped me suit up for the flight the following Saturday, I was not frightened at all. The butterflies in my stomach were due to my excitement in being with him. I could hardly wait to be airborne. But Philip's manner was less carefree than it had been the previous week. He seemed preoccupied.

The flight that day was smooth. The Hawkesbury River and its tributaries encircled Greater Sydney and I was astounded by its beauty — the shimmering water, the bushland and hills. But every so often I would see clearings in the forests and felled trees and my vision of cherishing and protecting nature stirred in me.

Philip brought the plane to land near a beach. I watched him take out the neatly packed portions of sandwiches, salad and fruit in precisely the order we would eat them. We used tin mugs and plates for our picnic but he smartened the setting up with a lace tablecloth over the rug and linen napkins.

'Apart from Uncle Ota, I don't know any other man with your domestic competence,' I told him.

'My mother wouldn't hear of a helpless male in the house,' he said. 'Although we had several maids, she taught my father how to iron a shirt, just so he'd know.'

'It sounds as if she was a very modern woman,' I said, remembering Miloš stomping around our apartment in Prague and demanding Marie and Mother help him get ready.

'She was twenty years younger than my father and what he described as "a healthy shock to the system",' said Philip. 'You remind me of her. It's very fashionable to be independent these days, but most women I know would still swoon if it would get a man's attention. You don't try to be fashionable, Adéla. I like that. It's just how you are.'

Silence fell between us. I understood Philip's preoccupation now. For there was one thing left that stood between us and our happiness in being together: Beatrice. She was the unmentioned barrier to love. Sooner or later we would have to talk about her.

I glanced at Philip's handsome profile. I would think of Beatrice later. All I wanted in that moment was to be blissfully happy. It might have been a false moment or a stolen one — for,

despite Beatrice's behaviour, Philip was still a married man —
but all I could think of was bathing in this sweet happiness a
little longer.

We returned to the cottage later than we had anticipated. The
sky was darkening.

'Come inside for a cup of tea before you go,' I told Philip.
'You need to warm up for the journey.'

Philip shook his head. 'I'll have to get going while I still have
the sun.'

He looked in the direction of the cockpit but made no move
towards it. 'What is it?' I asked.

He exhaled and clasped his hands in front of him. 'You know
those places I told you about? The Katherine River and Alice
Springs?'

'Yes.'

'One day I'd like to show them to you, just as you want to
show me the blue gum forest.'

A ripple of happiness ran up my spine. 'Yes, I would like that.'

Philip smiled and took my hand, kissing my fingertips. Then
he pulled me towards him and kissed me on the lips. His mouth
was soft and it warmed me despite the breeze that was sending
goose bumps up my legs.

'Until next Saturday,' he said, breaking away and reaching
into the cockpit.

'Stay,' I said.

Philip turned to me. His jaw set into a grimace. 'Beatrice ...
she won't give me a divorce, you know,' he said, looking at the
ground then back at me. 'Some mixed-up notion she has that it
makes her decent to be married although we live on different

sides of the globe. She even had the gall to say that divorce would be an offence to our religion.'

I had already guessed that Beatrice would not permit a divorce. I understood her character better now. No one could be happy without her permission. She did not want me to have what she could not. That was the reason she had tricked Philip into marrying her. Not because she had loved him.

'Stay,' I said, reaching out my hand.

'I can't marry you, Adéla.'

'But you love me?'

Philip's gaze softened. 'Yes. I've always loved you.'

He took my hand and we headed towards the cottage. The love we would share would not be the innocent, wide-eyed love of our youth. But it would be just as precious. We would flout convention, for what had obeying convention done for us except keep us separated for years? Philip was one of the country's finest doctors. I had shown Australia in all its glory to the world. What else did we need to do to prove ourselves to others? It was time to live for ourselves.

'I've got to wash my hands,' said Philip, when we reached the house. 'They're caked in grease.'

I gave him a towel from the cupboard and he headed towards the bathroom. I stood in the sitting room and imagined a cosy scene: Philip reclining in the armchair, marking flight paths on maps, while I wrote letters to government officials about why trees were more precious than 'progress'. A roaring fire crackled in the fireplace. I drank in the pleasure of the image, knowing that I had reached a point of bliss. I had found my life's purpose and my life's partner.

Something crashed in the kitchen. I rushed down the hall and turned on the light. The vegetable basket was upside down and carrots, beetroots and potatoes were scattered over the floorboards. MP poked his head out from the curtain under the sink, a cherry tomato clutched in his paws.

'So!' I said, happy to see him despite the mess he was making in my kitchen. 'Didn't I tell you it is not good to always be alone?'

Something blunt fell on my head. I glanced down and saw a candle lying near my feet. I kept a box of them on top of my kitchen cupboard in case of emergencies. I looked up to see another, slightly smaller possum sitting on the cupboard and peering at me.

'At last,' I said to MP. 'Good boy.'

I left the kitchen window open so that MP and his companion could leave when they had finished devouring my food and closed the door behind me. I would clean up the mess in the morning.

I walked out onto the veranda for one last glimpse of the sun setting over the valley. The cool air was bracing. A lone magpie drifted on the breeze. Something rustled in the bushes near the steps, perhaps an echidna or a wombat.

'Adéla!' Philip called.

I walked back into the house. Philip was in the sitting room with the towel in his hands. His face was pink and he smelt of rose soap.

'What was that crash?' he asked.

'Never mind,' I said, taking his hand and leading him to the bedroom.

He hesitated at the door. 'Are you sure about this, Adéla?'

'I have never been surer of anything. I love you,' I told him.

He took me in his arms and kissed me. Suddenly all the heartaches I had accumulated over the years vanished. I had been wrong in thinking that Philip and I could not be innocent or thrilled by life because of all we had been through. Everything was new and fresh. I saw us, young again, sitting together on the sands of Wattamolla beach, our future spreading out gloriously before us.

THE END

ACKNOWLEDGMENTS

Finishing a novel is like arriving home after a life-changing trip abroad. One's suitcase is filled with happy memories of the experiences and the people one met along the way. *Silver Wattle* was a sojourn mostly in my own country and I have so many people to thank for making it a wonderful journey that I am afraid I will not have enough space to mention all of them here.

The story is expansive and multi-layered and involves many characters; it has been mostly a seven-day-a-week project. Therefore, first and foremost I have to thank my family for their encouragement, especially my husband, Mauro, my father, Stan, and my three stepsons: Michael, Brendan and James. I would also like to thank my friends for their understanding of my schedule and hope they have not forgotten what I look like in the daylight!

I would especially like to thank my inspiring agent, Selwa Anthony, and wonderful publisher, Linda Funnell, who encouraged me through the many drafts it took to write the novel. Their care, interest and experienced advice found their way into the weave of the story. Special mention should also be made of my talented editor, Nicola O'Shea, who is such a joy to work with, and Kate O'Donnell, my diligent HarperCollins editor, who went to great efforts to accommodate my requests for 'more time'. Others I would like to thank at HarperCollins*Publishers* include: Shona Martyn, Publishing Director, for her unwavering support for me as a writer; publishing assistant Denise O'Dea; and the fabulous marketing, publicity and sales teams who put such energy behind sending my novels out to the wider world that I am in awe of how lucky I am to be published by such a dynamic, talented company.

In terms of research, I am especially grateful to the lovely Jana Rich and her husband, Dennis, who went to enormous lengths to help me confirm that my Czech references were correct and that the dishes in the novel were authentic. It was such a pleasure getting to know Jana and Dennis; it was worth writing the novel just to have met them!

For helping with my wildlife research, I would particularly like to thank Sonya Stanvic, Cilla Norris, David Williams, Gary Taylor, Nick Edards and Paul Ibbetson of the NSW National Parks and Wildlife Service. I should also make special mention of Sue Small and Ela Achtel who so graciously stepped into my role as Brushtail Possum Co-ordinator for the North Shore Branch of WIRES so I could meet my publishing deadline.

I would like to thank Debbie Sander of the Australian Film, Television and Radio School and Les Parrott for their helpful information on film technique in the 1920s.

Others who I would like to acknowledge include: John Scott, Aviation Historian; John McCulloch of the Australian National Aviation Museum; Ewen Simpson and Gerard Willems of the Conservatorium High School; Andrew Constantine of the Sydney Observatory; Gillian Simpson of the Australian National Maritime Museum; Helen Sartinas of the Immigration Museum; Simeon Barlow of the National Archives of Australia; Sally Orr of the Royal Flying Doctor Service in Queensland; Esmay Foster of the Kiama Historical Society; John Merriman, Local Studies Librarian with the Blue Mountains City Library; Kay Donovan; and Fiona and Adam Workman.

Finally, I would like to thank the helpful staff at the following libraries: Ku-ring-gai Library, Wollongong City Library, Leichhardt Library and the State Library of NSW.

Thank you to everyone for making the writing of *Silver Wattle* the trip of a lifetime!

AUTHOR'S NOTE

One of the great pleasures of writing *Silver Wattle* was researching the early Australian film industry. While it is not possible to list all my sources for inspiration here, some of my favourites included: John Tulloch's *Legends on the Screen: The Australian Narrative Cinema, 1919–1929*; Elsa Chauvel's *My Life with Charles Chauvel*; Simon Brand's *Picture Palaces and Flea-pits: Eighty Years of Australians at the Pictures*; Eric Reade's *History and Heartburn: The Saga of Australian Film 1896–1978*; and Ken Hall's autobiography, *Directed by Ken G. Hall*. The three-part DVD series *The History of Australian Cinema 1896–1940*, is an excellent starting point for anyone interested in learning about the beginnings of Australian film.

Debate continues today among film historians about the role of the Combine in the decline of the Australian film industry as it did in the 1920s between local film producers and distribution and exhibition agencies. While I found the debate fascinating, I resisted being swayed by either side and tried to present the argument through the characters' views as they would have seen them from their respective positions in the industry.

Angel, the brushtail possum joey, is reared on canned milk, but licensed wildlife carers are now trained to raise orphaned marsupials and have available to them special formulas and supplements to bring up these fragile creatures. Angel would have to have been a resilient possum to have reached adulthood on canned milk. Her upbringing in the 1920s was created in consultation with Sonya Stanvic, author of *Possums: Rescue, rearing, rehabilitation and release*, and Cilla Norris, an experienced possum carer with WIRES. Should you find an orphaned native bird or animal — or an injured one — do not attempt to raise or rehabilitate it yourself. Keep it warm and quiet and contact your nearest wildlife group or veterinary surgeon for further advice. As the brushtail possum co-ordinator for my local branch of WIRES and as a licensed wildlife carer, I have seen too many sad cases where a member of the public tried to raise a joey and did not call us until it was too late to save the possum. Also, never take an animal from the wild and attempt to turn it into a pet.

Applying a tourniquet and cauterising the wound was the standard method of treating snakebite in the 1920s, but this is not the current recommended first aid treatment and could lead to serious injury or death. It is best to familiarise yourself with an up-to-date first aid book before venturing off the track in bushland. Snakes are protected native reptiles and most bites occur because the victim was trying to kill the snake or pick it up. Have a healthy respect for snakes and their role in the environment and leave them alone — or observe them from a safe distance if you find them fascinating, as many people do. If *Silver Wattle* has sparked your interest in Australian wildlife and you would like to learn more, you can start by viewing the WIRES website at www.wires.org.au, contacting your nearest wildlife organisation or by visiting your local library.

While on the subject of native animals, possums were called 'opossums' in the 1920s and koalas were referred to as 'native bears'. To avoid confusing contemporary readers while maintaining some nuance of authenticity, I chose to use the term 'possum' while keeping koalas as 'native bears'.

Finally, to give a flavour of the Czech language to the novel, I used the diminutives for Adéla and Klára's names, Adélka and Klárinka, where appropriate. However, nouns in the Czech language, including names, change depending on their role in a sentence. I decided to stay with the 'a' endings in all cases to avoid confusing non-Czech readers. The Czech háček alters the pronunciation of the letters below it in the following ways:

š sounds like English *sh*
č sounds like Engish *ch*
ž sounds like the s in English *leisure*

For a straightforward guide on Czech pronunciation and grammar, I found David Short's *Teach Yourself Czech* very helpful.

I hope you experienced as much pleasure in reading *Silver Wattle* as I did in researching and writing the novel.

WHITE GARDENIA

In a district of the city of Harbin, a haven for White Russian families since Russia's Communist revolution, Alina Kozlova must make a heartbreaking decision if her only child, Anya, is to survive the final days of World War II.

White Gardenia sweeps across cultures and continents, from the glamorous nightclubs of Shanghai to the harshness of Cold War Soviet Russia in the 1960s, from a desolate island in the Pacific Ocean to a new life in post-war Australia. Both mother and daughter must make sacrifices, but is the price too high? Most importantly of all, will they ever find each other again?

Rich in incident and historical detail, this is a compelling and beautifully written tale about yearning and forgiveness.

WILD LAVENDER

At fourteen, Simone Fleurier is wrenched from her home on a Provençal lavender farm and sent to work in Marseilles. Her life there is hard and impoverished, but Simone discovers the music hall and a dream: to one day be a famous dancer and singer. But when war threatens, Simone makes a decision that will lead to great danger — yet ultimately prove that love, just like wild lavender, can grow in the least likely of places ...

Belinda Alexandra has created a tale of passion and courage that moves from the backstreets of Marseilles to the grand music theatres of Paris, from the countryside of Provence to decadent pre-war Berlin and jazz-age New York. *Wild Lavender* is a feast for the senses that will live on in the imagination long after the book is closed.